The Blood Line

WILL SHINDLER

The Blood Line

HODDER &
STOUGHTON

First published in Great Britain in 2023 by Hodder & Stoughton
An Hachette UK company

1

A CIP catalogue record for this title is available from the British Library

Hardback ISBN 978 1 529 38380 5
Trade Paperback ISBN 978 1 529 38381 2
eBook ISBN 978 1 529 38382 9

Typeset in Plantin Light by Hewer Text UK Ltd, Edinburgh
Printed and bound in Great Britain by Clays Ltd, Elcograf S.p.A.

Hodder & Stoughton policy is to use papers that are natural, renewable
and recyclable products and made from wood grown in sustainable
forests. The logging and manufacturing processes are expected to
conform to the environmental regulations of the country of origin.

Hodder & Stoughton Ltd
Carmelite House
50 Victoria Embankment
London EC4Y 0DZ

www.hodder.co.uk

'The light of lights looks always on the motive, not the deed, the shadow of shadows on the deed alone.'

– W. B. Yeats

PROLOGUE

It's choice, not chance, that decides your destiny, so they say. But none of this feels like something he's chosen. He's sitting by the window of the cafe drinking burnt coffee. It's well after rush hour and the stream of passers-by preoccupied with their phones has thinned out to a trickle. His table's illuminated by the white glare of the street lamp and he stares out unblinking at the office block on the other side of the road.

There are three other people in the coffee shop with him and he's careful to keep his face hidden. The scarf he's wearing is chin-high and, together with the baseball cap, doesn't give much away. He takes a sip of his coffee; hot and bitter, it helps calm his nerves. And he *is* nervous because already this wasn't how he imagined it would be. He's one of the bad guys now – and the bad guys are supposed to be terrifying, not terrified.

Lukasz Mazurek's head was pounding. It had been a long day, fiddly and irritating. He reasoned that if he put in the hours now, then he might give himself a standing chance of not having to be here again this time tomorrow. Just once this week would be nice.

'Go home, Lukasz,' said a warm voice from the other side of the office. He looked round and saw his boss, Lambeth Council's principal social worker, Nina Thornbury, getting to her feet. She was slipping on her coat as her PC screen went dark behind her. He straightened up, feeling every tense muscle in his back pinching as he did so.

'I can't – I've got to prepare a care plan for a meeting tomorrow. A fourteen-year-old girl with learning difficulties—'

'I know the case,' she said, interrupting. 'But that's not until 2 p.m. – you've got bags of time to finish it off. Come back to it fresh, you'll be better for it.'

He shook his head.

'I've got meetings all morning, a client visit at lunchtime and—'

Nina held up a hand in surrender.

'I won't argue with you – I know what you're like. You're big enough to manage your own hours.'

He shrugged helplessly.

'I thought I had hours to kill – trouble is, they fought back and won . . .' he said with a wry smile.

Nina laughed.

'Just wish I had a husband as patient as your wife,' she said.

'*Kurwa,*' he said under his breath, preferring, as usual, to swear in his native Polish. 'I meant to call her.'

He delved into the pile of paperwork on his desk, fumbling for his mobile. Nina gave him a wave and headed for the door. He found his phone and winced as he saw the message he'd missed by over an hour.

Helen
Running late? x   20:16

He quickly tapped out a reply.

Lukasz
Sorry! Leaving soon, I promise . . .☺   21:19

An answer came almost instantly. In his mind's eye, he could see her watching TV, her phone perched next to her on the sofa.

Helen
No rush. I've made a stew. Love you x   21:19

She was used to it and wouldn't be cross – just worried about him. There'd be a gentle prod about his health later, the familiar refrain that he was working himself too hard. He closed his eyes, trying to summon one last burst of energy. His stomach felt empty, his mouth tasted of old socks, and the thought of that stew was making him salivate. He ignored his complaining body and focused instead on the screen in front. It was just over twenty minutes later when he finally surrendered.

As he made his way out, he looked briefly at the coffee shop opposite. It was tempting to pop in and buy a bag of crisps to keep himself going, but he didn't want to risk missing the next train home. Another half an hour standing in the cold really didn't appeal. He hurried on, pulling his coat around him. Walking towards him was a man in a baseball cap staring down at the pavement. Lukasz tried to step out of his path and felt a sudden sharp pain in his midriff. Heat began spreading across his chest. He looked down and realised immediately he'd been stabbed, understood it with almost detached incredulity. The knife was still in the man's hand, blood dripping off it. Before he could react, his attacker thrust it in a second time. Now, the blade was deep inside, cutting through things he really shouldn't be able to feel, and his legs began to buckle. The man reached out an arm to steady him.

'*Shhh,*' he said.

The Labour MP for Wimbledon South, Claire Beacham, was watching the ten o'clock news with growing irritation. On

3

screen, a woman was standing amidst the packed green benches of the House of Commons and addressing the chamber. She was in her early forties, wearing a black trouser suit, with shoulder-length, mahogany-coloured hair, her eyes searching out her colleagues with good-natured intensity. The woman was Beacham herself, several hours earlier.

'According to a survey by Women's Aid, only five per cent of refuge vacancies listed last year could accommodate women with no recourse to public funds. I say again to the minister – we have to do better for victims of domestic abuse. Not by Christmas, not by next year. But now.'

She sat down sharply to a ripple of approval from the MPs behind her. A man in an immaculate suit stood up on the government side and approached the table of the House with an avuncular smile. He laid a smart ring binder down in front of him like a vicar about to give a sermon at the pulpit.

'We made it very clear when we set out our proposals on housing benefit that we would protect particularly vulnerable people such as the ones the Honourable Lady refers to. Those policies were the right ones then – and they remain the right ones now.'

The news report snapped back to the presenter in the studio and Beacham turned the TV off in disgust.

'Wanker,' she said, tossing the remote on to the desk in front of her. 'Wankers, in fact.'

'What's the matter?' asked the silver-haired man standing next to her. Grant Lassiter was her diary secretary and they were in Beacham's parliamentary office at Portcullis House. Though the building, a stone's throw across Parliament Square from the Palace of Westminster, was lavish, her office was not. Small and functional, it often felt more like a cell on long evenings like this.

'You've made the ten o'clock news, every major news website's carrying it and I've got interview requests from

4

several national radio stations for the morning. I'd call that a win,' he said. Claire exhaled.

'Yes, I suppose so. Not arguing. I'm just pissed off with myself, mainly – I think I could have done better. I was too' – she grasped for the right word – '*woolly*.'

'You're being too tough on yourself. Again,' said Lassiter.

'No, I'm not. This isn't self-deprecation, Grant – I wasted time this morning that I could have used to prepare myself better.' Lassiter looked disappointed and she immediately waved a mollifying hand. 'I'm not blaming you. It's my fault – spreading myself too thin again.'

'It's supposed to be my job to stop that from happening.'

'So we both failed. But you've got an excuse – you don't get paid enough.'

'That's very true,' he agreed and they both smiled. 'You've got an early start again tomorrow. I've booked you a taxi home.'

She looked up, annoyed.

'I don't need a car – it'll cost a small fortune. Public transport's fine.'

'What you need is a decent night's sleep, Claire. It's on me – you can return the favour some time.'

She shook her head wearily.

'I'll pay you back.'

'Whatever. It's waiting downstairs. And don't forget you're starting early tomorrow with talkRADIO at six-forty. I've emailed you the full list of interviews with times. I'll be up and on the end of my phone if you need me.'

She nodded and stood. She might just get six full hours of sleep if she was lucky, and the call of her bed suddenly felt powerful.

'Thanks, mate,' she said sincerely and reached for her coat.

★   ★   ★

'Smug fuckers, aren't they?' declared the driver as they pulled off. Privately Claire was grateful for the unexpected lift. It was a welcome chance to sit back and switch off. What she didn't need was a chatty driver.

'Who are?' she replied, trying not to be rude but hoping he'd take the hint.

'This government. Muppets, the lot of them. I heard you on the news sticking it up them earlier. My wife loves you.' He pointed at the Houses of Parliament as they began to cross Westminster Bridge. 'Always says you're the only one talking any sense in that place.'

She smiled. The compliment was rather nourishing after the day she'd had.

'Does she now. And what's this smart lady's name then?' she said, reclining back.

By the time they reached Wimbledon Parkside, the affluent part of south-west London where she lived, Claire had established the driver's name was Ivan, his wife was called Angie and that they'd been married for nearly forty years. He seemed a decent man who'd been through a bit in his life, and there was also a lack of self-pity which she'd rather warmed to. It had been an unexpectedly nice way to end a long day.

Walking up the drive to the large detached house she shared with her husband, she felt in unexpectedly good spirits. Sometimes talking to someone who didn't arbitrarily hate you because of your job was refreshing.

As she approached the front door, she saw a medium-sized brown box on the step in front of her. She assumed it was a late delivery from Amazon that her husband hadn't heard. He was probably blasting out the TV on full volume or the delivery driver hadn't bothered ringing the bell even though the lights were on. She hated it when they did that. Stooping to pick it up, she then shoved the box under one arm and fumbled for her keys.

'Have you been wasting money again, Michael?' she shouted as she entered the hallway. There was no reply, and as she walked into the kitchen, she saw her husband standing by the counter, buttering a slice of bread. Roughly the same age as her, with billowing black hair and matching beard, he possessed either a vaguely Christlike countenance or a satanic one, depending on her mood.

'What are you talking about?' he said, looking round.

'I found this on the doorstep,' she replied, placing the box on the kitchen table. 'What are you doing?'

'Making a sandwich. I've been on the phone all night and haven't eaten. Do you want one?'

'You beauty . . .' she said with feeling.

He reached for some more slices of bread from the loaf next to him.

'Nice performance today, by the way,' he said. 'You've been all over the news.' She didn't reply and he gave her a knowing look. 'If you tell me you thought you were shit, you can make your own sandwich.'

'I don't want to talk about it. It's all I've been talking about all day.' She pouted and took her coat off.

'So what's in the box?' he said, motioning at it.

'Don't know – at first I thought it was a delivery.' She flipped the box over, looking for some clues. 'But there's no writing or labels on it anywhere.'

'Are you sure it's safe?' said Michael, peering at the object in her hands uncertainly now.

She sighed.

'It's not a bomb – I know that much.'

'Carried many bombs, have you?' he said.

She rolled her eyes.

'I can *tell* – it's probably a gift from a constituent. Wouldn't be the first time, would it?'

'Cake with rat poison in then,' he said with an exaggerated eye-roll.

She made a face at him then shook the package and heard the rustle of plastic inside.

'Weighs a ton, whatever it is.'

'Maybe you should let one of the security people at Westminster open it?' said Michael.

Claire was too tired to be cautious so, using her door key, she scored the front of it open. Inside was a carrier bag. She lifted it out gingerly and immediately something dripped on to her shoe.

'It's *wet* . . .' Almost in slow motion, she saw her hands were now soaked in dark, red, sticky liquid. 'Fuck!' she said, dropping the bag. Something heavy hit the ground with a clunk and rolled across the floor. For a moment they both stared at it in disbelief. And through strands of bloodied hair, the sightless eyes of Lukasz Mazurek peered blankly back up at them.

I

Detective Inspector Alex Finn rolled out the blue mat and sat down on it cross-legged, focusing his attention on a framed picture hanging on the far wall of his flat. It was a painting of a small port with a perfect azure sky, some tavernas, and a handful of bright white yachts moored close by. He knew the place well – Fiscardo village on the Greek island of Kefalonia, a place he'd once visited with his late wife Karin. He stilled himself, slowed his breathing down and cleared his mind of everything except the image. Meditation was something that once upon a time he'd have poured scorn on, but in recent months he'd come to appreciate.

He was a tall, lean figure with short, grey-flecked brown hair and high cheekbones. Expensive Prada glasses adorned a well-moisturised face, giving him a slightly professorial look. He didn't fit most people's stereotype of what a murder detective looked like – but then he hadn't been one for a while. Finn was currently on a sabbatical from the job, after suffering from what he now accepted had been a breakdown just over six months before.

In the aftermath of his wife's death from a brain tumour just over two years earlier, he'd rushed straight back to work. At the time he'd thought it was the best way of dealing with his grief. As it turned out, he'd been wrong – horribly wrong. He hadn't been able to let go of her – *bereavement as addiction* is how it had been described to him. How close he'd come to

9

taking his own life the day that addiction finally overwhelmed him, he wasn't sure. The memory still made him shiver.

It had proven to be the catalyst for change that he'd needed. Since then, he'd been undergoing bereavement counselling, learning to enjoy life once again, and slowly easing his way back into a healthier state of mind. Now on the eve of his return to work, he felt rested, refreshed and just a little bored.

'Proud of you,' said Karin.

'Hush now,' he replied with a smile, focusing again on the picture.

Finn was a man of routine. After his daily meditation, he went for a swim. After the swim, he went for a walk and then there was a stop for a leisurely coffee at his favourite cafe on Wandsworth Common. Force of habit meant he still studied the news websites closely. He often pictured his colleagues at the Cedar House major investigations team going about their business, and he enjoyed following the progression of their investigations through the media. There'd been a frequent temptation to call in and see how they were doing, but his counsellor had made it clear that to do so would be rather defeating the point of his sabbatical.

As he sipped at his espresso, he flicked through the BBC News website on his phone. The world seemed a little less restless than usual – a Commons debate over domestic violence was dominating most of the headlines. But there were no reports of any fresh murders in south London and his return to work looked like it would be a gentle reintroduction. He watched the world go by for a moment, absorbing the sights and sounds around him. This particular routine was about to come to an end and he would miss it.

He spent his afternoon in the Marylebone office of his bereavement counsellor. One last session to put a cap on things for the time being.

'*Do you feel ready?*' she'd asked him and he'd only been able to shrug in response. He'd replied that they'd soon find out, but she didn't let him go without a warning:

'*Be on your guard, Alex. We've talked about triggers – you need to be aware if you feel yourself sliding again.*'

The conversation stayed with him on the tube journey home. His job would bring him into contact with death – he led a major investigations team, after all. And with it came the bereaved and with the bereaved came triggers. She was right – he would have to be on his guard. He looked around the carriage and saw a discarded copy of the *London Evening Standard* on a seat. The headline on the front page read:

'*Domestic Violence Bill disregards needs of victims, warn campaigners*'.

He flicked through the pages and again was struck by how quiet things were. If politics was the front page splash, it told you something. A quiet start the next day was probably not the worst thing. He was looking forward to going back, but there were some nerves too. He wasn't entirely sure how his colleagues were going to receive him after his time away.

That night he made a curry, slow-cooking it until the chicken was hanging off the bone. Spicy and creamy, it was rather sumptuous, even if he said so himself. He'd deliberately laboured over it – one last meal before the job consumed him again. Then, it would be the usual snatched bites to eat, as and when. He was just starting to think about bed when the call from DCI John Skegman came. Skegman was his superior at Cedar House and Finn sighed when he saw the name on the display. It felt like his dad was checking up on him. They'd spoken several times during his sabbatical – the DCI keeping abreast of Finn's progress. That was fine – but this call, the night before his return, felt a little unnecessary.

'How are you, Alex?' said Skegman.

'I'm good. So what can I do for you that couldn't wait until tomorrow?'

There was a slightly compressed huff of irritation on the other end and Finn smiled. He knew the face that usually accompanied that sound. The two men generally got on very well, sharing a mutual respect for one another's abilities. But the DCI was a pedantic and slightly humourless man; not someone you'd want to be trapped next to on a transatlantic flight.

'You been watching the news this evening?' asked Skegman.

Finn had seen the main BBC bulletin at ten but nothing particularly noteworthy had jumped out at him.

'Yes . . . why?'

'It's the MP who was in the top story, Claire Beacham . . . well, there's been an incident at her house tonight.'

Finn sat up, suddenly alert. It felt like Beacham had been subtly following him all day. He recalled the front-page piece in the *Standard*, the snarky exchange with the minister in the Commons that had been on the news. Skegman explained about the box she'd been left and the severed head it contained.

'Bloody hell – any idea who the victim is?' said Finn.

'No, not yet. Beacham didn't recognise him. So far we've had no fresh reports of a missing person or a body either – so it's early days.'

Finn dredged his mind for as much as he could recall about Beacham.

'What is she? The shadow minister for domestic violence?'

'Yes – "domestic violence and safeguarding", to give it its full title. But she's quite low-key most of the time – not one of those that can't keep their face away from the cameras. The only previous time she's called the police was over some online trolling.'

'So what do we think? Is this terror-related?' said Finn.

'The head is of a white male – we estimate in his late thirties or early forties. SO15 have been informed but they're letting us handle the initial investigation.'

Finn nodded. That made sense – counter-terror tended not to get involved until a proven link had been established. But the terrible murders of Labour MP Jo Cox in 2016 and the Conservative MP Sir David Amess in 2021 hung over the conversation.

'So the day Beacham asks a high-profile question in the House – this happens,' said Finn. 'Can't be coincidental . . .'

'No. I didn't think there was much point mucking around, Alex – thought you might want to go to the crime scene for yourself tonight and take a look. It's not too far from you.'

Finn felt his curry repeat and was grateful he'd only had the one can of lager with it earlier.

'Makes sense – who's there now?'

'Jackie Ojo.'

Finn smiled at the name. Ojo was as much a friend as a colleague, which was rare for him – he tended to keep his workmates at arm's length socially. With his full support, she'd been temporarily promoted from her rank as a detective sergeant to acting detective inspector in his absence. It was fifty-fifty whether she'd be happy to hand a job like this on to him or be sad to surrender it. The latter, if he was a betting man, he thought.

'And how's Beacham?'

'Pretty traumatised, as you can imagine. Very keen that we keep this away from the media for as long as possible. Jacks can fill you in when you get there. I'll text you the address.'

Finn was already crossing the room searching for some appropriate footwear. There was a pause on the other end of the phone.

'What is it, John?' said Finn, knowing full well what it was.

'Are you *sure* you're okay?'

It was a fair, if irritating question. Finn had deceived his colleagues before about his mental health. He couldn't blame the man for asking.

'Don't you worry about me – I'm fit and raring to go.'

2

A solitary uniform constable was manning the front gate of the Beachams' house when Finn arrived around half an hour later. Scene-of-crime officers were already there, literally crawling on their hands and knees all over the site. Finn flashed his warrant card at the PC and was greeted by a convoy of police vehicles parked on the gravel outside the front door. He steadied himself, trying to find his focus – from here, he needed to be on his toes – taking on board every last detail of what he could see and was being told. It usually came second nature, but after six months off, he found himself having to reach for it, which was unsettling. He helped himself to a white forensic suit, latex gloves and overshoes, and headed through.

Inside, the house had a warmth to it. Money had clearly been spent but it was tasteful rather than ostentatious – nice rugs adorned immaculate wooden floors, fine art in expensive frames hung on smartly painted walls. Talking to one of the CSIs in the hallway was the familiar figure of Acting Detective Inspector Jackie Ojo. A tall, no-nonsense woman in her early forties, clad in forensic apparel, she only noticed Finn when she saw the CSI's attention wandering in his direction. Immediately she turned to greet him. They'd exchanged a few texts during his absence, some work-related emails, but hadn't actually seen each other in person for months.

'Blimey – this is like a royal visit. You must be keen,' she said, her eyes displaying the smile her mask was disguising.

Finn shrugged.

'Don't know about that. Skegman hit me with this just before I was about to turn in for the night. So much for a nice, quiet return,' he said.

Ojo nodded, swiftly becoming more business-like.

'We can catch up properly later; you should come through and see this for yourself.'

He followed her into what ordinarily would have been a seriously impressive kitchen. Two sets of French doors dominated an entire side of it. A lavish lighting array ran down the length of the ceiling while a large white Formica dining table dominated the middle of the space. But Finn barely noticed the decor. His eyeline was following the ugly red smear on the floor to the object at the centre of everyone's attention. There were yellow forensic cones with black numbers dotted around, evidence rulers carefully placed next to some of the blood spots.

Crime scenes tended, by and large, to be quiet places. People working efficiently, keeping their conversation to the necessary and functional. But there was a special hush about this one as the forensic staff went about their business. The head had come to rest at an angle, so seemed to be staring up and past you from wherever you looked. The box it had fallen out of was where Claire had dropped it by the table, together with the bloodied carrier bag the head had been wrapped in.

Finn tried to picture what this man had been like in life, walking and talking, smiling and frowning like everyone else. He had floppy brown hair which looked like it might usually have been kept swept back. Some of it, caked in blood, had dropped on to his forehead. There was stubble on his chin too, perhaps the beginnings of a goatee. Tendrils of bloodied flesh were just about visible at the base like roots of a plant.

'Welcome back, boss,' said Ojo.

16

'Thanks,' replied Finn, matching her dryness.

'Can't say I'm too gutted to be handing this one over.'

'Really? I was worried you might be a bit pissed off.'

Ojo shook her head.

'Honestly, no. You might have warned me about the amount of red tape that comes with the job, the extra hours, the lack of support from above . . .'

'Ah,' said Finn wryly. 'You've discovered John Skegman likes to delegate . . .'

'That's what you call it?' She stopped herself, held up a finger. 'We'll get back to this. In the pub. Soon. When there isn't a severed head on the floor.'

Finn looked again at the strangely crestfallen-looking face on the ground.

'So what do we know?'

'The good news is this place is covered in state-of-the-art home security – and we've got some footage of the guy who left it.'

She led him out of the way of the forensic team who'd temporarily paused their work to let Finn take a look. They went out into the living room where a laptop was flipped open on a large wooden table.

'Digital forensics have uploaded the key bit already,' she said.

Ojo tapped at a key and he leant in. A reasonably clear black-and-white image showed a figure in a baseball cap, face masked by a scarf, carrying the box up to the front door, then turning on his heels and running.

'The street cameras must have him too,' said Finn. 'I saw a few when I arrived.'

Ojo nodded.

'Yes, there's decent coverage in the area – we should get an idea from which direction he came and went. Uniform have the description too and are making house-to-house inquiries in case anyone saw or heard anything.'

'Have the Beachams seen this footage?'

'Yes – but they weren't able to add anything and there's no guarantee this guy is the same one who actually severed the head. He might just be the delivery boy with no idea what he was dropping off.'

Finn nodded.

'Where are the Beachams now?' he said.

'Upstairs – we're just organising a hotel for them to stay overnight.'

'Do they have kids?'

Ojo shook her head.

'No, which is probably just as well in the circumstances,' she replied.

'How are they coping?'

'Both reacting as you'd expect – they're obviously pretty traumatised. She genuinely has no idea who the victim is or specifically why someone would do this.'

That was fair enough, Finn thought. Politicians were magnets for all sorts of crazies.

'Feels like a message of some sort,' he said.

'No shit.' Ojo rolled her eyes.

Finn smiled despite himself.

'I don't think it'll take us too long to identify who the victim is,' he said. 'A headless body's not exactly the easiest thing to dispose of and this looks pretty ... *fresh*.' He was aware as soon as he said the word that he could have been talking about a joint of meat in the fridge. 'I take it someone's running through all the current mispers in the system?'

'Yes, and we've also asked to be alerted immediately about any fresh disappearances that are reported in,' replied Ojo.

Finn furrowed his brow trying to recall something. 'I'm sure I've come across Michael Beacham's name before somewhere – remind me again what he does?'

'A lawyer of some sort – high-end property, I think.'

He concentrated again, trying to assimilate what he knew of the Beachams with the brief bit of Googling he'd managed before he'd left his flat.

'My perception of Claire Beacham is that she's genuinely pretty principled – she did some good work on domestic violence throughout the pandemic,' he said. 'From memory, she seems more of a constituency MP than someone trying to climb the greasy ladder.'

Ojo pulled a face immediately.

'I don't know about that – I've always found her a bit holier-than-thou. Jumping on to causes, banging a drum for a bit, and actually changing fuck all.' Finn arched an eyebrow and she looked around, as if suddenly aware of where she was standing. She shrugged unapologetically. 'You know what I mean,' she added, slightly more discreetly.

'Interesting,' he said. 'Shall we find out?'

Finn waited in the living room as Ojo went to fetch the couple, looking around, trying to get a sense of who these people were. Their taste was immaculate, that was for sure. Finn liked to think he and Karin had possessed a good eye, but everything – from the furniture to the artwork on the walls to the sculptures on the shelves – was exceptionally judged. In the framed photographs of the couple, he was struck by the broad smile on the MP's face. There was a cordiality to it you didn't tend to see too often in her public appearances. It would be interesting to find out whether his or Ojo's assessment of her was the more accurate.

It was now nudging half past one in the morning and when the couple entered the room a few moments later, they both looked understandably tired and upset. Finn's first thought was that Claire was smaller and more fragile than she appeared on television. She sized him up too as he introduced himself, then sat down on a sofa with her husband. Ojo joined Finn on the couch opposite.

'Are we in any danger?' asked Michael before they could begin.

'First of all, let me say I'm so sorry this has happened to you,' said Finn. After six months away, it felt odd trying to find the right tone again – dealing with people in shock. 'We'll try and complete our work here as quickly as possible to mini- mise the inconvenience. My instinct is that if someone wanted to hurt you directly, then you'd already know about it. Is there any reason you can think of why you've been targeted like this?'

He knew they'd already been asked the question but it was one you couldn't ask enough in Finn's experience, especially as the shock began to wear off.

'God, no – I mean, there's always some nonsense going on in the background. But there's nothing specific that comes to mind,' said Claire.

'Have you noticed anything strange in the last few days?' offered Ojo. 'Anyone hanging about outside the house, perhaps? Or maybe some unusual messages you've received?'

Claire thought about it, then shrugged.

'As I say – I get shit online all the time; it comes with the job. But you learn to ignore it. I've had death threats before, as well – but nothing that stands out recently.'

'When you say you get shit all the time ... what sort of stuff?' said Finn.

'You know – that I'm a whore, a bitch, a traitor, that I should be raped or hung from a noose outside parliament.' Finn saw Michael wince as she said the words quite matter-of-factly.

'But to my knowledge, nobody's suggested I need a decapitated head left on the front doorstep.'

'Digital forensics are already going through Claire's online accounts,' Ojo told Finn.

'Yes – that's not inconvenient at all. When can I get my phone and laptop back?' said the MP wearily.

Finn nodded sympathetically.

'As soon as possible – again, apologies for the hassle,' he replied. 'Is there any chance what happened this evening could be connected to the domestic violence debate you were involved in today? It was all over the news.'

Claire blew through her cheeks and shrugged.

'God knows. I mean . . . it's not the usual kind of thing that provokes the nutters. And why would they hurt this guy, whoever he is?'

'Until we identify him, I don't honestly know,' said Finn. 'Is there anything else you're involved with which we should know about?'

Claire mulled it for a moment.

'The only thing I can think of is a constituent of mine – Benjamin Ngomo. He's a young man in prison who I'm trying to stop the government from deporting.'

Finn looked up, interested.

'I haven't read anything about that?'

'That's because I haven't really started to make much noise about it yet – I wanted to get the domestic violence debate out of the way first. But it's something I've been working on behind the scenes with my team for a few weeks now.'

'It *is* the sort of issue that stirs up right-wing extremists,' said Ojo.

Finn nodded in agreement.

'It's a line of inquiry, certainly. Do you have any details you could send over?'

'Of course.'

'One other thing – is there any chance this could have been directed at you, Mr Beacham – and not your wife?'

'I can't see why. I'm a property lawyer; it's hardly the most controversial of occupations,' he said.

'So there's nothing you've been working on which might have provoked this?' said Finn.

Michael looked faintly surprised by the supplementary question and clasped his hands together.

'Most of my work right now is with the Doll Street Collective, if you've heard of it?' he said. Both Finn and Ojo shook their heads. 'They're a not-for-profit development trust trying to acquire some run-down old buildings near Borough. They want to regenerate them for the local community. My role's just to help them get the deals over the line and try and keep the developers at bay. Some of the local residents have lodged complaints about the proposals, but you'd expect that – comes with the territory. I can't see why any of that would prompt . . . *this*.' He motioned with horror at the direction of the kitchen.

'No, I can't either,' agreed Finn. 'And there's nothing else either of you can think of that we should know about?'

The Beachams both shook their heads.

'Will you be telling the press about what's happened?' said Claire.

Finn was getting a sense her political instincts were beginning to kick in. There was a sharpness behind her eyes, despite the tiredness.

'No, not until we've got a clearer idea what this is about – in case it is terror-related.'

'But you'll keep us informed?'

'Every step,' he replied, meeting her gaze head-on.

★   ★   ★

'So what do you reckon?' said Ojo as they stood outside the Beachams' house afterwards.

That was a good question, Finn thought. His instincts still felt strangely rusty after such a long time away and it was continuing to unsettle him.

'Let's see what develops overnight,' he said. 'The forensics and house-to-house inquiries may well give us something more concrete to work with by the morning, and we could have a name for the victim too.'

'I haven't even asked how you are yet,' said Ojo.

He smiled at her.

'Fine, thanks. Sorted a lot of stuff out while I was off – think my head's in a better place now. We'll see. To be honest, I was getting bored at home.' A thought struck him – a sense some-one was missing and he'd only just properly noticed it. 'Where's Mattie, by the way?'

DC Mathilde Paulsen was part of Finn's team at Cedar House and he'd been expecting to find her working in tandem with Ojo. Spiky, awkward and not worried about giving Finn a hard time if she felt he warranted it, she was another whose company he'd missed over the last few months.

'Been giving evidence in court all day – didn't think it was fair to spring this on her too.'

'How's she been?'

Ojo shrugged.

'Grumpy, monosyllabic, generally unapproachable.'

Finn smiled again.

'Normal then?'

'You got it.'

They both laughed, and as he made his way back to his car, Finn found himself feeling energised. It was good to be back in the swing of things. It was only as he started the engine that the image of that bloodied head came back to him, and he shivered unexpectedly. Someone somewhere would be worried sick about a man who hadn't come home and their nightmare hadn't even begun yet.

3

'A severed head. Are you shitting me? At this woman's house?'

Nancy Deen held up her phone. The Sky News website showed a stamp-sized picture of Claire Beacham addressing the House of Commons the previous day. Nancy's partner Mattie Paulsen was sitting on the sofa in their small Tufnell Park flat struggling to squeeze her foot into a shoe.

'Fuck these shoes,' she said under her breath. Tall, mixed-race, with a distinctive jet-black bob of hair, Paulsen spoke with just a hint of the Swedish accent she'd inherited from her father.

'Why isn't it all over the news?' said Nancy, now scrolling through her phone. Even though she hadn't been at the Beachams' house the previous night, Paulsen was already up to speed with what had happened. And she was already regretting sharing that information with Nancy. Momentarily giving up on the fight with her shoe, she explained the probable sequence of events that had unfolded, and why the Met would be sitting on the information for a few more hours.

'It's horrible. I like Beacham – I've always liked her,' said Nancy. 'She's one of the good ones. I think her heart's in the right place.'

'No blabbing about this at work, Nance,' warned Paulsen. 'To anyone.'

Nancy looked indignant. She was a social worker in east London and took a keen interest in her partner's job. But it wasn't entirely unknown for her to share with her workmates the odd titbit of information she'd gleaned from Paulsen regarding a high-profile investigation.

'When have I ever . . .?' she said, trailing off at the withering stare she was receiving. Paulsen's mobile rang, interrupting them. She looked at the display and her glare defrosted as she answered it.

'You could at least wait until I get into work before hassling me . . .' she said by way of a welcome.

'Hello, Mattie,' said Finn. 'It's nice to hear your voice too.'

Paulsen smiled, despite herself.

'How are you, guv?'

'None too shabby as it goes – thanks for asking.'

Paulsen's smile widened. There was a playfulness in Finn's voice she wasn't used to.

'So what have you been doing with yourself for the last six months?'

'Erm . . . making sourdough, mainly.'

She laughed out loud.

'Seriously?'

'We can save the catch-up for later,' he said hurriedly. 'Have you been briefed about the Beacham investigation?'

'Of course. Jackie spoke to me late last night,' said Paulsen, enjoying the discomfort in his voice and trying to shake the image of him baking bread.

'We've assembled a list of people who've made threats to Claire on her social media. Can you start looking into them? I'll email them over. Also – can you liaise with the pathologist who was at the crime scene last night? I want to know—'

'Boss!' she said, interrupting. She was still holding the errant shoe in her spare hand. 'Can this wait until I get in? There's not much I can do from here, is there?'

26

'Sure,' he said, sounding mildly chastened. 'Sorry, Mattie – it's just that I'm at my desk now, and I thought I'd get you all moving on this early. So we can get ahead on it.' There was a pause. 'No pun intended.'

Paulsen arched an eyebrow – now he was cracking gags, which *really* wasn't like him. She looked at her watch.

'You're at your desk now?'

'Yes. First day back. I've got quite a lot of catching up to do, on top of the investigation. Emails and suchlike.'

Paulsen tried to keep the smile out of her voice. He'd probably been there since five in the morning.

'Of course,' she said. 'I'm just on my way out of the door now – I'll see you when I get in.'

She put the phone down and looked up at Nancy.

'Jesus wept – I think I preferred him depressed,' she said.

'Inspector Goldenballs?' said Nancy.

Paulsen had never managed to quite sell Finn to Nancy for some reason. Even though the two had only met on the odd, brief occasion, Nancy hadn't quite taken to him. But then he could appear stand-offish and slightly aloof to those who didn't know him properly. Paulsen had seen Finn in any number of different moods over the years, but vaguely light and playful was a new one. With a heave, she finally forced her heel down into the shoe.

'Why does it feel like the day hasn't even started yet and I'd quite like to go back to bed?' she said.

Claire Beacham yawned. She and Michael had spent the night at a Premier Inn nearby in Tooting and were now helping themselves to its rather limp selection of breakfast options. On the plus side, the small restaurant area was completely empty, so there was no danger of being recognised. She'd spent the early part of the morning fulfilling her various radio

27

commitments, phoning in from their hotel room as if nothing had happened. Anyone listening wouldn't have guessed from the robust exchanges that anything was amiss, and she'd found it a good distraction from the horror of the previous evening.

Now though, it was all beginning to catch up with her. She'd scrubbed her hands over and over but still couldn't shake the oily sensation of the blood smeared on her fingers, or forget the sound that head had made as it dropped on to the floor.

She looked down without much enthusiasm at the wrapped package on the plate in front of her. She tore it open and shook out a rubber-looking croissant. Michael, who'd been helping himself at the buffet counter, came over and joined her, carrying some fruit in one hand and a small bowl of cereal in the other. He stared at it with little enthusiasm.

'We could still find a cafe or something?' he said.

Claire shook her head.

'This is fine and I need to get going soon.'

'Are you sure?' he said.

She smiled, reached across the table and squeezed his hand.

'I'm just tired. How are you doing?' she said with genuine concern.

Michael shook his head slowly.

'I can't unsee it. I don't think I'll ever unsee it. I'll certainly feel a lot happier when the police have caught the guy responsible. I can't believe how calm you're being about everything.'

She shrugged.

'What else can I do? The police will keep an eye on us for the next few days – and whoever did it would be pretty stupid to come back. Life goes on, doesn't it?'

Michael nodded in agreement and poured her some tea from a chipped white pot.

They'd first met when she'd been a firebrand young local councillor at the beginning of her political career. A property lawyer was an unlikely kindred spirit but she'd been instantly drawn to Michael. He believed passionately that everyone deserved an affordable roof over their heads and had dedicated his career to that principle. There was a genuine mutual respect between them that had endured too; a shared motivation to try and make the world just a little bit better for others. They'd 'rubbed along very nicely', as he liked to put it. Most importantly, he was supportive and caring, providing that outlet of sanity that she needed when the Westminster bubble felt too much.

Some things had changed over the years though. Not dramatically, but the edge had dulled from that early zeal with which they'd initially attacked their careers. She'd put it down to a natural levelling off that came with the passing of time. The pandemic – long, attritional and tiring – hadn't helped either. She still held the same ideals, fought for the same causes, but that desire to change the world wasn't quite as powerful as it had once been. Sketchy thoughts about standing down at the next general election had been coalescing at the back of her mind for some months, and last night's horror show had only served to sharpen her thinking. Other jobs were available that didn't deliver severed heads to your front door.

She watched Michael eating his breakfast, and took a sip of the lukewarm tea he'd poured for her. All this could wait. It would have to, at least for a while.

'So what's on the agenda today?' she said.

'Another meeting with the Doll Street Collective. There's light at the end of the tunnel now – we might even have a deal in place by the end of the week. Though by saying that out loud, I've probably jinxed it. What about you?'

'I'm supposed to be at Cromarsh Prison later, to talk to Benjamin Ngomo. I want to see where his head's at.'

They looked at each other for a moment and both smiled. 'Probably not the best choice of words,' she said. His smile faded.

'Don't you think you should be keeping a low profile for a bit? The police did advise it.'

'Not a chance – there's too much that needs doing, particularly with Benjamin's case. I can't hide away.'

He gave a resigned nod.

'I'm so glad you're fighting that one though,' he added. It'd been Michael who'd first been told about Benjamin's situation by a client and highlighted it to her, and he'd kept a keen interest in her progress. It wasn't the first time their shared ideals had found a way to cross-pollinate. She shrugged with frustration.

'Benjamin's got no one. And what the government is doing to him is wrong – just plain wrong.' She took a bite of the croissant. As suspected, it was pastry-flavoured chewing gum. Michael was squinting now over at the television showing *Good Morning Britain* in the far corner.

'How long do you think it'll be before we're all over the news?'

Claire sighed gloomily.

'Sooner rather than later. Better get ready to batten down the hatches . . .'

Finn had spent most of the morning so far ignoring the handful of well-wishers who were pleased to see him back. Most of his team weren't in yet, but his presence had been noted by a few uniform officers and some of the CID detectives working early shifts. He'd smiled pleasantly but not stopped to make small talk and had now sealed himself off in his office. There was plenty of admin to catch up on and he wanted to clear the decks as quickly as possible.

If the early word doing the rounds was that he was as terse as he'd ever been, that suited him just fine. Experience taught him that the Beacham investigation was likely to dominate everything else in the coming days and he wanted all his attention focused on that. It felt odd being back at his desk – the room even *smelt* the same – but he wasn't the same man and it was important not to lose sight of the journey he'd been on.

He'd found some plants on his desk when he'd first arrived – presumably Ojo's – and moved them discreetly on to a shelf out of his line of sight. He wondered how well she'd been received by the rank and file during her attachment covering for him. She could be fairly brusque, like him, but was also disarmingly honest, which he suspected would have gone down well with a lot of the troops. You knew where you stood with her. She was naturally open as a person, whereas he was notoriously closed. He checked himself – this was something his counsellor had encouraged him to try and change on his return. A couple of hours into day one and her early verdict would probably be: 'could do better'.

'Stop beating yourself up – you've barely started,' said Karin and he smiled.

Refocusing on his screen, he checked the time – he still had a good hour before his team would start arriving in numbers. He was starting to feel a few proper butterflies now, aware people would be scrutinising him, looking for any potential weaknesses following his time away. It was human nature, after all. Police officers needed to have total confidence in their leaders – their lives might depend on them one day. He wasn't sure what most of them had been told about his sabbatical, but he knew his absence would have been the subject of plenty of chat. There'd have been more than a few rolled eyes, fingers tapping at the sides of heads. Whatever advances there'd been in the wider world about understanding men's mental health, he wasn't certain they had quite permeated the Met yet. One thing he was clear about was that he'd need to hit the ground running.

'Guv.'

He turned and saw a uniform PC standing in the doorway.

'You got something, Rob?' said Finn.

He nodded.

'I think so. A misper reported late last night – we think he's a match for your murder victim.'

Finn felt a rush of adrenaline. He'd missed this.

4

'His name's Lukasz Mazurek,' said Finn. 'He's a social worker at Lambeth Council. His wife reported him missing in the early hours of this morning. Uniform managed to get a photograph of him, but only made a provisional match with the head that was left at the Beachams' this morning.'

'You actually look a bit different . . .' said John Skegman, screwing up his face as he peered up at him.

'New glasses,' said Finn tightly, wondering why his appearance was taking precedence over a beheading on their patch.

He was standing in the DCI's office at Cedar House. Like seeing Ojo the previous night, it was the first time they'd been together for some time. A small, wiry man with sharp, pointed features and a permanent five o'clock shadow, Skegman wasn't someone who tended to dominate a room when he entered it. But Finn had known him long enough not to underestimate him. There wasn't much he missed inside his station or within the detail of an investigation. He could also be bloody annoying.

'Mazurek's Polish by birth,' Finn continued. 'Thirty-six years old, came over with his family when he was thirteen—'

'He's an immigrant then? That might be relevant,' said Skegman interrupting.

Finn nodded.

'I know what you're thinking, but Claire Beacham's not known for being particularly outspoken on immigration. I'm not sure she's an obvious target for right-wing extremist groups. Domestic violence is her brief.'

'Doesn't rule it out though. Is there a potential link?'

'Possibly,' conceded Finn. 'There's another case – another immigrant Beacham's dealing with – but it's obscure and hasn't received much publicity yet.' He held up a file of paper-work. 'Benjamin Ngomo, a twenty-two-year-old of Congolese descent. He's being held in Cromarsh Prison for offences related to membership of an organised crime group. But his situation is very different. Mazurek had British citizenship, Benjamin doesn't. He was brought over when he was a small child and his parents never formalised his status. Despite growing up in this country, he's still effectively living on the same temporary immigration visa.'

'Why didn't his parents pursue it?' asked Skegman. Finn shrugged.

'Happens more than you think – just reading through some of the case notes, there are currently around 180,000 people in this country estimated to be in a similar position.'

'So what's Beacham's involvement with him?'

Finn glanced through the paperwork he was holding.

'The problem this kid's got is that he has a previous convic-tion – a suspended sentence for shoplifting.'

Skegman pulled a face.

'That shouldn't be enough to get you deported – even with this government?'

'It isn't – but they operate a "two strikes and out" policy. Benjamin's already been found guilty and his sentencing hearing is early next week. If he's given longer than a year, he'll face automatic deportation, and that's what Beacham's fighting.'

'Is it likely? What was he charged with?'

'Nothing too serious – but enough. Sounds like he was very

low level. Conspiracy to commit theft, conspiracy to handle stolen goods, and various drug-related offences. But add that to his previous conviction, and there's no way he's getting less than twelve months this time.'

Skegman's eyes narrowed as if he was remembering something.

'Which OCG are we talking about?'

'They were based in Guildford and mainly responsible for a number of armed robberies across the south London/Surrey borders last year.'

Skegman nodded in recognition.

'I remember now – the ringleaders were all jailed last month. So why haven't I heard about this boy's case before?'

'The media covered it lightly a few weeks ago, but not much since then, and Beacham wanted to get the domestic violence debate out of the way before she went big with it.'

Skegman pondered it for a moment.

'It's very specific and, frankly, quite small fry. Doesn't strike me as the sort of thing that would provoke such a graphic murder. And why pick Mazurek? Just because he's an immigrant too? Is there any obvious connection between him and Beacham?'

Finn shook his head.

'None that I've seen so far. And I agree, there are more high-profile MPs, more high-profile cases that an extremist could target if immigration was their issue. I doubt many people have even heard of Benjamin Ngomo.'

'Still – keep counter-terror in the loop on it. Has Mazurek been formally identified yet?'

'No, but Sami Dattani and Dave McElligott are on their way to talk to his wife. We only made the connection around an hour ago. In the meantime, we'll continue to look at any possible links there might be between Mazurek and the Beachams.'

Skegman's ratty little eyes were still scrutinising him.

'It's not just the glasses – have you lost weight, Alex?'

Finn went directly to the incident room and found it starting to fill now. Walking through, nursing a cup of instant coffee and scowling at no one in particular, was Mattie Paulsen. He'd genuinely missed that scowl and tried not to let his inner smile show.

'Sourdough?' she said, raising an eyebrow at him.

'It's all about the quality of the flour,' he replied, deadpan. 'Happy to show you some time . . .'

'Thanks, but I think I'm busy that decade,' she countered.

He grinned and so did she.

'Good to see you again, Mattie. How have you been?' he asked.

'Surviving,' she said. 'And you, guv?'

He considered it for a moment.

'Still alive . . .'

Paulsen laughed.

'Well, I suppose that's as much as we can hope for.'

'Let's see where we are by the end of the week,' he said. His face turned serious. 'We think we've identified the victim in the Beacham investigation.'

She nodded.

'I've just heard – what do you need me to do?'

'See if you can find anything that connects either Claire or Michael Beacham to Lukasz Mazurek in the first instance. Have you found anything interesting in that list of online trolls I emailed over?'

Paulsen gave him a sideways look.

'Give me a chance – I've only just arrived . . .'

Finn nodded apologetically.

'Sorry, I'm a bit ahead of myself.'

'Didn't get this with Ojo . . .' she said, rolling her eyes.

Finn shook his head, enjoying the banter. Some of those butterflies from earlier were beginning to dissipate.

'Speaking of – where is Jackie? She's usually first in.'

Paulsen looked awkward.

'I don't think it's anything to worry about,' she said.

'What isn't?' said Finn.

She continued to look uncomfortable.

'I think she's dealing with some stuff at home at the moment.'

'What sort of stuff?' he asked, unable to contain his curiosity.

Paulsen shrugged.

'Don't know exactly. A few issues with her son, I think.'

Jackie Ojo was a single mother to a nine-year-old boy and Finn was aware she also looked after her elderly mother. She juggled a lot, but rarely talked about it at work, let alone allowed the pressures to show. Finn knew only too well what the job could be like when you had other stuff distracting you.

'I ought to crack on,' said Paulsen and headed over to her desk. As Finn turned, he saw Ojo entering, as if on cue, through the main double doors of the incident room. He watched as she took off her jacket and hung it up, almost oblivious of everyone else. He recognised the hard determina-tion on her face – it was like an unspoken warning to her colleagues not to bother her unless it was absolutely neces-sary. He knew better than anyone that what you saw on the surface wasn't necessarily a guide to what was really going on in someone's head. She caught him looking, smiled briskly and settled down at her desk.

★   ★   ★

37

The woman hadn't stopped crying since they'd got there. DC Sami Dattani was sitting in the kitchen area of a small flat in Tooting. It was bright, cheerful, and completely at odds with the reason they were there. He'd just informed Helen Mazurek that a body had been found in the search for her missing husband, and also told her that they were confident it was Lukasz. What she didn't yet know was the manner of his death. That, to Dattani's eternal gratitude, would be left for the family liaison officers to break to her. They'd need to do that soon though. What had happened was bad enough, but you didn't want her piecing it together from a rumour on Twitter, or a newspaper headline once the media got wind of it.

It didn't help that his fellow officer hadn't said a word since they'd arrived. DC Dave McElligott was a tall man with glossy black hair, boyish features and, normally, a natural affable charm. But he'd been sitting like a sullen child at the kitchen table, watching the woman's pain with what looked like detached boredom, and it was seriously starting to piss Dattani off.

Helen spoke with a plummy Home Counties accent and, judging by a wedding photo hanging in the hallway, she'd been married to Lukasz for some years. It was disconcerting seeing the same man in the various other pictures dotted around the flat. The smiling, happy individual on the ski slope, the beaming son extending an arm around elderly parents. The only face Dattani could see was that bloodstained, yellowing one resting on the Beachams' kitchen floor. There was no doubting now that this was the same man.

'I'm sorry,' said Helen, composing herself. 'I just can't understand this. It's almost beyond my ability to—' She broke off again and held up a hand. 'Why can't anyone tell me how he died? Was it quick, at least?'

McElligott looked over at Dattani, and then so did Helen, following his lead.

'We won't know anything for sure until there's been an autopsy,' Dattani answered diplomatically. Strictly speaking, he wasn't deceiving her.

'I want to see him – when can I see him?' she asked.

Dattani shifted in his seat.

'We can talk about that when the FLO arrives,' he replied reassuringly, even if the words were carefully chosen.

Immediately, Helen looked overwhelmed again.

'Take as long as you need,' he continued, glancing over at McElligott, whose expression hadn't changed. What was wrong with the man? It wasn't as if they hadn't been in situations like this countless times before. He knew what was involved in these conversations and was usually far more engaged.

'It's okay. I want to try and help,' said Helen, composing herself.

'Can you think of anyone who might have wanted to harm your husband?'

'No. Not at all. He was the warmest, kindest person you could ever meet. He didn't have enemies.'

'What about his work – do you know if he'd upset anyone?' said McElligott.

'Not as far as I know. You'd have to check with them, but he was all about helping people – that's why he became a social worker. He loved it.'

'This is going to sound a bit left-field, but did Lukasz know the MP Claire Beacham or her husband, Michael?' said Dattani.

Helen looked confused.

'No – he wasn't really interested in politics.'

'He'd never met either of them to your knowledge?'

She shook her head and looked down, the pain visible again. They were interrupted by the sound of the front doorbell ringing. Dattani felt relieved – he sensed they'd got as much as they were going to get.

'That'll be DC Adams – she's one of your family liaison officers—'

'I'll get it,' said McElligott, springing to his feet. A few moments later, he returned with Adams, and as Dattani made the introductions, McElligott slipped outside. Dattani left the pair together. He'd got answers to the most immediate questions; Nishat Adams would be able to pick it up from here and he was happy to leave her to it. Right now, he was almost as interested in what was making McElligott act so detached. As he walked out on to the street, he looked around, but there was no sign of him.

'Fuck's sake, Dave,' he said under his breath.

McElligott had walked down a side street near to Helen Mazurek's flat and was leaning against a brick wall with his mobile pressed to his ear.

'Thanks for getting back to me – I really appreciate it,' he said. 'It's about the application I made for a bank loan earlier. I still don't quite understand why it was refused and I was wondering if—' He listened to the reply, trying to contain his frustration. 'Yeah – I realise all that, but my understanding was that I *would* be eligible. I was told it would be okay.' He stopped again. 'Look, mate – just talk to me like a human being. I'm a police officer, okay? So treat me with a bit of courtesy. I've got a pregnant girlfriend – and I could use some help here—' He listened for a few more moments and shook his head. 'Yeah, whatever – I get the message.' He shook his head and cut the call off. *'Fuck!'* he shouted to no one in particular.

'You alright, Dave?'

McElligott turned, unsure how long his colleague had been standing there.

'Yeah, mate, all good,' he replied to Dattani.

'Are you sure? You didn't seem at the races back there?'

McElligott gave him a sour glare.

'Oh, come on, how do you arrive at that?'

'Because you barely said a word to a woman who's just found out her husband's been murdered.'

McElligott looked like he might argue back, but then the fight seemed to go out of him.

'Things are a bit difficult at home at the moment. Zoe's suffering a bit – and with me working, she's having to do a lot on her own. We had a blazing row before I left this morning and I haven't been able to shake it off.'

Dattani's face softened.

'Sorry, mate – I didn't think. How long has she got to go?'

'About six weeks. That's why I'm a bit distracted.'

'Don't worry, I know how stressful it can be – especially when it's your first one.'

McElligott seemed to brighten up.

'Thanks, Sami, appreciate that.'

'We ought to head back – the governor wants to hold a briefing at ten.'

'Cracking the whip already, is he?'

He winked at Dattani, but as they turned to walk back to their car, the smile on his face darkened into something more serious.

'It's good to be back,' said Finn, surveying the room. 'I'm sure you've all missed me, but rest assured, I'm still as friendly and easy-going as I always was.' There was a ripple of laughter around the room. 'So let's get to it.' He pointed at a board behind him where photographs of Claire and Michael Beacham were pinned. There were photographs too of Lukasz Mazurek, alive and well, taken from his Instagram, and one of the forensic photographs of the severed head from the crime scene. There was also a screen grab of the intruder in the baseball cap caught on the Beachams' security cameras.

'Forensics overnight haven't really given us much to go on. The killer was careful – there's no fingerprints or DNA traces to work with, not from the head nor the bag and box it was carried in. And we still don't have a body – though judging by the lack of decomposition, it looks like the killing must have taken place pretty recently. The house-to-house inquiries haven't thrown up much either. Nobody saw this guy arrive or leave.'

'What about the street cameras?' said Paulsen.

Finn stepped over to the map of south London that dominated one side of the incident room. A red pin had been stuck in to mark the Beachams' house. He traced the route with his finger.

'They show him proceeding into the next road ... Tully Street, then on to Alden Way, and then they lose him.'

'So we've got nothing,' said Ojo.

Finn gave a slight grimace of frustration.

'Not as much as I'd like, put it that way. The early indications are that the Beachams didn't know Lukasz Mazurek and he didn't know them. That's not to say there isn't a connection – and right now that's what I want to establish. There's a reason this guy was selected, a reason he was killed in the manner he was, and a reason why the Beachams were targeted.'

'Unless it's a nutter,' offered Dattani.

'I think that much is pretty fucking obvious, Sami,' said Paulsen.

Finn nodded in acknowledgement before continuing.

'The other possibility is that this was a hate crime – Mazurek was a Polish immigrant and that might have been enough for someone.' He pointed at the picture of the MP. 'Claire Beacham started her political career in 2012 as a local councillor in Stockwell before joining the Labour group on the London Assembly in 2017. She was elected to parliament as the MP for Wimbledon South in 2019. Mazurek was employed as a social worker in Lambeth throughout that period – so there's plenty of potential for a crossover somewhere in there. Let's look into this man's past, every case he's worked—'

Finn broke off. Jackie Ojo had taken a call while he'd been talking and was now holding up a hand, signalling it was important.

'You got something, Jacks?' said Finn.

She nodded.

'Yeah, guv – looks like we've found the body.'

5

Finn sighed the moment he arrived. He was standing on a main road midway between Brixton and Clapham. A small alleyway in front of him and most of the adjoining street had been cordoned off. A couple of PCSOs were protecting the area while a full forensic operation began to unroll. Despite being some distance away, a television cameraman was already there, pointing his lens at the whole scene.

'I thought we might get just a little bit longer before they arrived,' muttered Finn.

'I didn't,' said Paulsen as they made their way towards the cordon.

The body had been discovered by a schoolboy who'd sneaked into the alley for an impromptu pee. He'd found the discarded machete next to a large industrial dustbin. Climbing up on to some nearby crates, he'd then seen what was inside the bin. The first responder's main task hadn't been to deal with a traumatised adolescent but to make sure the photos he'd taken were completely deleted from his phone. It was hardly a surprise though that news of the discovery had already travelled fast.

'Now that the world knows we've got a headless body, the next question's going to be about the location of the head. I'm not sure how long we'll be able to keep Claire Beacham's name out of this,' said Finn. 'These things have a habit of leaking . . .'

The Senior CSI saw them approaching and came over to greet them. After they'd donned the appropriate apparel, he led them up the pavement to where a series of numbered yellow cones began.

'It looks like the victim was attacked here first,' the CSI said, pointing at the ground. It was splashed with blood and Finn could see a clear trail of drops where the forensic investigation team had laid out the rest of the cones. 'My guess, given the small quantity of blood, is that it comes from some sort of puncture wound.'

Finn nodded in agreement. It tied in with what the forensic pathologist who'd examined the severed head believed had happened – that Mazurek had mercifully died prior to the decapitation.

'Makes sense,' he said. 'The killer stabs him first to incapacitate him, then probably finishes the job in the alley, then takes the head.'

They followed the CSI to the alley, where the forensic photographer was already working. Finn's eyes were immediately drawn to the machete lying on the ground where it had been found.

'He didn't even bother to try and hide it,' he said. 'He could have chucked that in the bin with the body.'

'Yeah, because that would have completely disguised the fact that someone was decapitated here,' said Paulsen, pointing at the sticky crimson sea by the bin's base. It was clear something major had happened here – there wasn't just blood on the ground, there was pink fleshy matter too. The forensic team had placed a small stepladder close to the cylindrical drum to allow a look inside without further contaminating the scene.

Finn climbed the ladder and peered down. For a moment it looked like someone was curled up asleep in there. There was blood pooling at the bottom and the stench, largely from the rubbish surrounding the body, was appalling. It smelt literally of shit, though it was hard to tell whether that was Mazurek's bowels releasing post-mortem or simply the discarded refuse of the local dog population. He looked at the fleshy stump at the top of the shoulders and remembered the bloodied tendrils at the base of the head in the Beachams' kitchen. He knew the various ways a body could become dehumanised in death but this was genuinely horrific. They could put a name to the man now, knew where he lived, who he lived with and what he'd done for a living. Lukasz Mazurek had definitely deserved better than this.

'We won't be able to retrieve the body out of there for a while,' said the CSI. 'There's a lot of ground to cover between here and the street.' Finn nodded and stepped back down on to the ground. Paulsen went up next, briefly looked inside for herself and, without altering her expression, stepped back down again.

Finn could see the forensic team were keen to get on. Space in the alley was tight and they'd been holding back while he and Paulsen were there. As they walked back up towards the main road, Finn pointed to a large grey building around two hundred yards away.

'That's where Lukasz worked. Uniform have already been taking statements; let's see if any of his colleagues can tell us anything.'

Paulsen didn't move. She was looking up and down the length of the street.

'The killer must have ambushed him. If the intention was always to take the head, he must have been watching from somewhere first, waiting for Lukasz to leave work and get close to that alleyway.'

Finn nodded and looked carefully around. He couldn't see any obvious CCTV cameras mounted close by.

47

'Possibly from a vehicle. Or maybe that coffee shop over the road,' he said. 'But you're right, this was pre-planned. After he killed Lukasz, he left the machete out in plain sight where it could be found, then made no effort to hide the mess round there. He knew we'd find the body in the bin and I don't think that bothered him in the slightest.'

Kenny Fuller pulled the woollen ski hat down over his head. He felt it itch against his balding scalp and, with a grunt of irritation, pulled it straight off again. He didn't like people staring at the back of his head – they always did the same thing; that little glance back as they passed him. In prison, he'd been nicknamed 'Smiler' because of the long scar that curved in a grotesque resemblance of a smile stretching across the back of his skull.

He'd acquired it in his twenties when he'd been sleeping rough in his home town of Liverpool. Some would-be gangsters had mistakenly thought he was dealing drugs on their turf and taken a twelve-inch blade to his head. The damage hadn't just been to the exterior. In his early forties now, he still suffered from splitting headaches, occasional moments of forgetfulness and, of course, the rages – the white-hot furies that came from nowhere.

He wasn't in the best of moods. The man he'd been dispatched to meet was someone he'd have quite comfortably never set eyes on again if he'd had any choice in the matter. Colin Jakes was also a former inmate of HMP Brazely. One of those people who couldn't quite wipe the smirk off their face even when there wasn't anything to be amused about. He also had a smart mouth – a tendency to add a little dig here or there, all in the name of 'banter'. But the boss had decreed that Jakes possessed a skill set that might be useful, so Fuller tried to remember the bigger picture.

He arrived at the pub where they'd agreed to meet and found Jakes sitting outside, nursing a half-drunk pint of beer. The younger man greeted him with that characteristic smirk and Fuller beat down the desire to wipe it off his face.

'Alright, Smiler,' said Jakes.

Christ, he wanted to hurt him, Fuller thought.

'It's Kenny out here. Do you understand?'

Another smirk.

'Right you are, Ken,' said Jakes. 'Can I get you a drink?'

'No, and you might want to finish that,' said Fuller, pointing at the beer. 'I don't want to have this conversation here.'

Jakes smiled agreeably and downed the rest of his drink. Fuller turned and started walking, forcing the other man to jog to catch up with him.

'So, what's this all about?'

'I've been sent to ask if you'd be interested in some work?'

Fuller was full-on marching now, just a little bit too fast for Jakes. It was deliberate – he could hear him breathing heavily as he tried to keep up. It would do him good; the man had developed a belly since leaving prison.

'Depends on what sort of work you're talking about, mate,' said Jakes.

Fuller looked around. Although it wasn't busy, there were enough passers-by to make him feel uncomfortable. He saw a side street and turned into it, checking they were completely alone before continuing.

'The man who employs me is planning something big and we need people. He thinks you're someone who might be able to help us.'

Jakes smirked again.

'When you say the man who employs you ... do you mean—'

'Don't be fucking stupid, Col,' said Fuller, interrupting quickly. The smirk didn't go away. A gust of wind blew an empty beer can over nearby and a dirty old bin liner wrapped itself around Fuller's legs. On a whim, he picked it up and kept hold of it. Jakes was watching him uncertainly. The smirk was beginning to fade a little now.

'I don't think that's for me, Ken. Since I got out I've been trying to keep my nose clean. I think I'm better than that sort of work now, to be fair.'

Fuller shook his head.

'What exactly does *"better than that"* mean?' he said, unable to keep his irritation hidden.

Jakes smiled pleasantly, held up his hands in mock surrender.

'Easy, fella – it's not a dig. I've been offered a job with a firm of builders. It's a fresh start, isn't it?'

Fuller stopped.

'The man I'm talking about was *very* keen to get you on board. Personally, I think he's wrong. I think you're a slippery fuck I wouldn't trust as far as I could throw.'

Jakes laughed.

'Yeah, well – good job you're not the brains of the outfit then, eh?'

Fuller smiled. Not because he was amused, but because he couldn't see any good reason now not to do what he was about to do. He looked around – the street was pleasingly empty.

'You're sure then, Col? Absolutely certain of that?'

Jakes nodded cheerfully.

'I'm sure, mate. Sorry.'

He smirked again. With a snarl, Fuller lunged and wrapped the bin liner around the man's head. In one quick movement, he pulled the now hooded figure towards him and connected a meaty punch to somewhere around the face. Jakes fell heavily to the ground, still enveloped in black plastic. Fuller dropped down and rained a torrent of rapid blows on to the bin liner until, finally, he ran out of breath. He stood up and watched blood leak out from under the plastic and on to the pavement. One of Jakes's legs began twitching.

'Cheers, *mate*,' said Fuller as he turned and walked away.

The man felt the cold air sting his cheeks and savoured the sensation. The Lauterbrunnen valley wasn't just one of the most beautiful parts of Switzerland, it was one of the most beautiful places in the world, as far as he was concerned. In the middle distance, he could see the 297-metre-high Staubbach Falls – the highest free-falling waterfall in the country. Every day the vista took his breath away.

He noticed a wooden bench further along the path, sat down and pulled out a thermos flask. As he poured himself a steaming shot of coffee, he leant forwards, breathing in the aroma. Sweet, slightly spicy, with just a hint of butter, the smell was exquisite. It was ground from fresh Hawaiian Kona beans, and he swore it was the best cup of coffee in the world. The beans cost a small fortune to import but he wasn't a man who liked to compromise. He was about to take a mouthful when his phone rang. He checked the display and immediately took the call.

'Colin Jakes is a no,' said a distinctive Scouse voice on the other end.

The man absorbed the information and took a sip of his coffee, savouring the taste like a fine wine before swallowing it.

'That is a shame. Do you have alternatives?'

'There's always alternatives.'

'Good, because I'm flying back this afternoon. We'll regroup in person tonight. And Kenny . . . make sure you have someone in place by the time we meet. Yes?'

He ended the call and stared out across the valley. It had been almost three years since he'd last set foot on UK soil, and he would miss this place. It hadn't been the worst location in the world to sit out a global pandemic, but there was something that he wanted, something he wanted very much. And when Ray Spinney wanted something, he was prepared to move heaven and earth to get it.

6

The social services office where Lukasz Mazurek had worked was even drabber than Cedar House, thought Paulsen. And that took some doing. She and Finn were waiting for Mazurek's manager, Nina Thornbury. They were sitting in a small meeting room adjacent to the main office watching Thornbury at work outside. She was talking to visibly shocked members of her team, who were still in the process of reassigning the dead man's caseload. It was only when Nina finally came and joined them that Paulsen could see how truly devastated she was.

In her early fifties, with grey-white hair, she possessed a hard-lined face set around warm eyes. Paulsen suspected she was someone pretty formidable in the normal run of things. But she was subdued as she introduced herself, and as Finn made his own introductions, her pain was all too clear.

'Lukasz was very *uncomplicated* . . .' she said. 'Yes, that's the best word to describe him. There was no side to him. He was diligent and had a lovely way with the public. He earnt people's trust very quickly – which is priceless in this job.'

Paulsen knew that only too well. Her partner Nancy was also a social worker and she felt a strange sense of associated pride. Thornbury could just as easily have been talking about her.

'When did you last see him?' asked Finn.

Nina explained that they'd both been working late last night, but she had left before him and hadn't seen anyone suspicious hanging around as she'd departed.

'Is there anyone you can think of who might have wanted to hurt Lukasz?' asked Paulsen.

'There are always going to be people unhappy with their situation and how they've been treated. So yes. And over the years, there were some who felt we – he – could have done better.'

'Any, in particular, that stand out?' said Finn.

Thornbury looked out of the window. It was only mid-morning but she looked shattered, her face devoid of colour.

'There was a twelve-year-old – James Hartley – who was murdered by his stepbrother in 2017. Edie Selwyn – a baby who was shaken to death by her mother in 2019. They were the most difficult cases he dealt with. The families and friends were all deeply unhappy with how things were handled and made complaints. But his conduct was exemplary on both occasions – there was never a question that he bore any responsibility. These things come with the job, as I'm sure you're both well aware.'

Paulsen nodded sympathetically. She'd seen Nancy deal with enough tricky situations already in her short career for that observation to resonate.

'Lukasz worked here for twelve years – but there were only two contentious cases that you can think of, involving him?' said Finn.

'Of course not, but they were the most significant – the ones I can remember, anyway.'

'We'll need to go through everything, I'm afraid,' said Paulsen. 'But there's nothing in the immediate past that springs to mind?'

Thornbury shook her head.

'Do you mind if I ask you about the MP, Claire Beacham?' said Finn.

She looked up with surprise.

'What's she got to do with this?'

Paulsen glanced at Finn, happy to let him field that one. He licked his bottom lip carefully.

'There's some evidence ... peripherally linking her with this.'

Thornbury sat back in her chair and digested the words, trying to make sense of the connection.

'Have you dealt with her at all?' said Finn, quickly.

'Yes, and I have to say I always found her interventions when she was a local councillor here very welcome. She's smart, clued-up and genuinely cares – the world could use more politicians like her, in my opinion. If she's somehow been sucked into this, then that's awful.'

'But there were no cases or anything else you can remember connecting Lukasz with her?' said Finn.

Thornbury shook her head.

'No. To be honest, since she was elected to parliament in 2019, we haven't had much to do with her – we're not in her constituency.'

'They didn't know each other personally then? Or perhaps Lukasz knew her husband?' said Paulsen.

'Not as far as I know.' She faltered and put her hand to her mouth. 'I'm sorry, this is just so hard to take in.'

'Perhaps you should take the rest of the day off,' said Finn. 'In the circumstances, I'm sure people would understand.'

Her expression immediately hardened again.

'If I go home, lots of things that need to be done won't get done. Lots of people who are counting on us will have to suffer that bit longer. Lukasz would definitely not want that. We've been pared to the bone here.'

Like the décor of the office, thought Paulsen, some things here were, in fact, exactly the same as Cedar House.

*   *   *

While Claire lived in the leafy suburbs of south-west London, her constituency office was located in one of South Wimbledon's less salubrious streets. Sandwiched between a betting shop and a newsagent, the converted Chinese takeaway bore the words 'Claire Beacham MP' on the front in simple white letters against a red background. A large portrait of her in the window beamed out at passers-by, while posters advertised the times of surgeries, together with details of local food banks. There were two main rooms on the ground floor – a front reception and an office behind, which carried the near-permanent odour of grease. Despite an extensive refurb, the smell betrayed its previous existence as the restaurant's kitchen.

When Claire arrived, she found Grant Lassiter at his desk talking to the other member of her team, researcher Rebecca Devlin. Attractive, in her early twenties, with flowing, long blonde hair, Rebecca was a graduate straight out of Sheffield University. She was someone Claire fancied she recognised a little of herself in – or at least the young woman she'd once been, anyway.

'Jesus, Claire – are you alright?' said Lassiter, rising immediately to his feet as she entered. She'd called and told him what had happened earlier that morning.

'I will be, though a cup of tea wouldn't hurt, Bex . . .'

Rebecca nodded furiously and hurried through to a small adjacent kitchen area.

'You should probably see this,' said Lassiter. He angled the laptop he'd been looking at towards her. On screen, the *MailOnline* headline read:

'*Severed head horror at MP's home*'.

'Right,' she said, leaning in to read the article.

'I was about to phone you,' he said. 'It's only just broken. We're being inundated with calls – press inquiries, mainly.' He looked at her with concern. 'It must have been absolutely horrific. Are you sure you're okay – seriously?'

She smiled reassuringly at him.

'Yes. I think so, anyway. Bit wobbly, I suppose – but neither of us was hurt and that's the main thing.'

'So how accurate is that piece?'

She simply nodded in confirmation and he looked down, ashen. Rebecca re-entered carrying three cups of tea on a tin tray. She handed Claire a chipped mug that bore the words 'Smile – it may never happen'. Beacham arched an eyebrow at her as she took it.

'I hope there's a shitload of sugar in that . . .' she said, before taking a sip and giving an approving thumbs up. She then explained to both of them the events of the previous evening, from the moment she'd arrived home to their unexpected overnight stay at the hotel. 'We'll deal with this in due course,' she said calmly. 'For the moment, let's put together a state-ment for the press. I'm not doing any interviews – tell them Michael and I are fine, we want to let the police do their jobs, and our sympathies go out to the victim and his family. And tell them we won't be making any further comment for the foreseeable.'

Lassiter nodded.

'I'll draw something up. The Chief Whip's office also . . .'

'I know. I've already spoken to them – I'm meeting him at 2 p.m. Can we reschedule my visit to Cromarsh Prison for as soon as possible? I really want the focus of the next few days to be on Benjamin Ngomo, not this.'

Lassiter shook his head.

'We won't get you in there until tomorrow morning, now.'

Beacham sighed.

'First thing then, please, Grant.'

He nodded.

'Claire – do you mind me asking something?' said Rebecca. 'It's just . . .' She faltered, as if embarrassed to ask the question. 'Are *we* in any danger?'

For a second, Claire was lost for words. Guiltily, she realised it was something she simply hadn't thought about in the rush of things.

'I can't say definitively. But the police say there isn't any evidence of a threat to my safety.' Rebecca didn't look overly reassured. 'Bex, if someone's trying to intimidate you, the best way to respond is to ignore them,' she continued. 'And until the police tell me otherwise, that's what I think we should all do.'

'I can't believe how calm you are,' said Rebecca. 'I'd be all over the place if something like that happened to me.'

Claire smiled smoothly. The smile she usually saved for the Commons or television interviews.

'Life goes on. I'm just going to go to the loo, and then we'll run through the diary for the rest of the day. Onwards and upwards, eh?'

It was only when she reached the toilet that the mask slipped. The sensation of the blood, dribbling between her fingers, just wouldn't go. Neither would the image of that head, rolling like a dropped cabbage across the kitchen floor – or the look on its face. She hadn't given herself time to properly take it on board yet and Rebecca's point was well made. What if the police didn't catch the killer? Just how much danger were they in, was she *putting* them all in? She looked into the mirror above the sink and saw something she hadn't seen in her own eyes for a long time – fear.

It was a nondescript warehouse on a nondescript trading estate in the middle of nowhere. Ray Spinney looked around approvingly at the vast empty space. His flight from Interlaken had gone without a hitch. A fake passport had allowed him to slip back into the UK without undue attention. He saw Kenny Fuller emerge from a makeshift office in the corner of the warehouse, and turned to the young man who'd driven him from the airport and smiled pleasantly at him.

'You can fuck off now, son,' he said. The man, who was still holding Spinney's bag, handed it over and did just that.

'Decent flight?' said Fuller as he joined him.

'Never mind that.' Spinney bent down and unzipped his bag, pulling out a copy of the *London Evening Standard*. 'I'm more interested in this.' The headline on the front page read:

'MP in beheading horror'.

A photograph of the alleyway in south London where Lukasz Mazurek's body had been found showed a cluster of police officers and CSIs caught in mid-conversation. A second smaller picture of the police operation outside the Beachams' house was next to it.

Fuller nodded.

'Yeah – I saw that earlier.'

'You know how important Beacham is. What is this and why's it happening now?'

Fuller shrugged helplessly.

'A coincidence – it's got to be?'

Spinney sighed. He stared across the warehouse as he considered it.

'I don't like coincidences. What we're trying to do is like any other project in life. The planning has to be perfect, to the nth degree. Any little wrinkle or unexpected development – you don't ignore. Because these things can come back and bite you on the arse – yes?'

Fuller nodded in agreement.

'You think someone knows what we're planning?'

Spinney shook his head.

59

'I don't know what to think.' He tapped the front page of the paper. 'But the lanky streak in the middle – I know him; I've come across him before. His name's Finn.'

His mind flashed back three years to the events that had caused him to leave the country in the first place.

'What do you want me to do?' said Fuller.

'Nothing. This isn't a job for you. We need information and I still have one or two people left inside the Met who can help provide it. I want to know everything about Detective Inspector Finn and his team. And then I want to find a way in.'

7

Finn was in the incident room the following morning catching up on his team's progress when Skegman entered, hovering awkwardly by the door. Finn recognised the look on his face; it always reminded him of a dog in a park just before it began to chase its tail and defecate. Something equally smelly was undoubtedly about to get dropped.

'I'm getting some heat from the super. I think *he's* getting some heat from the chief super . . .' began Skegman as he finally joined him.

'So you're transferring that heat on to me?' said Finn, taking no pleasure in being proven right.

Skegman smiled wolfishly.

'Happily. When an MP's involved, everyone gets a bit twitchy. So where are we with this?'

The DCI perched on a desk and looked at him expectantly.

'Not much further on, to be honest,' replied Finn. 'As far as the forensics go, the head's been swabbed for fingerprints and potentially foreign DNA – we fast-tracked the results but found nothing. They also used adhesive tapings to check for hair and fibres, but again – the killer was being careful.'

'What about the murder weapon?' said Skegman.

'No prints there either.'

'And Beacham – any idea why she was specifically targeted?'

Finn shook his head.

'We've established no clear links between the victim and the Beachams, and counter-terror say they haven't picked up any unusual chatter from their usual sources.'

Skegman was frowning as he listened.

'We're still at a very early stage with this,' added Finn.

'I'm well aware,' said Skegman testily. 'What about the guy with the baseball cap from CCTV?'

'Nothing – though we've given the press a screen grab with a plea for information and witnesses.' He gave a non-committal shrug.

'So what are the other options? That Mazurek was simply in the wrong place at the wrong time and this is the work of a lunatic?'

'We're looking hard through both his and Beacham's worlds for anyone with a serious grudge against either of them.'

'I imagine there's quite a few nutters buried in that. Especially in Beacham's case,' said Skegman. 'MPs attract them like flies to honey.'

'Yes – and we're taking them all seriously, knocking on doors where appropriate. But as I say, nothing's immediately jumping out.'

Skegman watched the room at work for a moment while he considered it.

'Perhaps you should think about getting a profiler in? It might help you narrow it down . . .'

It wasn't a bad shout, thought Finn. But before he could reply, Paulsen interrupted them.

'Guv – sorry to barge in but something interesting has just dropped,' she said.

Skegman swivelled round, interested, but she ignored him. It was something she quite enjoyed doing, Finn had noticed.

'What have you got, Mattie?' he said.

'Doesn't look connected to the Mazurek investigation, but I thought you'd want to see this anyway.' She produced a piece of A4 paper with an image taken from a CCTV camera. 'A man was beaten half to death in the street yesterday in Greenwich. An ex-con called Colin Jakes. He was caught on camera walking with this individual, moments before.' She handed Finn the print-out and he looked at a picture that showed the pair from an angle high and from behind. It took him a moment to see what had caught Paulsen's eye – the tell-tale scar stretching across the back of the larger of the two men's head. The slightly pixelated image exaggerated the curved smile even further, into something almost demonic.

'Kenny Fuller . . .' said Finn. 'Unless someone else has had an extremely unlucky accident.'

'I doubt it. Fuller was in HMP Brazely with Jakes until his release last year,' said Paulsen.

'Doesn't seem to have been a very happy reunion . . .' said Skegman.

Finn was more than aware of who Kenny Fuller was. Just under three years ago he was the prime suspect for the murder of a corrupt police officer inside Brazely jail. It was widely believed he was working on behalf of an organised crime gang leader known colourfully as the 'Handyman'. Ray Spinney had earnt the nickname from his penchant for using hammers, screwdrivers, hacksaws and various other household imple-ments to inflict the crudest possible damage on his enemies.

Spinney's main infamy came from masterminding one of the biggest armed robberies of the last decade. An armoured vehicle carrying cash from a cargo depot at Stansted Airport to a bank in central London had been held up and robbed in 2015. Millions had been stolen and never recovered. While many of the men who'd carried out the raid had eventually been tracked down and arrested, Spinney himself had evaded capture, and a certain mystique had grown around the Handyman.

Three years previously, a murder investigation had taken Finn close to a portion of the missing Stansted money and he'd had a brief brush with what Spinney was capable of. The memory was still sharp enough to make him feel uncomfortable. The man had a long reach: one of the reasons he'd been able to evade capture for so long was his ability to cultivate insiders within the police force. To Finn's knowledge, the names of many of those sources still hadn't been identified.

One of them was known though – he was the man Kenny Fuller had been suspected of killing inside Brazely Prison. An expensively appointed solicitor had managed to clear Fuller not long afterwards. Finn was privately convinced it had been Spinney who'd funded the lawyer. The Handyman was currently thought to be in Europe somewhere and high on Interpol's most wanted list.

'What was Jakes inside for?' said Finn. 'Do we know?'

Paulsen nodded.

'Armed robbery. He and two other men robbed a newsagent in Romford in 2016 and left the owner in a coma. Uniform have been given Fuller's description – I'll let you know if they get anything.'

'Can we talk to Jakes? What state's he in?' said Finn.

She shook her head.

'He's in a coma, with a fractured skull and a bleed on the brain. I think he'll be lucky to survive this, from what I've been told.'

'Sounds like karma to me,' said Finn.

'Surely just some sort of prison feud that spilt over?' said Skegman, shaking his head dismissively.

'Probably,' said Finn. 'Unless it wasn't. We know who was pulling Fuller's strings before . . .' he added thoughtfully. He couldn't see an obvious link to the Mazurek murder investigation, but the timing of it was interesting, to say the least.

Benjamin Ngomo was twenty-two years old, but not for the first time Claire Beacham thought he looked at least seven or eight years younger, as she and Lassiter entered the visiting hall of Cromarsh Prison. He was a muscular figure with finely chiselled features, and if he seemed small and alone, that's because he was. He had no family after both his parents had died in his teens. The only person he did have in his corner was his girlfriend, Emma, a barista at a coffee shop. The pair seemed genuinely devoted to one another, but with the forces currently ranged against him, it was a romance that looked doomed.

As things stood, he faced either deportation or a potentially long jail term after his sentencing the following week. He had no legal representation and hadn't been able to get legal aid. Though he'd been born in Kinshasa, his parents had moved to London when he was a child and he had no family in the Democratic Republic of Congo that he was aware of. He was terrified at the prospect of being deported there, and even in the brief amount of time that she'd known him, Claire could see what kind of toll that fear was taking on him.

After Michael had brought the case to her attention she'd been happy to take it on. A man – a boy, really – against the system: it was definitely her kind of fight.

'Hello, Ben,' she said warmly as they sat down. 'How are you doing?'

He shrugged, as if that explained everything. Claire and Lassiter exchanged a glance. 'I can only imagine how you're feeling,' she continued. 'But I just wanted you to know what we're going to be doing this week to raise the profile of your case.' He nodded without a great deal of conviction.

'You do want to know, don't you?' inquired Lassiter.

Benjamin bit the bottom of his lip, rested a hand on the table.

'What's the point?' he said finally. He always spoke quietly, Claire noticed, regardless of his mood. It gave him an aura of calm she wasn't always sure was accurate. Deeper currents, she sensed, flowed beneath the surface. 'They're going to do what they're going to do, whatever the court decides. But if you want to try – knock yourself out,' he said.

She leant in.

'You can't talk like that. This is why I wanted to see you today – because I can help you. I *will* help you – but you need to believe that we can do this. We're going to bang the drum loudly. I'm going to be talking about you in parliament, to the television cameras, to the newspapers – from the rooftops, frankly. And when I'm sure the world knows all about you, I'll ask the Home Secretary to review your case and make it impossible for her to say no.'

The words were defiant but Benjamin looked at them both as if he'd just heard white noise.

'I didn't kill anyone. I just drove people around, dropped off a few packages – did as I was told. So why do they want to do this to me?'

Again, the same soft, neutral voice.

'It's not you personally that they have a problem with,' said Claire. 'They want to make an example out of you. But they can be forced into U-turns – governments do it all the time. If you manage the situation correctly, they *can* be forced to back down. And you have to believe that I know how to do that.'

He met her gaze evenly as she tried to inject her conviction into him.

'I don't want to lose Emma,' he said finally. 'That's all that matters to me.'

'How is she?' asked Claire.

'Same as me – scared.'

'It's really important you both try and stay positive,' said Lassiter.

'Easy for you to say – there's people in here who want to hurt me. They know I'm talking to an MP and they don't like it.'

'The authorities are aware of that and are keeping an eye. It's not in their interests for you to get hurt; they want everything to be above reproach,' said Lassiter.

'Just hang in there, Benjamin, please. I want to show the world who you really are – not who the Home Office says you are,' said Claire.

She tentatively moved to take his hand, but he moved it away and looked down again instead.

'Whatever,' he replied.

'Must be awkward,' said Sami Dattani, placing a mug of grey tea down on Dave McElligott's desk. McElligott looked at it with disdain.

'Am I going to have to stick another teabag into that?' he said.

'My wife says I make the worst cup of tea in the world,' said Dattani, almost with pride. McElligott took a sip.

'She's not wrong.' He grimaced. 'What must be awkward?' he said.

Dattani nodded discreetly towards Jackie Ojo, who was standing with her back to them by one of the office printers.

'Jackie O. Last week she was running the place. Now the gaffer's back – she's kind of back in her box, isn't she?'

McElligott pulled open his drawer, fished out a sugar sachet and emptied it into his mug before stirring the contents with a biro.

'He hasn't changed – Detective Inspector Robot. I thought someone might have reprogrammed him while he was away.'

'Come on, Dave. Give the bloke a break – I think he's had it quite hard.'

McElligott rolled his eyes.

'I wouldn't mind having it hard on his salary.'

Before Dattani could respond, McElligott's phone vibrated with an incoming text.

'Zoe forgiven you everything already?' inquired Dattani. McElligott swiped the message out of view and stood.

'Do us a favour, mate, and cover for me; something's come up.'

'Sure – anything I should know?'

But McElligott ignored him, and instead strode purposefully towards the door. Out in the corridor, he read the message again.

A mutual friend tells me you need a loan. Call me on this number if interested.

8

Myriad thoughts were going through Dave McElligott's mind as he made the journey from Cedar House into central London. The instructions he'd been given were very specific and he was fairly sure, even now, that he had a sense of where things were going. Anonymous offers like these didn't tend to be acts of charity. The question he was asking himself was: just how far was he prepared to go to sort out his financial problems?

They'd kind of crept up on him; he couldn't quite work out how he'd allowed things to get as bad as they had. Zoe had been the best thing to ever happen to him. Before meeting her, he'd ambled through relationships and had no great desire to settle down. His colleagues at Cedar House didn't think he took life seriously enough.

He'd never understood why that was such a bad thing. If you were happy and living a carefree existence – well, wasn't that what everyone aspired to? What all these experts on TV were always preaching? As far as he could see, both his mental health and his finances had been just fine, right up until the point where he *was* taking life seriously.

He'd met Zoe in the pub and it had begun rather casually, like so many of his relationships. She didn't seem to take the world too seriously either and he liked that about her. He didn't believe in love – or at least the idea that a relationship could last and survive over many decades. You could count on one hand the number of happily married people there were at Cedar House. That was nothing to do with the job – that was just life, full stop, in his view. But he and Zoe had clicked – the relationship had intensified, not faded away like so many of his previous liaisons – and then she'd got pregnant.

Far from being upset or shocked by this turn of events, he'd found himself genuinely excited at the prospect of becoming a father. And that, in hindsight, was where the problem had begun. He'd sold his small bachelor flat and, ignoring any semblance of financial sense, bought a three-bedroom house in Croydon with money he didn't have. He wanted the best for his new family; enjoyed hearing the word *'family'* roll off his tongue. But the house he couldn't afford had proven an unmitigated disaster. He wished he hadn't hired such a clown of a surveyor now. The guy had come cheap but it wasn't what he'd spotted, so much as the ninety-nine per cent of what he hadn't. The roof, the damp, the electrics, the plumbing and just about everything else needed more than just a 'little updating and modernising'.

Zoe had little idea of the true scale of their financial difficulties. She'd bought into the idea that progressing the house would be a shared project for them over the next few years. Their dream home, taking shape one room at a time around their burgeoning family. His last few pennies had foolishly been spent on a new kitchen – just to give her the illusion that they were well on their way. It was a lie, of course, and for the first time that he could remember, Dave McElligott was genuinely scared. Finn, Ojo and the rest of them should be proud – because he was certainly taking life seriously now.

As he walked through Victoria station, he went through the mental arithmetic of it for the umpteenth time. He'd only wanted a smallish loan from the bank – one to simply tide him over. But now, with this fresh new possibility arising, he was beginning to wonder if he shouldn't go for broke. Be bold, go big, get rid of the problem and worry about the consequences later. He just needed to hold his nerve, find out what this was all about and make sure he came out on top.

'Balls of steel, mate,' he muttered under his breath as he headed towards the tube.

Ten minutes later, he found himself exiting Tottenham Court Road underground station at the intersection with New Oxford Street. He walked in the general direction of the British Museum, checking his phone for the precise location of the place he'd been directed to. It wasn't hard to find in the end, a small Italian-run cafe tucked between a Zara and a Starbucks. He entered, scanned the room, and when he saw the man who was sitting in the corner waiting, felt his blood run cold. The first thing that went through his mind, oddly, was a song.

'Who can rob at sunrise?
Sprinkle it with gold,
Cover it in diamonds and a miracle or two?
The Handyman. The Handyman can ...'

For a while after the Stansted heist, every officer in the Met knew that little ditty – a bastardisation of the old Sammy Davis Jr. classic. Dave had sung it himself in the incident room, back in the days when he enjoyed playing the fool for a cheap laugh.

There was no question who the man now sitting at the table was, even though he'd never laid eyes on him in the flesh before. But he'd certainly seen photographs of Ray Spinney and was sure that's who he was looking at. In person, the Handyman wasn't as physically imposing as you might have expected; a slightly built man in his early sixties with Brylcreemed silver hair. He was dressed in a grey shirt with a black waistcoat and dark corduroy trousers. To anyone else, he probably looked a bit like an old-fashioned barber on a lunch break. But he still carried a presence – a lined face that looked hewn out of granite and a steely gaze that was boring into McElligott across the room.

He knew even before he sat down what kind of Faustian pact was about to be offered. Spinney was renowned for his use of insider contacts. Corrupt officers who provided him with information and were presumably handsomely rewarded for their trouble. The only question for McElligott was whether he was going to use this opportunity to be the person who brought the Handyman down – or to clear his debts. He'd revisit that choice later.

'I'm guessing I don't need to introduce myself,' said Spinney, with a voice like dry reeds.

McElligott shook his head.

'Good. Then, I won't waste your time. Let me run through some facts before I ask you a question,' he said. He took a sip of his espresso before he continued – a sense he was getting his ducks in a row.

'Your partner's name is Zoe Kenwright. She works as a beauty therapist in Wallington. She's pregnant with your first child and her delivery date is in just under six weeks' time.'

McElligott wasn't surprised at the level of detail; information was, after all, the man's currency. He was intrigued though about how he'd found all this out. He now regretted over-sharing with various friends in different stations over the last few months. He was pretty sure none of them were bent, but once you put this kind of information out there – in conversations, texts and emails – then you left yourself open. It looked like that loose mouth of his might yet be his downfall. His late mother hadn't got that bit wrong.

Spinney broke down for him the full extent of his financial problems, projecting how much he could expect them to deteriorate over the next twelve months. McElligott held up a hand. He knew the numbers himself only too well.

'Alright – I get the message. You know my situation. What do you want and what are you offering?'

'I want a steer on the inquiry involving Claire Beacham and any other investigations that might be of interest to me.'

'A steer?' said McElligott.

Spinney opened out his palms.

'That's it.'

'Really? Because the specific terms of this are important. I want to know that nothing I'm doing will lead to anyone getting hurt – I won't have blood on my hands.'

It wasn't just a question of being principled: McElligott was well aware that if this arrangement was ever uncovered, this detail would be critical.

'There won't be. My business is like any other – it relies on the flow of information. The more people providing me with it . . . the better positioned I am.'

'And what do I get in return?' said McElligott.

Spinney smiled.

'I can make your financial worries disappear: 50K – in cash. How does that sound?'

Like sweet music was the honest answer, but Dave maintained his poker face.

'And if I say no?'

'Nothing will happen to you,' said Spinney, as if surprised by the question. 'If you refuse my offer, we won't meet again. But if you tell anyone about this conversation, that would be a different matter.'

McElligott nodded. It didn't take a genius to realise that information would leak fairly quickly back to Spinney if he did.

'Are you responsible for the death of that social worker?' he said, leaning in, looking the old villain in the eye. Even as he considered crossing a line, it was important to *set* a line. If this man was responsible for beheading Lukasz Mazurek, he wanted no part of it. Opening a flow of information was one thing – becoming an accessory to murders like that was quite another. Spinney took another sip of his espresso.

'No. But I do have a vested interest in the MP.'

'Why?'

Spinney almost looked amused by the question.

'You don't need to know. But any developments in that particular investigation, I want to be kept informed of.'

McElligott slowly weighed it up and nodded – he didn't really have much choice. And anyway – as far as he could see – apart from that one cop who died in Brazely, Spinney looked after his people. It was in his interests to keep them protected, after all. He thought about Zoe and her bump. Thought too about the house – what it might look like renovated and completed, the three of them enjoying it together with all the worry removed. Fifty grand was certainly enough to make a difference to his current predicament.

'Alright. You're on,' he said. Spinney smiled, displaying some immaculate white dentures. 'One thing . . .' continued McElligott. 'If I want to back out later . . . would you let me?'

Spinney rubbed the back of his neck thoughtfully and straightened his waistcoat.

'Our arrangement can be terminated at any time. The only golden rule is you don't ever mention it happened. Or I will come after you, your partner and your child, regardless of whether it is inside or outside Ms Kenwright's womb.'

McElligott put all his effort into keeping his face neutral.

'Then I'd say we have a deal,' he said.

For a man who'd just sold his soul, McElligott felt quite at ease with himself as he made his way back to Cedar House. This didn't feel like corruption, not in the sense that he'd always understood it to be. He wasn't stealing money or drugs from anyone, and the terms of the arrangement were quite straightforward. Whatever Spinney's interest in Beacham, McElligott didn't care.

This would be a short-term thing that he'd terminate at the first opportunity – once he'd sorted his finances out. He couldn't preclude the fact that Spinney might come after him again, would always have that hold over him. But the more he thought about it, the more he thought that was unlikely. There seemed a strange, old-fashioned quality about the man, a code of sorts – if you followed it, so would he. Honour amongst thieves and all that. And the simple truth was he didn't have much choice. Not now. He began to whistle softly to himself – that bloody tune was like an earworm.

'Who can rob at sunrise ...'

When he got back to Cedar House, he found himself in surprisingly good spirits. He winked at Sami Dattani as he slipped back behind his desk.

'Where did you go that was so urgent then?' said Dattani. 'You've been gone nearly an hour and a half.'

'Never say no to a pregnant woman when she summons you, Sami.'

Dattani looked at him with concern.

'Everything alright?'

'It is now,' he said confidently.

'Yeah, well – she's bound to be a bit emotional at the moment what with everything.'

'Too bloody right, mate.' McElligott smiled conspiratori-ally. 'Just don't let her hear you say that.'

Dattani grinned and turned back to his computer screen. McElligott looked around the room; everything was exactly as it had been before. Not that it wouldn't have been, of course, but the normality was still reassuring. There was just one more thing. He reached into his pocket and pulled out the burner phone Spinney had given him just before they parted. He put it on his desk and looked at it, the alien object amongst his clutter. He shivered, felt the hairs on the back of his neck rise, then opened his top drawer, threw the handset inside and slammed it shut.

9

To Finn's irritation, things hadn't progressed very far by the following morning. He had a feeling this was one of those investigations that would be solved by a piece of diligent police work at someone's desk rather than by a dramatic development from outside. The answer was buried in the history of these two people – Claire Beacham and Lukasz Mazurek. Somehow, some way, something important connected them and it was to be found in the paperwork his team were still busy sifting through.

He watched as Dave McElligott strutted into the incident room looking pleased with himself. McElligott had in truth never been one of his favourites – Finn had always considered him something of a man-child. He liked his officers to be serious about their work and had never warmed to the facetiousness that the DC frequently displayed. But even he could see something had changed while he'd been away. There was a new air of confidence, maturity even, that hadn't been there before.

'What are you grinning at?' said Sami Dattani suspiciously as McElligott swung off his jacket and wrapped it around his chair.

'I'm going to be a dad, Sami – why wouldn't I be happy?'

Dattani, who had two young kids of his own, pulled a face.

'Enjoy this bit, mate – in six weeks' time, you'll be knee-deep in shit and so tired you won't be able to spell your own name.'

McElligott beamed.

'Bring it on – I can't wait.'

Settling down at his desk, he logged into his computer, lifted a sheaf of paperwork from his in-tray and began to get to work.

Finn had taken in the whole exchange with interest. There was definitely a swagger to the man now that hadn't been there previously. He wondered if it was simply impending fatherhood, then briefly felt a spike of something himself. If that was what it was, it was an emotion *he* was in no danger of experiencing any time soon.

'Guv – we've pulled something off the CCTV,' said Paulsen, interrupting his train of thought. She was holding up an iPad.

'What have you got?'

'It's from the road adjacent to the alley where the body was found. The key street camera which should have picked up where the killer first intercepted Lukasz is out of action.'

Finn rolled his eyes.

'Of course it is . . .'

Paulsen held up a finger.

'But . . . one of the CSIs spotted a security camera at an e-scooter shop close by. Have a look at this.'

She passed him the tablet, where some grainy footage of the high street had been paused, and he pressed play. For a moment there was nothing but an empty pavement, then the figure of Lukasz Mazurek appeared at the top of the screen. Even in this reduced, pixelated form, it was recognisably the same man whose head Finn had seen on the floor of the Beachams' kitchen. It was jarring seeing him in life like this, knowing where the evening was taking him. Into view came a figure in a baseball cap, a scarf wrapped around his face. Finn paused the footage.

'Have we got screen grabs of this?' he asked.

Paulsen nodded.

'It's the same height, build and clothes of the man who dropped the package off at the Beachams' house just over an hour later. I'm certain it's the same person.'

'So maybe it is just a lone actor?' he said, then resumed the playback.

The first stabbing was so quick it was almost hard to see – the second wasn't. The killer appeared to prop Mazurek up briefly before putting an arm around him and walking him out of the camera's line of sight.

'That's it – but we've now also got witness statements from the coffee shop opposite saying someone matching that description was waiting in there for at least half an hour before,' said Paulsen.

'Did they get a better description?'

'He had the cap and scarf on throughout, but the barista swears he was a white male, possibly in his early thirties. Forensics are in there, but given the amount of time that's elapsed, I think the chances of recovering anything useful are slim.'

Finn nodded.

'So potentially a single white male acting alone – it certainly fits a particular kind of profile. Have you found anything in Claire Beacham's social media?'

Paulsen exhaled.

'Nothing life-enhancing. I hope she doesn't look at that every day. It's pretty toxic.'

'Anything unusual?'

She shook her head.

'It's all rather one-note – and as you know, we've already been talking to the most prominent trolls. They all had alibis for the night of the murder. But there's a lot of misogynistic stuff in there too – I'm beginning to think that's a more likely motive than the far-right link.'

Finn mused it for a moment.

'So maybe it's to do with her domestic violence brief? How far have we got looking through Lukasz's case files?'

'We're still ploughing through them – but you're talking years' worth of material; it's going to take a while,' said Paulsen.

'I'll see if uniform can lend us some extra bodies to assist. Get Dave McElligott to help you if you're struggling in the meantime.'

He glanced over again at McElligott and, just for a second, the two men caught each other's eye. The DC looked away instinctively.

Something about it irritated Finn.

'Is it me or has Dave changed while I was away?' he said.

Paulsen shrugged.

'Can't say I've noticed.' She thought about it for a moment. 'Can't say I *would* have noticed . . .'

Finn smiled, but his gaze lingered on the man in the far corner.

Claire Beacham was sitting outside a cheap, cheerful coffee shop close to the constituency office in South Wimbledon. If the people passing by recognised their elected Member of Parliament enjoying the sunshine on a bright Saturday morning, then they didn't seem to be letting it show. It was freezing, despite the good weather, but she liked it out here when she needed a break from the dingy office, and the general anonymity she was able to enjoy was welcome too. Her hands were wrapped around a takeaway coffee cup for warmth and she smiled politely as one of the shop's staff began wiping down her table.

Standing a few yards away, a finger in one ear, her mobile jammed to the other, was Rebecca. Claire knew it was Grant she was speaking with and was happy to let her act as a filter between them. There was only so much she could hold in her head and this way of working meant her aides didn't bother her with anything that wasn't a priority.

Rebecca finished the call and came over looking concerned.

'Grant's just been getting an update from the police. They're going to formally confirm to the media in the next hour that they found the head of that man at your home.'

Claire shrugged.

'It's no biggie; they warned me they'd have to. They're just rubber-stamping what the whole world knows anyway – it's been all over the papers and the internet for the past forty-eight hours.'

'So how do you want to play this?' said Rebecca.

Claire mulled it for a moment.

'I'll do a single, pooled interview . . . I know I said I wasn't going to, but I've changed my mind. I can turn all this attention to our advantage – use it to start pushing Benjamin's case.' Rebecca made a note in the large pad she was holding.

'Grant also wanted to check you've got everything you need for next week.'

The Home Secretary was due to make a statement to the Commons regarding some proposed amendments to the government's immigration policy. Claire had targeted it as the opportunity to launch her first salvo in the Benjamin Ngomo campaign and was scheduled to ask a question.

'Yes, I think so – it's quite handy how things have fallen, I suppose, with all the media attention coming my way.' Almost as soon as the words had come out of her mouth, she realised what she'd said. 'Sorry – I didn't intend it to sound like that. You know what I mean . . .'

Rebecca smiled.

'Yes – it's what we do, isn't it? Try and maximise situations.'

Claire took another sip of her coffee, pulled a face when she realised it was tepid.

'How are you doing, Bex? I know it's been a difficult couple of days. It wasn't what you signed up for, really, was it?'

Rebecca laughed, though it sounded slightly forced.

'I'm okay, though I don't mind admitting I had a few beers last night.'

Claire frowned.

'I don't want to sound like your mum, but be careful with that. It's easy to fall into the habit in this line of work. You'd be surprised how big a problem it is.'

'You sound like you're speaking from experience?' said Rebecca.

Despite the fact they were alone, Claire still checked before she answered. She liked Rebecca, and knew too how politics could chew up and spit out people like her – the young, impressionable ones at the start of their careers. She didn't want to see that happen to her. When she spoke, she kept her voice low.

'I suppose I do. When I was younger, I had a real problem with booze for a time. I was ambitious – played hard, drank hard – was a bit of a cliché, frankly. But then I had a bad experience . . .' She faltered. 'I don't want to say too much about that; I haven't even told Michael about it. But I suppose, ultimately, more good came from that than harm. I learnt from it.'

'They say everything happens for a reason,' offered Rebecca.

'And I've always thought that was bollocks,' said Claire and they both smiled. 'I don't mind admitting I was bursting for a drink myself last night, but I'm glad I didn't have one.'

Rebecca looked puzzled.

'But I've *seen* you drink – wine and champagne at some of the events we've been to.'

Claire nodded.

'That's different. A glass to be sociable when I have to be. I'm not an alcoholic – the odd one doesn't do me any harm. But it's when you're vulnerable – when you're stretched ...' She shook her head. 'That's when you have to watch it.'

Rebecca was listening carefully and didn't seem to know what to say.

'Just between the two of us, eh?' said Claire.

'Of course,' said Rebecca.

'I'm so sorry – I completely forgot,' muttered Jackie Ojo, a mortified look spreading across her face. Finn was standing awkwardly by her desk. He'd been trying to catch up with the other investigations he'd inherited on his return. As usual, the MIT were fighting battles on several different fronts simultaneously. He'd asked Ojo about one in particular – a schoolboy who'd been stabbed to death in broad daylight by a group of youths two months earlier – and uncharacteristically, he hadn't heard back from her. Even more unusually, she seemed genuinely flustered by the error.

'It was on my list of things to do – I'm so sorry, guv. I'll have it on your desk by the end of the day,' she said. 'By the way – I've just received an update on Colin Jakes, the guy we think Kenny Fuller assaulted the other morning. He's still in a coma but the doctors are now formally saying they can't put a time frame on when, if ever, he'll wake up. Here's the thing though – I checked in with the National Crime Agency too. They've heard whispers Ray Spinney might be back in the country. That's surely no coincidence.'

Finn rubbed his chin thoughtfully.

'Why would he take the risk of coming back to the UK?'

'The NCA say there's chatter he might be planning something.'

Finn felt the same discomfort he'd experienced the previous day when Spinney's name had come up. Who knew how many assets the man still had within the Met. The idea made him queasy. He shook his head. 'It's not our problem – it's the NCA's. We've got quite enough to be focusing on.'

Ojo nodded; the guilty look reappeared on her face.

'I'm sorry about that paperwork – I'll get it done this afternoon, I promise.'

Finn looked at her for a moment, not bothered if his concern was showing.

'Is everything alright, Jacks?'

'Of course – I'm fine.'

'Are you sure?'

'Jesus – you're one of them now, aren't you?'

He looked at her, bemused.

'One of what?'

'You've had a bit of therapy and now you think you're God's gift to psychoanalysis.'

He shook his head, not having it.

'I don't need to be a therapist or a police officer to notice you deflected my question.'

She grinned.

'Fair enough. There's a few issues at home at the moment that I suppose are probably distracting me,' she said. 'Nothing big, nothing I can't cope with.'

'Want to talk about it over a drink tonight?'

Finn and Ojo had an irregular habit of meeting for a drink two or three times a year at a wine bar in Clapham. Ranks were checked in at the door and a full and frank exchange of views regarding life at Cedar House would ensue. It was something else he'd missed during his time away. Jackie could drink most people – Finn included – under the table. He'd been going easy on his drinking, but suddenly felt a great desire to throw that out of the window for one night. Besides, he sensed something wasn't quite one hundred per cent with his detective sergeant and wanted to get to the bottom of it.

'If I can persuade my stubborn mother to babysit my even more stubborn son, then yes,' she said. Finn smiled, but as he turned to head back to his office, the mask slipped to a look of genuine concern.

IO

It didn't just feel like a zoo, it sounded like one at times, thought Benjamin Ngomo. He was standing patiently at a bay of small phone kiosks on D wing at Cromarsh Prison. He could hear the usual cocktail of men chatting, shouting and laughing around him. There was the occasional yell that could be anything – a boisterous game of table tennis or someone's fingers being broken.

He focused simply on the man in front, currently talking on the phone Ben was queuing to use. The guy was a lifer – but still seemed hell-bent on dictating to his wife how his family should be living their lives. He was micromanaging everything from where they should be eating to where they should be going at the weekend, in patient, patronising terms. Benjamin wondered idly if they actually obeyed his instructions or simply humoured him on the phone each week.

Finally, the man gave way and Benjamin stepped forwards. He picked up the receiver, looked around carefully, then made the call.

'*Hey* ...' came a warm greeting and he felt his heart lift immediately. Emma was far more than just his girlfriend – she was his best friend too. They'd been together for just over a year, and despite his incarceration she'd stuck by him. That didn't feel a surprise either – the connection between them had been instant and strong and right now she was just about the only thing keeping him going.

'Hey yourself,' he replied.

'You sound tired. Are you sleeping okay?' she said. He loved the sound of her voice, just a hint of a cut-glass accent but down to earth with it.

'What do you think? I've been trying to work out the number of days I might have left if this goes against me – I mean, I could be on the plane by the end of the week,' he said.

There was a silence as the implication hit her.

'I didn't realise it would be that quick. What are we going to do, Ben?' she said.

He shrugged, checking to see whether anyone was eaves-dropping. Behind, a young man waiting for the phone glared at him.

'What will be, will be.'

'You can't just roll over and accept it.'

'What else can I do?' he said. 'I've got no control over what happens, have I?'

He heard Emma sigh.

'What about that MP – she must be able to do something.'

'I wouldn't get too excited about her. I think she's full of shit,' he said. 'She's just using me – it's all propaganda. As soon as I'm on the plane, she'll be finding someone else to do the same thing with. That's all it's about with people like that.'

'So what? Let her use you,' said Emma. 'She's all you've got. Have you seen though? She's been in the news.'

Benjamin hadn't seen – he'd never been particularly inter-ested in current affairs outside of prison, let alone in his current predicament. Emma brought him up to speed with the severed head and its connection to Claire Beacham. His eyes widened as he slowly tried to make sense of it.

'It's intimidation – because she wants to help me ...' he said, the panic rising in his voice.

'Shhh,' said Emma. 'You don't know that. Like you say, you might only have days left and she's the best thing you've got going for you. So you help her – you do everything she says. And when this is over – you and me, we'll disappear, we'll go somewhere where no one will ever find us. Hold on to that thought.'

'Where's that going to be then?' he said, softening.

There was a pause.

'I dunno – Blackpool, maybe.'

He could hear her smile as she said it. One began to spread across his own face too.

'*Blackpool?*' he said.

'Or Chipping Sodbury – wherever. But just you and me.'

For a moment he felt a wave of pure happiness. Just the very idea of it was like a window into what could be – then hot on the heels came the reality of his situation. That he was likely to be imminently deported and he may never set eyes on her again.

'We aren't going to Blackpool and you should forget about me. This severed head – it's hardly a coincidence, is it?'

'I don't care,' she said immediately.

'You know what I mean.'

'And you heard me – there's no chance of me letting you go.'

He could hear her breathing heavily on the other end now; hear his own breath too.

'*Come on, mate, I ain't got all fucking day …*' said the man behind, but Benjamin ignored him – he did have all fucking day frankly.

'Do me a favour, Em – trust no one. Not that MP, or anyone else. It's just you and me, yeah?'

★   ★   ★

Ray Spinney loved Whitstable in the sunshine. He'd grown up in these parts and a walk through the town centre and along the beachfront always brought the memories flooding back. His parents had run a guest house just five minutes' walk from Tankerton Beach and on this visit, he was disappointed to find the old turn-of-the-century building had finally gone. Rightly or wrongly, he felt safe in the area too. He knew – because he'd checked – that the police didn't know of his connection to it. His parents were long since dead and he'd lived most of his adult life in and around London. A few familiar shops and businesses appeared to have become victims of the pandemic but as he surveyed the seafood market by the beach, it all still felt and smelt very much like his childhood.

Waiting by one of the giant wooden groynes that subdivided the pebbled beach was Fuller. Wearing cheap mirrored sunglasses and a beanie hat on his head to hide his tell-tale scar, he looked faintly ridiculous.

'What have you done?' snarled Spinney by way of greeting.

'What do you mean?' said Fuller, surprised.

'Colin Jakes – why didn't you tell me that you smashed his skull into pieces? Our new friend Mr McElligott tells me the police have footage of you with him. Your description has been circulated – you're a wanted man.'

Fuller was momentarily nonplussed as Spinney spat the words out.

'I couldn't help it. He's got a smart mouth on him,' he said. 'I know I shouldn't have – but he's no loss.'

Spinney controlled himself.

'Are your brains leaking out of that gash in the back of your head? We've already got a random element in play with Beacham, and now you, quite needlessly, have created a second problem.' He leant in until he was almost nose to nose with Fuller. 'That temper of yours is going to be the death of you, Kenneth.' Behind them, the sea swept across the shingle. 'You keep your head covered until the job is done and you stay indoors as much as possible until then, too. You do not attract any more unnecessary attention – am I clear?'

Fuller looked chastened.

'Do you want to postpone the job – wait for things to calm down a bit?'

Spinney scowled at him.

'We have a date and we have a plan. My question for you now is . . . do we have the personnel?'

Fuller nodded quickly.

'Yeah – I've recruited the last one. We've got a full team now and we're ready.'

He told him who he'd found in place of Jakes. Another ex-con – disaffected and hungry to change their circumstances. Spinney listened in silence.

He often thought pulling off a job like this was like constructing a house. First of all, you needed an architect – someone to meticulously draw up the plan. To estimate the cost, determine timelines, think through every eventuality until you had something that was completely watertight. Then you brought in the builders – people with a different skill set, but no less important to the outcome. The artisans to execute your plan. And just like building a house, the key was to avoid cowboys.

'This is the largest team I've ever assembled,' said Spinney when Fuller was finished. 'As you know, I usually prefer small numbers – but the nature of this job is different. I need to know each and every man can be relied upon. And I need to know their weaknesses too. Because someone will let us down – experience has taught me someone always does.'

Fuller shook his head.

'Not this time – they all know how much money they stand to make from this.'

'We're only as strong as our weakest link,' said Spinney. 'And trust me – somebody will get greedy. So we need to have some leverage – an ability to control them after the job's done.'

Fuller reached into his pocket and produced a thumb drive.

'These are the details of the whole team – just like you asked. It's a full dossier on every one of them. Who they are, what they can do and how they perform under pressure. Also, their personal details – who their wives and girlfriends are, where their kids go to school and everything else you need to know. Have a look through – if you've got any doubts, it's not too late to make changes.'

Spinney took the thumb drive and nodded approvingly.

'And they all know their roles?'

Fuller nodded.

'We've been doing dummy runs at the warehouse for the last fortnight. So far, everything's gone like clockwork.' He looked at Spinney hesitantly. 'I'd be happier if we had a few more insurance policies in place—'

'That's in hand,' said Spinney, cutting in. 'Our new friend at Cedar House can help us there. Leave that to me – you just make sure those men are ready when I need them to be ready.'

Spinney looked out across the sea. It wasn't far from here that he'd kissed his first girlfriend. He wondered what that version of him would have made of the man he'd become. More than likely he'd have been disgusted.

'Do you mind me asking?' said Fuller suddenly. 'Why did you come back for this job? You didn't need to – you could have stayed in Switzerland. You were safe there, it wouldn't have made any difference.'

Spinney smiled, took in a lungful of salty air.

'Because this is personal.'

'. . . and I've written to Lukasz Mazurek's wife to offer my deepest condolences. I don't want to say too much more because I think we all need to respect the family's privacy. What's really important is that the individual who was responsible is caught and brought to justice. I don't want to give this person any more publicity either – because that's what they're seeking. So what I'd like to focus on instead is the appalling injustice that one of my constituents Benjamin Ngomo is now facing . . .'

Michael Beacham was watching the clip of his wife – taken from the lunchtime news – on a laptop in his office. As ever, she looked composed and was hitting precisely the right notes. With the Doll Street deal moving to a conclusion, he'd come in on a Saturday to continue working on it. He envied her – he was still struggling with what had happened. Even he was surprised at the extent to which it had unnerved him and he'd found it hard to keep his concentration since. He'd been home alone when the box had been dropped off. That thought wouldn't leave him either – that the killer might have peered in through a window and watched him for a while.

There was a knock at his office door and he snapped back into the moment, flipping his laptop shut. He'd lost track of time a little, almost forgotten someone was coming to see him. He composed himself, opened the door and found a smartly dressed silver-haired man in his early sixties smiling at him. Andrew Colleter, a wealthy philanthropist who shared many of the same ideals as the Beachams, was the driving force behind the Doll Street Collective. Michael liked him – he was calm, determined and didn't let obstacles get in the way. When he wanted something, he had a long track record of making it happen. And regenerating a run-down street in south London into a major new social enter-prise for the local community had become a passion project for him.

'Thanks for coming in on a Saturday, Andrew – it's a bit saner round here at the weekend. We can talk in peace,' said Michael.

'Never mind that,' said Colleter. 'How are you? I saw what happened, obviously. Are you okay? How's Claire?'

'We're fine,' Michael lied. 'Life goes on, doesn't it?' he added, remembering the way Claire had said something simi-lar in the Premier Inn. He hoped he sounded as convincing. He talked Colleter through what had happened as quickly as possible, keen to move the conversation on. It didn't take long to get to business.

'So where are we with the consortium?' said Colleter.

The group he was referring to were his co-investors. A small collection of businessmen who'd come together to support and co-finance the Doll Street venture. It was a complex deal and Michael was the key broker charged with holding it all together.

'Everything's fine – we're just crossing i's and dotting t's . . .' he said. Colleter smiled and then so did Michael as he realised what he'd said. He held up a hand by way of apology. 'God, I'm tired. You know what I mean . . .'

'It's understandable in the circumstances. So what kind of time frame are we talking about?' said Colleter. 'I was hoping we might get this done by the end of the week. It's been a long road.'

Michael shook his head apologetically.

'And it might be a little longer – but hang in there, Andrew, we're almost over the line.'

Colleter smiled and put a hand on Michael's shoulder.

'When this is finally completed, I'm buying you and Claire dinner. No arguments. It'll be somewhere with Michelin stars and it'll be on me.'

After he'd gone, Michael sat back down at his desk and put his fingers to his temples. After a few seconds, he flipped open the laptop again and typed into Google: *Los Angeles real estate*. A list of results came up and he began to flick through them.

'Keep your eye on the prize,' he murmured to himself, hoping to God that Claire would forgive him when this was all over.

I I

'. . . is the appalling injustice that one of my constituents Benjamin Ngomo is now facing. He's been told he faces deportation to the Democratic Republic of Congo and has no legal representation or legal aid to fall back on. This is a man who's lived almost his entire life in this country, but the Home Secretary has apparently deemed deportation to be conducive to the public good . . .'

How exactly did the woman's hypocrisy not climb up through her oesophagus and strangle her, the man thought. He was watching the lunchtime news with a cup of tea and a biscuit. To his disappointment, Beacham still had that smug *I know best* tone about her voice. There was no sign that what he'd done had shaken her in the slightest. It had certainly shaken him though.

He couldn't stop thinking about the feel of the blade as he's sawed through Mazurek's neck, the grid of steel on bone. He hadn't forgotten the accompanying noise either. And then there was the blood – more than anything else, that's all he could see in his mind's eye; the red haze creeping around him while he knelt.

He put his teacup down and turned the television off. He'd had quite enough of Beacham's sanctimonious face. He checked his phone – there was a missed call from his sister and he felt a twinge of guilt. He was going to break her heart. Eventually, he'd be caught and all this would come out. The nagging irritation of it was that despite everything, he still felt he owned the moral high ground. That what he was doing was right – not that he expected anybody else to see it that way, but when you knew the history, truly *understood* why . . . then it all made a kind of sense.

And that's what infuriated him – because people would judge him later. The jurors discussing him wouldn't get it. The judge passing sentence would deliver one of those patronising homilies those privileged old duffers enjoyed dishing out. And as for the court of public opinion . . . well, he'd be a monster, wouldn't he? But he wasn't. If just one of those people – a juror, a lawyer, a journalist – had been through the experience he had, then they might see that.

He was equally convinced there was a silent majority who'd understand his actions completely. In his mind, he was doing it for them – the disenfranchised of this country who had no voice. The people Claire Beacham claimed to represent.

Breathing out, he felt better; his little pep talk to himself had helped calm his nerves. He thought briefly again about that alleyway and the blood. That first cut. He'd found the strength then and he'd need to find it again.

Because tonight he was going to see a doctor.

'. . . *but the Home Secretary has apparently deemed deportation to be conducive to the public good. I urge the government to think again about young men like Benjamin – to choose compassion over cruelty. This wilful destruction of people's lives is inhumane and doesn't represent the true values of our country.*'

'Christ – she's hard as nails,' said Jackie Ojo. 'You'd think she'd take some time out. I would.'

'That's not how a politician's hardwired, is it?' said Finn. 'Every situation's an opportunity.'

Beacham's interview was getting a second spin on the evening news and Finn was sitting on a sofa in Jackie Ojo's living room, watching it with great interest. Neither of them had planned to be there. They were supposed to be spending their Saturday night in a bar in Clapham, several bottles deep in red wine by now, but Ojo's mother had scuppered that plan. She'd rung her daughter complaining of several minor ailments that were either related to her back, her legs, or her respiratory system – Finn couldn't tell. Despite Ojo's best attempts to reassure her, a decision was taken that postponing their night out might be for the best.

It was raining hard as they left Cedar House and on a whim, Ojo had invited him back to her place with the offer of a take-away. Remembering his counsellor's advice not to seclude himself away, Finn had accepted and now here they were. He'd enjoyed himself too. From the little he'd been told about Ojo's mother, he'd been expecting a frail old woman full of aches and grumbles. In her seventies and surprisingly glamorous, she'd proven to be warm and engaging company instead. Distracted by their surprise guest, she'd shared a string of anecdotes about his detective sergeant's younger days. Far from being embarrassed, Ojo had laughed along, clearly enjoying the memories.

Jackie's son Cassian had been a tougher nut to crack. Initially, he was sullen and silent, though Finn suspected that was more to do with shyness. It was once they'd started chatting about football that he'd begun to come out of his shell. And when Finn began to talk about the great American sports coaches he studied so obsessively in his own spare time, he hit the jackpot.

The boy listened raptly to tales of NFL coach Vince Lombardi, who terrified his players into becoming champions, and basketball coach Phil Jackson – the man who harnessed Michael Jordan and the rest into legends at the Chicago Bulls. His mother had quietly removed their dirty plates and empty silver food trays, observing carefully while they talked.

After Cass and his grandmother retired to their respective bedrooms, Finn and Ojo settled down in the living room with a couple of cans of beer. He felt strangely awkward. Though the two of them frequently put the world to rights in wine bars, this seemed to have a slightly different feel to it.

'So it turns out you're actually quite good with kids,' said Ojo, turning the TV off once the news had finished. 'Who knew?'

'I wouldn't go that far,' he said. 'Though I have to say, we did kind of hit it off.'

Ojo chuckled and took a sip of her beer.

'You did fine, he liked you. I've seen him when he doesn't take to someone and you didn't get that treatment. Trust me – you'd have known about it.' She shook her head. 'I still can't figure out what's bothering him though.'

'Maybe the problem isn't him – maybe it's you,' said Finn, immediately thinking he could have phrased that better.

'What's that supposed to mean?' she said, instantly confirming the suspicion.

He held up a hand.

'You've been dealing with a lot. Covering for me, handling Skegman, raising your boy, looking after your mum ...'

'Are you saying I can't manage that?'

She was looking genuinely pissed off now.

'No – I'm just saying everyone needs a break sometimes. I didn't realise that myself until I had one. You can burn yourself out in this job without even noticing. I almost did.'

He hadn't told Ojo about his near suicide attempt the previous year. He was pretty certain she wasn't close to anything like that, but he remembered all too well his conviction in the months before that there was nothing essentially wrong with him. He'd ploughed on with almost disastrous consequences.

'I *am* tired, you're right about that,' she said, after thinking it through for a moment. 'But I couldn't afford to take some time out even if I wanted to. Which I don't, by the way.'

Finn was starting to understand why so many people offered him advice – it was a damn sight easier when you could see the problem in someone else, but not yourself.

'Are you never tempted to find someone? I'm sure it's a lot easier when there's two of you,' he said, aware of his own stunning hypocrisy on the subject.

Ojo arched an eyebrow.

'You are feeling brave tonight.'

He shrugged.

'At times since Karin died, it's seemed like the entire world has felt entitled to comment on my private life – now you know what that's like.'

Ojo smiled despite herself.

'Fair enough. No – I've got my hands full as it is with Cass and Mum. If the right man were to rock up, then fine, but they're not exactly queuing up outside – in case you hadn't noticed . . .'

Finn looked around the room thoughtfully. It was enviably stylish and you could sense the pride taken in the place.

'Sometimes it feels like everyone is telling me I need to meet someone new. But I like being on my own – and then I see you, and you seem pretty comfortable with it too,' he said.

Ojo smiled gently, glanced up at the ceiling.

'But I'm not alone, am I? That's the difference.'

And afterwards, in a way that he could never have expected, those words would come back to haunt him.

★   ★   ★

Claire looked around her kitchen, trying and failing to banish the memory of what had occurred in the same room only a few days before. The police forensic operation there had finished and the place was now sparkling clean, as if the whole horror show had never happened. But in her mind's eye, the red smear across the floor was still there and that head was still staring dolefully back up at them. Ever since it had happened, the memory of the oily blood on her fingers had been making her nervously interlace them.

Night-time was a particular purgatory – if she wasn't lying in bed awake thinking about it, she was asleep dreaming of it – the appalling images remixing in her subconscious to find new ways to haunt her. The worst of it was that it was *distracting* – taking her concentration and time away from the things that mattered, that she needed to be focused on.

Michael was standing by the hob. A pot was on the boil next to a pan full of a bubbling tomato sauce.

'I thought I'd make spaghetti puttanesca,' he said, smiling as she entered. 'Just about found everything we need in the cupboards.' For a moment, as she stared at the lurid red contents of the pan, she thought it might just be the straw that broke the camel's back. She didn't know whether her husband's attempts to drive them both back towards some sort of normality were helping or making things worse.

'Good. Smells great,' she said, deciding to opt for the former. 'How's your day been?' Through the windows she could see the rain pounding down hard and she found the sound of it strangely comforting. She took a seat at the kitchen table and he told her about the meeting with Colleter earlier.

'Has Doll Street hit a snag then?' she asked. 'It seems to be dragging on a bit.'

He waved a hand airily.

'Just the usual nonsense you get with deals like this right at the death. Are you sure you don't want some wine?' he said, reaching for a bottle of Burgundy on the counter and pulling out the cork. 'One won't hurt, surely – after the week we've had?'

She was sorely tempted but shook her head.

'You seem a little more like your old self,' she said, watching as he poured himself a large glass. Briefly, there was a flicker of uncertainty behind his eyes. That, like the rain, was oddly reassuring too. They *shouldn't* just be carrying on as if nothing had happened. He turned to quickly check on the sauce again, then swivelled back round.

'Claire, tell me honestly – do you feel safe?' he said, ignoring her question. 'We could move out for a while if you like? Go and stay with my parents in Berkshire. You could work just as easily from there for the time being.'

Their safety was an issue that had permanently hung over them since she'd been elected – a fact of life they'd almost got complacent about until this week. The murders of MPs Jo Cox and David Amess over the last seven years had focused every MP's mind on the issue of their personal security. She gave the suggestion some serious consideration, mindful too of the concerns Rebecca had shown about their collective safety. The windows of the kitchen were now fully steamed up as the rain continued to crash down outside. She shook her head.

'We're not going anywhere. I'm not surrendering to anyone – and yes, I *do* feel safe, even if there's no logic behind that at all,' she said. 'How do you feel about it?'

He shrugged.

'At least we've got each other,' he said. 'That's what will get us through this.' He took another sip of wine and smiled.

⋆　　⋆　　⋆

Dr Ruth Vance felt shattered. At forty-two she was getting old, she thought. Just an ordinary day at work was enough to knock her out now. Maybe it was her age or maybe it was the pandemic – since it had begun that seemed to be the permanent way of things, she'd noticed. It was late and even though she'd seen her last patient out the door some time ago, there was still plenty in her in-tray keeping her busy. At least four other doctors were probably doing exactly the same thing in their own rooms right now. The GP practice in Tooting was spread across an old Edwardian house and at this point – as it was every night – they were all racing to avoid being the last to leave.

She put away her paperwork, locked her drawers and slipped on her jacket. It was only when she stepped outside that she noticed the terrible weather. Needless to say, she didn't have an umbrella. She was halfway down the street when she realised there was a whole catalogue of things she really should have done before leaving. A patient she should have called, a hospital doctor at the Royal London she needed to check in with, and some training courses she'd meant to get organised. Now she'd have to come in early the next day to make up the ground.

'Bugger,' she said to herself, ignoring the impulse to turn around.

She carried on for a few moments, thinking instead about the evening ahead – the glass of Pinot Grigio that would soon be in her hand. The chicken . . .

'Shit,' she said, doubling down on her muttered cursing. The chicken she'd forgotten to defrost before she'd left for work that morning. Beans on toast with Pinot then. She increased her pace as the rain continued to hammer down.

Twenty minutes later she was home.

'Solo?' she called out into the empty flat. Somewhere inside she heard a muffled *miaow*. 'I'll feed you in a minute if you want to show your face.'

She waited but there was no sign of the animal. She kicked off her sodden shoes, dumped her bag on to the ground and hung up her jacket on a hook by the door. Stifling a yawn, she caught a waft of her own dried sweat and began to anticipate a long soak in the bath after she'd eaten. She walked down the hallway, opened the door to her bedroom, and before she knew what was happening, a hand had shot out of nowhere and coiled itself around her neck.

She shrieked – part in shock, part in terror – and the arm tightened its grip. He swivelled her around and pushed her on to the bed. She looked up at the face of her attacker and saw cold eyes staring back down at her. Her mind spun. The best-case scenario was that this was just about sex. Sex and theft maybe. She looked up at him again, trying to place the face – she was sure she'd seen it before somewhere.

'Please . . .' she said in a hoarse whisper.

He moved swiftly forwards and punched her hard in the face. She saw blood explode from her nose and fell back on to the bed.

'I don't want to hear you speak,' he said.

He reached into his pocket and pulled out a knife, which was when she knew this wasn't about sex or possessions. He leant forwards, grabbed her jaw and forced her mouth open.

'Shhhh,' he said, and put the blade inside.

12

Dave McElligott woke in a pool of sweat with the sunlight streaming through his bedroom window. He turned and looked over at the other side of the bed. As usual, Zoe had risen before him. He could hear the electric shower roaring in the bathroom and was relieved that was still working at least. Somewhere between yesterday and this morning, the early confidence he'd taken from the deal he'd struck with Spinney had evaporated. Perhaps he shouldn't have spent the evening on the internet reading up on the Handyman.

It was the tabloids who'd come up with that nickname originally. The first victim attributed to him was stabbed through the eye with a screwdriver, while the second had his skull staved in with a claw hammer. The man seemed to be working his way through the toolbox. And the more he read, the more McElligott felt uncomfortable. There was a running theme too – Spinney appeared to have a very vindictive streak. There was also a firefighter who'd stumbled across a portion of the Stansted heist money and kept it. He'd subsequently committed suicide and at the time, Finn thought it was Spinney who'd pushed him over the edge, but they'd never been able to prove it.

McElligott stared up at the ceiling and breathed out. As long as they stuck to the terms of their agreement, he should be fine. But he had no leverage over this man. If he told Skegman everything and they arrested Spinney straight away

– there's no way he'd simply be allowed to walk away unscathed. And his imagination wasn't slow in offering some deeply unpleasant possibilities – a power drill, perhaps, or a blowtorch.

'Alright, sexy . . .' purred Zoe as she entered the room. She had a towel wrapped around her head and was wearing a white dressing gown that had fallen open, unable to contain the large bump around her midriff.

'Did you hear the storm last night?' she said. 'I swear I thought the roof was caving in, it was so loud.' She turned and smiled at him. 'I love lying in bed during a good storm.'

She looked radiant, he thought – literally, in the shaft of sunlight coming through the window. He remembered Spinney's threat to her in the cafe, thought about what he'd read online, and shivered.

'What are you up to today?' he said, trying to sound casual. Zoe slipped off her dressing gown and began selecting some clothing from the wardrobe.

'Busy one at work – it's funny, everyone's telling me I'll miss it when we're knee-deep in puke and nappies, but I'm pretty certain I won't. I hate working Sundays . . .'

She took the towel off her head and shook her long blonde hair. Now standing naked, she looked absolutely stunning but he felt no desire, just nausea with almost white noise in his ears.

'Do you want some breakfast?' she said. 'There's still some bacon left in the fridge – I could do you a cheeky fry-up before I go?'

He gave a decent impersonation of his old charming smile – the one that had hooked her.

'Go on, then – if you put a gun to my head . . .'

She grinned back and started to dress. In truth, it was going to be an effort to force any food down. He'd reminded himself too about DS Mike Godden – the officer on the Stansted investigating team who Spinney had also turned. McElligott was determined he wasn't going to end up like him – shanked in the shower of some godforsaken prison somewhere. He'd find a way out of this, he decided. Duck and dive like he'd always done and come out smelling of roses.

There was an unfamiliar buzzing from the drawer in his bedside table.

'What's that?' said Zoe.

'New work phone,' he lied.

The feeling of nausea increased as he reached across and plucked the burner from the drawer. There was a message on the display.

We need to talk.

It looked to Finn like Ruth Vance had simply been tossed aside. She was lying in a heap with her head hanging over the edge of the bed. Blood had dripped down her chin on to the white linen duvet cover and into a sticky puddle on the carpet below. The bed was soaked in dark crimson; the killer had removed her tongue and inflicted multiple stab wounds to her torso. The forensic pathologist was pretty certain the mutilation had taken place before death. A brief flash of a woman with no tongue trying to plead for her life went through Finn's mind and he banished it instantly.

There'd been no mystery over how the killer had gained access to the flat. A bathroom window had been smashed and the small garden patio adjacent to it was reasonably discreet. Finn wondered how long they had waited inside the flat and what had been going through their mind. A clock on the mantelpiece above a wrought-iron fireplace was ticking quietly in the background. It was easy to imagine the killer hiding in the shadows here, working themselves up to it with just that ticking for company.

Finn gave the dead woman on the bed one last look then walked through to the hallway where Paulsen was talking to one of the DCs from the homicide assessment team. She saw Finn emerge and broke off to join him.

'There's a bloodied fingerprint on the bedroom wall. We're waiting to see if it's a match to one taken from that industrial bin where Lukasz Mazurek's body was found.'

Finn processed the information, but it felt more than a coincidence. Two grotesque murders which involved mutilating the victim, in the same week, within a few miles of one another.

'It doesn't match anyone in the system though. That much we do know,' continued Paulsen. 'Whoever they are, they don't have a criminal record.'

'What do we know about the victim?' said Finn.

'Her name's Ruth Vance – she's a GP at' – she checked her pocketbook with a blue latex-gloved hand – 'the Westly Hill Practice in Tooting. She was single and lived here alone. As far as we've been able to establish, the last person to see her alive was her final patient last night.'

Finn stepped back to let one of the CSIs walk through to the bedroom.

'If the killer knew who she was – then it's a fair bet he knew she was out during the day, and would have known roughly what time she'd return too,' he said.

Paulsen nodded.

'Neighbours on the left are a young professional couple who were out until late last night. They knew Ruth quite well – they're pretty shocked, said she was kind and friendly, and didn't know why anyone would want to hurt her. And there's a vacant rental property on the right.'

'What about the other flats in this building?' said Finn.

'A young couple live on the second floor. They were the ones who called it in – they heard some unusual noises from down here and when they came down they found the door open. There's also an elderly man who lives alone on the top floor who didn't see or hear anything.'

'And I take it we've found no sign of the missing tongue or the murder weapon?'

Paulsen shook her head.

'So why this woman – and for that matter, why Lukasz?' she said. 'Or are they just random choices?'

'Could be,' said Finn. 'But if you were going to kill someone randomly, there's easier ways of doing it than risk being spotted breaking and entering. Why not intercept her on her way home? That's what he did to Lukasz.' He shook his head. 'Just like with him, the killer knew her routine. He'd done his homework – knew where they both worked. I wonder if that's significant? Given their proximity, there's got to be a decent shout this is someone who might have dealt with both of them in their professional capacities.'

Paulsen nodded slowly.

'If Lukasz was beheaded to send some sort of message to Claire Beacham, then what's *this* about – why the tongue?'

'I don't know yet, either,' said Finn. 'But it's starting to feel symbolic – like there's something specific being communicated. I spoke to Claire on the phone first thing. She and her husband had a quiet evening in last night with no nasty surprises. I don't think that tongue's just disappeared though.' He looked around the flat grimly. 'I suspect we'll find out soon enough where it is.'

Rebecca Devlin settled down at her desk and took the lid off the large Starbucks cappuccino she was holding. She wasn't wild about working on a Sunday morning – but it came with the territory when things were busy. She swallowed a mouthful of her drink, largely in part to blot out the ever-present smell of stale frying oil that permeated Claire's constituency office. Times like this almost made her yearn for the lockdown days of working from home.

Grant Lassiter was already at his desk. Unmarried, without any immediate family, he seemingly only lived for his job and she suspected he was a lot more relaxed about working at the weekend than she was. It was actually hard to imagine what else he'd be doing and where else he'd be. Lassiter had been floating around the backwaters of Westminster for years serving different politicians in a variety of equally invisible roles. Rebecca wasn't sure whether he loved the job, loved the MPs who employed him or simply now didn't have many other career choices.

'You're late,' he said without looking up.

He was fastidious about her timekeeping, which was vaguely ridiculous given that she was giving up her time freely. She didn't like that about him, either – the obsequious way he was with Claire compared with the patronising tone he took with her. But she was confident enough in her own relationship with the MP that she wasn't too concerned with what Lassiter thought or did.

She took another slow, deliberate sip of her coffee and found a stray piece of headed paper to use as a coaster before answering.

'Sorry – my bus was delayed. They're always rubbish on a Sunday . . .'

He carried on silently scrolling through a document he was studying on his laptop. Rebecca watched him for a moment and assumed the matter of her timekeeping was now closed.

'Have you spoken to Claire since yesterday – is she okay?' she volunteered.

He looked up as if noticing her properly for the first time since she'd walked in.

'Yes . . . she seems fine, thank God. The police have finished at her house so I think she's just happy to get back to some sort of normality. Honestly, she's extraordinary. There's quite a few I've known who wouldn't have reacted like that, trust me.'

Rebecca switched on her own laptop and waited for it to creak into life. Like Lassiter's, it was a refurbished old model that had been supplied by Claire after she'd been elected.

'Isn't that a worry though – that she's just putting a brave face on things?'

Lassiter had resumed his studied concentration again and went back to ignoring her. Rebecca waited then shook her head silently to herself.

So much for the glamorous career in politics, she thought – sitting in the former kitchen of a takeaway restaurant being treated like a small child by a middle-aged never-was-been. She wanted more – much more. She was ambitious and this was just a stepping stone. After all, David Cameron had begun his political career as a researcher and had gone on to become Prime Minister. For the moment she had little choice but to shut up and accept the status quo. But there'd come a day when men like Lassiter would brag about having known her once, would forget how they actually treated her.

'Could you go through the mail, please?' he instructed. There was a pile that had accumulated over the previous few days.

'Of course,' replied Rebecca.

She walked over to the stack of post Lassiter had nodded at and deposited it on her desk. Amongst the sheaf of envelopes was a large brown padded one with no writing or address label on the front.

'What's this?' she said, holding it up.

Lassiter looked up and shrugged.

'Why don't you find out?'

Rebecca smiled tightly and tore the package open. It was when she tipped its contents out into her hand that her smile quickly disappeared.

13

Claire Beacham's house was just as nice in daylight, thought Finn. It helped of course that there wasn't a major forensic operation underway this time. Arbitrarily, it struck him how serene the place felt too – well away from the main road, there was an enviable hush about it inside. Paulsen was with him, and as before, the Beachams were sitting together on the sofa in their living room.

They'd been in shock on his first visit – now he sensed genuine fear. Michael seemed tightly wound in particular – the frown on his face hadn't dropped since they'd arrived. The discovery of Ruth Vance's severed tongue in the package at Claire's constituency office – and the very strong possibility that her murderer was the same person who'd slaughtered Lukasz Mazurek – had clearly spooked them both.

'It doesn't make any sense – I just don't understand it,' said Claire.

'Nor do we, frankly,' said Finn. 'Not yet, anyway. But I'm hoping you can help us join some of the dots.'

Claire held out both her hands as if explaining something to a child. Finn recognised the gesture – he'd seen her doing the same thing in the Commons.

'I've never heard of this woman. She's never been my GP – I've never come across her socially or professionally. I don't know why someone would wish to harm her – or indeed, target me.'

'Is it just some far-right nutter?' said Michael. 'Surely you must have some idea by now?'

'Ruth Vance was white, heterosexual and came from St Albans originally,' said Paulsen. 'The far-right angle that we thought might be a factor in the first death looks far less probable now.'

'But not impossible,' said Finn quickly. 'We're obviously looking into Dr Vance and trying to find out as much as we can about her.'

Paulsen looked across at Claire.

'The fact they sent the' – Paulsen broke off, struggling for a moment to find the right description – '*package* ... to your constituency office at least confirms something – that this is specifically being directed at you, not your husband – and is related to your job.'

'We'd kind of worked that one out for ourselves, thanks,' said Michael, layering on the sarcasm. 'He's a maniac – quite clearly.'

Finn still wasn't sure what he made of the man. He seemed like a decent person, but there was something a little highly strung about him too. Though, perhaps in the circumstances that was understandable. He suppressed a small burst of frustration – the feeling he was still a little ring-rusty and that his radar about people was almost – but not quite – back to where it had been before his sabbatical.

'There's literally no connection – however peripheral – you can think of?' he said to Claire. 'Have you ever visited the Westly Hill Practice, for example? Or maybe come across someone who's had an issue with that practice?'

'I can only repeat myself, Detective Inspector. Until you mentioned her name, I'd never heard of this poor woman – or her doctor's practice,' said Claire.

'This is an escalation, that's what concerns me,' said Michael. 'The first murder wasn't a one-off – this is a psychopath with a serious grudge against my wife. Surely you should be offering us some increased protection now?'

'I don't want that,' said Claire immediately. 'I just want to focus on my job – there's a lot of important work coming up and I'm not being locked away out of sight.'

'No one's saying that,' said Michael. 'But it's just common sense, don't you think?'

'Is there any evidence of a direct threat to my safety?' said Claire, addressing the question to the two detectives.

'No, but I think some additional protective measures wouldn't hurt,' said Finn. 'We're not talking about round-the-clock surveillance. We can talk through some options with you if you like.'

Claire waved a hand almost dismissively.

'What kind of options?' said Michael, more interested.

'A panic alarm here, similar to the one you have installed at your constituency office,' said Finn. 'A personal alarm you can carry around with you. And I'd also suggest some extra covert cameras in addition to the security system you currently have. We can put that in for you too.'

'Fine,' said Claire. 'But I'm not curtailing my movements or dropping anything from my diary because of this.'

Finn nodded.

'Is there anything in your past we should be aware of?' he said. 'Something that's come back to you, perhaps, that you haven't mentioned previously?' He deliberately kept his tone neutral rather than accusatory. 'It might not necessarily be obvious – anything that someone might have held a grudge over, for example?' For a split second, he thought he saw something in her reaction. Vulnerability perhaps, in a face used to masking it. But she shook her head.

'No – there's nothing. If this is meant to do more than just intimidate me – if there's some sort of message hidden in all of this – then I simply don't understand what it is.'

'Do you think she's telling the truth?' said Paulsen as they walked down the Beachams' front drive to Finn's car. He stopped and turned to look back at the house one more time.

'I'm in the wrong job . . .' he muttered.

Paulsen gave him a withering look as she waited for him to answer her question.

'You don't need a house this big. *They* don't need a house this big,' he continued, apparently to himself. He looked back at the property again. Why did they have a place that big? It looked like it probably contained at least a couple more bedrooms on the top floor. He wondered why the Beachams didn't have children – or had they bought it intending to start a family perhaps? He refocused.

'Yes – in answer to your question – I think she *is* telling the truth,' he said. 'They both looked pretty freaked out to me. I think their priority is to see this guy caught – why would she lie about any of it?'

'Because she's a politician and they all lie as easily as they breathe,' spat Paulsen.

Finn looked over his shoulder, checking they were far enough away from the house to be out of earshot.

'In my experience, that's a cliché. Believe it or not, I think the vast majority of them do actually have a genuine desire to make the world a better place.'

'Bullshit,' snorted Paulsen. 'They're all in it for themselves – the only thing they care about is personal power and ambition.'

'For some, I'm sure. But I'm not convinced that's Claire . . .'

'So what do you think is going on here? Clearly, the killer has some sort of grudge against her?'

They reached his car and both climbed inside. He sat behind the wheel for a moment considering the question.

'I think there *is* a connection between Claire and the two victims, for sure. But I believe her when she says she doesn't know what it is. She looks genuinely mystified.'

'The killer seems to think she should know.'

Finn nodded.

'Maybe,' he said. 'Or perhaps he's simply overestimating his own importance to her and she genuinely can't recall anything useful. That said – did you see her face when I asked if there was anything in her past?'

Paulsen nodded.

'Yeah – she reacted. She definitely remembered something.'

'It could be anything. But I think it might be worth taking a deep dive into her personal history. It's possible it's something she didn't want to say in front of her husband.'

'So maybe we should interview her separately?' said Paulsen.

Finn considered it.

'If she knew something that would help the investigation and she didn't want Michael to know about it, she'd come forward of her own volition.'

'Or she's holding something back from us. I'm telling you – they're liars,' said Paulsen.

Finn gave her a sideways look.

'Mattie – even by your standards, you seem to be in a foul mood today. At least I think so – it's never the easiest thing to tell with you.' She arched an eyebrow at him which he ignored. 'Is something the matter?' he said.

She sighed and leant back in her seat.

'Sorry, guv. Yes – I had a row with Nancy last night. It's still pissing me off, to be honest.'

Finn was nonplussed for a moment – caught in a corridor of uncertainty about whether to push any further. Paulsen sighed.

'I'm thinking about applying for a vacant sergeant's job at the west London MIT. Nancy doesn't like it. She thinks I'm settled at Cedar House and shouldn't move yet.'

He was lost for words, caught by surprise and not sure what to make of this. His first, immediate reaction was irritation – why did she want to go? He beat the feeling down and tried not to let it show.

'Yes. As it goes, I think you *should* be thinking of applying for a sergeant's job at this point in your career.'

She brightened at his approval.

'But I can see Nancy's point of view too,' he added. 'If you're happy doing something – why would you want to change that? There's no rush. When the time's right, I'm sure you'll move on up.'

'Anyone would think you don't want to lose me,' said Paulsen.

'Ebb and flow is the nature of this job,' said Finn airily.

Paulsen produced one of her unexpected, wide smiles.

'I'd prefer to be a sergeant at Cedar House – that would be my first choice,' she said.

He didn't give her any encouragement.

'As you know, we've got four sergeants in total – and I don't see any of them moving on any time soon. So it looks like that's a decision you'll have to make.' His jaw tightened and he started the engine.

Dave McElligott had been waiting at the old bandstand for nearly three quarters of an hour. He felt uncomfortable and was certain he looked it too. Spinney had provided specific directions and insisted on this park in Beckenham for their meeting, which seemed odd as it was pretty public. He looked around, saw young mothers walking past with their toddlers and hoped they hadn't noticed the awkward-looking, very obvious police officer, sitting there like a spare part.

He'd calmed down a little following the summons from Spinney earlier. The fact he'd walked straight into a fresh murder investigation had actually helped. Nobody was too bothered with him and he'd been able to slip away relatively unnoticed. But he'd need a decent excuse on his return. Given that it was all hands to the pump, the fact that he'd disappeared for a great chunk of the morning would be picked up on. It didn't help that his new employer clearly wasn't a great timekeeper.

'Mr McElligott,' a voice rasped suddenly.

'Jesus!' he said, turning to see Spinney standing behind him. He must have crept up unseen from the other entrance to the park. Wearing a navy overcoat topped by an olive-green trilby hat, he looked like a rather stylish grandad enjoying the Sunday morning sunshine. He'd made no attempt to hide his features, which was bold given that he was one of the most sought-after men in Europe.

'You're taking a chance, aren't you?' said McElligott.

The Handyman sat down, removed his hat and placed it on his lap.

'Not really – do you see any CCTV cameras close by? Or do you think some of these young people have a detailed knowledge of Interpol's most wanted?'

McElligott looked around again. He had a point – they could be sitting there stark naked and he wasn't sure anyone would notice. In the middle distance, two young women were talking animatedly by the swings while their children played. A middle-aged man was engrossed in his phone while his dog crapped contentedly a few feet away.

'So what is it you want?'

'I need you to do something for me.'

Spinney then began to outline exactly what that entailed. As he listened and the shape of the plan began to become clear, Dave McElligott's eyes widened and his heart sank.

'Hold on, mate – that's not what we agreed before. Why would you need me to do that?'

Spinney bared his teeth.

'Because I do.'

McElligott shook his head.

'You said you just wanted information – a steer on the Beacham investigation. Not this.'

Very slowly Spinney turned his head to look out on to the park. The two women by the swings were still talking as their children screamed in pleasure. The man with the dog was fumbling with some disposable gloves as he prepared to clear up after his animal.

'This isn't a pick-and-mix, son – you don't get to choose what you fancy doing. It's all or nothing now. Do you understand?'

McElligott realised then the mistake that he'd made. There wasn't a choice nor had there ever been one. It felt as if his life, Zoe's, and that of his unborn child were all hanging on what he said next. His mouth felt dry and he licked his bottom lip.

'It's complicated – I take it you've heard about what happened last night?'

He told him about Dr Ruth Vance and where her tongue had been discovered and there was a flash of what seemed like genuine emotion in Spinney's eyes. It was hard to read what that emotion actually was though – like trying to decipher how a lizard might be feeling.

'I'll need to know all about that investigation too. Every last detail you have, yes?'

Increasingly McElligott was thinking no, but he wasn't going to say it. He'd already tried saying no once in this conversation and could see how dangerous that word might be. The granite expression on the old man's face pretty much confirmed it too. The pretence that this was an arrangement between equals was already starting to crumble.

'We have an agreement – and now you will fulfil your part of it,' continued Spinney.

McElligott slapped in his knee in frustration.

'What you're asking me to do … I can't just make that happen out of nowhere. It'll take time to organise—'

'Then I suggest you get started immediately,' said Spinney, cutting in. 'There's a ticking clock on this, Mr McElligott. Consider that your first and last warning.'

Without waiting for a reply, he put his hat back on, stood and walked away.

14

By lunchtime, some sixteen hours after Ruth Vance's murder, Finn had gathered his team together to regroup. It wasn't exactly a briefing in the truest sense of the word – that would be stretching things. This was more a case of circling their wagons, seeing collectively what they'd gathered and trying to extrapolate some sort of sense from it all.

There was a flat mood in the room that Finn had picked up on almost immediately after he'd returned. News of Dr Vance's death was beginning to trickle out in the media. A lone woman killed in her own home was the stuff of nightmares. Radio news bulletins were carrying the story and the Safer Streets for Women Twitter feed was already talking about a vigil later that evening. John Skegman had just issued a press release in response, urging the local community to be vigilant and promising increased patrols in the area over the next few days.

But it was the connection to Lukasz Mazurek's murder that was underpinning the atmosphere in the incident room. There was now hard evidence to confirm what they'd all known since the package with the tongue had been found at Claire Beacham's constituency office.

'Forensics have confirmed the fingerprint picked up at the scene matches the one from the alleyway where the first body was found,' said Finn. 'It's the same guy – but the bad news is, it isn't a match for anything we've got in the system.' He let that sink in for a moment before continuing. 'What we have got is a new image of the killer taken from a camera at Beacham's constituency office. You'll have seen it on your email earlier – this is an expanded version that digital forensics have cleaned up.'

He pointed to a mounted widescreen TV next to where he was standing. On it was an image of a dark figure, again with a baseball cap and scarf wrapped high around their neck. The man's eyes and brow were more clearly visible on this one, as well as some hair on the side of his head which was poking through the cap's strap. He was clearly carrying a padded envelope in one hand.

'It's timed at just before 5.45 a.m. It doesn't give us much more – but from this, we can say fairly categorically that he's a white male, and I reckon we can be about seventy to eighty per cent certain he's got black hair.'

'Looks like he's in his thirties to me, guv ...' said Sami Dattani, squinting at the image.

Paulsen frowned.

'You can't say that, Sami – it's impossible to tell.'

Dattani shrugged.

'It's not an old man though, is it?'

'What about the CCTV from Dr Vance's street – was there any camera coverage there?' said Ojo.

Finn shook his head.

'No, it was a backstreet – but we're looking through some of the cameras on the adjoining roads. Uniform haven't picked up anything useful from the door-to-doors.' He took a moment to gather his thoughts, then resumed.

'So what connects these three people?' he said, pointing at the pictures of Claire Beacham, Lukasz Mazurek and Ruth Vance that were pinned up on the boards behind him. Graphic photographs of the crime scenes were also there as well as the two earlier CCTV grabs of the man in the baseball cap. A rough timeline for the night Mazurek had died had been constructed and a second one, even more nascent, for the latest murder was now alongside it. 'A politician, a social worker and a doctor. It's someone who's been on a journey with all three and for whatever reason has chosen to hold Beacham accountable,' he continued.

'Except we can't find a single thing in common between them,' said Paulsen.

'It's not a given it's about their jobs either,' said Ojo. 'In fact, I'm not sure that's helping us – just think of them as three separate people. The connection might be something from their personal lives.'

Finn nodded in agreement; the fact that Ojo had contradicted him and was addressing the troops as if she was still acting DI didn't bother him. She'd earnt that authority in his book. The conversation was interrupted as Dave McElligott tried and failed to slip in unnoticed at the back of the room. As heads turned, he held up a hand apologetically.

'Sorry I'm late, boss,' he said. 'I was following up on a call from a member of the public. Reckoned she saw someone fitting that description,' he said, nodding at the TV screen. 'Turns out there's a lot of people in Tooting who wear baseball caps . . .'

Ojo rolled her eyes. Finn simply looked irritated.

'Use your discretion, Dave – resources are thin enough without you wasting time on wild goose chases.'

McElligott nodded.

'Sorry, it sounded legit – the way she was on the phone it seemed worth a conversation in person.'

Finn moved on.

'I'd like to have a good look through Ruth Vance's patient lists to see if there's anything that connects her to either Lukasz Mazurek or Claire Beacham.'

'I've already approached her practice with a data protection form,' Dattani cut in. 'Hopefully they'll appreciate the circumstances and waive the usual concerns about patient confidentiality.'

'If they don't, let's make sure we get an application for a court order in promptly,' said Finn.

'There is one small thing . . .' said Dattani, looking slightly uncertain now. 'She did work at a practice near Oval up until eighteen months ago.'

'Wasn't Beacham a local councillor in Stockwell before she became an MP?' said Ojo.

Finn nodded.

'Same patch – it's worth following up given Mazurek's history in the area as well. Look at the dates, Sami, and see if you can pin down exactly when all three of them would have been working there. It's a starting point if nothing else.'

Dattani nodded.

'Mattie – have a look through Vance's social media. See if any of the people trolling Beacham show up there. Jacks – I'd like you to pull together everything we know about Claire's personal history. Previous jobs, previous relationships – that sort of thing.' He explained the brief reaction he and Paulsen had observed when they'd spoken to her earlier.

'What I don't get,' said Ojo, 'is why this guy simply hasn't gone after her directly?'

'Because I think he holds her responsible for something,' said Finn. 'I don't know what that is – or what the two victims did – but as I said this guy is holding her to account for it.' He stopped and looked around the room. 'And we could be racing against time here. Because there might be other people he's got a grievance with too. The faster we can find out what connects these three – the better our chances of putting this to bed.'

★   ★   ★

It happened on Zoe's lunch break. She hadn't been aware of the large man with the beanie hat who'd been following her from the moment she left the salon where she worked. She'd pottered into a few shops and he'd discreetly waited, watching from a distance. For a few minutes she'd stood on a street corner WhatsApping a friend and he'd halted, pretending to window-shop. He'd been waiting for the right moment and, in the end, one presented itself.

Zoe took a seat on a bench in the middle of the high street. Fishing into her bag she pulled out a Boots sandwich, a packet of crisps and a bottle of Diet Coke. She was happily munching on the crisps when he sat down next to her. Though it was a large bench and she was sitting at one end, he deliberately placed himself right beside her, almost squeezing her in. Out the corner of her eye, she could see him glancing at her.

She grabbed her things as if to leave and he gave her a pleasant smile.

'Do you mind – I'm absolutely parched?' he said with a thick Scouse accent.

Before she could react, he took the bottle of Coke from her, removed the top and took a long swig from it.

'Ahhh. Lovely,' he said, turning to look at her properly. The initial shock on the pregnant woman's face had turned to concern and she tried to get up. A thick hand grabbed her by the wrist and restrained her.

'Sit down, Zoe,' he said.

Concern turned to fear.

'Who are you? How do you know my name?' she said, frozen to the spot now.

'Don't get yourself agitated, love. A woman in your condition . . .'

He smiled at her pleasantly, let go of her wrist then reached across with the palm of his hand and placed it on her stomach. To anyone passing by they simply looked like a pair of old friends enjoying the sunshine.

'We don't want to get this little one stirred up, do we?' he said.

He gently pressed, exerting just the smallest amount of pressure. Zoe began to tremble and he pushed a little harder. She made a sound that might have been a whimper and he leant in close.

'I've got a message for your boyfriend . . .' he said.

'Calm down – just calm down,' hissed McElligott trying to fight his own rising panic. He'd been at his desk when Zoe had called. She was back home now and out of her mind with fear. Aware Sami Dattani was watching him – again – he'd turned his back and listened as she explained the encounter on the bench. He felt light-headed now – like he might pass out, hot as well, sweat patches forming under his arms. Any pretence that he could control this situation was well and truly shot to pieces.

'I owe some people some money, alright? Gambling debts.'

He whispered the words, hoping to God no one else in the room could hear them. 'There's nothing to worry about – I've got the cash in the bank and I'm paying them off this afternoon.' For an impromptu lie, it was the best he could manage and would have to do. 'This guy was just trying to spook you to put pressure on me. I'm so sorry this happened – but it won't ever happen again, I promise.'

Damn right, it wouldn't, he thought. He shouldn't really leave her alone, ought to make up some story and take the afternoon off – but after his jaunt this morning he knew he wouldn't get away with it. He'd seen that familiar look of irritation on Finn's face during the briefing. He'd always felt the DI had never really liked him and the feeling was mutual.

There was now another problem to add to all the rest. What Zoe had told him in the morning about the storm – *'I swear I thought the roof was caving in'* – wasn't far removed from the truth. The wind *had* caused some serious damage to the roof. It was yet more money that he didn't have. Rationalising his thoughts, he knew there was only one real option left to him now. Necessity had pushed him to a point he'd never wanted to reach.

He made the call out in the car park. Standing in the shadows at the back of the building, he was well out of sight, not even wanting to risk his colleagues catching a stray glance of what he was doing. He waited for it to connect then heard that now familiar dry voice again.

'Alright – message received,' McElligott said straight away. 'I'll do you what you want – but I need the money now. You pay me today – fifty grand in cash – and it'll happen. But after that – you never, ever go near Zoe again. Do we understand each other?'

Ray Spinney was in excellent spirits as he took a sip of his tea. The vacant house he was using was empty and out of the way. There was a string of properties across the UK he knew he could safely use and this one midway between London and Kent was perfect for his needs. The neighbours kept themselves to themselves and it was quiet. He'd handled many people like Dave McElligott in his time. Weak men, nearly always kept in check by a combination of carrot and stick. Not only had he reassured the stricken detective on the phone, but he'd also immediately arranged delivery of his payment. Fear made people malleable, money made them willing, and the combination was a powerful one. The boundaries were now established between them: McElligott knew if he stepped out of line the threat was real – but if he played the game so was the reward.

The Assam tea Spinney was drinking tasted brisk and malty. He took a spoonful of sugar from a small bowl on the kitchen table and held it under the surface of the liquid, slowly infusing it as he considered his next move. After a moment he reached for his mobile and called Fuller.

'Your lunchtime trip had the desired effect. If you're happy that everyone's fully drilled, then we're almost ready to proceed.'

'Is he going to comply?' said Fuller.

'Yes,' said Spinney calmly. 'Now that you've refocused his attention, I expect our new friend to move quite quickly.'

There was a pause on the other end of the phone.

'I don't trust this bloke. He's not the type you usually use – he sounds flaky. Why do you need him to do this – aren't there others?'

Spinney sighed. The truth was, in the intervening years while he'd been in Europe, his network of insiders within the police service and elsewhere had diminished drastically. Some had taken early retirement, while others had simply moved on. The once easy flow of information he'd built his empire on had been reduced to a trickle. To some extent Fuller was right – a few years back he wouldn't have bothered with men like Dave McElligott – but these were different times. It was also important to keep that particular truth close to his chest. Weakness in this game meant vulnerability – and vulnerability could be fatal.

'As I told you in Whitstable – I need him because of that severed head that turned up at Beacham's house. And now there's been a second murder. It complicates things. Having a man on the inside of that police investigation is useful.'

'So we're just waiting on him then?'

'Yes, so let's use the time profitably. Why don't you give the tree one final shake for me.'

There was another pause.

'You know I've done that. That's all I *was* doing up until you flew back. I got nothing. What's the point in doing it again when we're ready to go?' said Fuller.

Spinney kept his temper in check, his voice even.

'If we can still get the prize by easier means – then why take unnecessary risks? Just do it. Belt and braces. When I'm convinced we've exhausted every avenue, then I'll give you the go-ahead.'

He ended the call without waiting for a reply. Everything was more or less where he wanted it to be and now it was time to think about what would come afterwards – the next stage of it. There were conversations he needed to have. He'd learnt his lesson from the Stansted heist, knew that there was a trick to making large sums of money disappear. Those preparations were also in hand, so why did he feel niggled?

He checked the internet on his phone – the murder of the doctor in south London was beginning to build some traction in the media, but there was no mention yet of her severed tongue or confirmation it was linked to the murder of the social worker. The police were obviously holding that back. It was a wrinkle he didn't like and this particular venture – more than any other he'd undertaken – needed to go perfectly, whatever obstacles presented themselves.

15

'I know I keep saying it, but I need you to stay calm, Benjamin.'

Claire looked up at the wall clock in her office at Portcullis House. It was the start of a new week and already her time felt short – she was due in the Commons later and wanted to make the most of this phone call. She'd hoped to visit him in person again but there just wasn't any space in her diary, so a phone call would have to suffice.

'I am calm. But so far, all you've done is talk. Once that judge passes sentence, I'm finished,' said Benjamin. 'And then how interested will you be in me?'

She rubbed her eyes with her spare hand. Sometimes the remorseless distrust from the public really ground her down. It was frustrating with this case in particular because she genuinely wanted to help Benjamin and try to right a wrong. With everything that was going on in her life, it was something to focus on, something to help shut out of her mind what had happened to Lukasz Mazurek and Ruth Vance. Also the pervading sense of guilt she felt – that somehow, in some way she didn't fully understand, she bore a responsibility for their deaths. She recalibrated quickly, trying to find the words that would cut through.

'You're right. All I do is talk. Because that's *my* weapon – that's how I win. And I can win this for you.'

There was a long silence and she could picture precisely the intense, brooding expression that was likely on his face. 'I want to try and come and see you in person again before your court appearance,' she continued. 'Hopefully, there'll be more I can tell you then. But if there's anything you need, any questions you have – don't hesitate to call my office.' She waited for a reply but one didn't come. 'There's a lot of people trying to help you, so don't give up,' she said and ended the call.

'That didn't sound great,' said Lassiter who was sitting opposite. Claire shook her head.

'He just doesn't trust me. He's convinced he'll be on a plane by the end of the week.'

Lassiter smiled supportively.

'All you can do is what you're doing – keep reinforcing the message. Eventually it might get through.'

Claire nodded.

'How's Rebecca doing?' she said.

'She's okay,' said Lassiter. 'Still a bit shaken obviously. I gave her the chance to take the day off but she didn't want to.'

Claire looked concerned.

'Where is she now?'

'Grabbing a coffee. I'll check on her when she gets back. More importantly – how are *you* doing?'

Claire pinched the bridge of her nose while she thought about it – how *was* she doing?

'Apart from feeling permanently shattered, you mean?' She shook her head. 'It's just the weirdest thing – it feels like my life is running in parallel to this horror show. I can't do anything about it except get on with the job and trust the police to do theirs. But it's hard not to feel *some* responsibility for what's happening – even though I know that makes no sense at all.'

Before Lassiter could respond, Rebecca burst into the room clutching a copy of the *Evening Standard* in one hand and a coffee cup in the other.

'You need to see this . . . it's all over the lunchtime editions,' she said immediately, opening the paper and putting it down on Claire's desk in front of her. The headline read:

'Fury as Doll Street deal collapses'.

Claire's eyes widened in surprise as she skimmed through the article.

'What is it?' said Lassiter.

'Doll Street's been bought out by some property consortium. The whole regeneration project's collapsed,' said Claire, scanning the article. She looked genuinely shocked.

'I thought that was almost over the line?' said Lassiter.

'So did I . . .' said Claire, already reaching for her phone again. Lassiter and Rebecca exchanged a glance.

'Answerphone,' said Claire to herself in frustration as the call connected. 'Michael, it's me – I've just seen the story in the *Standard* about Doll Street. Is it true? Are you okay? Give me a call when you can.' She looked at her two aides as if they possessed all the answers. 'He must have known this was coming – he's been working on it for months. Why didn't he say something to me?'

She remembered his vague dismissal of the subject over the weekend.

'Maybe with the two deaths . . . he didn't want to give you something else to worry about,' said Rebecca. 'He was probably just trying to be kind . . .'

Claire glared at her and the words trailed off. Lassiter was looking concerned.

'There's going to be fallout from this, Claire – Doll Street was a huge project. They were going to provide social housing, jobs – an entire mixed-use neighbourhood . . .'

Claire turned her glare on him.

'Don't you think I know all of that? And because of my connection to Michael, I'm going to get drawn into this.

There'll be no shortage of Tory MPs making cheap jibes about it, not to mention the press – it's a free hit. No one will be listening to a word I have to say about Benjamin – it'll get swallowed up.'

'Are you sure?' said Rebecca. 'The whole House knows what you're going through with these murders. There'll be cross-party support for you.'

Claire looked at her again as if she was insane.

'That's a lovely thought, Bex – but this is politics. What would we be doing if this was a Tory?'

Rebecca thought about it for a second.

'Going for the jugular?'

'Exactly,' said Claire. 'What the hell happened – why didn't he say something?'

She repeated the words almost to herself and ran a hand through her hair as she tried to get her head around it. Looking out of her window, she could see the familiar outline of New Scotland Yard just behind Parliament Square. A scrum of reporters was gathering close to the iconic triangular sign at the front of the building. She knew what they were there for – she'd taken a call from the police earlier. That seemed about a hundred years ago now. She felt as if she was at the centre of a perfect storm.

'I can confirm that we are formally linking the murder of Dr Ruth Vance in Tooting to the murder of Lukasz Mazurek in Lambeth last week,' said DCI John Skegman to the waiting pack of journalists. Because of an MP's involvement, the graphic nature of the deaths and the high media interest, Skegman had been summoned by the chief superintendent to brief the press at the Met's headquarters. They'd released the two screen grabs of the man in the baseball cap and were now making a renewed appeal for information.

'Can you confirm a body part from the second victim was sent to Claire Beacham?' shouted a reporter. Skegman had been expecting the question. They'd agreed with Claire's consent and Ruth Vance's family to release that information too.

'We're aware those rumours have been circulating online. What I can confirm is the cause of death is believed to be as a result of multiple injuries and that the body had been subject to mutilation. Some evidence was subsequently retrieved from a package delivered to Ms Beacham's constituency office in South Wimbledon.'

There was a ripple of almost ghoulish satisfaction at the detail.

'Do you know why these two people have been targeted and what their connection is to Claire Beacham?' one of the television reporters asked. Skegman turned to address him directly.

'Just like Lukasz Mazurek, Dr Ruth Vance was a respected member of the community. She absolutely did not deserve the brutal and appalling way she was murdered. And on behalf of her family, I would ask you all to give them some privacy at this very difficult time.'

'You haven't answered the question, DCI Skegman,' said the same reporter. 'Is there any indication why Claire Beacham has been specifically targeted by the killer?'

Skegman shook his head.

'All I can tell you is that Ms Beacham's been extremely cooperative with us and we're continuing to investigate the motive for these murders.' There was another volley of questions and he waited for them to subside before he picked up again. 'It's critical that we find the man in those photographs and we're asking the public's help to do that . . .'

*　　*　　*

'. . . *anyone who thinks they might have seen him or recognise who he is should get in touch with us immediately.*'

'He's loving it,' said Jackie Ojo witheringly. They were all in the incident room watching Skegman's performance live on the BBC News channel. In a separate development, the strapline running across the bottom of the screen read '*Breaking news: London regeneration project collapses*'.

'I don't know about that,' said Finn with the faintest hint of a smirk.

He was watching the screen with some enjoyment. The DCI had palmed off enough press briefings to him over the years. There was something undeniably satisfying in seeing him squirm in front of Her Majesty's press corps.

'Doll Street was Michael Beacham's deal,' said Paulsen, pointing to the banner at the bottom of the screen. 'Do you think it might be relevant?'

Finn nodded; he'd been thinking hard about it ever since the news had broken.

'The timing's interesting, to say the least,' he said. 'But if someone had a problem with any of that, then you'd think Michael would be the target. It's worth a conversation with him, certainly. If you can get hold of him, that is – I suspect he's a pretty wanted man right now.'

On screen, Skegman had wrapped up the press conference and was now walking back up the steps into New Scotland Yard as the coverage cut to the presenter in the studio.

Finn shook his head. Satisfying though it was to see his boss taking the heat, he was well aware the pressure was now on them all. The press interest, already intense, was only going to increase from here. There was nothing to suggest the killer was finished, either. Finn's last six months spent meditating, attending therapy and drinking lazy coffees in cafes now felt like a blur. Every second mattered and he'd almost forgotten how that felt. It wasn't simply that he'd missed this – he'd *needed* this sense of urgency in his life again.

As Ojo and the rest of the team started drifting back to their desks, Paulsen remained where she was.

'There's something else, guv. I just took a call from a contact at the NCA. They're hearing a *lot* of chatter about Ray Spinney at the moment.'

Finn frowned. It wasn't their problem – that was one squarely for the NCA – but Spinney's presence out there was nagging at him too.

'Have they got anything new?'

'Not really; they still haven't picked up Kenny Fuller for assaulting Colin Jakes. They also seem to think that whatever Spinney's planning is imminent. They were asking me if I'd heard anything.'

Finn looked surprised.

'Why?'

'Because they're in the dark. I don't think they have a clue what's coming – just that something *is* coming . . .'

Dave McElligott was hovering close by, looking awkwardly down at some paperwork, and Finn realised he'd been standing there for a few minutes.

'You got something there, Dave?'

McElligott looked up quickly.

'Yes, I've just been talking to Ruth Vance's parents. There's a few bits and pieces about her background that I can fill in for you.'

He seemed oddly self-conscious as he said the words.

'Okay – I've got five minutes now if you want?' said Finn.

McElligott nodded, and for a moment Paulsen seemed to pick up on his discomfort, too, before leaving them to it.

It was a waste of time, Fuller thought privately. He could understand why Spinney wanted it done, but he hadn't expected the outcome to be any different than it had been before. The young man in front of him was the last on the list of people he'd been revisiting.

'Please. If I knew, I'd tell you, I swear . . .'

Fuller looked at him dispassionately. He was sitting in the man's kitchen and he'd even been made a cup of tea. An attempt to try and keep things civil. He picked up the mug and casually threw some of the hot liquid at him.

'*Jesus* . . .' cried the man, howling in sudden pain. Most of it had landed on his clothes, though a little had caught his throat which he was now rubbing furiously.

'Mr Spinney wants to be entirely sure that you're not holding something back from us.'

'Why would I lie? Seriously, why would I do that?'

Fuller shrugged.

'Some kind of misplaced loyalty, perhaps?'

Fuller rose from his chair and went over to the kitchen cabinets. He opened them up until he found what he was looking for.

'What are you doing?' said the other man nervously.

Fuller pulled out the food mixer, placed it on the counter and plugged it in. He put the lid on and assessed the chute normally used for pouring liquids in. He switched the device on and watched the blades whirring around noisily for a moment. He wondered if there was just about enough space to squeeze a finger into that chute. It would take some effort, but you probably could do it. He turned back around to the man still fussing at his burnt neck.

'I haven't got time to mess around. So if you know something – now's when you should probably speak up.' The blades whirred again.

A few minutes later he left the flat, pulling his hat down over the back of his head. He walked over to his car and pulled his phone from his jacket pocket.

'I've tried everyone. Nobody knows and no one's lying about it, either.'

'You're a hundred per cent sure?' said Spinney.

Fuller smiled.

'One hundred per cent.'

In the small anonymous house where he was staying, Ray Spinney sighed. Deep down he hadn't expected any other answer. His adversary was a formidable one, someone who knew him inside out. He'd genuinely hoped it wouldn't come to this, but now he saw little room to manoeuvre.

Once McElligott fulfilled his side of their arrangement, the operation would go ahead as planned. He'd tried one last time to pursue this peacefully and it hadn't worked.

He looked over at the television in the corner of the room. A business correspondent in a sharp suit was explaining the implications of the collapse of the Doll Street regeneration project. A picture of Michael Beacham briefly filled the screen. Spinney's hand slammed down on the table in front of him in a sudden burst of unexpected rage. He controlled himself, breathing heavily for a moment.

'Alright then, if that's how you want it . . .' he muttered. 'Cry havoc and let slip the dogs of war . . .'

16

It was weird how the feel of a room could change, thought Dave McElligott. He'd worked at Cedar House for almost six years and this incident room was like a home from home. He'd always enjoyed the craic with his fellow officers. Now as he looked around, it felt like he was behind enemy lines. Nothing was different, of course – the usual low-key hubbub of quiet chatter and ringing phones. But he was acutely aware that he now actually needed to do the deed and acquire the information Spinney wanted so badly. Since he'd got in that morning, he'd found himself actively avoiding even thinking about it. Hearing Finn and Paulsen talking earlier, inadvertently discussing the very robbery he was now actively helping to engineer, had brought the scale of it home.

He was a mass of contradictions about what he was being asked to do. One minute the decision was made, another and it felt like he could still turn things around if he so chose. If he went to Finn and confessed everything, then this could all be over very quickly. And then he remembered what Zoe had told him about the man she'd met during her lunch break – how he'd touched her stomach, touched his baby. He thought too of Colin Jakes, lying now in a hospital bed with permanent brain damage. And then there was the way Spinney had spoken to him in the park, outlining in no uncertain terms what the nature of their relationship was. Goosebumps were rising on his arms – what had he got himself involved in?

Glancing down, he saw a familiar coffee-stained mug on his desk. Emblazoned on the side in dark capitals were the words: 'Keep calm and date a police officer!'

It had been a present from Zoe that used to make him smile. She'd been in pieces since her encounter with Spinney's thug and he'd been quizzed hard about his 'gambling debts'. He'd bobbed and weaved, turning on the charm to maximum, and somehow had managed to calm her down and reassure her. But what had struck him later was the way she was looking at him. A sense that something in their relationship had been permanently altered.

And now, quietly, here it was – the actual moment of betrayal. Of his colleagues, his girlfriend, the very values his parents had given him once. His hand snaked out almost unwillingly towards his keyboard.

'Dave – have you had a chance to look at that forensic report I sent you earlier?'

The voice was sharp and hard. Looking up, he saw Jackie Ojo standing by his desk. He honestly had no idea what she was talking about.

'What report?' he said.

'The one from the lab? They've been cross-checking some of the evidence that's been gathered at the different crime scenes.'

He vaguely remembered reading and ignoring the email earlier.

'Not yet.'

The slight condescension on Ojo's face was turning to thinly disguised anger.

'I marked it urgent – I don't suppose there's any danger of you pulling your head out of your arse?' she said.

He could feel his own temper rising now, knew instantly it was probably the suppressed emotion of the last few days finally making its way to the surface.

'With respect, you're not acting DI any more – so don't talk to me like that,' he said. He could see heads around the room turning towards them. The last thing he needed was to draw attention to himself. Ojo's face was hardening as she geared up for a confrontation.

'I'll get on it – alright?' he said quickly, cutting her off before this could escalate further. He rose to his feet and strode to the door, leaving the detective sergeant hanging. Finn had caught the whole exchange and came over to join her.

'What the hell was all that about?' he said.

She looked at him, genuinely dumbfounded.

'I wish I knew.'

'I think I can help,' said Dattani. 'Don't be too hard on him – Dave's under a lot of pressure at the moment.'

He explained the conversation he'd had with McElligott on the day they'd interviewed Helen Mazurek and also the conversation he'd overheard in the street outside her flat.

'He's got a new baby coming and financial problems by the sounds of it – you can't blame him if he's a bit touchy,' he said.

Ojo was already shaking her head.

'It explains a few things but it doesn't excuse behaving like a child,' she said, still steaming. 'We're in the middle of a double murder investigation – that's where his focus needs to be.'

Finn's jaw tightened.

'We've all got our pressures, Jacks – haven't we?' he said lightly. There was a small moment between them and she softened. Finn turned back to Dattani. 'Thanks, Sami, I'll try and grab Dave for a chat and see how he's doing.'

McElligott had gone straight to the toilets and shut himself inside a cubicle. He was sitting with his head in his hands trying to pull himself together. He couldn't remember ever unravelling quite like this before. Even worse, it was being noticed – just about the worst thing possible in the circum-stances. He was cocking this up before he'd even done anything. As if on cue, there was a buzz in his pocket and he pulled out the burner phone. On the display were two words.

Tick tock . . .

'I'm not condoning the crimes committed by anyone – it's the process of deportation which is fundamentally wrong.' Claire looked around the green leathered benches of the Commons, punching out each word carefully. 'People like Benjamin Ngomo are being bundled out of the country without due process or consideration. The Home Office has got it wrong time and time again on immigration – I call on them to think twice in this instance and not add to that long and shameful list.'

She sat down and fixed the Home Office minister opposite with a sharp stare. He stood, studiously ignoring her gaze, and approached the table of the House.

'Well, Mr Speaker – the honourable lady speaks of a long and shameful list. I think perhaps today of all days, that's a little rich . . .'

There was a ripple of schoolboy smirking on the benches behind him. Claire didn't allow her expression to change. She'd expected something like this – nothing direct, of course, but she knew the collapse of the Doll Street deal and her husband's involvement wasn't simply going to be ignored. There was an unwritten rule, usually observed by MPs of all parties, that the sins of the family stayed out of the chamber. Don't mention your opponent's spouse or they'll go for your father or son, was the general thinking. Out of the corner of her eye, she could see the Speaker watching like a hawk. The minister had trod the line but not crossed it and her heart was sinking – she knew whose sound bite would make the news and so did he.

Afterwards, as she walked through parliament's ornate central lobby, she was stopped several times by concerned well-wishers. Whatever political point-scoring had been going on in the chamber wasn't reflected outside of it. The murders were front page news and Claire's photograph was accompanying each and every article. There was cross-party support – a sympathetic Conservative, a Liberal Democrat she'd worked with on several domestic violence issues in the past – and some from her fellow Labour MPs too. She made time for all of them, appreciating the genuine concern being shown. She could see it in their eyes though – *there but for the grace of God.*

Unusually though, even as she spoke to them, she was struggling to keep her focus. Deep down, a beating drum had been distracting her since she'd seen the news about Doll Street. It wasn't the murders, what had just happened in the chamber, or even Michael that was occupying her mind. All she could think about was how badly she wanted a drink.

'We're being bombarded with interview requests again,' said Lassiter a few minutes later as she returned to her parliamentary office. The room, more than ever, felt like a bunker.

'That's hardly a surprise after everything that's happened today. Out of curiosity – what are they interested in the most: the human body part we were sent yesterday or a failed multi-billion-pound business deal my husband was supposed to be brokering?' she asked. Lassiter looked at her sheepishly.

'Both, I think we can safely assume.'

She checked her phone.

'Michael still hasn't called me back – or even sent a text, for that matter.' She shook her head, not bothering to hide her anger. 'I take it he hasn't called the office either?'

Lassiter shook his head.

'Call me a taxi,' she said.

'Just tell me what the *fuck* happened,' said Andrew Colleter coldly.

It struck Michael Beacham he'd never heard Andrew swear before, and the way he overemphasised the word made it sound awkward. He was glad, all things considered, the conversation was taking place on the phone. It was a delayed discussion too – Michael had deliberately laid low for much of the afternoon trying to take the heat out of this.

'I'm still attempting to get to the bottom of it, to be honest. As far as I can tell, we were gazumped.'

'You must have had an inkling this was in the wind though? How could it get this late and you *not* know?'

'I'm sorry, Andrew – I really didn't. It would have been a business decision by the vendors, purely and simply. I've no doubt when we get to the heart of it – in some form – that will be the explanation. I know how much this meant to you and I'm so sorry.'

'And that's all you know?'

'Yes,' said Michael. 'The vendors are under no obligation to tell me anything.'

There was some heavy breathing on the other end.

'It did mean a lot. Not just to me – but to a whole community. I want to know what happened. In forensic detail – all of it.'

The line went dead and Michael sighed.

'I'd like an explanation too.'

He looked up and saw Claire standing in the doorway of his office. She'd clearly been listening for a while and he recognised the expression on her face, knew that tone of voice. This was going to be a trickier conversation.

'Claire . . .' he began.

'Why didn't you tell me this was coming?'

He rose from his desk and came round to join her.

'Because I didn't think this would actually happen.' He ran a hand through his mane of black hair. 'There's a whole load of extremely unlikely things that needed to occur at the same time – and it seems they clearly did. It's just rank bad luck.'

'So why didn't you return my calls earlier? You know better than anyone how this would land. I've just been humiliated in the House, and I've got the press lining up to take shots at me. *On top of everything else.*'

He held his hands up.

'It's just been crazy here. I wanted to find the time to talk to you properly about it. And we will – tonight. That's a promise.'

She didn't look convinced.

'At least tell me who this consortium that bought Doll Street is? No one seems to know a thing about them.'

He shrugged.

'Property developers – that's all I know. A suggestion there might be Saudi money involved. It was always a possibility that someone might come along late in the process and blow Colleter's offer out of the water. Ultimately, it's just business – that's the only way to view it.'

She still had that dispassionate look on her face and it was beginning to unnerve him.

'Tell me this has nothing to do with those two poor people who died?' she said.

Michael spluttered with indignant astonishment.

'Absolutely not – why on earth would it? *How* could it?'

Claire looked out of his window for a moment then shook her head.

'You're lying to me about something, Michael. I don't know what it is – but you're not telling me the whole truth.' She held his gaze but he didn't reply. She turned to leave.

'Claire . . . you have to believe that everything I do is for you. All of it,' he said.

She whirled back around and for the first time he thought he saw a glimpse of some warmth coming through but then she turned again and left. He waited a few seconds then told his PA he didn't want to be disturbed for the rest of the day. After shutting the door of his office, he walked over to his desk and unlocked the bottom drawer. He pulled out the mobile phone he kept in there – and made a call. The voice that answered was as dry as old leaves.

'We're fine – it's done,' said Michael. 'I don't anticipate any further problems.'

'Good,' said Ray Spinney and the line went dead.

17

Dave McElligott was back at his desk and no happier. The same problem was in front of him and the day wasn't getting any younger. Paranoia was also now starting to bite. The text he'd received had unsettled him. *Tick tock.* It was as if Spinney knew he was having doubts about this. Briefly, he'd considered – then dismissed – the thought that someone else in Spinney's employ might be in the building, watching and reporting back. More realistic was the concern that someone was out there stalking Zoe from a distance again. That if he didn't get a move on and do this, the next text might be even blunter – or worse.

He rubbed his forehead, trying to think pragmatically about how he could actually do what had been asked of him. It wasn't straightforward but he'd formed a few thoughts about his next step. He'd need to slip away again and hope nobody asked any awkward questions.

'Dave – have you got a minute?'

He looked up and saw Finn approaching. There was a warmth to the question rather than a bark. What was it about today that no one would just leave him alone?

'Sure,' he said, affecting a smile.

'Yo Yo's?'

Inside, McElligott felt a little piece of himself die.

Yo Yo's cafe was something of a Cedar House institution. Situated on the opposite side of the road, it was a useful place to escape to when the station's walls became too claustrophobic. Its formidable proprietor Yolande probably knew more about the workings of the station than John Skegman, given the amount of gossiping that went on in there. Retreating there was another of those little work routines that Finn had missed during his sabbatical. He was pleased to find Yolande's espresso still as hot as a furnace and as bitter as hemlock.

'I just wanted to check that you're okay?' asked Finn. 'You seem a bit tense at the moment . . .'

YoYo's was unusually quiet for the time of day – it felt like the words were echoing around the whole cafe and McElligott seemed uncomfortable as he shifted in his seat.

'I'm absolutely fine, boss,' he said sheepishly. 'Look, I'm sorry about earlier with Jacks. I'm just a bit on edge – what with the baby and everything. That's all it is.'

'Are you sure? We've worked together for quite a few years now – I'm not sure I've ever seen you like this before.'

'Like what?' he replied with a bemused smile.

'Jumpy, making small mistakes – under pressure, frankly.'

Again, McElligott looked more like a schoolboy in with the head teacher than someone having a friendly coffee with a colleague.

'Honestly – I've never been in this situation before. You don't have kids, do you?' he said. Finn frowned awkwardly.

'No, I don't.'

'This is my first and I can tell you, it's an emotional roller coaster. I wasn't really expecting that. Everything's happened in such a rush and now the baby's almost here . . .'

He shrugged helplessly and Finn nodded sympathetically.

'I can understand that. What I wanted to say was that my door's always open – you don't have to bottle things up. That's not how I want things to be in my team. I suppose that's one of the big things I learnt in my time off.'

'Thanks, guv,' he said. 'I'll keep that in mind.'

Later, much later, after blood had been spilt, McElligott would look back on that conversation as the last chance he'd had to change course. He'd remember the kindness Finn had tried to show him too. But he hadn't told him about Spinney and wasn't going to now. He'd lied to the man's face and knew that if he ever was discovered, then Finn would remember that conversation as well. The clarity of that strangely helped to settle him down. He cleared the screensaver on his desktop and searched out the information he needed. It didn't take too long to find. He scribbled it on a Post-it, slipped it into his back pocket and stood. He'd make the call outside and use the burner phone again so it couldn't be traced back later. He stood and swung on his coat. Sami Dattani was watching him once more from the adjacent desk.

'Everything alright, Dave?'

'Why does everyone keep asking me that today?'

'Because I've never seen the boss take you across the road for a coffee before.'

It felt like the gods were deliberately trying to chuck obstacles in his way now.

'Yes, mate, everything's alright. In fact, it's more than alright.'

He gave Dattani a wink with something of his old swagger and walked out.

Finn walked back to his office feeling slightly unsettled by his conversation with McElligott. He was trying to understand why impending fatherhood was having such a profound effect on the man. Maybe he was being forced into doing a lot of growing up fast, or perhaps he simply didn't want to be in that situation at all. Finn knew little of his circumstances, but it struck him how many of his team seemed to be struggling with personal issues of one kind or another since he'd returned. Jackie Ojo with her family, Paulsen at a crossroads with her career. His sphere of influence over these things was limited, but he couldn't help feeling slightly responsible anyway. After six months away, it was like finding a well-tended garden beginning to show signs of neglect.

As he settled back at his desk, Paulsen poked her head round his door.

'I might have something, guv – I'm not sure.' She held up some paperwork. 'I've been digging into some archive material of Claire's press coverage to see if there was anything interesting. These are from six years ago when she was a London Assembly member. The first one is from the opening of a new library in Stockwell.' She handed Finn the article. 'Look carefully at the picture.'

Finn studied the black-and-white photo closely. Claire was standing by the reception desk of the new facility with what appeared to be a team of beaming librarians. The headline read:

'Council opens new library and heritage centre'.

At first sight, it seemed standard fayre. What did stand out was that Claire was wearing dark glasses, which was odd given that they were indoors.

'Not sure about those sunglasses – it's a library in south London, not a film premiere,' he said.

'Look at her face,' said Paulsen.

He did as she asked and this time he could see what seemed to be a dark outline around her right eye and temple.

'Is that shadow around her eye?' he said. 'Or bruising?'

'I think it's bruising. If you look closely, there's actually something that resembles a cut as well. And that might explain why she's wearing the sunglasses,' said Paulsen.

'Maybe she'd had some sort of accident?'

'Which is entirely possible – and on its own, it's hard to say anything conclusive about it. But . . .' She brandished another piece of paperwork. 'It was only a few weeks later that she started publicly speaking up about domestic violence. This is from the opening of a women's refuge in Brixton.'

Finn looked at the new picture – this one had been taken outside. Claire appeared visibly more comfortable in it, her smile more natural. Ironically she wasn't wearing sunglasses in this and there didn't seem to be any marks on her face either.

'You think someone was abusing her?'

'I may be adding two and two and getting five – but I think it's a possibility,' said Paulsen.

Finn considered it, looked at the two pictures again.

'Interesting. It's not much to go on, but if she was herself the victim of domestic abuse then I'd like to know who was responsible – because that's someone I'd like to be talking to quite soon. What do we know about her relationship history – was she with Michael at that point?'

Paulsen shook her head.

'No, according to one profile of her I found, her boyfriend then was a university lecturer called Ian Gilfoyle. And what's really interesting is that it isn't too long after that second picture was taken that she meets Michael Beacham.'

Finn nodded approvingly at Paulsen's logic and the digging she'd been doing.

'So she appears in public with what appears to be bruising on her face, suddenly becomes very interested in campaigning against domestic violence and then splits up with her partner soon afterwards. Where's this Gilfoyle now?'

'He's a lecturer at the London School of Economics.' Paulsen smiled. 'And he's expecting us in around half an hour . . .'

Rebecca Devlin was having doubts. The murders were undoubtedly a big part of the way she was feeling. She wouldn't forget the sight of a human tongue in the palm of her hand, flopping like a half-dead fish – or the clammy feel of it. Now there was this whole Doll Street business to contend with too – a different kind of problem. She'd never taken to Michael Beacham if she was honest – there was something a bit disingenuous about the man. The way he always greeted her when they met, as if permanently surprised to still find her employed by his wife. Add Lassiter's condescending attitude and the paltry salary she was on, and it was no surprise she was having misgivings. It wasn't as if Labour was even Rebecca's party, but it had been a first rung on the job ladder. She'd already begun thinking about alternatives and extending some feelers.

Most of her morning had been spent on the phone talking to various campaign groups who might be sympathetic to Benjamin's case. The idea was to try and hold a rally after his sentencing and provide Claire with a platform to make a grandstanding speech for the cameras. She'd then nipped out to run some errands for Lassiter before finally grabbing a late lunch break. While she'd been eating she'd caught Claire's exchange with the Home Office minister on her phone. And as she made her way back into Portcullis House, she wondered what kind of mood she'd find the MP in. She soon found out.

'Here she is . . .' said Claire without looking up as Rebecca entered the office. She was on her own with no sign of Lassiter, which was a bonus.

'I've got some good news – there's plenty of interest in the rally,' said Rebecca. 'If everyone I spoke to delivers what they promised, then we could be talking about two to three hundred people taking part.'

Claire took a large swig from a white teacup on her desk.

'Well, isn't that the dog's bollocks,' she said loudly and that's when Rebecca noticed the half-drunk bottle of vodka next to the cup. If there was any doubt that Claire wasn't drinking her usual Earl Grey, she ended it by topping up her drink with a large measure from the bottle.

'Are you—' said Rebecca.

'Drinking? Yes, I am, and yes, I have had rather a lot. It's been a bit of a day, in case you hadn't noticed,' said Claire, cutting her off. 'Don't worry, I'm not going to start dancing naked down the corridor, I'm not *that* drunk.'

She explained the conversation she'd had with Michael in his office and Rebecca tried to make sense of it.

'You genuinely think he's lying to you?'

Claire nodded.

'I can always tell – he's got a face like a cocker spaniel when he lies. Why did he have to pick now though?' She faltered. 'Isn't there enough shit coming our way?'

The last mournful question made her sound like a small child, thought Rebecca.

'I don't understand – why would Michael lie to you about this? There's no reason.'

Claire smiled sourly.

'Isn't there? I can't prove it, but I think the property developers got to him somehow.'

'*Got to him?* You mean financially?' said Rebecca, astonished. Claire nodded. 'But why? As I understood it, Michael only took on Doll Street because he believed in the principle behind it.' This whole conversation was making Rebecca feel uncomfortable. The alcohol was loosening Claire's tongue and she wondered if that was something they both might regret later.

'We all change, Bex,' said Claire. 'That's the hardest thing about politics – as you age, so does your world view. That fire *you* have – to do things, to change the world – it cools, believe me. It becomes something else. Money and security can quietly overtake your principles without you even noticing.'

She took another big swig from the teacup.

'Are you sure you don't want a coffee?' offered Rebecca gently.

Common sense finally seemed to hit Claire and she nodded, putting the cup back down. There was a small kettle in the corner of the room which had proven a lifesaver over the years. Rebecca filled it with the bottled water they kept for the purpose and switched it on.

'Maybe I deserve this . . . people in glass houses shouldn't throw stones,' said Claire.

'How do you mean?' said Rebecca, rooting around inside a cupboard for a jar of instant.

'It's not like I haven't told Michael a few lies of my own over the years.'

Rebecca remembered the conversation she'd had with Claire outside the cafe in South Wimbledon on Saturday morning – how she'd struggled with alcohol after some sort of incident in her past.

'We've all got our secrets. There's no rule you have to tell your partner everything about yourself. Some things are best left buried in the past, aren't they?'

A mirthless smile spread across Claire's face.

'Ain't that the truth,' she said.

The kettle had boiled and Rebecca poured out a cup. She grabbed some milk sachets and a plastic stirrer and brought the collection over.

'That thing I was telling you about before,' said Claire. 'When we were having coffee the other day . . . it was a long time ago – something that happened with an ex. But it had a profound effect on me and I'm not sure I've ever really got past it. It's always *there*,' she said, tapping the side of her head.

Rebecca had no idea how to respond, but could sense Claire was restless, in the mood to talk.

'You don't have to tell me anything if you don't want to,' she said.

Claire looked at her almost shyly.

'Can I trust you, Bex?' she said. 'Properly trust you, I mean.'

'Of course.'

And so she told her. The revelation hung in the air between them.

'So now you know . . .' said Claire. 'Please say something.'

'That's awful, terrible,' said Rebecca. 'I'm so sorry.'

She ran a hand through her hair as she tried to think of something a bit stronger to say, something to match what she'd just been told. Claire seemed to be sobering up fast and the look on her face suggested she was already regretting how much she'd said. It struck Rebecca then just how lonely the woman seemed to be. Take Michael out of the equation and there didn't seem to be too many people in her life she could turn to.

'Just between us, eh?' said Claire.

'You don't have to worry,' said Rebecca. 'Honestly – you can trust me . . .'

18

The first thing that struck Finn was just how different Ian Gilfoyle was to Michael Beacham. Physically, they couldn't be more dissimilar. Gilfoyle had a closely shaven scalp and wore a pair of slightly ostentatious designer glasses. In his mid-forties, he looked like one of those media analysts who popped up on television occasionally to deconstruct how soap operas work. But Finn could see how he and Claire might have been an item once. When he spoke, with just the vaguest hint of an Irish accent, there was a slight intensity about him. A passion behind the eyes that suggested he wasn't a man who did things by halves.

They were sitting in the front room of a flat not far from Hampstead Heath. Finn guessed he must have been living there for some years and would probably make a comfortable profit on it one day. It was a bit neglected, with peeling walls and dated furniture, but felt like a classic academic's man cave. Wall-to-wall shelves of books, documents and folders were sitting side by side with an array of rather thirsty-looking houseplants.

'You must have been doing some deep old diving to find out about me and Claire. I didn't think anyone still remembered that,' said Gilfoyle.

'It was in a newspaper cutting I found,' said Paulsen. 'A profile of Claire when she was an up-and-coming politician.'

Gilfoyle smiled.

'She hasn't done badly for herself since then, has she?' he said. 'So, what is it you think I can help you with?'

Finn was well aware of the danger of making any assumptions. They didn't know if Claire had ever been abused by someone, let alone whether Gilfoyle was the culprit or not.

'How would you describe the relationship you had with her back then?' he said.

Gilfoyle regarded him pleasantly.

'Am I under suspicion for something? I mean – I follow the news – are you essentially trying to establish whether I chopped some poor fella's head off the other day?'

'We're just trying to colour in some aspects of Claire's past,' said Paulsen.

He nodded and looked away for a moment.

'Volatile, I suppose. Ultimately, that's why we split up. We're both quite headstrong characters.'

'So you argued a lot then?' said Paulsen.

He nodded.

'Were those arguments always verbal – or did it ever get more serious than that?' said Finn.

'If you don't mind me asking – is there anything in particular that's prompted you to ask me that?' he replied.

His tone was reasonable rather than defensive and the two detectives exchanged a glance. Paulsen pulled from her bag the print-out with the photograph from the library opening and passed it to Gilfoyle.

'Do you remember this particular event?' she said.

He looked down and studied it.

'Yes, I do – that's *my* Claire. Not the one you see on TV these days.'

'We think she's wearing dark glasses in that picture to hide some bruising to her right eye,' said Finn.

Gilfoyle seemed almost amused.

'And you think I might have been responsible?'

'Were you?' said Paulsen.

'No – she was very hungover that morning. She'd got drunk the night before and had taken a tumble – we had a small concrete patio back then. I virtually had to tip her out of bed to get her to that library in time.'

'She'd *"taken a tumble"*?' said Finn. 'You're aware how that sounds?'

Gilfoyle nodded.

'Yes – I suppose it does seem rather limp. But it is what happened.'

'Claire began her campaign against domestic violence not long after that picture was taken,' said Paulsen.

'I know – better than anyone,' said Gilfoyle. 'And it's something I hugely respect her for. Some of the work she did during the first two lockdowns was absolutely magnificent.' He shook his head. 'But this isn't what it looks like.'

'So what is it then?' said Finn.

There was a pause. A sense he was lost in a memory for a moment. He looked up at them awkwardly.

'I wasn't hitting her – she was assaulting *me*.'

Both police officers were momentarily lost for words. Finn's mind started to race – as if the picture he'd been forming had suddenly been reframed.

'There is an argument that you *would* say that,' said Paulsen, reacting first, '. . . if you were abusing her.'

'And I accept that,' Gilfoyle said, nodding. 'But why don't you go and ask Claire yourself if I ever raised a hand to her.' He faltered again and a genuine sadness seemed to overtake him. 'For a time, there was a real spark between us – but then she started drinking quite heavily and the alcohol changed her. The first time it happened, she punched me. The second time was a kick – and I ended things before there was a third.

It absolutely broke me at the time.' He breathed out, hard. 'But from what I can tell, the collapse of the relationship was the best thing that could have happened to her. She kicked the booze and went from strength to strength afterwards.'

'Can you remember when the drinking started?' said Finn.

Gilfoyle rolled his eyes.

'It was a long time ago – all I really remember is that it was quite sudden. She didn't have a history of it and it didn't feel like it had been building for a while – it just came from nowhere.'

'And you don't know what prompted it?' said Finn.

Gilfoyle shook his head.

'At the time I just put it down to the pressure she was under – or, to be more accurate, the pressure she was putting herself under. She was – and I assume, still is – a workaholic.'

'And you think that brief experience with you is what prompted her campaign against domestic violence?' said Paulsen.

Gilfoyle nodded.

'I'm convinced of it. I think the feelings of guilt had a profound effect on her, helped her springboard into becoming something better.'

He seemed to stop himself again.

'But?' said Finn, sensing there was one.

Gilfoyle looked down at the picture again, of the young Claire Beacham forcing a smile from behind the sunglasses.

'Sometimes when I watch her on television, I can't quite forget how good an actress she can be.'

'You shouldn't have come here – it's a really stupid idea,' said Benjamin with real anger as Emma settled down in the seat opposite. The rest of the visitors' hall at HMP Cromarsh was doing surprisingly little business and they had plenty of privacy. Petite, with a pretty, elfin face and a short chestnut bob, she smiled warmly as if they were at the table of an expensive restaurant about to peruse some menus.

'Don't be stupid,' she said. 'I had to—' She broke off, a catch in her voice as the emotion caught up with her. Benjamin desperately wanted to lean across and kiss her, for all sorts of reasons – reassurance, fear, sadness and lust all rolled into one – but he could only shake his head. She frowned as she noticed something.

'You're hurt?' she said.

There was some light bruising under his left eye. He brought up a hand and rubbed at it absently.

'Someone took a swing at me over breakfast.' She opened her mouth to reply, but he cut her off quickly. 'I have no idea why – might just be the way he thought I was looking at him.' He shrugged. 'It's a prison – shit happens.'

Emma looked desperate.

'I hate this. I want to be in court tomorrow – for your sentencing.'

'No,' he said immediately. 'I don't want you there and you know why – it's not safe for you.'

'Don't be ridiculous, it's the safest place I could possibly be.'

'No,' he repeated emphatically. 'Please, Em – for me. I've got enough to be thinking about, without worrying about you too.'

'But it might be the last chance I ever get to see you,' she said plaintively.

'Not necessarily. There's no reason you couldn't get on a plane and . . .'

He stopped as the reality of what he was saying struck him. In a few days, he could be living on a different continent, living who knew what kind of life.

'That MP was talking about you on TV earlier,' said Emma, deliberately changing the subject. 'She's done a good job of explaining your situation. People now know what's at stake – that even a light sentence means you'll probably get deported. They're going to hold some sort of march for you in central London after the hearing.'

Benjamin rolled his eyes.

'A march – big deal, because that'll really make a difference. Perhaps they can do a hard-hitting leaflet campaign while they're at it.' He shook his head. 'I'm sorry, Em – I just feel like I'm letting you down.'

'Don't be ridiculous, this isn't your fault. None of this is your fault – it's *mine*.'

Her face hardened as she said it.

'Promise me you'll stay away from court tomorrow,' he said. 'Don't go to work either – just stay out of sight until this is all over.'

'Okay – I won't come if that's what you really want, but I'm not hiding away. I'll be at work, thinking about you. If I can, I'll visit you again afterwards – assuming they don't bundle you on a plane straight away.'

'Beacham must think it's not going to be immediate otherwise she wouldn't be organising this march,' he said.

They looked into each other's eyes for a moment, shutting out the surroundings, shutting out the situation, shutting out everything.

'We're lying to all of them, aren't we?' said Emma.

'So Finn's not still moping about his dead wife then?' said Nancy Deen. She and Paulsen were standing in the queue at a Tesco Express in Archway. They were both tired and hungry after long days at work, their moods worsened at finding the fridge and cupboards bare on their return. Paulsen paid for the two pizzas she was holding and put them into a bag with a bottle of Malbec.

'No, he's been different since he returned – kind of laid-back,' she said as they made for the exit.

'*Laid-back?* The stiffest man in Great Britain?'

Paulsen shrugged as they exited the shop and began walking up Archway Road.

'I kind of like it. I've not seen him like this before, and after the last few years I'm not knocking it.'

'So how does Inspector Goldenballs feel about your desire to move on?'

Paulsen scowled.

'Do you have to call him that? I don't even know why you *do* call him that . . . you don't even know him that well.'

'I like it and it sort of feels like it fits. You haven't answered my question.'

Paulsen's scowl intensified.

'Hard to read – but he does that deliberately.'

'Are you sure about all this?' said Nancy. 'That you *do* actually want to leave?'

Paulsen was silent, and for a moment the only sound was their footsteps on the pavement. They'd already had one row about this and neither particularly wanted another. Nancy hadn't hidden her view before that she thought the timing was wrong.

'I suppose it's kind of bound up with my dad . . .' replied Paulsen finally.

Her father had Alzheimer's. For the most part, the worst ravages of the disease hadn't yet struck him but it felt like the oncoming storm was getting ever closer.

'How do you mean?' asked Nancy carefully.

Again there was a silence.

'I can't control what happens with him. But my job, my career . . . that I *can* steer. Does that make sense, Nance?'

Nancy considered it.

'It's giving you a sense of empowerment at a time when you feel completely powerless . . .' she said. Paulsen nodded almost imperceptibly. 'That's understandable, but it's also a bit dangerous,' continued Nancy.

'How do you mean?' said Paulsen.

'You're making a career decision based on an emotional reaction. To compensate for what you can't affect and change. But you're happy at Cedar House – more settled than I've ever seen you before. Why risk messing that up, what's the rush?'

'Because the deadline for the application is tomorrow. If I'm going to do this, I need to decide tonight.'

Nancy nodded, and they walked the rest of the way home in silence.

Ray Spinney had just finished a light dinner of poached chicken breast and steamed vegetables when Dave McElligott finally called. He drained his glass of white wine, switched off the Rachmaninoff adagio he'd been listening to and considered the information. Then he went to look at the maps. They were the best Ordnance Survey charts money could buy and he had them pinned up across the walls of one of the rooms of the empty house.

There was one map for each wall – one for each job. In his mind, he needed to visualise every aspect of the operation. Thanks to McElligott, the final elements were now in place. He also knew the personnel who would be with the money, where they lived, where their partners worked and where their children were schooled.

He spread the plan out in his mind and looked for any potential holes he'd missed. He'd been studying the profiles of the people they'd recruited, knew every last detail about them too. You couldn't ever say any plan was foolproof, but he was as comfortable as he'd ever been before a major job. And that was just as well because the stakes had never been higher. As ever, he'd given some thought about where and what he would be doing while it was underway. A new art gallery had opened up in Canterbury that had caught his eye. He'd get there early, have some coffee outside if the forecast held and the sun was shining.

The only nagging doubt was the MP. According to McElligott, Finn and his team didn't seem to have much of a clue who was behind these murders. They were vicious and grotesque – and Spinney knew a bit about that, why you might choose to kill people in that way. Invariably, it was to make a statement, send a message – to intimidate. And right now he needed the Beachams out of the firing line and off the front pages. His assumption had always been that politics being what it was, something would come along and displace Doll Street from the headlines fairly quickly. He'd factored that into the plan from the start – what he hadn't anticipated was these deaths keeping the focus on both Beachams for this long.

He sighed – you couldn't legislate for everything and he might be overthinking things, a familiar flaw. He took one last look at the maps on the four walls then called Fuller.

'We have all the information now. I'm formally giving you the go-ahead to proceed tomorrow. Gather the men together and brief them. Then you can release them for the night – but make sure they stay off the piss.'

'You're happy with everything? There's still time to make changes if you want,' said Fuller.

Spinney considered it one last time.

'Yes, I'm happy. I'll email across to you the exact timings and routes.'

'And the NCA – do we need to worry about them?'

Spinney smiled.

'No. I rather think we don't – thanks to our friend, DC McElligott.'

'I just hope there aren't any surprises,' said Fuller.

'Follow what I send you to the letter and there shouldn't be,' said Spinney. 'And hold your nerve – don't deviate or improvise. The next time we speak will be when it's over.'

He ended the call and looked out of the window. An evening walk suddenly felt appealing. He grabbed his coat and began quietly whistling to himself.

19

Dave McElligott slept fitfully that night. His mind hadn't stopped turning over with worry as the hours ticked by. He glanced over Zoe's sleeping form towards the bedside clock next to her. It was now just after five. He lay back and stared at the ceiling. All he could hear was his partner's shallow breathing and the sound of his own heart beating. What he'd set in motion was about to begin.

At that moment across London, a small white van was parking up on a trading estate close to Heathrow Airport. Inside, the National Crime Agency officer leading a small surveillance team radioed in and confirmed their arrival. Half a mile away, in a side street behind the estate, the commander leading a multi-vehicle armed response team did exactly the same. At the centre of their attention – roughly equidistant between them – was a large grey security ware-house containing over twenty-five million pounds in gold and diamonds.

An informant – or CHIS, as the modern terminology labelled them – had supplied intelligence that this was Spinney's intended target. He'd given up not just details of the that, but also names of some of those involved and also a rough timescale of when the attack was expected. Late the previous evening an anonymous call had been received by the Crimestoppers charity providing the very same specific infor-mation. The two corroborating pieces of information were enough to convince the NCA to deploy. Now here they were, in the half-light of dawn, quietly waiting.

In his bedroom McElligott could picture the scene all too easily. He'd made this happen, manipulated the CHIS, made that final phone call himself. Now, all he could do was let things play out. He sat up, put his head into his hands and slowly began to rub his temples.

Claire Beacham began her day in a filthy mood. She and Michael had spent the evening talking and he'd done nothing to calm her doubts about him. He flat out denied that he'd sold out the Doll Street Collective and maintained the story he'd given her in his office – that the deal had imploded at the very last moment. Not only did the suspicion that he was lying linger, it had strengthened. She was also full of regret about the conversation with Rebecca in Portcullis House, both the drinking that had preceded it and the personal information she'd disclosed. They were both things she'd been very careful to manage over the years. In the space of an hour, she'd somehow polished off half a bottle of vodka then spilt her most closely guarded secret to a twenty-something researcher. With a big day ahead, she felt distracted, irritable and full of self-loathing.

She'd gone straight to the constituency office in South Wimbledon early, for a FaceTime call with Benjamin. They were allowed with prisoners so long as you were on their visitors list and aged over eighteen. They were also recorded and monitored by a member of the prison's staff, which perhaps explained why Benjamin hadn't been overly keen on the idea. But Claire had wanted to make sure she spoke to him before his sentencing later. She wouldn't be able to make it there herself, but wanted to look him in the eye and reaffirm her commitment before he left. In a short time, he'd be transported to the Inner London Crown Court where he'd be held in a custody cell until his case was called. It could potentially be a long day with the worst of outcomes.

Grant had set everything up with an iPad on her desk and after a bit of fiddling, the line connected and Benjamin's face flickered into view. He seemed unexpectedly pleased to see them which took her by surprise, but Claire was encouraged by it. He was visibly nervous, that sullen hard-to-reach persona she'd encountered in person now replaced by something more fragile. She felt for him – on this day of all days he had no family to support him. All he had was his girlfriend and an MP. It was his life in the UK that was at stake, but he had the feel of an inmate on death row.

'How are you?' she began with.

'I just want to get this over with.'

'It probably won't take long once you're in the dock. It'll be straightforward for the judge.'

He shook his head irritably.

'It doesn't matter how long it takes – if he gives me more than twelve months, we both know what that means. And he will, won't he?'

Claire had checked and double-checked with legal experts. The answer had come back the same each time. Despite the relatively mild offences he'd been convicted of, the nature of them, combined with his previous conviction, would give the judge little option and she didn't want to give Benjamin false hope. Any chance of saving him from deportation lay in the wider battle with the Home Office.

'I wish I could be there for you but we don't know when you're going to get called so it's almost impossible.' His face dropped. 'Once it's done, I don't want you to panic – I'll be straight in touch and we'll work out our next move then. I want you to know we're working really hard to keep the pressure on and I'm also confident we've got public opinion on our side. You mustn't give up – whatever unfolds today.'

He nodded mechanically.

'So, how quickly could it happen afterwards? When could they put me on a plane? Tonight? Tomorrow morning – when?'

His voice was almost monotone; the real pleading came from his eyes.

'I honestly don't know,' said Claire.

Scott Upson was in hell and he couldn't quite work out how it had happened. He drove the Securicor van to the same building society in Wallington high street, once a week, every week. The routine was always identical. He and his colleague Kelly parked outside, picked up four large metal cash boxes containing nearly five million pounds in total, transferred them to the van and then drove the 2.4-mile journey to the cash depot. He liked working with Kelly – she had a mouth like a sewer and wasn't scared of anything. They were both trained in emergency procedures too – and even though they'd never had to draw on that knowledge, neither of them were complacent. They knew what could happen at any given moment on any given day.

What he hadn't been ready for was the phone call he'd received over breakfast that morning. At first, he'd thought it was some sort of nuisance call, some idiot trying to convince him he was eligible for a payout on an accident he hadn't had. The voice was calm and reasonable, friendly even. And then they'd mentioned St Lucien's Primary School and Mrs Wheeler. She was his daughter Esme's teacher. The man continued for a few more minutes, outlining the various entrances and exits to the school, lesson times and specifically what Mrs Wheeler was wearing to work this morning. Finally, with the same sort of tone you might use to give directions to a lost tourist, he'd talked about his lack of compunction at hurting young children.

'What do you want?' Scott had stammered.

And then the man had told him. Warned him not to say a word to Kelly or the police, had even broken down for him, minute by minute, how this was going to go.

They'd picked up the cash boxes as normal from the building society and were now driving back across south London to the depot. Kelly was prattling on about some man she'd met in a club over the weekend. She was describing what they'd got up to and what she was planning to *get* up to with him again. But Scott wasn't listening to a word.

They'd been on the road for nearly six minutes since they'd left the high street and were passing a stretch of scrubland close to Carshalton. Scott's eyes hadn't left the clock on the dashboard. Exactly on cue, a navy blue sedan raced out of nowhere and with a screech of tyres, swerved to block their path. Two men clad in black, wearing ski masks, jumped out brandishing guns. Much later those weapons would be identified from the dashcam footage as an AKM Kalashnikov assault rifle and a Mossberg 12-gauge pump-action shotgun.

Kelly stayed remarkably calm; the armoured vehicle had bullet-resistant glass, after all, and had been designed to withstand an attack exactly like this. The men moved silently round to each side of the vehicle and pointed their weapons at the two occupants. Kelly was already reaching for her phone to call for assistance when Scott simply opened his door and stepped out.

'Scott – what the fu—' she started to shout in astonishment, but one of the men was already inside.

'*Get out of the van and lie on the fucking ground!*' he screamed.

For a moment it looked like she might try to resist but then she saw the size of the shotgun being aimed at her. She opened the passenger's door and did exactly as she'd been told. Scott and the other gunman walked round to the back of the vehicle.

'*Scott!*' Kelly yelled and the man next to her smashed the butt of his rifle into her skull. She fell forwards on to her knees with a cry of pain, rubbing the back of her head as blood began to ooze into her hair. Terrified, Scott opened up the back of the van. Not a word was exchanged – it wasn't necessary. The two men took the cash boxes back to the car, where a third man had kept the engine running. They then forced the two stricken security guards at gunpoint into the back of their own van. They left them face down on the floor with plastic ties around their wrists.

At the same time, two other cash-in-transit vehicles were being robbed in precisely the same fashion. One was close to a golf course in Bexleyheath, the other by a common near Orpington. Three simultaneous armed robberies on three separate armoured vehicles – fifteen million pounds in cash stolen in less than three minutes. In west London, oblivious to what was happening, the NCA team continued their pointless surveillance of the security warehouse. In Canterbury, Ray Spinney strolled slowly around an exhibition of abstract landscapes. Very briefly he glanced up at a clock on the wall of the gallery before continuing on to the next painting.

In his cell, Benjamin had changed into a suit for his court appearance. He'd been thinking about his parents all morning. The irony was they'd only come to the UK for his sake – a small child, who they'd worked so hard to build a future for. Like all parents, they'd wanted a better life for their son than they'd had for themselves. If they knew how things were turning full circle, they'd be spinning in their graves now. He'd also been thinking about Emma, and what would happen to her once he was gone – that particular worry never left him. The door to his cell opened and two prison officers walked in. One, Benjamin knew quite well – a middle-aged, greying man called Terry; the other, younger with blonde hair, he didn't recognise.

'Come on, son, it's time . . .' said Terry in his thick Lancastrian accent. He smiled sympathetically while the second man simply scowled.

A short time later they were on the move. Benjamin was handcuffed, with Terry sitting alongside him in the back of the prison transport van.

'Want a Polo?' the older man offered, again with a pleasant smile. He pulled a tube of mints from his pocket and Benjamin nodded. 'You'll have to stick your tongue out, lad . . .' he said, motioning apologetically at the handcuffs. Benjamin opened his mouth and Terry fed him the sweet. It was welcome – his mouth was dry as a desert and tasted of old socks.

'Feeling nervous?' said Terry.

Benjamin nodded.

'Don't be.' The prison officer sucked on his mint for a moment. 'Do you know what my old man always used to say when I was worried about something? *Courage, mon ami, le diable est mort!* The French sounded strange delivered in his broad northern accent. 'It's a quote from somewhere, don't ask me where. It means, *Take courage, my friend, the devil is dead!*

He smiled encouragingly at Benjamin, who considered the phrase for a moment.

'Except he isn't,' he said quietly.

In the front, the driver was feeling an increasing sense of dread. He'd been feeling it all morning – since the phone call he'd received while he'd been getting dressed. The man with the calm, dry voice who seemed to know everything about him. In his mirror, he could see a dark blue sedan behind them. It had been there for a few minutes now.

'*In one hundred yards, turn left into Melbourne Road,*' intoned the vehicle's satnav, and the driver swallowed. He followed the instruction and saw the blue car do the same. Further ahead he caught a quick glimpse of a black-clad figure waiting by a row of parked cars. At the sight of the prison transport, the man walked out into the centre of the road and stopped. He turned and pointed the Kalashnikov he was holding directly at the oncoming vehicle. The driver slammed his foot on the brakes and the blue sedan swerved past and stopped. Before he could react, two more masked men carrying guns jumped out and sprinted towards them. They were screaming, and though he couldn't hear the exact words through the thick protective glass, there was no mistaking their meaning.

In the back of the van, the sudden stop had thrown Benjamin and his escort on to the floor. They could hear the shouting outside and understood instinctively what was happening.

'Please,' said Benjamin quickly, twisting to hold out his handcuffed wrists. 'It's me they want.'

Terry hesitated for a second, then nodded and quickly unlocked the cuffs.

'Don't do anything stupid—' he began to say but was interrupted as the back doors were pulled open. Two black-clad men were pointing guns at them.

'*Get out of the van now – move, move, move!*' one of them shouted, in what sounded like a Scouse accent. Terry rose to stand in front of Benjamin and held out his hands, palms up.

'Easy, lads – just take it easy,' he said.

'*I said move!*' the gunman screamed again.

Terry jumped out of the van but seemed to catch his foot on the way out. The trip made him stumble sharply forwards as he hit the ground. What happened next almost occurred in slow motion – the nearest gunman turned and fired his shot-gun straight at the prison officer's chest. The impact slammed Terry's body backwards, blood exploding everywhere. The second gunman, the Scouser, was now screaming at the first.

'*No!*'

Benjamin took advantage and leapt *through* them. He hurtled down the road, half expecting to hear the sound of a shot, feel the next bullet rip into his back, but it didn't come. He could hear more loud shouting behind him, then footsteps in pursuit. Fuelled by adrenaline and terror, he sprinted for his life.

20

It didn't take long for the events of the morning to become national news. The atmosphere at Cedar House was sombre, reflecting the mood at police stations up and down the country. Prison officer Terry Merchant had died at the scene, despite the best efforts of paramedics to save him. Most of the incident room was transfixed by the coverage on the BBC News channel. A reporter was standing by a cordon tape close to the scrubland near where Scott Upson's van had been robbed of several million pounds in cash.

'*It's too early to say whether the assault on the prison van in south London is connected to the attacks on the three security vehicles – but it is clear that these were a series of well-planned, coordinated raids . . .*'

'No shit, Sherlock,' said Jackie Ojo, who was watching with Paulsen. Finn, who'd been on the phone, came over to join them.

'I'm trying to get some sense out of the NCA – but as you can imagine, it's not a brilliant time to call. They were caught with their trousers down – apparently they'd received hard intel that Spinney was going to hit a security warehouse close to Heathrow. They'd deployed there . . .'

'He sold them a dummy?' said Paulsen.

'Looks like it.'

Finn walked over to the expanded map of Greater London that was permanently pinned across one of the walls. He stuck coloured flags into the four places where the raids had taken place.

'These locations aren't coincidental,' he said, pointing at the map. 'The attack on the prison van took place around twenty minutes after the synchronised assaults on the security vans – when the police response would have been at its most stretched.'

'You think Benjamin Ngomo was the primary target then – not the money?' said Ojo.

'Not necessarily,' said Finn. 'More like they were giving themselves the maximum chance of pulling off all four attacks successfully.'

'But *why* would Ray Spinney want Benjamin?' said Paulsen, frowning.

'The timing could just be coincidental,' said Ojo. 'If anyone wanted to help Benjamin escape, then surely it would have been what's left of the OCG he used to work for?'

Finn shook his head.

'What the NCA knows so far suggests that these were all linked. In each case, the attackers knew the routes the vehicles were taking. There were four teams of three – two men to carry out the robberies together with getaway drivers. The raid on the prison transport followed exactly the same pattern.'

'How could they know the routes?' said Paulsen.

Finn shrugged.

'We know, historically, Spinney has contacts inside the Met. If it turns out he used any of them to help him do this – then there are people wearing the uniform who cost Terry Merchant his life.'

Ojo and Paulsen exchanged a glance as the implication sank in.

'He's been doing this for years,' said Ojo. 'Using insiders to pull off major robberies like this. How come no one's ever put a stop to it, properly rooted out the rotten apples?'

Neither Finn or Paulsen had an answer for her.

'I'm more interested in whether this connects to our investigation,' said Finn. 'Benjamin's been on our radar all week. He's Claire Beacham's pet project. It feels way too much to be a coincidence.'

'I'll ask it again then . . .' said Paulsen. 'Why would Ray Spinney want a petty criminal who's facing deportation?'

'I've no idea and I'm not sure he's got him yet, either,' said Finn. 'The boy's disappeared. At first, it was thought he'd been taken, but the NCA told me the early witness statements are suggesting he managed to get away.'

Ojo was looking back up at the television where a mug shot of Benjamin taken at the time of his arrest was now on screen.

'That's an awful lot of shit circling the Beachams right now. Two murders, Doll Street . . . now this. None of it adds up in any way I can make sense of.'

Finn nodded; she wasn't wrong. Every day seemed to be bringing something new, the stakes increasing each time, and there they were – Claire and Michael Beacham continually connected to it all. The most frustrating part was – like Ojo – he still couldn't see any kind of pattern to it. Some of this *could* be coincidental, Doll Street and Benjamin, but his instinct said otherwise.

And that's, irritatingly, where his instinct seemed to stop. The pressure was on – from the killer, from Skegman, from the media, even Ray Spinney now – and for a fleeting moment, he felt slightly overwhelmed by it all. He'd assumed that his initial rustiness would clear quickly after a few days back. But a week had gone by and he was still feeling one step behind everything.

'I agree – it's mounting up,' he said quickly, aware Ojo and Paulsen were looking at him. 'I think we're going to need another chat with Claire.'

At his desk, Dave McElligott was watching the television coverage, aghast. A man had died – that hadn't been the plan and that was on him. The task Spinney had set him was to create the decoy at Heathrow. He'd needed a CHIS registered with another police officer to do it and at first he'd thought the task would prove beyond him. To find one who fitted the bill and could be pressured into turning – without giving away his own involvement – seemed nigh on impossible. Then he'd had his first stroke of luck since this whole nightmare began. A name came back to him – someone who through pure chance had been accidentally arrested by a uniform PC at Cedar House the previous year.

They'd had to apologise profusely to his handler and kick him loose, but Dave had remembered him. He'd found the name in the database then passed his details on to Spinney. From there he guessed it had been a simple matter of dispatching someone to gently persuade the luckless man to supply the false information back to his handler, who in turn would have immediately relayed it to the NCA. After that, all they'd had to do was corroborate the lie with a well-timed call to Crimestoppers. The line Dave McElligott insisted he wouldn't cross, he'd sailed over, and the outcome had been catastrophic.

The attempt to kidnap Benjamin had turned into a clusterfuck and the boy was now free. God only knew how Spinney was going to react. One thing McElligott was certain of was that he'd been complicit in a man's death. Whatever happened next, however this played out – things could never quite be the same again.

Kenny Fuller rarely felt fear. He was used to inflicting it, but it had been a long time since he'd genuinely been scared himself. Benjamin had been too fast for them – he'd hurtled away like an Olympic sprinter and their pursuit of him had bordered on farce. Fuller had many strengths but speed wasn't one of them. He and the other gunman both knew Benjamin needed to be brought back alive, so shooting him down hadn't been an option. Neither was winging him – it's not like either of them were crack shots. There was too much traffic for the getaway car to have gone after him and they hadn't wanted to put too much distance between themselves and their only means of escape. In the end, all they'd been able to do was stand and watch as their target hared into the distance.

The aftermath of the robberies had been as slickly planned as the raids themselves. The money was taken by the individual teams to three separate locations where Spinney's laundering operation was ready to kick in. Fuller and the other two men on his team had dumped their getaway car and transferred to a new vehicle before driving back to the warehouse to rendezvous with Spinney. The gunman who'd shot Terry Merchant had gabbled excuses at first. He tried to explain that he thought the prison officer had been trying to jump him.

'The guns were for show,' said Fuller in his Liverpudlian drawl. 'You knew that – you were told explicitly that no one was to get hurt. We were there to get the boy.' The man had quietened down as they drove on and Fuller suspected the full implication of his mistake was starting to dawn on him.

When they arrived at the warehouse, Spinney was already waiting for them. He was with the cash boxes from the raid in Wallington, together with the three-man team who'd stolen them. Fuller explained what had happened while Spinney listened with his usual inscrutable expression. After he'd finished, the gunman who'd fired the fatal shot tried to explain himself. He was babbling again – useful babble, as far as

Fuller was concerned. Spinney listened impassively, then walked slowly over to him and Fuller found himself holding his breath.

'Thanks to you, there'll now be a whole extra dimension to this. The Prime Minister will be on the news tonight pretending he cares about the individual you shot . . .'

Suddenly a bony fist shot out and struck the man in the abdomen, followed by an uppercut that put him on the ground. Purposefully Spinney walked over to a nearby wall where a metal bucket and some cleaning materials had been left.

'I've acquired a certain reputation over the years,' he said, picking up the bucket together with a bottle of bleach. He unscrewed the bottle and casually squirted some into the stricken man's face. The man on the ground howled in agony as Spinney emptied the rest into the bucket.

'And sometimes it doesn't hurt to remind people why . . .'

Savagely, he grabbed the man by the hair and pushed his face deep into the bucket of bleach and held it there. He looked like someone patiently waiting for a kettle to boil. After a few very long moments, he yanked him back up and threw him to the ground. The man's face was now scarlet red and he was screaming in agony, clawing at his eyes as a white froth foamed around his mouth. Spinney wiped his hands and turned to face the others.

'The money you're owed will be paid directly into your accounts later today. I trust I don't need to remind anyone to follow the plan. Keep your heads down, stick to your normal routines and keep your mouths shut.'

Their eyes were still on the shuddering figure on the floor and unsurprisingly they all nodded obediently.

'Good lads – thanks for today,' said Fuller. 'There's a shower round the back – change into your civvies and make sure you leave everything you wore on the job here. We're burning everything.'

The men nodded and gratefully began to disperse. Spinney waited for them to leave and then joined Fuller.

'I didn't come back to this country for the money.'

'I know,' said Fuller. He looked up deliberately and held Spinney's gaze. 'And I'm sorry about the boy. What do you want to do?'

Spinney considered it, the agonised cries of the man behind them the only noise for a second.

'The only positive is that he isn't in the hands of the authorities any more. There's only so many places he can go – we just have to find him before they do.'

Benjamin felt like he hadn't stopped running. He was conscious of being caught on CCTV and just wanted to get himself out of sight as quickly as possible. He had no money, no phone, just the suit he was wearing. Keeping away from the main roads, he finally found a construction site in a back-street somewhere near Kennington. It appeared to be deserted and he slipped in, collapsing inside the framework of what appeared to be a new block of flats under construction.

The obvious person to call was Emma, but he didn't have the means – and trying to steal a phone wasn't worth the attention it might draw. He didn't know where she lived now, not the exact address, anyway – she'd moved into a new place after he'd been arrested. And he didn't know where she worked either, other than it was a Starbucks somewhere near the National Gallery.

He knew full well Ray Spinney had been behind the attack on the prison van. A man like that didn't forget certain things, didn't just disappear. The image of Terry Merchant flying backwards kept replaying in his mind, the spray of blood exploding from his chest as if on a loop. Small kindnesses, like the warm smile he'd given him in the cell that morning, the peppermint in the van, others over the months in Cromarsh – they all added up. He could only hope it hadn't been as bad as it looked and the man was okay.

Outside he could hear the world getting on with its business and he tried to focus on what his next move should be. He didn't have many friends he could turn to and it wouldn't be fair on them anyway. Spinney would be frantically searching for him now and anyone who got in his way would . . . well, he'd already seen how far the man was prepared to go.

Sitting against a bare concrete wall, he pulled his knees up and hugged himself. He had one of the most dangerous men in the country desperate to find him and a government falling over itself to put him on a plane. The one person he really wanted to talk to was his mum. She'd know the right thing to do. But she wasn't here, and as the wind blew through the empty husk of the building, he began to cry.

21

Only once since he'd returned to work had Finn thought about his late wife. Progress, his counsellor would have said. He'd been wondering what Karin would have made of Claire Beacham. She'd been a good judge of people; it's what had made her an effective solicitor once. He'd been trying to break down his feelings about the MP as he and Paulsen made their way to her constituency office in South Wimbledon. What he'd told her before was true – he didn't share the popular stereotype of politicians as liars and frauds. He genuinely didn't have Beacham pegged as one of those, so her presence at the centre of so much of what was going on continued to trouble him. Ian Gilfoyle's description of her as an actress hadn't left him either.

Funnily, Gilfoyle's revelations had in fact only strengthened Finn's instinct about her. He liked people who'd had to battle their way to achieving something in life. Beacham had plainly possessed more than a few demons once. But she'd fought and overcome them to come out stronger, and that was certainly something he could get on board with. She was a mass of contradictions caught at the centre of far too many unanswered questions.

When they arrived, her slightly obsequious aide, Lassiter, made them all a round of teas and coffees then left them alone in a small, rather unglamorous back office. The instant he laid eyes on her, Finn found himself reappraising the woman again. He'd seen a few different sides to her so far. Shocked after the death of Lukasz Mazurek, then assured and strong in the House of Commons, despite Ruth Vance's severed tongue turning up at her office only the day before. The person in front of him now looked like she'd had all the wind blown out of her sails. Her cheeks were hollow and the expression behind her eyes even emptier. She seemed to have aged in a matter of days.

'I just didn't see this coming,' she said. 'Right now, the only thing that matters is that Benjamin is found safely. The National Crime Agency's asked me to do a bit with the media later, an appeal for him to turn himself in. I doubt it'll do any good, to be honest – he wasn't particularly listening to me before, so I'm not sure that he'll start now.'

'Did the NCA tell you who they thought might be responsible for the attacks this morning?' asked Finn.

She nodded.

'The man behind the Stansted heist . . .' She tailed off. 'I just can't make any sense out of that. I genuinely had no idea there was even a connection between them. I thought Benjamin was just the sort of person I *should* be working for. A man with no resources or family, taking on a hostile government all on his own. I wanted to try and help him – now it turns out I'm not sure I knew who he was at all.'

'He might still be that man,' said Paulsen. 'If this was a rescue, he'd have gone willingly with these people. Instead, he ran away.'

Claire nodded.

'I'm not sure the Home Office will see it that way. A prison officer died – it's catastrophic in terms of my campaign to try and prevent his deportation.'

'If you don't mind me saying . . . you seem to be at the centre of a *lot*, right now,' said Finn. The look on Claire's face suggested she was more than aware of that fact. 'As far as our investigation into the two murders goes, is it possible there might be a connection with Benjamin? I know you discounted the idea previously – but are you sure you've never been sent any kind of message to leave his case alone?'

She looked confused by the question.

'What kind of message?'

'Ray Spinney specialises in these kinds of graphic killings,' said Paulsen. 'It's why the press calls him the Handyman. It's possible he might have murdered Lukasz Mazurek and Ruth Vance to make some sort of point to you. Was there perhaps an approach before that you didn't recognise the significance of at the time?'

It was a theory they'd discussed in the incident room before they'd left. The introduction of Spinney into the mix – however peripherally – had cast a shadow over the whole inquiry. Claire shook her head.

'No – nobody's ever said a word to me about Benjamin. I've consciously been raising my profile in recent weeks with the domestic violence work though. Most of the crap I've received has been connected to that.'

'One last thing – Doll Street. The timing is unfortunate, to say the least. Is there anything you can tell us about that that you think might be relevant?'

That produced the most interesting reaction of all, Finn thought. For a second her eyes blazed with anger.

'No. I think that was just corporate greed – pure and simple.'

Paulsen looked troubled as they walked back to Finn's car a short time later. She glanced back at the photograph of Claire that hung in the constituency office window.

'Maybe it's me . . .' she muttered.

Finn frowned.

'I don't follow?'

She took her time before she answered, trying to articulate how she was feeling.

'Every time I see that woman, instinctively I kind of warm to her. She seems genuine, principled . . . decent.'

Finn remembered Paulsen's earlier scorn for politicians.

'You've changed your tune,' he said.

'She changed it for me. It's different when you can actually look someone in the whites of their eyes. She's not the person you see on TV . . . when you meet her, she's real.'

'And yet?' said Finn.

'I think she's holding something back. I don't know what – or how relevant – but *something*.'

Finn digested this and nodded. It tallied with his own growing suspicion about her.

'One other thing . . .' said Paulsen. 'And this is what I can't work out – I keep coming back to why Spinney wants Benjamin . . . it's not to help him, judging by the way he ran off. So why?'

'To hurt him – to silence him for some reason?'

Paulsen shook her head.

'He doesn't need to do that – the guy was more than likely going to be in another continent by the end of the week.'

Finn realised she was right.

'Alright – for information then. Because he knows something important,' he said.

'That occurred to me too – but it doesn't make sense, either, when you think about it. We know Spinney has people everywhere. Do we really think he doesn't have someone on the inside at Cromarsh who couldn't have put pressure on him? Why did he need to physically *take* him, and why did Benjamin run rather than let that happen?'

They were passing an electrical shop where several large widescreen TVs were showing photographs from the heist scenes. Finn shook his head.

'It's not our problem – that's for the NCA to investigate. Our focus is on finding out who that man in the baseball cap is and why he killed Lukasz Mazurek and Ruth Vance. For what it's worth, I think your assessment of Claire is correct though – we don't know everything about her yet. Or how Doll Street and Spinney figure into this – if they even do.'

Paulsen said nothing and he gave her a sideways look.

'Did you apply for that detective sergeant's job in the end?' he said.

'Yes,' she replied simply and walked on.

Michael Beacham stared at the burner phone on his desk as if it were radioactive. He'd been in a meeting when a BBC breaking news alert on his phone first made him aware of the raids that had taken place that morning. It was the attack on the prison van which had caught him by surprise – the robberies, he'd been expecting. Benjamin Ngomo was someone Ray Spinney had first brought to his attention several months before. Someone Spinney had wanted Michael to push in front of Claire as a case of interest. He'd assumed it was just an associate of Spinney's he'd wanted to help out. But now a man had died and suddenly the stakes were a hell of a lot higher. It made no sense, followed no logic, but it felt like he'd played a part in that man's death too.

The Handyman's first contact with Michael had come out of the clear blue sky earlier that year. Once he'd got over the shock of it, to his own surprise he hadn't run straight to the police. The deal that had been put to him had been thought through – it was carefully designed to catch his attention. He'd always thought of himself as a genuinely principled, ethically governed man. But now in his middle age, Michael Beacham had discovered that even he had a price.

Over the previous twelve months, he'd picked up on his wife's growing disenchantment with politics. They hadn't had a conversation directly about it, but there'd been throwaway comments, a weariness about her that he'd watched slowly develop. More disturbingly, the same seemed to be true of their marriage as well. He'd felt for some time that there was a growing lack of any kind of emotional centre to their relationship. Something was missing and instinctively he believed he knew what it was. Something that had *always* been missing: children.

Claire had always made it clear she didn't want them, had never wanted them. She'd never really given him a good reason why. It had just been there from the start and he'd understood and accepted it. It had never been something he'd felt strongly about himself – until now. The more he thought about it, the more he felt it had become the elephant in the room of their marriage – that it was at the heart of everything. They'd idly talked once about relocating to California, restarting their lives with a complete change of direction. New jobs, new careers, new outlooks.

That conversation was the only time he'd ever got a sense from her that there might be some regret.

'*Maybe we could think about kids if we went over there ...*' she'd said. And he'd remembered those words and the way she'd said them. He'd thought about the idea of moving more and more and had privately begun to investigate it. And then Ray Spinney had come along at just the right time with just the right offer.

He'd called him at the office, bold as brass on his direct line, explaining who he was and inviting Michael to Google his name. Calmly and without emotion, he told him that he was planning another major robbery. Afterwards, he'd need to launder the proceeds, together with the remnants of the Stansted heist and the funds from multiple other criminal operations. There were only so many ways major sums of money like that could be laundered in the UK – and real estate was one of the most effective methods. Michael guessed he must have read about Doll Street and identified it as the perfect vehicle.

Though he didn't know it, the terms he was being offered were roughly the same as had been presented to Dave McElligott and countless others: work with me and you'll be rewarded handsomely, speak of this and it'll be the worst mistake of your life. The sum being suggested was certainly eye-watering, but Michael, no stranger to a negotiation, initially turned it down. Spinney came back higher, and again Michael refused him.

This went on for a while, until finally, the offer became one he simply couldn't say no to. Though the Beachams had hardly been struggling for money, what was on the table was life-changing. It was a once in a lifetime opportunity and the cost in return seemed relatively low. The Doll Street regeneration project, while undoubtedly worthy, was the sacrificial lamb.

It wasn't completely straightforward to achieve – he was simply a property lawyer. But he had access to all the major players, and in the end, he'd been able to cajole, manipulate and steer them all to the desired outcome. Once the deal went through, he'd intended to sit on his payout for a few months then tell Claire a white lie about where it had come from. He'd take her out for dinner and show her the properties he'd short-listed in the San Fernando Valley. The dream could become a reality; they could start a family away from the prying eyes of politics and everything that came with that life. A fresh start with enough money to do whatever they wanted.

But then Lukasz Mazurek had been murdered and his world had been tipped upside down. Michael had done his homework on the Handyman by that point and knew full well what he was capable of. Spinney had sworn blind it was nothing to do with him and indeed seemed concerned himself by the development. Today's move on Benjamin Ngomo had come as a surprise though and would heap yet more unwanted scrutiny on to Claire. He recalled too how important it had been to Spinney to persuade her to take up his case.

Now Michael was starting to wonder what the endgame of all of this was and whether he'd been told the whole story. He stared again at the burner phone on his desk as if it were a hotline to hell itself.

22

The following morning, Finn found himself in a small greasy spoon in Brixton. For a man who was quite discerning about where he ate, it wasn't his natural venue of choice. The place was cramped, packed out and smelt of grease.

'Say what you like about you lot – and I have – but this about the only time the words "full English" really work for me,' said the Glaswegian sitting opposite, before taking a sip of the Red Bull accompanying his meal. 'So what is it I can do for you?'

'I need your help,' said Finn. The man opposite looked concerned for a moment and Finn raised a hand. 'Not for me – it's to do with an investigation I'm working . . .'

Murray Saunders was someone Finn had become close to in the nearly two years since they'd first met. In his early forties with a lived-in face, he looked slightly older than he was – his brown hair seriously greying now at the sides. He ran an Alcoholics Anonymous group close to Cedar House which Finn had stumbled into by chance one afternoon. At the height of his bereavement, he'd fled the incident room in the midst of an investigation and he still wasn't quite sure what had drawn him to Murray's meeting that day – alcohol wasn't one of his problems. Perhaps it was curiosity or just an instinctive gravitation to someone used to listening.

The pair had remained in contact and struck up an unlikely friendship. In many ways they were chalk and cheese – Murray was a working-class man from the East End of Glasgow who frequently found Finn's rather refined tastes a source of great amusement. Finn, for his part, didn't mind being the butt of the joke. There weren't many people in his life he bantered with and he found their slightly odd friendship strangely relaxing.

There was also the small matter that the Scotsman had saved Finn's life the previous year. The day when everything had coalesced and he'd seriously considered ending things – it had been Murray who'd stopped him and begun the process of leading him back into the light. He was fairly sure too that his friend's caustic sense of humour masked a personal sadness of his own. Finn still didn't know what it was, but assumed it must be alcohol-related. He'd probed gently a few times and got the clear message to back off. They were two middle-aged single men who'd bonded through a shared knowledge of pain. He owed the man a lot, even if the price was a fairly incessant stream of piss-taking.

The Scotsman took a bite from a piece of fried bread he was holding then wiped his mouth with the back of his hand.

'Aye – I saw you plastered all over the front page of the *Standard*. Couldn't just creep in the back door, could you?'

Finn braced himself. This was never going to be straightforward – it never was with Murray – but he suspected it might be worth the investment of a little time.

'So what I wanted to ask you—'

'We'll get to that,' Murray interrupted. 'Right now I'm more interested in what's going on in your head. How are you? And no bullshitting me.'

Finn sighed.

lose yourself for a while. And when things turn violent – well, there's often a lot of self-loathing fuelling that too.'

And just for a second Finn saw something in *his* face – the same as had been on Gilfoyle's.

'Yes, but why? Where does that come from – where *did* that come from in her case?' he asked.

Murray didn't miss a beat.

'Something traumatic, I'm guessing, something that sent her on a sudden downward spiral. I don't know if it's got anything to do with your murders, and I can only speak from a distance – so don't take this as gospel – but I suspect something must have happened to trigger it. She may have dealt quite well with it at the time, moved on from drinking and lashing out. But that doesn't necessarily mean it's gone away – that it's not still sitting in there, somewhere inside here.'

He pointed at his head, then speared another sausage.

Benjamin had spent the night in the building site. His range of choices had been so limited that he'd almost been paralysed by them. With nowhere to go, no plan that made sense, he'd stayed where he was. Not surprisingly, he didn't sleep particularly well, and woke early as cold rain drizzled down through the gaps in the structure above. His stomach was cramping with hunger pangs – he hadn't eaten since breakfast at Cromarsh Prison the previous day. Unable to resist, he'd gone out foraging on the deserted streets. Walking past some rain-soaked bins, he'd seen the remainder of half a loaf of bread still in its plastic wrapping. Now back at the building site, he'd found a handful of slices that weren't covered in green mould and was greedily wolfing them down. He'd also passed a bundle of newspapers lying on a newsagent's front doorstep. Curious to see if he'd made the headlines, he couldn't believe the splash on the front page of the *Sun*.

'*London under attack! Man dies as raiders strike to seize millions*'.

Now he was reading the story properly with his soggy breakfast. Within a few seconds, the full scale of what had happened the previous day became clear, as did the identity of the dead man. It wasn't a surprise that Terry Merchant hadn't made it, but until he read the confirmation in black and white, Benjamin had clung to the hope that somehow he'd managed to survive the point-blank blast. When he turned to page two of the newspaper, he saw his own face staring back up at him and that's when his heart began to pound.

He felt like the most wanted man in Great Britain. Looking around the deserted site, he realised he couldn't stay here much longer. There was no telling when the workmen might return. He thought about Emma and felt a wave of emotion – she must be worried stiff about him, be waiting for him to make contact. He looked down again at his picture. Weirdly, it didn't really look like him – a terse mug shot, which, a bit like a passport photo, didn't actually reflect his appearance. He knew he wouldn't get away with it for long, but in his suit, he might just pass for another commuter on their way to work on a grey morning. He rose to his feet with the vague beginnings of an idea.

Claire Beacham's morning had begun in Westminster where she'd been speaking at a meeting of the All-Party Parliamentary Group on Domestic Violence. It felt good to have something to get her teeth into and she'd spent the previous night working hard in preparation for it. Things with Michael remained tense though. They weren't a couple who had big screaming rows as such, but you knew things were bad when the atmosphere became overly quiet and courteous between them.

They'd discussed Doll Street further and she was still convinced he was lying to her face. It wasn't just a small deception either – it felt to her something of a quite different magnitude. Sooner or later there'd be a reckoning, but with Benjamin still missing and her work pile mounting up, it would have to wait. They were both managing to compartmentalise the murders – but at least on that front they had some common ground. Neither was in a rush to talk about them any more than they already had done – there was only so much speculation that was helpful. Until the police made an actual arrest, all they could do was try and carry on as calmly as possible.

When she returned to the parliamentary office at Portcullis House, she was surprised to find Lassiter already there waiting for her.

'Where's Rebecca?' she said. 'I was expecting her here earlier to help prep me for the meeting. Everything went fine but she should have let me know if she couldn't make it – it's not on, really.'

But even as she spoke she could see from Lassiter's face that something wasn't right.

'Rebecca has quit with immediate effect. She emailed to tell me while you were in the meeting and it seems she already has a new job. There's something you should see.' He picked up a print-out and handed it to her. 'This went up on the Right Way Forward website at nine o'clock this morning.'

Right Way Forward was a right-wing political blog with a decent track record in exposés that had claimed one or two high-profile scalps in the past. Claire read the headline:

'Boozy Westminster drink culture lets us all down'.

The byline credited the writer of the article as Rebecca Devlin. Claire skimmed through the piece – it was an account of a 'recent political researcher' and her experiences, amongst others, of finding the MP who employed her drunk in their office, together with details of the frequently sexist treatment she'd received from another member of her staff. It was cleverly written with no names mentioned. There was no suggestion the article's author and the anonymous subject of the piece were the same people either. But anyone who knew who Rebecca Devlin was wouldn't take long to put two and two together. Claire sat down, shocked, on the corner of her desk.

'I can't believe it. Why would she do this to us? I trusted her, considered her a friend . . .'

She remembered with horror the confession she'd made to Rebecca in the same office only days before. That, at least, hadn't made it into print.

'Because she used us,' said Lassiter. 'It's as simple as that.' He shrugged. 'That's the business we're in.'

Claire looked crestfallen.

'I honestly don't know how much more I can take. It just feels like one thing after another at the moment.'

Lassiter looked up at her awkwardly.

'Is it true?' he said. 'Were you drunk?'

She met his gaze and slowly nodded.

Finn was watching his team work. It felt to him like there was a slightly strange atmosphere in the incident room. There was something niggly in the air and he couldn't put his finger on why. Jackie Ojo's row with Dave McElligott earlier that week summed it up. He glanced across at McElligott and the DC immediately looked away – it's what criminals usually did under interview, thought Finn, when you'd caught them in a lie. And it wasn't the first time that had happened since Finn's return from his sabbatical.

'I think I've got something,' said Paulsen, interrupting his train of thought. She looked uncomfortable and there was a familiar look of minor irritation on her face.

'Are you sure?' said Finn. 'You don't look entirely convinced.'

'That's because it's *extremely* tenuous.'

'I'm open to tenuous right now,' he said.

She held up some paperwork.

'I've been going back through Lukasz and Ruth's case files. We've already been through them once in detail and found no obvious links – so I was looking at them with a slightly wider view. Thinking a bit more outside of the box. I suppose I was looking for a tenuous connection and I found one.'

She perched on a desk next to him and he motioned at her to continue.

'Do you remember Baby T?' she said.

'Of course,' replied Finn, a frown of his own now developing.

Baby T was a notorious case of child abuse. A two-year-old who'd died at the hands of abusive parents despite receiving numerous visits from social workers, police and health professionals over the previous year.

'But that was one of the most high-profile cases of neglect in recent memory,' he said. 'There was a full inquiry and everyone connected with it either lost their jobs or were moved on. If either Lukasz or Ruth had been involved, it would have flagged up immediately.'

Paulsen nodded.

'I said it was tenuous. Ruth was the mother's GP – very briefly before she left to take a job at the practice in Tooting.

There wasn't much overlap and it was a long time before the death of the child. I requested the records and I think they only met on one occasion.' She glanced down at the paperwork. Finn knew, in the circumstances, the practice would have waived the usual riders about patient confidentiality. 'She went to see her about a chest infection, so it was nothing significant,' Paulsen continued.

'But there's a connection to Lukasz as well?'

'Yes, he was one of the very first social workers to go and visit the parents. Again, he only went there the once – well before things got serious, and the case got passed on to others afterwards.'

Finn recalled their conversation with Lukasz's boss the day after his murder.

'Baby T wasn't one of the cases Nina Thornbury highlighted when we spoke to her,' he said slowly.

'She wouldn't.' Paulsen gestured at the document. 'It was before her time and the briefest of preliminary visits. He recommended that the family needed increased support – in hindsight it makes for interesting reading.'

Finn thought about it for a moment.

'Baby T's parents are both in prison now. Everyone responsible for that child's death was identified and punished – the head of children's services at the council was sacked by the Children's Secretary at the time.'

'I think it's worth pursuing,' said Paulsen.

He pondered it. There was an insistence in her voice and a challenge in her eye. He'd been like that once – hungry and ambitious, wanting to prove a point to the world. She really might be about to leave Cedar House, he realised with a slight melancholy.

'It's a connection, however slim,' he agreed. 'More than that, Claire Beacham would have been the local councillor in

Lambeth at the time.' They both took a moment to let that sink in.

'Another coincidence? They're mounting up ...' said Paulsen.

Finn nodded.

'I agree. Why don't you look into it – see if you can find something a bit more concrete ...'

23

Paulsen had visited HMP Brazely several times since she'd joined the major investigations team – she'd first encountered Kenny Fuller there on her first full day at Cedar House nearly three years ago. But as she sat waiting in one of the jail's visiting rooms, she couldn't ever remember feeling so curious about an inmate she'd come to see. Freya Appleton had, for a time, been one of the most notorious women in the country. She'd allowed her abusive partner, Brandon Challis, to torture her two-year-old son Thomas to death over an agonising series of months.

At her trial, the defence had tried to make the case that she'd been too afraid of Challis to interfere. But the prosecution had proven beyond any reasonable doubt that she simply hadn't cared enough to intervene. They described a woman more interested in her own priorities – partying, binge-drinking and smoking weed – than the welfare of her child. The post-mortem found his broken body had sustained over sixty injuries in total. Throughout, Challis swore blind that he alone hadn't caused them.

Paulsen had forced herself to read through some of the grim details of the case before she'd set off. She remembered the photo of Freya that had appeared in all the papers back in 2017. A not unattractive blonde with oversized glasses, staring at the camera with an almost Mona Lisa-like smile. It had become an iconic image – the smug expression successfully managing to enrage an already appalled public. So she found herself surprised by the person who shuffled into the room, accompanied by a prison officer. Freya had clearly put on weight during the intervening years. Her hair was now lank and brown and her face had filled out too. Though she still wore glasses, these were more functional. She looked a very different person to the one the world remembered.

Paulsen greeted her pleasantly and explained that they needed her help regarding a current investigation. She'd thought hard about how to broach this – in truth, there was very little reason for the woman to assist her with anything.

'At some point in the future, you'll be eligible for parole,' she said. 'Anything you can do to help us now I'm sure will help with that process when the time comes.'

She was well aware of how woolly that sounded – so was Freya by the look of sour contempt that was spreading across her face.

'I'm sure it will, dear,' she said.

It took a lot to throw Paulsen, but there was something detached and mocking about the woman's tone that got straight under her skin.

'This may sound quite obscure – but do you remember a doctor's appointment you had at the Bridge Park Practice in Lambeth in November 2015?'

Freya looked genuinely surprised by the question.

'You've come all the way here to ask me that?'

'Specifically, do you remember a Dr Ruth Vance?'

Freya thought about it for a moment.

'I remember the name, dear. But I'm not sure I could put a face to her. It was a long time ago and I've seen a lot of professionals over the last few years – as I'm sure you can imagine.'

Just for a second, there was a hint of that smile from the photograph, a glint of something else in her eye. Paulsen was already finding her unnerving – the use of the word 'dear' as condescending as it was intended to be.

'She was the GP you saw regarding a chest infection.'

Freya thought about it a little more – or at least gave the impression she was.

'I don't know what you want me to say – I remember having a dickie chest and I was prescribed some antibiotics – that's it. Can't say I remember too much about it.'

'Did you ever come across Dr Vance outside of the practice?'

With a slightly exaggerated look of mystification, Freya shook her head.

'What about a social worker called Lukasz Mazurek?'

'Who?'

Paulsen controlled herself.

'You met him in March 2016. He was one of the first social workers who visited you and your partner' – she deliberately paused – 'with regard to Thomas.'

If she thought mentioning the boy would produce a reaction, it didn't.

'I'm sorry, dear – but we're not having much luck, are we? Like I say, I've met so many of them over the years. Maybe I met this one, maybe I didn't.'

'He came and saw you on Thursday, March 17th 2016.'

'As I say, it's a good few years ago and I don't really have a head for dates.' She smirked.

Had she put an emphasis on the word 'head'? Again, Paulsen had that slight sense of being toyed with.

She made a quick calculation – either Freya was telling the truth and genuinely couldn't remember either of these two encounters, or she could and had no intention of helping her. Paulsen sped through her remaining questions as efficiently as possible, not wanting to extend this. Afterwards, driving back to Cedar House, it felt like she'd been in the company of something utterly soulless. It was only too easy to imagine that woman watching television with the same detached amusement while her child was screaming in agony in the next room. The thought turned her stomach.

'Do you believe she's telling the truth?' asked Finn later. He was speaking to Paulsen on the phone as he headed to Lambeth Council's social services department to meet Nina Thornbury.

'I think so,' she replied.

Walking close to the site where Lukasz Mazurek had been beheaded, he could see the forensic operation there had now finished. People were passing the alleyway without giving it a second look, but he couldn't stop his own eyes from being dragged there.

'You don't sound one hundred per cent?' he said.

'I'm not – she's the sort who could have been lying just for shits and giggles.'

'What about Claire Beacham?'

'Says she never met her – didn't even know who she was.'

'That might well be true,' said Finn. 'There's no reason why they would have ever met.'

He stopped outside the main entrance to the council building. 'See if you can find anything at all that connects Beacham directly to the Baby T case,' he said. 'Before I talk to her about it, I want to make sure we've checked every angle.'

'So you think it's a decent lead then?' said Paulsen.

He smiled but didn't allow it to show in his voice.

'I think it's worth being thorough . . .' he said.

A few minutes later he was sitting in the coffee shop opposite the council building. Nina had suggested they talk there rather than in her office and he could understand why. If he thought the mood in the incident room was a little strained at the moment, it was surely nothing on that place. Finding out one of your colleagues had been beheaded just yards from the office probably would have that effect on morale. Not that the cafe felt any less creepy. They knew from witness statements that the killer had waited inside before confronting Lukasz and it was hard not to imagine him sitting there quietly stalking his prey.

'Have you made any progress?' asked Nina, stirring a cup of strong-looking tea.

'I'll be honest – not as much as I would have liked,' said Finn.

Nina smiled unexpectedly.

'Yes – I know that feeling. It can make you feel rather small sometimes, can't it?'

He smiled back – there probably were more similarities in their two roles than he'd considered before. They were both in charge of understaffed, underfunded teams, and their jobs often involved getting to the heart of situations that the world didn't really want to help them unlock.

'How are you bearing up?' he said.

Her smile faded and something wearier replaced it.

'It's going to take me a fair while to get over this. When you've worked with someone that long, it's hard. Lukasz didn't deserve this.' She shook her head, almost in irritation at herself. 'I'm sort of sick of saying that too – it's all any of us have been saying since it happened. It won't bring him back.' She took a sip of her tea and her face became more business-like. 'So you mentioned something about Baby T on the phone earlier?' she said.

He explained the very threadbare link they'd found and she immediately looked sceptical.

'That case was before my time.' She shrugged. 'I mean, it's partly why I'm in the job – there were a lot of vacancies after the inquiry – but Lukasz had nothing to do with that one.'

'As I say – one of the files we found showed he visited the family early on,' said Finn.

She nodded.

'I had a look through everything we've got before you came – there's a lot, obviously. You're right, Lukasz did go there, just the once. He flagged it up too – and reading through his notes, he clearly had some concerns. But it looks like no one listened to him. And that's the story of the whole Baby T case, really – it was passed on to others who weren't quite so conscientious.' She shook her head. 'Lukasz didn't do anything wrong there – in fact, I'd say he did everything right.'

Finn listened and nodded, but there was something about that sentence that troubled him and he couldn't quite put his finger on why.

A minute's silence was held that morning for Terry Merchant at New Scotland Yard and by his colleagues at HMP Cromarsh in south London. At his desk in the incident room, Dave McElligott was looking on the internet at a picture of the Home Secretary, the Mayor of London and the Met Police commissioner standing with their heads bowed at police headquarters. It had emerged Merchant had only been a couple of months away from taking early retirement.

When McElligott left home that morning, a builder was already working hard to fix the hole in his roof. It was hard not to feel like Merchant had died simply for that. He hadn't, of course, but he couldn't shake the sense of direct personal responsibility. Zoe hadn't forgiven him for her encounter with Kenny Fuller yet, either, and he was convinced the worst was yet to come. Finn's briefing with the team later only confirmed his fears.

'I thought it wouldn't hurt to round up where we're at,' said Finn, addressing the room. A picture of Ray Spinney pinned to one of the boards behind him seemed to be staring directly through McElligott.

'As far as the link to Spinney goes, we know the driver of the prison transport was threatened in the same way as the drivers of the Securicor vehicles. The timing and method of attack means it's safe to assume it was part of the same operation. For whatever reason, Spinney wants Benjamin Ngomo. The NCA were caught blindsided on the day because they'd been tipped off that a security warehouse in west London was the target.'

'Do the NCA know how that happened yet?' asked Ojo. 'They wouldn't have deployed unless they were really sure about the source?'

McElligott looked down at the floor, trying hard to keep any kind of reaction off his face. This time last week, all he'd been thinking about was becoming a father.

'A CHIS has admitted he was intimidated into giving them the false information,' said Finn.

Ojo looked horrified.

'How did they manage to identify a CHIS?' she said.

'Current thinking is that it must have been a leak from within the police service,' said Finn. He let that sink in for a moment. 'You'll have seen the commissioner's comments to the press today – he's promised Terry Merchant's family that everyone responsible for his death will be brought to justice. That's more than lip service – they've got digital and technology specialists working in conjunction with anti-corruption investigators from the Directorate of Professional Standards to try and trace the culprits.'

McElligott felt a flush of heat, rising nausea with it. He focused everything on controlling himself.

'Claire Beacham doesn't know why Spinney would want Benjamin and says no one has ever warned her off trying to help him. I've asked the NCA to keep us in the loop if they find anything that assists our investigation,' continued Finn. He stopped and glanced down at his notes for a moment.

'A new line of inquiry we've been pursuing this morning is a potential link to the Baby T case from 2017. It's slim, but we've found that both Lukasz Mazurek and Ruth Vance met separately with Freya Appleton and Brandon Challis between November 2015 and March 2016.'

Ojo was frowning.

'I've been thinking about this, guv – and I've got to say I'm struggling with it,' she said without being asked. Finn motioned at her to continue. 'You might have found a connection. But what the hell's the motive? Appleton and Challis are both in prison. Just because there's a nominal link to something doesn't mean a thing on its own,' she said. 'There has to be a reason and I can't see how there can be one. Aren't we just wasting time ploughing through yet more historical paperwork?'

Finn was already nodding.

'Possibly – I've spoken to Claire this afternoon, and although she was a local councillor in the area at the time, she didn't have any direct involvement with the Baby T case. But . . . a link is a link, nonetheless. It's something that connects Lukasz, Ruth and Claire. In fact, it's the *only* thing we've found where you can draw even a tenuous line between those three. If there's more information to be found, then let's find it – because then we might get a step closer to a motive.' He turned to Dattani. 'Sami – do you and Mattie want to go through the list of council officials who lost their jobs after the inquiry? Maybe one of them can tell us something.'

'What have you got in mind?' said Paulsen.

'Were there any other contacts with the family involving

Lukasz and Dr Vance that didn't make it into the official paperwork? For example, off-the-record stuff, or maybe because it was just too small to mention?'

Paulsen nodded but Dattani looked troubled.

'So are the DPS going to be looking at us then? Because of the link to Benjamin Ngomo?'

'Why? Have you got something to hide, Sami?' said Paulsen.

The rest of the room tittered but McElligott just felt the sweat now starting to stick to his back.

'No, of course not – and if they want to talk to me, then no problem. But it would be nice to know where we stand before they come knocking,' said Dattani.

Finn nodded.

'They know about Claire's campaign to stop Benjamin from being deported. She's an obvious line of inquiry given how much is circling her at the moment. My understanding is Cedar House *is* on their radar. There's nothing to worry about – because we've got nothing to hide.'

Dattani nodded, unimpressed, and headed back to his desk.

Ojo came over and joined Finn.

'Did you mean that? You're certain we're clean?'

He shrugged.

'I hope so,' he said, but it wasn't lost on him that given the sheer number of people who worked at Cedar House – including the civilian support staff – it was impossible to rule anything out. He gave her a sideways look. 'I'd still like to get very drunk in a wine bar sometime soon, by the way.'

She grinned unexpectedly.

'Hell, yeah – I reckon we've earnt that. Saturday night?'

'You're on – it's a date,' he said a little bit too loudly, before adding awkwardly: 'You know what I mean . . .'

She rolled her eyes at him and walked away.

★ ★ ★

Dattani was still looking bothered as he settled back down at his desk.

'What's the matter?' said McElligott.

Dattani shook his head.

'I don't like the idea of being investigated. Nine years I've put into this job – I deserve better than that. All because some piece of shit somewhere sold themselves out to buy a new car or something.' He looked up at one of the wall-mounted TVs; it felt like the news channels seemed to be showing the scenes from New Scotland Yard earlier on a loop. 'If I ever get my hands on one of them . . .'

McElligott looked at his face – it didn't seem like an idle threat.

'Yeah . . .' he said. 'It makes you feel sick.'

24

By early afternoon, Benjamin was in central London attempting to blend in with the crowd. As the city went about its business, he'd tried to move casually and not attract attention. A member of the gang he used to work for had once told him how many CCTV cameras were in operation on the capital's streets. He couldn't remember the precise number but did remember the warning – *'In the centre, there's probably one on you everywhere you go.'* With that in mind, he was amazed he hadn't been picked up yet. He'd gambled that for a limited time he could get away with it and, so far, his luck had held.

He knew Emma worked at a Starbucks close to the National Gallery. He had no idea whether it was north, south, east or west of Trafalgar Square – or even what his girlfriend's definition of 'close' actually was – so methodically, starting south on the Strand, he'd gone into every branch of the coffee shop that he could find. All he needed was a few seconds to scan the room and he was gone before anyone could look too closely at him. If they did, they might have noticed how filthy his suit was and just how much fear was etched across his face.

He finally found the right one in a small side street off St Martin's Lane. At first, he hadn't recognised her – but that was no coincidence. She was wearing the coffee chain's trademark green uniform, together with a peaked hat and far more make-up than normal. When he walked up to the counter, he wasn't sure she'd recognised him either until she spoke.

'Toasted bacon roll and a venti cappuccino?' she said first, as if confirming an order, her face betraying absolutely no emotion whatsoever. He barely managed to nod and she smiled politely. 'There's plenty of seats downstairs – I'll bring it down to you if you like?' She looked him hard in the eye. The penny dropped and he headed immediately for the staircase. It was a small shop out of the way of the main bustle, and downstairs it was empty. He collapsed in a heap, able to relax for the first time since he'd left the building site. A few minutes later Emma joined him and they hugged each other hard and then kissed.

'You've got bad breath,' she said gently.

'I know,' he said and she kissed him again.

He sat down and began to devour the food and drink gratefully.

'You look terrible,' she said, sitting down opposite him.

'I don't really care how I look,' he said. The radiator by the table was hot and it felt like heaven.

'Are you okay?' she asked. There was a brief pause as the absurdity of the question dawned on them both.

'Yeah, never better,' he replied.

They both found small smiles from somewhere. Hers faded first.

'You can't stay here, Ben.'

'I didn't know where else to go. I can't believe you're working today – what if someone saw you?'

She looked at him incredulously.

'I work here every day. I've got to earn – I can't hide just because of this situation.'

'What if you were recognised?'

Her face hardened and something passed between them.

'It's been like that for months and I haven't been. You almost didn't know who I was upstairs. Besides, it's not me who's got the problem right now, is it? You've got to hand yourself in.'

He shook his head straight away.

'No – they'll stick me on a plane for sure now.'

She reached out and took his hand, then leant in and kissed him again.

The food, the warmth and the kisses were starting to make him feel like a human being again for the first time in months. She pulled back and looked him in the eye.

'If you don't give yourself up, then sooner or later they'll catch up with you and deport you anyway.'

He took a sip of his coffee, looked down at his filthy trousers.

'We could run away – get out of the country.' He checked himself as he realised what he'd said. '*Together*, I mean. Go to France or somewhere.'

She shook her head sadly.

'How are we going to do that? You haven't got a passport and the whole world is looking for you. If you turn yourself in, it'll count in your favour. It's your only move.'

He looked crestfallen.

'I could stay with you – no one would know.'

'How long for?' she replied.

He shrugged helplessly. She reached into her pocket and pulled out her phone and opened the BBC News app.

'Look . . .' she said, handing him the device. A video clip of Claire Beacham looking directly at the camera began to play.

'Benjamin – I know you must be scared and confused but nothing's changed. There are people who want to help you, but to do that you must surrender yourself.'

He paused it and passed the phone back.

'That woman's going to protect me from Ray Spinney? Seriously?'

223

She squeezed his hand gently.

'Ben, *someone's* going to get you – that's a given. What you've got to decide is which is the least worst option?'

'The money's been broken up and the three holding sites are now empty,' said Kenny Fuller. He and Spinney were walking through Clowes Wood, a forest favoured by walkers between Whitstable and Canterbury. Fuller was holding an umbrella to protect them both from the drizzle. Spinney's eyes were fixed firmly on the muddy path ahead. In theory, the laundering operation was a fairly straightforward one.

He liked to operate what was commonly known as a smurfing network. It was a technique that involved breaking up the stolen cash into multiple smaller amounts. These were then paid into several hundred individual personal bank accounts – the sums being just small enough not to attract any attention. Later the people who owned them – all Spinney loyalists for one reason or another – would invest the cash into a newly created shell company. And it was that business that had just agreed on the deal to acquire the Doll Street buildings.

For most people, it was something that would take years of meticulous planning to get right, but Spinney had put this together in a matter of months. As far as Fuller was concerned, it was a work of art and the man next to him was a genuine artist. But as they walked, Fuller knew too that the money almost didn't matter, that Spinney considered the operation a failure because of Benjamin Ngomo's escape. You could feel his repressed fury coming from every pore.

'You've seen the news?' said Spinney. 'Beacham's made an appeal to him.'

He spat the words out as if they had individually crossed him.

'Do you think it will work?' said Fuller.

Spinney considered it as the rain tip-tapped on to the umbrella.

'It depends on how he views his situation. The death of that prison officer hasn't helped us. He'll be petrified, won't be thinking straight.'

'I've put the word out there. If he reaches out to anyone – we'll know.'

Spinney looked at him sourly.

'We know where he's gone – to the only person he can go to.'

A young woman with a couple of Labradors in tow was walking towards them and Fuller waited until she'd passed.

'If we'd been able to keep eyes on Cromarsh . . . get someone else in there, even,' muttered Fuller.

Spinney glowered at the woodland ahead as if he could set it ablaze with his eyes alone. An early attempt to use an inmate at the jail to extract the information he wanted had failed. Benjamin was young and capable and had fended off the attack with ease.

'It takes time to cultivate insiders and I've been out of the country for too long. We are where we are.' He shook his head as he thought it through. 'Once the authorities find the boy, they'll rearrange his sentencing as fast as possible and the Home Office won't waste a second putting him on a plane. They'll just want rid. If we're going to put this right, then we need to do it quickly.'

He was interrupted by a phone buzzing in his pocket. He pulled it out, saw the name 'Dave McElligott' on the display, and dismissively slipped it straight back into his pocket.

'There are still some big positives – the robberies came off,' said Fuller. 'You did it again – and even if the lad's deported, there may be another way to . . .'

Spinney silenced him with a look.

'You're underestimating the person we're up against. Benjamin Ngomo is the key and he's slipping out of reach.'

Fuller considered his next question carefully, but he was genuinely curious about the answer. For as long as he'd worked for Spinney, he'd never known the man to fail. One way or another, he always found a way to get what he wanted. He was a person who prided himself on being one step ahead – whether it be of the police, the government or other criminals. But for the first time that Fuller could recall, he seemed genuinely defeated.

'What will you do if the boy does get away from us?' he asked.

There was a long silence, long enough to make Fuller question whether he should have even gone there. When Spinney did finally speak, it was with a snarl of fury – as if he couldn't keep it contained for a moment longer.

'I'll tear London apart with my bare fucking hands.'

Claire Beacham and Grant Lassiter spent the remainder of their morning in school. They were at Rycrofts – an independent co-ed day school – for a long-standing diary engagement. After a brief tour of the facilities, Claire gave a talk to a group of the students about her role as an MP and then fielded some questions. Throughout, she was very much the Claire Beacham everybody knew from their TV screens. Strong, opinionated and self-deprecating. She suspected the kids had been told not to ask about the much-publicised murders but one broke ranks and did anyway. She hadn't missed a beat and answered him honestly – it was shocking and scary, but life had to go on, she explained.

It was a performance though – inside she felt more brittle than ever. Distant from her husband, betrayed by Rebecca, and with the ever-present shadow of a killer still stalking her, it was hardly surprising she was struggling. Rebecca's online article had provoked a call from the Chief Whip. It had been sympathetic in tone but came with a coded warning. A one-off mistake could be forgiven; further incidents of a similar nature might not be so easy to overlook.

Journalists had been circling too, but without any hard evidence to stand up the story, it was a difficult one for them to run. The damage had been contained, but she knew it had added to the general smell around her at the moment. As that policeman, Finn, had observed, *'You seem to be at the centre of a lot, right now.'*

Even the usually loyal Lassiter was subdued during the school visit, and while driving back to the constituency office, she decided to lance the boil.

'Come on, Grant – what's bothering you? The psycho who's stalking me, Rebecca screwing us over – or the fact she caught me drinking?'

He licked his lips – a trait of his when he was nervous, she'd observed.

'If you were struggling, you should have told me. I might have been able to help. It's what I'm here for,' he said. She looked across at him as if he were slightly mad.

'Of course I'm bloody struggling. In the circumstances, I'd have thought that's pretty sodding obvious,' she said.

'Then why didn't you call me – why get drunk in the middle of the day like that? In some ways, you were lucky it was Rebecca who found you.'

For an instant, Claire recalled the conversation she'd had with her that afternoon, remembered what she'd told her, and shuddered. Lassiter caught the look on her face.

'Have you told me everything, Claire – or is there something I should know?'

She briefly contemplated lying. But she trusted Lassiter implicitly and felt she owed him at least something resembling an honest answer.

'No. Some things are just too personal. It doesn't have a bearing on the work or the current situation. Everything you need to know, you know. I suppose with everything else that's going on, I was feeling vulnerable, and when you're like that, all sorts of things start floating to the surface.'

He nodded, quietly digesting this. She guessed he was weighing up whether to push her further.

'You've got a surgery at the constituency office at four o'clock.' He hesitated. 'I still think in the current circumstances we should be doing these on Zoom . . .'

She was already shaking her head.

'Not a chance. Now more than ever. I won't allow any of this to stop me from helping the people who I'm there to help. The people who elected me—'

'*I know* – you don't need to give me the lecture,' said Lassiter, interrupting.

She nodded.

'We'll have police protection on site – it'll be fine,' she said.

'There's nothing in the diary until then,' he said. 'Why don't you give yourself a few hours off – it sounds like you could use them.'

Her phone rang before she could answer. She took the call and smiled almost immediately with relief.

'Oh, thank God,' she said. 'It's Benjamin – he's handed himself in.'

25

The National Crime Agency had interviewed Benjamin as soon as he was back in custody. He was still being held at a central London police station when Finn and Paulsen arrived for their turn with him. He'd been charged with escaping from lawful custody, despite his protestations about what had actually happened. The law had given the NCA little choice in the circumstances but to arrest him. Once Finn and Paulsen had finished their interview, he would have to appear before a magistrates' court on that charge before being transferred straight back to Cromarsh Prison – this time accompanied by maximum security.

Finn tried to get a quick steer from one of the NCA officers on what they'd learnt but got little change. He recognised that particular tight-lipped response – whatever answers they'd been hoping for, they clearly hadn't got.

'We're not interested in the cash raids – that's not our problem,' he said to Paulsen as they made their way down to the interview room. 'All we need to know is whether Spinney's connected to our double homicide. Let's try and keep this focused.'

Benjamin looked tired and belligerent as they introduced themselves. A duty solicitor was with him, looking almost as weary.

'What is it with you people? Can't you just talk to each other?' snapped Benjamin after the formalities were completed.

Finn explained why they were there and the two murders they were investigating.

'In case you hadn't noticed, I've been in a cell for most of the year. Or are you lot just trying to pin anything on me now so you can get me out of the country faster?'

'Of course not,' said Paulsen. 'We just want to establish whether those deaths are connected to Ray Spinney in any way. Given how much Claire Beacham has tried to do for you, I'd have thought you'd want to return the favour . . .'

Slowly he nodded, acknowledging the point, which Finn found interesting. He could simply have told them where to go. It was a place to start if nothing else.

'So why did Spinney come after you?' said Finn.

'Again? I've literally just been through all this.'

'I'd like to hear it for myself.'

'Yeah – cos I've got all the time in the world, haven't I?' said Benjamin. Settling himself, he began to talk, explaining how he'd first fallen in with the organised crime gang who'd employed him. Most of his work was either as a delivery boy running errands or as a driver ferrying people around. He asked no questions, avoided trouble and made enough money to survive. At the top of the tree, running things remotely from abroad, had been Spinney. A distant, ghost-like figure whose name tended to focus people's minds. Benjamin had never met him and, to all intents and purposes, hadn't given him much thought.

Finn listened patiently. All of this sounded perfectly credible and totally in sync with what he knew about how Spinney operated.

'So why did he send gunmen in to try and free a relatively junior member of his gang – why did a prison officer die for that?' asked Paulsen. 'There are bigger fish than you locked up who he's made no effort to help.'

Benjamin looked at her wearily.

'I'm coming to that. Not long before we were arrested, there was a meeting – some kind of summit. All the main players were involved – and not just from the gang I worked for, but others too. Spinney must have been running them as well.'

'And was this conference in person?' said Finn.

'No, it was all online. But I overheard a lot of it – they had it on a speaker. It meant nothing to me at the time but it was clearly important.'

'So what were they talking about?' asked Paulsen, not making much effort to hide her scepticism.

'Basically, it was Spinney laying out how he saw the future direction of things. What he wanted to do, how he wanted to do it – who he was going to do it with.'

'And, presumably, you've just given the NCA all this valuable information,' said Paulsen.

'No.' They both looked at him questioningly. 'Not until they give me some assurances about my future.'

'You want to make a deal?' said Paulsen.

Benjamin didn't answer. It certainly explained the reaction of the NCA officers they'd seen earlier, thought Finn.

'That's why he came for you – because you know his secrets and he's worried you'll give them all up?' he said.

'Of course. No one else will say anything – the man has a reputation of being able to get to people. But I've got nothing to lose in my situation, have I?'

'Did you ever hear Claire Beacham's name mentioned?' said Finn.

Benjamin shook his head.

'No – not until she contacted me in prison about my case.'

'And you're sure about that – she was never someone of interest to the gang you worked for, or to Spinney, as far as you were aware?'

'No.'

Finn smiled pleasantly.

'Then we won't keep you any longer – we can get the rest from the NCA.'

Paulsen glanced at Finn sharply then leant forwards.

'What specific piece of information do you have that Spinney wants so badly?' she said.

He sized her up for a moment.

'Nothing I'm going to share with you.'

'So there is *something* specific then?' she said.

'Mattie . . .' said Finn.

Benjamin shrugged and crossed his arms.

'What the hell was all that about?' snapped Paulsen as they left the interview room and walked out into the corridor. 'Didn't you want to push him harder? He told us absolutely nothing.'

'I know,' said Finn, stopping. 'I think he's lying and I'm willing to bet that he lied to the NCA too. Whatever the reason Spinney wants him, he'd rather be deported than tell us.'

'So this isn't about some key piece of intel he's going to use to negotiate with, then?' she said.

Finn shook his head.

'No, because if he actually had something, he'd have used it by now. But as I said before – that's the NCA's problem. Our only interest is the connection to the Beachams – and I'm satisfied there's nothing for us here.'

He'd regret that later.

The man wasn't sure who was worse – the politicians or the journalists. These people weren't even human, he thought. They weren't dictated by conscience or any kind of morality. Their actions were driven simply by the news agenda – nothing else. He'd killed two people to make a point – to send a message – and it was barely being mentioned any more. These armed robberies were all anyone seemed to want to talk about. A dead prison officer was apparently worth more column inches than a dead social worker or doctor.

And through it all, there was Beacham again – making it all about her. He'd watched her appeal for this missing prisoner several times online now. The earnest face with the furrowed brow, eyes focused sincerely at the camera, the slight deepening of her voice. It was as if the two people he'd killed simply hadn't touched her. And he could believe that too – because he knew her of old, knew who she *really* was. He had a plan but was wondering now if he shouldn't alter it, be a bit more flexible. Whether what he was doing was actually having any effect at all. What was the point of sending a message if it wasn't being received? He wanted to look her in the eye for himself. Then he'd know – and then maybe he'd simply end things there and then.

'Only one way to find out . . .' he muttered to himself.

Claire had taken Lassiter's advice and given herself a few hours off. She'd met an old friend for lunch and enjoyed a much-needed blowout. This time the only vice she'd indulged in had been calories and she'd studiously drunk mineral water throughout. There'd been very little mention of severed heads, her husband, or treacherous researchers – just a lot of laughter and catching up.

The news about Benjamin had lifted her too. She would go and visit him once he was back in prison and see where they were at. But she was relieved that he seemed to be unhurt, and the fact that he'd voluntarily handed himself in would do their cause no harm at all. Now she was refocused on the task immediately in hand, which was her scheduled weekly surgery at the constituency office in South Wimbledon.

She'd enjoyed these in the beginning after she'd first been elected. It was one part of the job that felt removed from all the bullshit of Westminster and was more about directly helping people in need. The most common issues tended to involve housing or benefits cases, but interspersed was also a sprinkling of those you couldn't help. The people who wanted to murder their neighbours, or who thought they were being bugged by the Russians. Or simply the lonely, the ones who had no one else to talk to and came to her for a chat instead.

You never quite knew what you were going to get. Since the murder of Labour MP Jo Cox in 2016, it had been standard advice for all Members of Parliament to have a panic button installed at their offices. Given her current circumstances, a uniform officer armed with a taser was also present this time. She'd almost forgotten about the ongoing threat. Almost – the memory of Lukasz Mazurek's blood-smeared head on her kitchen floor was never too far below the surface of her thoughts. The gaggle of journalists waiting to photograph her as she arrived, another reminder.

As she got underway, there seemed to be more people than usual amongst the familiar faces seeking updates on ongoing issues. There was a Mr Angry with a long-standing grievance against HM Revenue and Customs over a tax demand he deemed outrageous and unfair. A worried-sick single mother trying to get the correct medical care for her eleven-year-old. And a group of residents well behind on their rent, up to their eyes in debt, facing the possibility of mass evictions and prosecutions. She dealt with them all patiently and meticulously, receiving the usual varying degrees of gratitude and disappointment in return.

Around an hour in, she took a quick five-minute break to grab a cup of tea. As Lassiter went out to make it, there was the sound of raised voices from outside. It sounded like someone just leaving had got into an argument with one of the journalists out on the pavement. The cry of 'fucking vultures' rather gave it away. The police constable walked out to see what was going on, and as Claire waited alone, someone else slipped in.

He was a muscular man in his early thirties with a mop of jet-black hair, wearing a black T-shirt that showed off thick biceps and the hint of a complex tattoo design. His eyes were cold blue, and even before he spoke, she sensed something wasn't quite right. The way he was looking at her, for a start – usually, people were so interested in making their point they barely noticed her. But this one's gaze had been searching her out from the moment he entered.

'Hi – how can I help?' she said warmly, trying to put him at ease.

He didn't reply but his breathing became heavier. She glanced across at the panic button discreetly attached to the wall next to her desk. Outside there was still the sound of raised voices.

'You don't remember me, do you?' he said, the tone neutral.

Claire smiled.

'I'm sorry – I see a lot of people, remind me of your case again?'

He shook his head and casually reached down as if to scratch an itch. When he brought his hand back up again, he was holding a small knife. He turned it slowly so she could see just how sharp the teeth on the blade were.

'Don't make a sound,' he said.

She didn't even dare look at the panic button again, let alone try and reach for it. This was the man who'd decapitated Lukasz Mazurek, mutilated and killed Ruth Vance, and now he'd come for her – she was sure of it. His eyes were blazing with fury – not the 'normal' animosity you received as an MP; this was something else: a boiling rage and resentment.

'You don't know who I am, do you?' he said quietly as if reading her mind. 'But I remember you.'

Afterwards, when she remembered it, she couldn't be sure if she'd yelled in pure terror or actually called for help. Either way, the uniform officer was inside the room almost instantly. He saw the knife and immediately began reaching for his taser, but the man was too fast for him. He thrust the blade straight into the fleshy part at the top of the PC's leg where his stab vest ended. The officer howled in agony as blood spurted from the wound. The man turned to look at Claire and their eyes met – the hatred in his, deep and primal.

26

The police officer could have died if the paramedics had only been delayed by a few minutes. When Finn and Paulsen arrived at the constituency office, Jackie Ojo was already standing outside dressed in full forensic apparel. The attacker had fled the scene almost instantly after stabbing the PC, making no effort to harm Claire. Whether that was deliberate or because he'd been interrupted was hard to tell.

'The officer's name is PC Paul Irwin,' Ojo told them. 'He severed an artery in his leg and they reckon he lost nearly five pints of blood. LAS got him to St George's Hospital just in time.'

Finn nodded. After the death of Terry Merchant, this was another high-profile incident that had so nearly ended in another fatality. And almost predictably, the MP for South Wimbledon was once again at the heart of it.

'How's Claire?' he asked.

Ojo pulled a face.

'If she didn't have PTSD before . . .' She nodded at the constituency office, where a blue-gowned CSI was just emerging holding an evidence bag. 'I mean, it's literally a bloodbath in there. The good news is we've got a screen grab of the guy from the camera outside, as well as fingerprints and DNA samples. The bad news is Claire swears blind she doesn't know who he is, and the early checks haven't given us a name.'

Finn frowned.

'What name did he give when he made the appointment?'

Ojo glanced down at her pocketbook, which she was holding in a latex-gloved hand.

'Gary Foreman. We're obviously checking it out but it's almost certainly fake and it didn't ring any bells for Claire or her aide.'

'Where is she now?' said Paulsen.

Ojo motioned at a car parked on the other side of the road within the police cordon that had sealed the street off.

'I asked her to wait for you – there was nowhere else for them to go.'

Finn looked over and could see Claire and Lassiter sitting inside. He and Paulsen crossed the road as Ojo headed back inside the constituency office.

As they approached, the pair got out of the vehicle to greet him. Finn was relieved to see there seemed to be a healthy amount of colour in Claire's cheeks. She welcomed him with a small smile of recognition.

'I'm told that the officer – PC Irwin – is going to be alright. I just want to place on record my thanks to him. He may well have saved my life.'

She sounded stiff, robotic almost, Finn thought – just like a politician issuing a formal statement, in fact.

'Are you both okay?' he asked.

'What do you think? You're damn lucky this isn't a murder investigation,' said Lassiter, jumping in before Claire could answer, a tremble of emotion in his voice.

Finn met his gaze, not dodging the accusation.

'I know. If it's any consolation, we've certainly got more to work with now – we know what he looks like, at least. I know you've already been asked this, but are you sure neither of you recognised him?' he said.

238

'That's such a hard question,' said Claire. 'He asked whether I remembered him. And that's the thing – there *was* something familiar, but I just can't place him.'

'You meet a lot of people in the course of your work,' said Paulsen. 'Is it possible he's someone you could have met briefly and forgotten?'

Claire shrugged.

'Of course it is. And you're right, I do meet members of the public all the time; I might well have met this man before. But with respect – I'm not sure that's the issue, is it?'

'How do you mean?' said Finn.

She took a deep breath.

'You didn't see the rage in his face. I looked him in the eye and there was genuine hatred there.' She visibly shuddered as she remembered. 'Pure, undiluted venom – and the thing is, I genuinely don't know what it is I'm supposed to have done. Surely, I'd remember that, just as much as his face?' Before she could continue, her phone rang and she glanced down at the display. 'That's Michael – I ought to take this, he'll be worried sick,' she said. Finn nodded and she walked away, pressing the phone to her ear.

'She's just about holding it together,' said Lassiter discreetly once she was out of earshot. 'But after what's happened this afternoon, I think we're going to need some proper protection – whatever she might feel about that.'

'I agree,' said Finn. 'I'm extremely concerned about her safety. This was an escalation – the best thing would be for her to move out of London for the next few days, or at least until we've made an arrest.'

'Good luck persuading her to do that . . .' said Lassiter.

Finn frowned.

'If she won't, then she needs to at least cancel all her forthcoming engagements and keep an extremely low profile for the time being. I'd suggest working from home – and staying there, frankly.'

Lassiter looked helpless.

'I'll do my best – but I think you may need to reinforce this yourself,' he said.

'Don't worry, I will do,' said Finn.

Lassiter nodded, mollified.

'I need to make some calls of my own,' he said. 'All I'm trying to do is protect her if I can – it's supposed to be my job. And I don't think I'm doing it very well at the moment,' he added.

Finn nodded sympathetically as he turned and walked back to the car.

'Does she need protecting though?' said Paulsen suddenly as they watched him go. 'This guy could have killed her if he'd wanted – he was armed and had the opportunity – so why didn't he? Always assuming this is the same man . . .'

They couldn't say it for certain, but the new CCTV image suggested the same height and build as the suspect in the baseball cap and they were confident the fingerprints would soon confirm a match. Finn pondered it. A killer who'd murdered two people to send a message and then turned up in person – and for what reason? Simply to intimidate? There were links, possibly, to the death of a baby – or possibly not.

And then there was the Ray Spinney connection, though surely the Handyman wasn't behind this. Finn was growing convinced of this after their conversation with Benjamin earlier and also because this felt so *personal*. Spinney was motivated more by money, and when people crossed him, he tended to deal with them quickly and directly. This kind of elongated campaign didn't feel like his modus operandi. But the link remained there, nevertheless. The same week Claire began publicly promoting Benjamin's case, Spinney had tried to kidnap him. Was that really a coincidence? The whole thing was a mass of contradictions and he was struggling to see the wood for the trees.

Again, there was that nagging feeling of irritation that his thought process was sluggish – that six months in therapy and sitting on a meditation mat had dulled his senses. With it came a sudden rush of fear that he might not ever get back to what he'd once been. He suppressed the emotion quickly.

'Do you know what?' he said. 'I think we might need to get some help in on this one.'

By the time they returned to Cedar House, a picture of the man who'd nearly killed PC Paul Irwin had already been circulated to the media. The near-fatal attack was already topping the evening news bulletins. The Met was coming under fire from some of the correspondents, and politicians that were being interviewed for reaction. They wanted to know why the police weren't doing more to protect an MP and, predictably, John Skegman was furious. Finn suspected there'd been some pressure on him from above as well.

'It's not how it works,' said Skegman, shaking his head as Finn stood patiently in front of his desk. The DCI's narrow little eyes were darting around in impotent fury. Finn had known him long enough to know that was most people's equivalent of a major tantrum.

'I know – you don't have to tell me that,' said Finn. He meant it too – there hadn't been a direct threat to Claire Beacham's life until this afternoon and the amount of protection she'd been receiving had been appropriate. Anyone in the job would know that – frankly, so did most of the politicians criticising them. The other thing none of them knew was how resistant Claire had been to receiving any extra security.

'It's gone above my head now, anyway,' said Skegman. 'The commissioner's taken it upon himself to speak to Beacham

241

this evening. It's absurd – it's all for show.' He shook his head and Finn had a degree of sympathy. He was right – the commissioner's words of reassurance weren't much more than PR. Finn had already spoken to Claire, just as he'd promised Lassiter. They'd taken an immediate review of her security arrangements and temporarily suspended any work at the constituency office. There'd be no media coverage of her movements over the next few days and a police car would be parked permanently outside her home until the threat had ended. There'd been no pushback from her this time on the issue.

'So what's your next move?' said Skegman.

'Since you asked . . . Neil Plaskitt.'

Skegman looked up.

'Really?'

Finn nodded.

'He's in YoYo's now, going through everything we've got.'

The longest day of Dave McElligott's life had been extended by the unfolding drama in South Wimbledon. It was now early evening and the incident room smelt of stale sweat and cold coffee. He'd spent most of the afternoon unsuccessfully trying to contact Spinney. Is this what happened, he thought, when you'd outlived your usefulness? You were dropped and fed to the lions? The lions in question hadn't made their presence felt yet but his paranoia was going through the roof.

He kept telling himself he was safe – he'd taken every precaution to protect his identity. No breadcrumb trail could lead back to him, and yet the fear had been rising with every passing hour. He slid open his top drawer and discreetly removed the burner phone to check for any messages – there was still nothing. He quickly tapped out another text of his own. To his surprise, this time there came an instant response.

Call me.

It felt like a defibrillator had just issued a jolt of electricity directly to his heart. He instantly rose to his feet and was about to head for the door when Finn swept in with Skegman. McElligott checked his watch and realised he'd forgotten they'd called a briefing earlier and sat back down again. The walls seemed like they'd moved another inch or two in around him.

Criminal psychologist Neil Plaskitt was young, prodigiously talented and held an unashamedly high opinion of himself. But Finn had a healthy regard for his abilities and didn't mind the ego that often came with them. Slightly overweight with a crop of ginger hair, he was someone who had clearly taken a fair bit of stick over the years – you didn't need to be a psychologist to work that out. Finn suspected the overconfident exterior was actually a hardened protective shell he'd developed as a defence mechanism. Whatever changes were sweeping the globe, some old coppers of a particular vintage hadn't necessarily got the memo and could be fairly brutal with their banter. Finn introduced him to the room and explained why he was there.

'I just think we could use a steer about this guy – I don't think he's a random nutter. I think there's a reasoning behind what he's doing and Neil can help us understand it.'

'Usual caveats apply,' said Plaskitt with a light Geordie twang. 'I don't claim anything I ever say is one hundred per cent reliable – but these are my impressions from looking at everything you've got so far.' He looked around the room as if waiting to be challenged and then continued.

'This is someone who feels personally wronged. There could be any reason behind that. The way this MP's voted on something in parliament, for example – whether that had a consequent impact on this guy's life. The anger from him that she talked about seeing today feeds into that too.'

'Hold on,' said Ojo, interrupting. Plaskitt glared at her, irritated at being stopped in full flow. 'If it's something like a parliamentary vote – then it could be about *anything*. And we've been through all the potentially controversial votes she's been involved in. There was nothing you wouldn't expect to find – she's a left-wing, liberal MP.'

Plaskitt almost sneered in response.

'So this guy's a far-right nutter then, only he's not a member of a prescribed organisation so he's not showing up anywhere. Or he could have met her once on a march or a rally and has got the hump because she didn't give him the time of day. I can only give you a general idea.'

Ojo gave him a tight smile which he didn't return. Finn arched an eyebrow at her and she gave him a sour look back.

'What do you make of the body mutilations – the severed head, the removal of Ruth Vance's tongue?' said Finn, turning back to Plaskitt.

'It's symbolic, isn't it – you don't need me to deduce that for you.' He blew through his cheeks. 'A social worker who didn't *think* something through, a doctor who didn't *speak* up or said too much. Question is whether the victims were random choices, merely symbolic of their professions – or whether these two individuals were specifically targeted.'

'So why hasn't he simply killed Claire Beacham if he hates her so much?' said Paulsen. 'He had the perfect opportunity.'

Plaskitt turned as if a schoolkid had just asked a painfully obvious question.

'Because he holds her accountable, above *everyone* else. It's about trying to teach her a lesson – and I think that's why he didn't harm her earlier, because he hasn't finished doing that yet. I think today was about seeing for himself whether she was getting the message.'

'By implication, you think there could be more deaths then?' said Skegman who was watching from the back of the room. Plaskitt looked non-committal.

'I wouldn't bet against it – because at some point he'll want to reveal what this is about, and I think if this was over he'd have done that.'

He looked around the room but there were no further questions, just stony silence.

27

It wasn't until almost nine o'clock that Dave McElligott finally left Cedar House for the day. The burner phone was sitting in his breast pocket like a hot iron next to his heart. With difficulty, he'd resisted the temptation to phone Spinney immediately and drove a couple of miles before parking up in a side street. To his irritation, his fingers were shaking as he finally made the call. He calmed himself while he waited for it to connect. He needed to come across as strong, and more to the point – *relevant*. That was his way out of this.

'I've counted three missed calls and four separate text messages from you on this phone. I hope you're not panicking, Detective Constable,' said the voice on the other end. As usual, it sounded as dry as old parchment, and he'd seemingly made a point of pronouncing the word *cuntstable*. McElligott composed himself. Across the road, two youths were walking along, laughing noisily, and he waited for them to pass.

'Of course not. But the NCA is trying to find out who your sources are. As far as I can tell, they're determined to track down every single person inside the police service who's ever helped you. They're throwing major resources at it this time because of the death of that prison officer.'

'You think I don't know that? Haven't already prepared for it? You very much sound like a man who's panicking to me.'

'Since you asked – *were* you prepared for it?' replied McElligott. 'Because I'm betting that the last thing you wanted was an unnecessary death. And you assured me nothing I was going to do would result in anything like that, remember?'

Time seemed to stand still while he waited for an answer. Somewhere, at the end of all this, was a future with Zoe and his child. Everything in between was just the necessary connective tissue and that's how he had to view it.

'These things aren't an exact science. What happened wasn't my preference and the extra attention it's brought on you is regrettable,' said Spinney. McElligott exhaled silently.

'Why did you ask me to call you?' he said. 'Since clearly you aren't simply returning my calls and texts?'

'Because of the attack on that police officer at Beacham's office in South Wimbledon this afternoon. Tell me what you know.'

'Quid pro quo,' said McElligott. 'I'll tell you – if you tell me why Benjamin Ngomo is so important to you.'

'Don't piss me about, son,' came the instant response. There was audible irritation in his voice and McElligott knew he'd gone too far. He quickly explained what had happened in the incident room earlier – that Finn had brought in a criminal psychologist, and what Neil Plaskitt had subsequently told them.

'Has Michael Beacham's name come up in any of this?' Spinney said after another long pause. McElligott hadn't been expecting that and the question threw him.

'No – not as far as I'm aware. Why?' he said.

'If it does – you tell me immediately.'

McElligott decided not to push the point.

'Sure. What about the NCA? Do you want me to—'

But the line was already dead.

'Fuck's sake . . .' he said.

The conversation had done little to lift the weight of pressure on his shoulders. His heart felt heavy, the guilt still toxic.

Another phone in his pocket – his personal one – was vibrating now. When he looked, it was a message from Zoe.

Where are you?

He took a deep breath and started the engine.

Tony Whitcombe saw the headlines about the police officer who'd been stabbed in South Wimbledon while he was attacking a burger in McDonald's. A private insurance fraud investigator, he'd spent most of his afternoon in Romford trailing someone who used to work as a bin man in east London. The individual in question had hurt his back on the job and been offered a decent settlement, but was holding out for nearly £250,000. Whitcombe's clients had recently received an anonymous letter claiming the same man's passion for playing amateur rugby every week appeared to have discreetly resumed.

A quick trip to the Essex/London borders had yielded some helpful pictures of the guy enjoying some pretty active midweek training. Job done, and with an empty belly, he'd rewarded himself with a Big Mac and fries at London Bridge on his journey home. Glancing through the day's news on his phone, he'd read about the attack at the constituency office. What had happened to that young woodentop was a useful reminder about why he'd chosen to leave the police service.

Whitcombe had quit a few years before off the back of a messy divorce. Most of his colleagues thought he was having a midlife crisis but in truth he'd been thinking about it for a while. He'd never been a career animal, happy enough ambling through life as a constable. But the break-up of his marriage was the trigger he'd needed to move in a different direction.

Out on the streets, every day, serious injury or death hung over you like a shadow. Every small moment held potential threat – the suspect reaching for their ID who pulls a knife instead, or the drug addict pointing a dirty needle at you. He'd seen all sorts of shit happen to his mates over the years and couldn't help wondering whether they'd been unlucky or whether he'd simply been riding his own good fortune. Investigating insurance fraud – by and large – was a lot less dangerous.

He bought a copy of the *Standard* to read on his train home. He hadn't really taken in the Claire Beacham stuff that week, though he'd been aware of it. The severed head had been pretty shocking and he assumed it was some far-right nutjob. But when he looked at the CCTV image of the suspect who'd attacked the PC earlier, it triggered something at the back of his mind.

He stared at the image for a few moments, unsure if he recognised anything in the blurry face or not. He read the story again – more closely now. The name of the second victim, Dr Ruth Vance, rang faint bells as well, but he couldn't put his finger on why. He thought about it but couldn't retrieve the memory – if there even was one to retrieve. The likelihood was that he was probably just tired after travelling a long way to stand behind a tree in Essex for half the afternoon. He'd met a lot of people over the years, heard a lot of names.

He lived in a small flat in Brockley and after getting home, he immediately uploaded the rugby photographs he'd taken then settled down in front of the TV with a beer. He'd also kept the newspaper – which was unusual as normally he didn't bother – but those names and faces were still faintly triggering something at the back of his mind. He was snoozing on his sofa when the doorbell woke him with a start. There was a strong temptation to ignore it, but then he thought it was probably his neighbour finally coming to collect the parcel he'd taken for her earlier that week. He dragged himself to his feet and went to see. A dark figure wearing a red baseball cap was standing at the door looking at the ground. Instantly he recognised the silhouette from the newspaper.

Before he could react, the man raised his hand and Whitcombe saw he was holding something – a small, clear plastic bottle. He held it up and sprayed it at him. Whitcombe felt a jet of liquid squirt in his face, smelt the ammonia, and then his eyes were burning and so was his skin. The man pushed him back into the hallway, following him in and shutting the door behind them. Whitcombe fell back on the floor, his hands instinctively scratching at his eyes with burning fingers.

In the blur of the little he could see, the black and red shadow was leaning over him now. He took one hand from his face and held it blindly out to try and protect himself. The intruder grabbed his wrist and pinned it to the floor. Suddenly there was a loud sharp crack and then new pain, agonising and appalling, like nothing he'd ever felt before. There was a wave of dizzying nausea and just before he passed out, he remembered who that man was and where he'd seen him before.

28

Finn slept badly that night and had strange dreams. Memories of long-dead family members resurfaced, images from his childhood mingling with the present. On waking, he felt restless and the feeling lingered for a while. For the first time since he'd returned to work, he felt alone again. He'd known Tony Whitcombe – not well, but had come across him when the man had been a police constable. The guy had quit in his mid-forties so had served for over twenty years. There would be a lot of shocked ex-colleagues this morning coming to terms with what had happened.

He'd gone straight to the crime scene the previous evening – the body had been found by a neighbour coming to collect a parcel from Whitcombe. That hadn't been accidental – the killer had left the front door wide open for the world to see just as at Ruth Vance's flat before. He'd severed Whitcombe's right hand at the wrist before stabbing him to death. It didn't take a genius to work out that the severed appendage was probably already en route to Claire Beacham in some form. Every step possible was being taken to try and prevent it from reaching her. She'd been informed of the murder and once again had no prior knowledge of the dead man. Despite attempts to dissuade her, she'd been bullish about continuing with her duties as close to normal as she could. The security with her now though was round the clock.

After his difficult night's sleep, on a whim, Finn didn't bother with his usual highly regimented morning routine. Instead, he went to the cafe by Wandsworth Common that he'd taken such a liking to during his sabbatical. He wanted to give his mind some thinking time before he went in. Whitcombe's death raised some interesting questions. Neil Plaskitt had suggested that the killer might be targeting symbolic victims. A social worker and a doctor – and then he'd almost killed a police constable. Later on the same day, he *did* kill a former PC. Had the intention been to murder an officer in front of Claire? And was the attack on Whitcombe a swift attempt to make up for that failure? If so, then why a former officer? The logic didn't quite add up. And now there was a severed hand to follow the head and the tongue. That surely was symbolic, as well – but in relation to what?

His train of thought was disturbed as the waitress brought him a bowl of porridge with a double espresso. He let the coffee's aroma hit his nostrils and spooned some honey from a small dish on to the porridge. Again there was a sense that Whitcombe had been specifically identified. Finn hadn't needed to check the files to know that the PC had been stationed in the same part of Lambeth as Baby T. But there was no record of him being involved in that case in any way. The early indications were that nothing connected him to the other victims – let alone Claire Beacham.

'*Which obviously means there is something – you just haven't found it yet,*' said Karin. Finn smiled and swallowed a mouthful of oats. She was right, of course – *something* bound the three victims to Claire. Something very specific, which the killer held her ultimately responsible for. The devil was in the detail – it had to be.

He shivered as his overnight dream came back to him unbidden. It hadn't quite been a nightmare but it had been unpleasant. The investigation had occupied almost all of his thoughts since he'd returned to Cedar House and his time spent with the bereavement counsellor now felt a distant memory. He remembered her warning on their last meeting – not to fall back into old destructive habits. In truth, he wasn't behaving much differently to how he'd been before he'd taken his sabbatical. He was shuttling back and forth from an empty flat, with not much thought for anything except the investigations in progress.

His counsellor had reinforced the importance of breaking that cycle and he was aware he was neglecting those around him once more. It would be good to finally have that drink with Jackie Ojo – to check how things were at home with her. Also, he wanted to catch up with Paulsen and see where her head was at regarding leaving. That had been nagging away at the back of his mind too, bothering him. But as he drained his espresso, his thoughts were with Claire Beacham. She'd looked at breaking point at the constituency office the previous day and he could only wonder how she was feeling this morning.

Claire laughed. Michael had brought her breakfast in bed – something he'd never done in living memory. He was being very careful around her – like a scolded puppy with big doleful eyes, as he laid the tray of cooked food down next to her.

'What on earth . . .' she said, looking down at the food.

'We had frozen sausages in the freezer that needed using up,' he explained.

'They've been there for months . . .' she said and laughed again. He looked at her nervously and she waved a hand at him. 'I'm okay – if I didn't laugh, I'd be in pieces. What else can I do?' The smile quickly disappeared though. 'I'm going to get grease all over the bed . . .' she said, before taking a sip of tea from a large mug.

'It doesn't matter – just relax,' he said. He went and peered through the curtains, saw the armed response vehicle parked on the opposite side of the road.

'Poor sods,' he muttered under his breath before coming back and sitting on the edge of the bed.

As she looked at him, despite everything that had happened between them recently, she could see there was genuine concern in his face.

'How many more deaths are there going to be?' she said quietly. News of Tony Whitcombe's murder so soon after the incident at the constituency surgery had almost felt inevitable when they were told about it. After each appalling incident came the hope that no more would follow, and yet here they were again. Another killing, and still nothing to help them understand why it was happening. Michael sat down on the edge of the bed.

'This isn't on you,' he said. 'This is on *him*. You can't be held responsible for what this nutter's doing.'

'Can't I? I've seen him now – looked him right in the eye.' She shuddered as she remembered him. '*He* certainly thinks it's on me.' She pushed the tray of food to one side but wrapped two hands around the mug of tea as if her life depended on it. 'I'm sorry – I know you meant well, but you'll understand if I don't have much of an appetite this morning.'

He nodded.

'So what are you going to do?' he said.

She blew out through her cheeks.

'I know what I feel like doing – just lying here all day. But I can't.'

'Why not? It sounds a brilliant idea.'

'Because there's Benjamin, for a start – I can't drop the ball on that just because of everything else that's going on.'

Michael shook his head.

'The police have made themselves very clear – they think you should get the hell out of London for the time being. After what happened yesterday – don't you think you should?'

She ignored him, swung her legs out of bed and stood, draining the tea.

'I want to go ahead with the rally in Parliament Square later. I was going to make a speech there and I'd still like to. Everything else I can do from home.'

Michael looked dismayed. The rally had been rescheduled after Benjamin had handed himself in and he'd assumed she'd yield to the firm advice she'd been given.

'Claire—'

She shook her head, cutting him off.

'It's important to show these people – the killer, for a start, plus the government, the press, the public – *everyone*, that I'm not going to be silenced or stopped from doing the right thing. You remember that, don't you? Doing the right thing – why that's important?'

She grabbed her dressing gown and headed to the bathroom.

John Skegman's mood wasn't much improved on the previous day. As Finn stood in his office again, the DCI had a selection of the morning papers spread out on his desk. The attack on PC Irwin in South Wimbledon and the murder of Tony Whitcombe were covered on most of the front pages. Politicians from across the spectrum were saying all surgeries with the public should be switched to Zoom as a matter of course now.

'There's a lot of people higher up the food chain wanting to see some progress, Alex. Please tell me – with two new crime scenes – you've got something,' said Skegman. The question wasn't aggressive, the tone more apologetic. Finn knew that the last thing the DCI would want to do is put more pressure on them at this point. Despite everything, Skegman wasn't the sort to throw people under the bus, and Finn suspected he'd been shielding the incident room from much of the heat coming from above.

'If you look through Tony Whitcombe's CV, he was working at Brixton police station at the same time Lukasz Mazurek was a social worker in the area and Ruth Vance was working there as a doctor. And all of that coincides with Claire Beacham's stint as a local councillor for the patch. It's that period of time we're focusing on.'

'And you've got nothing except Baby T which connects them?' said Skegman.

'I wouldn't even go that far. There's nothing that connects Claire or Whitcombe to Baby T.' Finn shrugged. 'But we're going through it all again with a fine-toothed comb in case there's something we missed.'

'And there's no sign of this severed hand yet?'

Finn shook his head.

'No. We're assuming he's not stupid and won't be delivering it in person – but you can bet he's trying to find some way of getting it to Claire. We're obviously trying to circumvent that.'

'And no idea what it means?'

Finn shrugged.

'Beyond the obvious – did Mazurek not think? Did Dr Vance say something she shouldn't? And as for Whitcombe . . .' He shrugged again. 'Who knows . . .'

'What have forensics given you?'

'That Whitcombe's killer is definitely the same individual who murdered the other two – and the same one who attacked PC Irwin too.'

Skegman relaxed back in his seat.

'We've got good pictures of this man – and they're all over the media today. Someone must know who he is.'

Finn looked at him awkwardly.

'There's something else. I've just been speaking to Claire's aide, Grant Lassiter. She's adamant she wants to attend the rally they're holding in Westminster today for Benjamin Ngomo.'

Skegman rolled his eyes.

'Fuck's sake.'

'We've no legal right to stop her – even if the idea's insane,' said Finn. 'But there's worse places than Parliament Square. We can protect her properly there and it's easy to seal off. There's camera coverage of every single blade of grass. We might be able to use it to draw him out . . .'

Skegman considered it.

'Or we could get her killed. I see where you're coming from, but in the first instance, we have a duty of care. Have another word with her – try and get her to see sense. If you can persuade her to take a holiday somewhere north of Aberdeen, even better.'

Finn shook his head.

'She's adamant she wants to do this.'

Skegman produced a razor-sharp smile.

'Then use your charm, Alex.'

With the constituency office a crime scene and off limits, Claire made good on her promise to work from home. Michael had also taken the day off – given what had happened, it didn't feel right to leave her on her own, despite the presence of the patrol car outside. As she worked, he'd quietly slipped into the garden and was sitting on a wooden bench looking up at the grey-black clouds scudding overhead.

Like his wife, he was feeling numbed by the events of the last twenty-four hours, of the last few days – of even the last weeks and months, to be fair. If anything, it had just strengthened his determination to push through his plans to start a new life for them abroad. He was also convinced that Claire would be more receptive to the idea now. His relative calm was interrupted by his phone – the burner he kept in his pocket permanently now.

'How are you, Michael – is everything okay?' said Ray Spinney.

The question took him by surprise. In all the time dealing with this man, he'd never heard him begin a conversation like that. There was almost something like a genuine concern in his tone.

'Yes, I am. *We* are. Claire's alright but obviously a bit shook up.'

'What have the police said to you?'

Suddenly it was obvious and he realised how slow he was being. Of course Spinney wasn't concerned about their well-being. He was concerned that the police were digging into their lives and was worried that those inquiries might start turning towards the Doll Street deal.

'Don't worry – they're not investigating *me*. We're fine, Doll Street's fine, everything's on track.'

There was a long pause – as there always seemed to be when they spoke. But then, Spinney had never been what Michael had quite expected. Perhaps, lazily, he'd thought a man with the nickname the 'Handyman', with a CV like his, would be a certain type of thug – like the Godfather or some-thing. Instead, he'd found him an extremely cerebral person – a sense of someone playing chess on several boards at once. It made him a damn sight scarier than the simple one-dimen-sional gangster he'd originally taken him for.

'I hope your wife *is* okay . . .' said Spinney unexpectedly.

Again Michael struggled to make sense of it – he hadn't imagined the slight change in tone he'd heard, the actual *emotion* in his voice.

'Thank you,' he said, unsure of where this was going.

'Do you mind me asking you a question?' said Spinney. 'A personal one, I mean . . .'

Michael looked around to check he was still alone, that the back door to the house was still firmly closed.

'Sure,' he said, wondering what on earth was coming. 'Go ahead . . .'

'Why did you get involved with me? You didn't need to.'

Michael thought about lying, then wondered what the point would be, so he told him the truth. He explained about his desire for children, why he wanted to relocate with Claire to California and why Spinney's money was crucial to that plan.

'. . . because in the end, it's about family,' he said. And even as the words came out of his mouth, he reminded himself the man he was talking to was a killer, was responsible for the death of prison officer Terry Merchant and countless others.

'Yes, it is – always. The rest is irrelevant – family is *everything* . . .'

The line went dead and Michael tried to make sense of the conversation. There'd been a catch in the old villain's voice at the end, and if he didn't know better, he'd swear it sounded like sadness.

29

Benjamin was standing at one of the phone bays on D wing at Cromarsh Prison again. His brief excursion into the outside world already felt like a distant memory. The mood in the jail was different too since his return. There was a tension amongst the prison officers, even those who usually showed a little warmth. You could smell the fear on them. The death of Terry Merchant had hit them hard and been a reminder of the dangers of their profession.

Benjamin had been nervous too about how he would be received by the other inmates. The whole incident had been national news and the last thing you ever wanted was to be high profile inside. He hadn't been sure what to expect – whether the prison staff would hold him responsible for what had happened to Merchant, or whether he'd be a target for some of the other prisoners. But nobody was getting in his face or making much noise about it – if anything, everyone was giving him a wide berth. They all knew who'd tried to break him free.

Spinney had people everywhere – Benjamin had already learnt that when he'd first arrived at Cromarsh and another inmate had tried to attack him. He'd fought that one off and there hadn't been a follow-up, at least not until the assault on the prison transport. The fight he'd got into over breakfast earlier in the week he'd thought was a one-off, but he wasn't so certain now. He knew he'd need to be braced for anything, but was also aware it was a problem that he wouldn't have to worry about for too much longer. The threat of deportation was looming again and that ominous sense of a ticking clock had returned. His cellmate was a Romanian guy built like a tank who could barely speak any English. It was a mixed blessing not having someone to talk to – but he'd spent the night lying on his bunk feeling more suffocated than ever.

'Hey …' said Emma and he smiled at the sound of her voice, pressing the receiver closer to his ear so he could drown out the noise around him. 'How are you doing?' she said.

'I'm okay,' he lied.

He looked around, suddenly self-conscious, but no one was watching.

'How's it been?'

'Like I've never been away.'

She made a small sound that might have been a laugh or a sigh, he couldn't tell which.

'I think you did the right thing handing yourself in. It'll help you later,' she said.

He wanted to tell her it felt like a death sentence but didn't.

'Feels like we're back exactly where we started. Only this time I'm scared about what Spinney's going to do now that he knows where to find me again.'

'He'll do nothing – just like before,' said Emma firmly. 'Remember, he had to wait until you were on the move before he could try anything. He can't get to you in jail – or at least, not in the way that he wants – or he'd have done it already.'

Behind him, someone somewhere was squawking like a crow. He looked around and waited until the screeching subsided.

'None of this matters, anyway – I've got a new date for my sentencing hearing. It's on Monday, next week,' he said.

'I want to come and see you.'

'Not a chance. And if you do come – I won't go to the visit-ing hall,' he replied immediately.

'Ben . . .'

'*Please*. I'm begging you.'

He heard her sigh.

'Alright. We'll see,' she said finally.

'We won't.'

'We'll talk about it later.'

'We won't.'

There was a silence and he shook his head, even though she couldn't see him.

'Are you being careful?' he said.

'Of course – and I'm the last person you need to worry about. You just make sure you look after yourself.'

He could feel his eyes stinging and controlled himself. You couldn't show weakness in here; even the slightest hint that he'd been crying would bring hell down on him. He forced his face into a neutral expression, aware people were queuing behind him now to use the phone.

'It just feels like everything's hanging by a thread,' he said.

Use your charm, Skegman had said. As Finn sat in Claire Beacham's living room, he envied – not for the first time in his life – those to whom the quality came easily. Those people who could turn it on like a tap.

'*You're not one of them, Alex,*' said his late wife unhelpfully and he banished her with a tight smile as Claire handed him a cup of tea.

'I've forgotten if you take sugar,' she said as she sat down on the sofa opposite. 'I feel like I've seen so much of you lately I ought to know . . .'

'Yes, I do,' muttered Finn, slightly embarrassed. Michael Beacham quickly jumped to his feet and headed to the kitchen, leaving them alone. Claire smiled awkwardly at him.

'Is there really no progress at all in finding this man?' she said. Finn was aware she'd been reassured by the Met commissioner himself that everything that could be done was being done. Now, all he could tell her was that they were no nearer to an arrest than they had been since this had started. The fact was, though CCTV had caught the suspect's escape from the constituency office, the camera footage only went so far. Over a hundred people had rung the incident room after seeing the pictures – but not one single call had led to a solid lead yet.

'He's still out there – and that's why going to this rally today really isn't a good idea,' he said. Claire held up a hand as if stopping traffic.

'I have no intention of going on the march itself – but I do want to make my speech in Parliament Square this afternoon. It's important to do it for lots of reasons.'

'Then you won't be surprised if I tell you we think that's a very bad idea too.'

He almost admired the certainty on her face, knew too that this latest appeal was hitting the same rocks as all the previous ones had.

'I'm sorry – but I *need* to do this. The Home Secretary is making a statement to the House later – it's the perfect moment to put pressure on her.' Finn tried to interrupt but she waved him down again. 'If I'm in Parliament Square leading from the front – despite everything that's happened this week – it *will* have an impact. Trust me.'

Michael slipped back into the room clutching a sugar bowl and Finn helped himself to a couple of teaspoons. The slight interruption helped diffuse the atmosphere. Michael sat down, still looking like a worried schoolboy. He'd been lucky, Finn thought – the whole Doll Street outcry had quickly been displaced in the news headlines by the other events of the week. But there was still something about the man's skittishness he wasn't quite sure about, even if his nerves were pretty understandable in the circumstances.

'How do you feel about this?' Finn directed the question at Michael.

'The rally? I think it's a terrible idea,' he replied.

Claire's face hardened.

'And that's exactly why I want to do it – because *no one* is there for Benjamin. It would be easy to just go along with both of you and do the safe thing – but it could cost him everything, and I'm not going to let that happen.'

Now it was Finn's turn to think. He'd met Benjamin Ngomo, talked to him for himself. He'd seen enough to understand why Claire was fighting so hard for him. He understood the reasons she was giving too. It rankled with him as well that this psycho who'd killed three people might also claim another kind of victim – Benjamin didn't deserve that. But he also remembered Skegman's comments about their duty of care for the MP.

'There's plenty of other ways you can fight his corner. As you say – you have the platform in the House of Commons later. You don't need to put yourself at risk out in the open,' he said. Claire simply shook her head.

'I don't suppose if I begged ...' said Finn, only semi-seriously.

'It wouldn't make the blindest difference,' said Claire, poker-faced.

Finn nodded, acknowledging he couldn't stop her.

'If we proceed, there'll be an extremely heavy police presence, obviously, and there's a lot we can do in that environment to protect you. But you need to be aware there's no situation that's one hundred per cent watertight. I can't completely guarantee your safety.'

'I'm fine with that,' said Claire.

'One other thing: if we agree we're going to do this – we do it my way.'

Claire smiled, *properly* smiled at him this time, and he had to fight to stop himself from returning it.

'Of course,' she said.

There was a knock at the living room door and Finn looked up to see one of the PCs who'd been watching the Beachams' property outside. Excusing himself, he rose and went to join the officer in the hallway.

'There's something you need to come and see,' said the PC.

Finn followed him out into the Beachams' driveway. A terrified-looking teenager was being held by a second uniform constable.

'He told me just to leave it by the front door – I don't know what's in it, I swear!'

Finn followed the boy's gaze. On the ground in front of them was a box.

30

An hour later and Finn was back in his office trying to wolf down a sandwich while he had a spare moment. His brief moment of peace came to an abrupt halt as John Skegman came crashing through his door. Not for the first time, he thought there was a special place in hell for those who interrupted people eating at their desks.

'I gather there's been a development?' said Skegman.

Finn nodded. The box had been removed swiftly from the Beachams' house and opened by forensic officers in a sterile police laboratory. Predictably, it had contained Tony Whitcombe's missing right hand.

'The kid who delivered it says the man approached him on a trading estate a couple of miles away. We think the boy's a dealer and the killer targeted him because there's no cameras in the area,' Finn explained. Paulsen was downstairs taking a statement from the boy in question. 'He slipped him a twenty-pound note to deliver it and told him not to look inside,' continued Finn, wiping some stray tomato seeds off his chin. 'Probably a good job that he didn't.'

'Did the kid get a description?' said Skegman.

Finn nodded.

'Yes – it's a match for the man who stabbed PC Irwin at the constituency office. I'm pretty sure forensics won't pull anything useful off that box though. Not if the previous deliveries are anything to go by.' He shook his head and threw the empty sandwich container into a bin under his desk. 'He thought it out – just like he's thought out every step of this so far.'

'How's Claire taken it?' asked Skegman.

Finn had already rung and confirmed the grisly discovery. At least on this occasion, they'd prevented it from reaching her.

'Better than you might think – she was expecting it. But we need to find this guy, because, like us, she's beginning to wonder just how many more there are going to be.'

The man looked at his reflection in the bathroom mirror and lifted the clippers to his scalp. He shouldn't have gone to Beacham's constituency office – in retrospect, it had been a mistake. An act of hubris that had derailed his carefully constructed plan. But the temptation to look the woman in the eye, to see the fear there, had been so strong. And it *had* been there – just for a second, he'd seen it, harvested it, and felt a high better than any drug.

Her lack of recognition wasn't a surprise though. What else had he been expecting? But he'd fucked up and there was no getting away from that. Now the world knew broadly what he looked like and he needed to change that. It wouldn't be the first time, after all. He ran the clippers over his head and watched dyed black hair drop into the sink. It didn't take long and afterwards, he picked up the cheap glasses he'd bought at the chemist earlier. They made him look older, with perhaps a touch of the hipster about him too. Different enough.

Running a hand over his newly shaven scalp, he sat down at his kitchen table and considered the state of play. He'd wanted Whitcombe to pay, just like Mazurek and Vance, and now they all had. There was satisfaction in that, at least – but his impatience had probably cost him his best chance of killing

Beacham. He'd never get that close to her again, not now. You never saw this happen to the bad guys on TV – their plans were always foolproof – but real life was different. He remembered how scared he'd been, waiting in that cafe for Mazurek. The nerves he'd felt waiting for Ruth Vance to come home, the look of terror on Whitcombe's face at the end almost matching his own. And then he thought again about why he was doing this and didn't regret a thing.

And if he couldn't kill Beacham, then there were other ways he could get to her. Things that would rest on her conscience – and he knew, better than anyone, what living in that particular circle of hell felt like. He picked up the flyer he'd printed off earlier. There was a picture of that young man who was her current pet project. The words 'March for Benjamin' were written below it. The rally was due to begin at the BBC's headquarters at Broadcasting House at the top of Regent Street. The demonstrators would then make their way down through central London to Parliament Square to hear Miss High and Mighty make her speech.

It was the perfect opportunity for what he had in mind, but would take some planning and there was little time for that. There were a crazy number of cameras in the area and you could bet they'd all be looking out for him – the lone wolf. And that's exactly what he'd be – because everyone knows what a lone wolf amongst a flock of sheep can do . . .

31

'I'm sorry, mate – she sounded convincing on the phone,' said Sami Dattani. He and Dave McElligott were walking across Plumstead Common back to Dattani's car. The early blue skies above had given away to a gathering of ominous-looking black clouds. They'd just been interviewing a woman who'd rung the incident room, convinced she recognised the man pictured in the newspapers. The empty bottles of vodka in the recycling box outside were their first clue that she might not be the most reliable. The half-opened one on the kitchen table inside had both of them exchanging weary glances. Ten minutes later they were satisfied her ex-husband wasn't the killer of three people, just a man deserving of some considerable sympathy.

'No worries – not the first time, not the last time that'll happen,' said McElligott. 'Good to get out of the station, to be honest,' he said, pulling his jacket around him.

'What do you reckon is keeping the DPS then? I thought they were supposed to be talking to us all imminently,' said Dattani, frowning. 'You know, about whether any of us are supposed to be bent or not,' he added with clear contempt.

McElligott glanced across at him.

'That's really bothering you, isn't it? Got something to hide, Sami?' he said, trying to affect a little of the old cheekiness. Dattani threw him a glare back. Paulsen had used the same gag earlier and it was starting to piss him off.

'Don't be ridiculous. And yes – it is bothering me. Heard a rumour this morning they picked someone up in Islington. A DS, supposedly.'

'Got a name to go with that?' said McElligott.

Dattani shook his head.

'No – but he's fucked whoever he is.'

'What happened to innocent until proven guilty?'

Dattani stopped.

'Of course he's fucked – just think it through, Dave. First of all, the press is going to be all over him – the corrupt cop that cost Terry Merchant his life. Then when the trial happens, there's no judge that isn't going to throw the book at him. And then try and imagine what life inside would be like? It's bad enough if you're a cop – but in this instance, it's probably the screws you'd be looking over your shoulder at.'

McElligott nodded mechanically.

'Maybe these poor sods didn't have a choice – maybe Spinney threatened their families too. Like the security guards in the robbery.' Dave just about managed to make the words sound casual. The rain was starting to spit now with the promise of something heavier. Dattani was already shaking his head.

'No way. If it was me, I'd have gone straight to the boss and told him. It's not even a choice. Do you want that hanging over your head for the rest of your life? Even when you come out of prison – what are you going to do? One quick search on the internet and there it is. I mean, you'd never work again – anywhere. And what about your family while you're inside – they'd be pariahs, probably. Shit like this doesn't get forgotten.'

They'd reached the car and Dattani unlocked it with his key fob. There was a rumble of thunder above.

'Suppose you're right,' said McElligott.

'Sorry, mate – didn't mean to go off on one. I guess what's really pissing me off is the thought it could be anyone. People we know, for Christ's sake.'

As they drove back to Cedar House, McElligott sat scrolling through his phone to avoid further conversation. His head still hadn't quite caught up with his heart, he realised. Intellectually he understood what he'd done, why he was in the position he was. And it all still made sense: the pressure of his finances had felt crushing, the responsibility he bore to Zoe and his unborn child even more powerful. And yet . . . there was still a strange bemusement at how he'd managed to get himself quite so knee-deep in shit.

'Do us a favour, Sami,' he said suddenly, as they passed through Eltham. 'Drop us here, would you?' Dattani looked across at him, confused. 'I need to get some stuff for Zoe – I promised her I would and I just don't know when else I'm going to get the time today. I don't want to hold you up – I'll get the train back to the nick.'

Dattani shrugged and stopped to let him out.

'Are you sure you're alright, Dave?' he said.

'On fire, mate.' He winked at him. 'I'll see you when I see you.'

Dattani smiled uncertainly before accelerating away. McElligott stood and looked around the nondescript patch of suburbia he found himself in and began to walk as the rain came down.

Dattani's words had cut deep. Dave's main concern overnight had been the anti-corruption investigation, although he was still convinced there was no way his part in this could physically be traced. He didn't trust Spinney as far as he could throw him, but could see no reason why the man would sell him out – at least not yet. There was no obvious advantage and he still needed him as a pair of eyes and ears on the murder inquiry. But it was all about – to paraphrase Donald Rumsfeld – 'the known knowns and the known unknowns'. He couldn't be one hundred per cent sure his position was watertight and now Dattani had outlined a whole bunch of scenarios he hadn't fully thought through. All he'd been thinking about was discovery and how he'd manage that if it came to it. He hadn't thought too much about prison – or the potential lifelong ramifications for Zoe and his child.

He'd wanted to get out of the car simply to be alone and to give himself time to think. Now he was seeing a whole spread of deeply unpleasant options branching out in front of him. A world in which the only way Zoe could get through this would be to totally disassociate herself from him. A son or daughter he'd never meet, whose only knowledge of him would be by reputation and what he'd done. That thought was almost too much to bear. He took refuge under a deserted bus shelter and called Zoe.

'Hey – what's up?' she said.

He watched a steady stream of water tipping down a drain by the kerb as the rain continued to pound down.

'Nothing really. Just thought I'd say hello.'

He could easily imagine the smile beginning to spread across her face.

'You daft sod,' she replied.

'How's the roof holding up in this rain?' he said.

'It's fine – the builders did a good job.'

He thought for a moment of that future he'd imagined, the one where the very mention of his name would repel and disgust her.

'Love you,' he said.

Ten minutes later he was sitting on a bench at Eltham railway station waiting for a train to take him back to Cedar House. His mood matched the weather – he felt like he'd pissed his life away. Every opportunity he'd ever been given he hadn't properly taken. Instead, he'd watched people like Jackie Ojo grafting their way up the ladder, seen relative newcomers like Mattie Paulsen leapfrog him to become the rising stars. Meanwhile, good old Dave trundled along behind them, the cheeky chappie who kept everyone's spirits up. Now the life he'd wanted when he'd bought that house in Croydon was in danger of being yet another false start. He looked at the electronic board above the platform, but the times of the trains had been replaced with the words:

Fast train approaching – stand away from the platform edge.

There was no visible sign of the oncoming train but he slowly rose to his feet and looked around – only a few other passengers were waiting there, taking refuge under the platform's leaky roof. He caught the eye of a tall guy in his twenties holding a rucksack who was standing a few metres away. The sound of the high-speed train approaching was audible now, getting louder with every second. He was a burden, he thought. To Zoe, to a child who might grow to hate him, to his colleagues, to his parents – to just about everyone in his life. The train was now visible, hurtling towards them. He glanced down at the electrified tracks and took a faltering step forwards. The guy with the rucksack was watching him hard. The train was speeding closer and McElligott took another step.

'Mate—' The man's voice cut through like a whip crack. All he did was catch Dave's eye and shake his head, but it was enough. The train fired past, the wind ricocheting around them in its slipstream.

'Fucking hell,' said McElligott involuntarily. The man with the rucksack came straight over and for a moment they looked at each other and neither of them knew what to say. And in that instant, Dave McElligott finally understood what he needed to do next.

★   ★   ★

It took a lot to throw Finn, to completely knock him out of his stride – but this conversation had managed it. He stared at McElligott's face, unsure whether he felt overpowering sympathy or a desire to beat him senseless. The DC had come to his office with the same brooding demeanour he'd been carrying all week and had asked for a chat, stressing it was urgent. Finn had been utterly unprepared for what came next. McElligott then explained, in dispassionate forensic terms, exactly what he'd done and why he'd done it.

'Terry Merchant's death . . .' he'd concluded. 'That's on me – I take responsibility for that.'

About the only thing Finn was prepared to give himself credit for was the fact that he'd sensed all week that something had been seriously up with the detective constable. But he'd taken his earlier explanations of the pressures of starting a new family at face value. He'd always found McElligott facetious and irritating – but every nick had one like that. At heart, he was a good officer and Finn had always been able to separate people's personalities from their abilities. But he'd misread this horribly and there would be a price to pay for that mistake.

'Say something,' said McElligott.

Finn watched Mattie Paulsen stride down the corridor outside, scowling at the world for no reason as usual. On the other side of the door, it felt like he'd entered a different dimension or something. Of all the emotions coalescing – betrayal, anger, empathy, disbelief amongst them – the one rising to the surface was hurt. He was taking this personally, he realised.

'Why didn't you come to me first, straight away – when he first made contact with you?'

'I know it's hard to understand now but I felt . . . boxed in – like I had no choice.'

'Money? It was just for money?'

'Initially. But then Spinney began to threaten Zoe—'

'You knew who you were dealing with,' shouted Finn, interrupting.

'She's *pregnant*.'

Finn rubbed the back of his neck while he thought it through.

'You're finished as a police officer and you'll go down for this.'

McElligott nodded.

'I know.'

Finn shook his head.

'How much did you tell him about the murder investigations in progress?'

'Everything.'

The answer came without hesitation. Now he'd committed to confessing, he didn't seem to be holding anything back. Finn visibly controlled himself.

'You do understand Spinney might still be behind those deaths – that you've kept him a step ahead of us right the way through.'

'I don't think he is – but he has an interest in them for sure. I just don't know why.'

Finn tried to process every angle of this, a feeling he still hadn't properly grasped the full implications of it.

'I won't be able to help you.'

'I'm aware of that too. But I just want to say this: I could have continued, not said anything and tried to bluff this out, but I chose not to do that.'

He said the words as a statement of fact rather than with any pride. Finn's fury was already cooling into icy contempt.

'And you want credit for that?'

'Be honest, sir: you never liked me, did you?' said McElligott.

'Like or dislike never had anything to do with it.'

32

Skegman's reaction to the news wasn't much different to Finn's. He listened in silence and then sat motionless while he tried to make sense of what he'd just been told.

'Where is he now?'

'In my office, with a "do not disturb" sign on the door – it was the most discreet place I could think of leaving him.'

Skegman nodded. It made sense – Finn's office was in the sterile, MIT part of Cedar House with access controlled by a security keypad.

'Anyone on the door?'

Finn shook his head.

'This came from Dave – I don't think he's going anywhere. I don't think there's anywhere he *can* go now.'

Skegman thought about it.

'Brief someone you trust and put them in there with him while he's here – just in case. He'll need to be formally suspended from duty immediately – then arrested and charged.'

He said the words like a factory controller authorising a shipment.

'Of course – but I thought you might want to do that somewhere away from here. From what I can tell, the DPS have been keeping news of their other arrests as quiet as they can. I think they want to keep Spinney in the dark for as long as possible in case there's a chance of catching him.'

The delayed anger was now starting to catch up with Skegman just as it had with Finn earlier.

'How could he be so stupid?'

Finn relayed the financial issues that McElligott had told him about and Skegman pinched the bridge of his nose.

'There'll need to be an immediate review of your investigation, to establish the potential impact on it. Any tactics or sensitive information which have been disclosed to him will also need to be looked at and changed if necessary,' he said.

'He's been out all morning with Sami and hasn't been party to any of the planning for the Parliament Square operation . . .' Finn faltered as he realised what he was saying. They'd been housing a corrupt officer, someone working for one of the most dangerous men in Europe, and even though he'd seen something hadn't been right, he'd still missed this. Who knew how much damage had been done. 'This is my fault,' he said. 'I'd have caught this before my sabbatical, spotted the warning signs.'

Skegman shook his head.

'He didn't just fool you.' He glanced at the clock on his wall. 'There's plenty of time to examine the fallout later. Right now you need to be concentrating on Parliament Square.'

Skegman was right – it was now midday, with Claire's speech at the rally due to take place at 6 p.m., before the Home Secretary addressed the Commons at seven. There was a lot to do if they were going to keep her safe and Finn realised his attention was split. The emotion was all on McElligott, but his head needed to be with Claire now. If he wasn't careful, the day could still get a lot worse.

'I better get back to that – what do you want to do about Dave in terms of the rest of the team?'

'Let's keep this between ourselves for now,' said Skegman. 'I'll inform the DPS and the NCA immediately and they can fight it out between them. They'll both want him moved for questioning, whichever way that goes, and that's fine by me. The faster he's out of the building, the better.'

'We're going to have to tell the rest of the station what's happened at some point,' said Finn.

Skegman nodded.

'That can wait. Let's get today out of the way first. Do you have a rough idea of how much has been leaked?'

'Yes – Dave genuinely doesn't think Spinney's behind these murders and that's my sense too. So in terms of damage to the inquiry – I think it's probably minimal.' He shrugged help-lessly. 'But we've only got his word for that and I honestly don't know how much that's worth any more.'

Skegman rubbed the back of his neck.

'So why's Ray Spinney so keen to know what we're doing?'

'Because of Claire,' said Finn. 'And whatever the hell his interest is in Benjamin Ngomo.'

Skegman's frown deepened while he tried to join the dots.

'Is she corrupt, is that it? In his pocket or something?'

'I don't think so. But perhaps it's the threat of his imminent deportation. We know Spinney wants Benjamin, we just don't know why. If he's kicked out of the country, then he'll take whatever that information is with him. Claire might just be his best chance of keeping him here.'

'And we still don't know what that information might be?'

Finn shook his head.

'Not a clue. Before I wasn't so sure we *needed* to know, but all of this is starting to feel interlinked now.'

'And Dave doesn't know what it is, either? He's not holding that back?'

'No. At least I don't think so – he seemed to want to get everything off his chest. And if I was Spinney, why would I tell him that anyway – just in case he *was* caught?'

283

Skegman's frown had given way to something flatter now, his ratty little eyes narrowing as reality started to bite.

'This is going to kill us. Our standing, I mean . . . this station, not to mention our own individual reputations. He's properly fucked us, Alex.'

That assessment was about right, Finn thought. Within the service, people would point and query why the officers around McElligott hadn't picked up on what was going on. They were supposed to be detectives, after all, and he'd made fools out of all of them.

'I better get a shift on . . .' he said, thinking that could be added to the list of things to worry about later. Skegman was already reaching for his desk phone.

'I'll let the NCA and the DPS know what's happened, then bring Dave up to me.'

Finn moved to leave, then stopped and turned back.

'You're right when you say it might kill us,' he said. 'But it might very well kill Dave for real.'

Skegman simply nodded.

Finn escorted McElligott up to the DCI's office and left them to it. Despite everything, he found himself almost admiring the man's strange calm in the circumstances. Almost. Like everyone else, he'd read the obituaries of Terry Merchant in the media, seen the pictures of his grieving family. He still couldn't quite connect the immature, attention-seeking DC he knew with the haunted figure he'd left sitting with Skegman. As he turned to his computer, there was a knock at his door and Paulsen entered without waiting to be invited, clutching a sheaf of paperwork.

'Guv, I think I've found another connection between the victims – and a name to go with it this time.'

Finn instantly banished all thoughts of McElligott and gave her his full attention. She passed him a photograph of a wiry-looking man in his thirties with light brown hair. At first glance, he didn't look anything like the dark muscular figure from Claire's constituency office.

'What am I looking at here, Mattie?'

'His name's Daniel Best – he's Baby T's biological father.'

Finn looked at the picture again more closely – the name and face did ring a faint bell.

'Freya Appleton left him for Brandon Challis, didn't she? About a year or so before the murder?' Paulsen nodded in confirmation. 'He was pretty dignified, as I remember – made a strong statement to the press outside court on the day Appleton was sentenced.'

Paulsen passed him another piece of paper – a photocopy of a newspaper article this time. There was a picture of the same man on the steps of the Old Bailey, surrounded by photographers. Again Finn studied the face closely.

'He's certainly got good reason to be angry about what happened – but what's his connection to the three victims?'

'I only found it once I started looking into Tony Whitcombe. There was a domestic at Freya Appleton's flat about four months before the boy died – I mean there were a *lot* of call-outs there at that time, as far as I can see, but that was the first. Best had gone round to confront Challis. Whitcombe was one of the PCs who responded to it.'

Finn thought about it for a moment, again with a sense of déjà vu.

'Just like Lukasz Mazurek was one of the first social workers to visit Appleton and Challis. Did Best have any contact with him too?'

'Sort of, but nothing that's on the record – that's why it hasn't come up before. I emailed Nina Thornbury at Lambeth Council earlier to ask her the same question. She rang me back a short time ago and said one of her colleagues remembered

285

Best turning up at their offices once without an appointment. He was apparently pretty emotional and it sounds like Lukasz might have dealt with him. Nina didn't mention it before because she didn't know it had happened until today.'

'And Ruth Vance?'

Paulsen nodded, almost a touch of smugness about her expression now.

'She was Daniel Best's GP and she had an appointment with him several months before his son's death.'

For the first time Finn could feel some of the dots on this investigation beginning to join. This felt like a breakthrough, Paulsen's smugness not misplaced.

'Do we know what about?'

'No, the practice wouldn't tell me – but I went back through the Baby T files and there *is* something we missed before. We didn't spot it because it was small and buried in the paperwork.'

'Let me guess . . .' said Finn. 'Ruth Vance wrote to Lambeth Council social services to express her concerns about Daniel Best's son after meeting with him.'

'Exactly that – and it never got properly followed up,' said Paulsen. 'The inquiries that followed the murder all focused on the doctors who'd been treating Thomas directly before he died. No one remembered the GP who'd flagged it up months earlier.'

Finn laid out both photographs of Best in front of him.

'Could this really be the same man who was at the constituency office yesterday? They look completely different people to me.'

'These pictures are old,' said Paulsen. 'He might have bulked up since then, dyed his hair. But look at his features – the eyes in particular I think are very similar. I think it's a decent shout . . .' Finn did as she suggested, looked one more time, and slowly began to nod in agreement. 'I've left messages for Claire to call me back,' Paulsen continued. 'But here's the thing – I checked and Best met with her too when she was a local councillor in the area. It's on record.'

'Again – do we know why?' said Finn urgently.

'No, I've just got a time and a date – and it was right before Thomas's murder.'

Finn met her gaze – a moment of shared adrenaline. It felt like the clincher.

'Can we make a DNA match with Thomas Best?' he said.

'I've already asked the lab to get on to it.'

Finn nodded.

'This is excellent work, Mattie, really excellent.'

He saw the pride in her eye, both in what she'd done and in his respect. And even in the immediacy of it, he wondered if this might just be the moment when they lost her.

'What do you want to do?' she said.

'Let's pick Best up – as fast as we can, preferably before that rally gets underway.'

Before Paulsen could respond, Sami Dattani interrupted them.

'Guv – I think there's a bit of an issue with Dave. He's gone AWOL and I can't raise him either. He's been acting strange all day – all week, for that matter. I'm a bit concerned, if I'm honest.'

Finn tried to look him in the eye and failed.

'He's with the DCI, Sami. I'll fill you in later.'

33

The raid was organised quickly and efficiently and Finn took no chances with it. Daniel Best lived in a one-bedroom flat in Streatham Hill, the same home he'd once shared with Freya Appleton. A full pre-planned firearms operation was quickly mobilised and after a briefing at Cedar House, deployed just under two hours later. Six armed officers wearing full protective gear were joined by a team of specially trained search officers from the Territorial Support Group, led by a POLSA sergeant. If Best was their man, then the proof needed to be watertight. There was already enough scrutiny on Cedar House, and Finn knew that would only increase once the news about McElligott emerged.

Finn and Paulsen waited in an unmarked car in the adjacent street while the raid proceeded. One armed officer covered the rear of the building while two more covered either side, cutting off any potential escape routes. The TSG sergeant smashed the door open with an enforcer and his team swarmed in behind him. In their vehicle, Finn and Paulsen could only wait patiently, watching a couple of elderly neighbours chatting by their front doors, blissfully unaware of the drama playing out only a couple of hundred feet away. After a few seconds, Finn's radio crackled into life.

'*All clear – it's empty. The target's not here,*' said the sergeant.

'Bollocks,' said Paulsen, speaking for all of them.

Standing in the small living room a few moments later, Finn looked around, trying to get a sense of the man. The place was smart but sparse, with few obvious clues. A framed picture of baby Thomas was on the mantelpiece, another one on a side table by his bed. It was functional, a place where someone existed rather than lived.

One of the TSG officers pulled him over and pointed at a dark jacket draped around a chair. Finn couldn't see what had caught the man's attention, but when he looked more closely, the large dried blood patches on the fabric were clearly visible. A scarf matching the one from the CCTV footage was draped underneath it.

'Jesus – it really is him. You were right, Mattie,' said Finn, almost under his breath. There was satisfaction at confirming the killer's identity but no elation. Part of him still couldn't quite square the image of the man who'd spoken so eloquently on the steps of the Old Bailey with the butchery they were investigating now.

In the kitchen bin they found a knife strapped in black masking tape and wrapped in plastic. As he watched it being carefully transferred to an evidence bag, Finn was fairly certain it was the same weapon that had been used to stab PC Paul Irwin at the constituency office. Paulsen called out to him and Finn went back through to the living room and re-joined her. She was holding in a latex-gloved hand a flyer for the rally in central London in support of Benjamin Ngomo.

'Well, I guess that explains where he's gone . . .' he said. 'It was probably a bit too much to hope he'd just nipped out for a carton of milk.'

Behind the face mask she was wearing, Paulsen looked confused.

'He's not that stupid, surely?' she said. 'He must know the route will be crawling with police and that Parliament Square will be the most protected patch of land in the country.'

Finn nodded.

'All true – but it still feels to me like he's going to try something.'

Paulsen surveyed the flat as if it held the answer somehow.

'Why would he hold these three people responsible for what happened to his boy? Freya Appleton and Brandon Challis were convicted of the murder. More than that – the inquiry named every official who was deemed responsible and he hasn't gone after any of them.'

'I can't answer that – but I've got some suspicions,' said Finn. He took a breath and gave himself a moment to think. 'I need to head into Westminster to oversee the operation there. We're literally running out of time now.'

'Why don't you just call the march off? It's madness to go ahead with it,' said Paulsen. 'Claire can't attend a rally that isn't being held.'

Finn was torn.

'What can Best actually do? Like you say, it's all loaded against him, and it's a fantastic chance – maybe our only one – to catch him. I think we have to take it. It's Claire he wants and there's no way we'll allow him to get to her.'

The truth was, it wasn't Finn's call to make. It went above his head – Skegman's too, for that matter – but he knew the DCI had been making the case to the powers that be to let them proceed. It was a statement of trust in Finn's judgement that he hoped didn't prove misplaced. He could almost hear the questions that would come afterwards if this went tits up – *'Are you sure DI Finn was mentally fit enough?'*

For all that, proceeding with the rally still felt like the right call. More than anything else, he had to learn to trust his own judgement again.

'So what do you want me to do?' said Paulsen.

Finn looked around the flat one more time, his eyes settling on the picture of Thomas Best on the mantelpiece – the twinkly smile of a dead child.

'This is a man who lost his son in the most horrific circumstances possible. Go and talk to the people who know him. Let's see if we can't try and fill in some of these gaps.'

34

Emma stared at the little boy and watched him lick the top of his chocolate cream frappuccino. She reached behind her and grabbed another thick syrupy concoction and passed it to his mother, who greeted it with equally greedy anticipation.

'Mind if I take my lunch break now?' she asked her shift supervisor, who gave her a quick nod as he turned to take the next customer's order. As usual, she took the short walk down to St James's Park to eat the sandwich she'd made at home earlier. If her colleagues watched her closely, then they might have noticed that she never removed her green work cap when she went outside. Instead, she pulled it even further down and kept her gaze very much directed at the pavement.

As she got closer to the park, she saw the crush barriers in place for the rally later, the podium being erected for the speeches. She wouldn't be joining them, much as she wanted to. There'd be TV cameras and photographers and she couldn't take the risk. Anyway, it all seemed a little too late. She'd run out of ways to comfort Benjamin. There'd been so many phone calls over the last few months where she'd tried to keep his morale up, but it now felt like she'd run out of words.

More than anything else, after the week just gone, she simply wanted him to be safe, however this played out. She was almost wondering if being deported might not be the lesser of two evils. And evil was the right word – she knew that better than anyone. Sitting down on a bench close to Horse Guards Parade, she watched the tourists meandering up towards Buckingham Palace, before retrieving her lunch from her bag.

She'd originally met Benjamin when he'd been working for the organised crime gang. They were people she'd known only too well herself and he'd stood out from the rest of them immediately. There was a quietness about him that she'd liked – most of the men she'd known in her life were the very definition of toxic masculinity. Their identities came from physical strength, not showing weakness, and rejecting any displays of emotion.

But there was none of that about him and it fascinated her, given the world he was operating in. As she got to know him better, she found someone who was also genuinely interested in her. Again, there hadn't been too much of that over the years. He yearned for family and companionship, perhaps because he'd lost everyone close to him so early in his own life. It was something else that they shared. For a time, they'd enjoyed the tantalising possibility of starting their own family – but all that now felt like a distant daydream.

Time, she finally accepted, had caught up with them. The crowd would gather in Parliament Square and Claire Beacham would trade barbs with the Home Secretary in the House of Commons later. But after the shouting stopped, Benjamin would be sentenced and the government would finally get their way. And then she'd be alone again, still looking over her shoulder. Sooner or later, the one thing she feared – even more than losing Ben – would happen; it felt as inevitable as everything else.

Over my dead body, she thought with a sudden rush of fury.

She finished off her sandwich and threw a remaining bit of crust for the pigeons to feed on. As they clustered around, she delved into her bag again and extracted a mobile phone. It was a burner, of course; one she'd bought for this purpose some months ago. She hadn't wanted to use it unless it was absolutely necessary and now it felt like the moment had arrived. *Over my dead body.* The words repeated in her mind. She punched in a number – one burnt into her memory – and put the handset to her ear. The voice that answered was exactly as she remembered, dry as dust, with that ever-present base note of menace. It made her shiver.

'Who is this?' growled Ray Spinney.

'Hello, Dad,' she said.

Spinney had been walking alone through Clowes Wood when he took the call. He hated being cooped up and had begun to enjoy these walks in the Kent woodland. They helped with the increasing sense of despair he was feeling, not that there was anyone close enough to observe this. Fuller's main job now was to make sure the stolen money was reaching the laundering network. There were other networks in play too, to make sure the correct amount of money was there to complete the Doll Street purchase, and Spinney had been busy juggling plates. But all the way through had been that underlying sense of failure. It was an unfamiliar sensation, together with the helplessness that came with it.

As he walked through the woods he'd been considering his next steps, limited though they were. Benjamin's decision to hand himself in had pretty much taken any element of control he had over the situation out of his hands. He'd all but decided to return to mainland Europe again, when out of nowhere – here she was, the person this had all ultimately been about. When he heard her voice, his heart missed a beat. Violent criminals like Fuller and his ilk were just children, tools in a toolbox to be used, but Emma Spinney had power over him like no other living human. She was his greatest achievement and simultaneously his greatest adversary – because she knew him better than anyone else.

'Hello,' he said. 'Don't suppose you fancy telling me where you are?'

He strained to listen to the ambient noise behind her. There was heavy traffic, the sound of bird wings flapping, small children laughing too. She was somewhere public, not even bothering to make a call like this discreetly, which he found oddly irritating.

'You know I'm not going to tell you that,' she said.

'So why have you called me then?'

'Because I want you to leave Benjamin alone.'

Spinney's mouth curled into a smile and he took a lungful of the clean forest air.

'I think it's pretty obvious that's out of my hands now.'

'Is it?' she said. 'I know what you're like – you've got slugs under every stone and you never give up when you want something. So I'm asking you, begging if you want – if you've got people in Cromarsh – leave him alone.'

'If I had people in Cromarsh, we wouldn't be having this conversation.'

There was a moment of silence and he guessed she was trying to work out whether he was lying or not. The truth was he *did* have people in the prison, but not enough of them and not in the positions he needed them to be.

'Just let me go, Dad,' she said. 'Forget me.'

'Not a chance. Not today, not ever. I *will* find you . . .'

'And then what will you do?'

He breathed heavily down the line, unable to answer the question.

'You're absolutely nothing without the threat of violence, are you?' she said. 'Tell me – what will you do when you find me?'

'Emma . . . I'm your blood. Your only blood—'

'Don't I know it,' she said, cutting in. 'Didn't seem to bother you when Mum was dying of cancer, did it? You could have helped her – used all that stolen money of yours to make her final days easier. But you didn't lift a finger. So much for blood.'

'Your mother and I split up years ago . . .'

'She died in agony. I was there.'

For a moment he was transported to another time and place. He'd met Emma's mother Angela in the late 1990s, just before his criminal career had really taken off. He'd been in his late forties and all but given up on the idea of a lasting relationship – it wasn't as if letting people into his world came naturally – but Emma had come along as a surprise a few years later and stolen his heart. While his feelings for Angela eventually calcified and died, his love for his daughter had only grown stronger. He'd never thought that his bloodline mattered before she was born – but as he'd got older, living his life in the shadows, she'd become *everything*. His only problem had been telling her that.

What he hadn't foreseen was the schism that had developed between them. Initially, he'd screened her from the full extent of what he did for a living, but she wasn't stupid and he was careless in front of her. Despite his protestations, she slowly began to fully comprehend who and what he was. The crack in their relationship became too wide to bridge and she disowned him, breaking his heart in the process. The thing he now wanted from his remaining time on this Earth was to get her back – irrespective of her feelings on the matter.

'Do you know what?' she said. 'These last few years – when you disappeared to whatever stone you crawled under – I hoped Covid would get you. That you'd die alone somewhere, forgotten and ignored. If there was any justice for Mum, that's what should have happened.'

The words stung but he didn't let it show.

'I'm not just going to let you go, Em. You understand that, don't you?'

'Of course I do – you made your point when you murdered that prison officer. But you're never, ever going to find me and *you* need to understand that.'

He felt his temper rising as it always did when someone blocked him.

'Surrender isn't in my nature, love. It's not what I do. I will *always* be looking for you.'

'And Benjamin won't ever tell you where I am. So please, I'm asking you – leave him out of this.'

Spinney gave a reedy chuckle.

'If I get even a chance, I'll break every bone in his body and I won't think twice about it. Alternatively, you can end this and agree to see me.'

She took a sharp intake of breath and briefly he thought he'd got through to her.

'I'll take my chances. Like you say – if you could get to him, you already would have. If he's deported, then there'll be no one left who can tell you where I am.' She paused to let that sink in. 'So know this – I'm my father's daughter. And if you ever find yourself in a room with me again, I swear I'll do all that shit to *you*, old man. And worse.'

The phone went dead and Spinney couldn't stop a smile from slowly spreading across his face.

35

Mattie Paulsen hadn't visited many betting shops in her life – in fact, she couldn't ever remember setting foot in one before. On the odd occasion when she'd walked past an open door, they'd looked to her like a home for the living dead. Blank-faced punters in need of a good wash, staring at TV screens and charts trying to divine some sort of profound meaning from them. There was an off-putting waft of fast food and stale sweat too which always seemed to accompany the places. She was currently standing in a branch in Peckham that was doing nothing to challenge her preconceptions.

A quick phone call had confirmed that Daniel Best's employment details were still up to date. He'd been working here as a cashier when Freya Appleton and Brandon Challis murdered his son. It didn't take Paulsen long to see from the staff's wary reaction that they'd all been on a journey of their own with this too. There was a side to stories like Best's that the public never saw, she thought. People having to carry on after tragedy, and those around them forced to accompany them whether they liked it or not. His colleagues here had probably been the same ones slapping him on the back and buying him beers when Thomas was born.

The shop's manager was a hard-faced woman called Stella who wouldn't have looked out of place on one of the Territorial Support Group teams. She showed Paulsen to a small kitchen area behind the cash tills and got straight to it.

'What's happened to Dan?' she said.

'We need to find him as a matter of urgency and I was wondering if you might be able to help?' said Paulsen.

'He's been off sick all week – I've no idea where he is.'

'What's the matter with him?'

Stella sized her up for a moment, as if she was a punter querying a mistake on a betting slip.

'Stress. It's not really a surprise – his mother died of cancer last month. It'd been coming for a while, and I don't think he's got anyone left now, so he's on his own. I won't lie to you; we were all a bit concerned when we heard she'd finally passed. I think she did a lot to keep him out of trouble over the last year or so.'

'What do you mean by trouble?' said Paulsen.

For the first time, Stella began to look uncomfortable.

'There have been ... some disciplinary issues with him.' Paulsen raised an eyebrow and Stella sat up, straightening her red company top. 'Inappropriate behaviour – nothing sexual, I should add,' she said hurriedly. 'But there were some problems with his temper, snapping at colleagues – punters as well – that sort of thing.'

'How bad?'

'He didn't cross any lines, but he's been treading on a few for a while. There's been a fair bit of tolerance, what with his mum's illness and everything. You have to understand – we do get some testing situations here at times. The clientele isn't always the easiest and there's obviously the situation with his son to factor in too. So we've probably let quite a lot go that we wouldn't have done with another member of staff.'

'How do people get on with him here – is he popular?'

She mulled it.

'There's sympathy for him – after everything he's been through. The pandemic made things worse – I don't think all that time in lockdown helped up here.' She tapped the side of her head. 'But I don't want to give you the wrong idea about him – Dan's basically a decent bloke.'

Paulsen digested this for a moment.

'Have you ever heard him talk about the MP, Claire Beacham?' Paulsen asked.

Stella nodded immediately.

'Oh yeah – he hates her. Blames her for Thomas's death.'

Paulsen felt a jolt of adrenaline and fought to keep the reaction from showing on her face.

'Has he ever explained why?'

'No – just says that she's got blood on her hands. He's never elaborated on that and none of us have ever pushed him when he brings the subject up. I know he was never happy about the inquiry that happened – said the real villains had gone unpunished. I think we all just assumed he needs someone to blame to help him deal with it. I mean, everyone blames MPs for something, don't they?'

Paulsen listed the names of the three murder victims, but Stella shook her head blankly.

'No, never heard him mention anyone else. It's only ever Beacham he seemed to have a problem with.' Suddenly it seemed to dawn on her why she was being asked. 'Oh God – what's he done?'

When Paulsen returned to Cedar House, she found Finn up to his arms working on the security operation for Parliament Square. The rest of the team was working flat out too on the hunt for Best, but there'd been no sightings of him. Claire had been kept up to date with developments and was still intent on making her speech later. Neil Plaskitt was also in the incident room, watching the activity there with a detached interest.

Finn listened carefully as Paulsen updated him with what she'd learnt from her trip to the bookies. He called Plaskitt over and got her to share it with him too. The psychologist looked like he was sucking on a non-existent sweet for a moment as he thought the information through.

'Sounds like his mother's death was the trigger – but this has been festering,' he said finally, before catching the look on Paulsen's face and giving her a sour glare. 'Yes, I know that sounds obvious, but the inquest into his son's murder and the inquiry that followed should have brought him some closure. It clearly didn't, and that's because sometimes things can be *too* neat. The killers are in jail, the authorities who messed up all lost their jobs. Everyone culpable was identified.'

'I don't understand,' said Paulsen. 'Are you saying that wasn't enough for him?'

Plaskitt nodded, almost dismissively.

'Exactly that. Intellectually, all the outstanding questions were answered. But emotionally, I don't think he can stop asking himself *why* this happened and why it wasn't prevented. Essentially that's why he's killed these people – because it's helping to give him that sense of closure.'

'But what did he think they'd all done?' said Finn.

Plaskitt shrugged.

'You'll have to ask him that. I can only give you the shape of what I think this is about.'

'And Claire?' said Paulsen.

'She's clearly the biggest villain of the lot, for some reason – but again, only he can tell you why.'

'We know they met – when she was a local councillor,' she said.

'That's the interesting thing,' said Finn. 'I spoke to her while you were out and she remembers that meeting. It was brief – because she had to leave for an appointment – but she said she followed it up afterwards and wrote to him. There was no comeback and everything seemed pretty straightforward – or so she says.'

'What was the meeting about?' said Paulsen.

'Thomas, obviously. She couldn't really remember the detail of it – a range of concerns he had about the situation. I suspect he could see the threat to the boy was very real and no one was listening. He—'

Finn broke off because Skegman was standing in the door-way. The DCI caught his eye and motioned at him to join him.

'Anti-corruption investigators are with Dave McElligott in your office,' said Skegman once they'd returned to the privacy of his own office. 'They didn't want to wait – I suspect the news will be all over the station within the hour.'

Finn, out of nowhere, had a burning urge for a double Scotch.

'Do you want me to say anything? Sami's radar's already on full alert,' he said.

'No,' said Skegman. 'This is out of our hands now. I'll give you the all-clear just as soon as it's given to me. Where are we with Best?'

Finn explained what Paulsen had discovered and Plaskitt's interpretation of the situation. Skegman nodded.

'If Beacham really is the one he blames for his son – for whatever reason – then the only way he can get closure is by finishing the job. But if that's what he wants, why didn't he do it at the constituency office when he had the chance?'

Finn blew through his cheeks.

'Maybe the PC interrupted him before he could. But the rally later is a bigger stage – right at the heart of government. It becomes less personal and more symbolic. If that's how he's thinking. I mean – it has all been symbolic with him so far, with the head, tongue and hand.'

'So what's your plan?' said Skegman.

'There'll be personal protection officers with Claire at all times and a covert surveillance team close by. There'll also be an arrest team on hand in case Best is identified before he gets to the square. There'll be two armed response vehicles patrolling the area and some armed officers on foot as well. I've asked Jackie to be at the Special Operations Centre in Lambeth. She can monitor the CCTV feeds and stay on top of the communication links with the teams on the ground.'

'And where will you be?'

'In Parliament Square.'

Skegman gave him a sideways look.

'Shouldn't you be at the Operations Centre overseeing it?'

'Probably,' said Finn.

There was a knock at the door and Ojo entered, looking at Finn.

'Sorry to interrupt. We've just had a call from Claire Beacham's office. It's Benjamin Ngomo at Cromarsh Prison – he wants to talk to you and Claire immediately.'

Finn frowned with frustration.

'I'm up to my eyes. Is it important?' he replied.

Ojo nodded.

'Apparently.'

Finn looked at the clock on the wall and rolled his eyes.

'What are you doing right now, Jacks?'

'I'm sorry,' said Ojo forty-five minutes later as she met with Claire and Grant Lassiter outside the main gate of Cromarsh Prison. 'The DI sends his apologies – but he's obviously got his hands full right now.' She glanced over at the personal protection officer who'd escorted Claire. He nodded in acknowledgement then headed back to wait in his car.

'That's okay – in the circumstances, I quite understand,' said Claire.

'Any idea what this is about?'

'No,' said Lassiter. 'He just called us out of the blue, said it was extremely urgent and he didn't want to do it over the phone.'

A short time later, the three of them were waiting in a side room near the jail's visiting hall as Benjamin was brought in by a prison officer to join them. He looked jumpy straight away and barely seemed to notice Ojo as she introduced herself. He waited until they were alone and then explained exactly who his girlfriend was.

'Emma *Spinney*?' said Ojo. 'As in, Ray Spinney's daughter? Why the hell didn't you mention this before?'

'Because I couldn't – I had to protect her,' he said evenly.

Her jaw hadn't actually dropped, but suddenly lots of things seemed to make more sense – even if she didn't quite understand the how or why yet. Lassiter was frowning while Claire simply looked bemused.

'Emma's father is the man behind those armed robberies?' said Claire slowly. 'Behind the Stansted heist too? The same person responsible for Terry Merchant's death?'

Benjamin nodded.

'Is that why he tried to free you – because you're her boyfriend?' said Ojo.

'Yes – but that wasn't to help me. He hasn't seen her in years and he's desperate to find her. I'm the only person who knows where she is.'

Ojo let that sink in for a moment.

'The man has people everywhere – he got an ex-police detective murdered at Brazely Prison a few years ago. Are you telling me he couldn't have got to one inmate in here to get this information from you?'

Benjamin smiled unexpectedly.

'He did try when I first arrived – he got someone to have a go, but I was able to fight them off and they didn't try again. His preferred tactic is to use leverage – he likes to threaten people close to you. Except he couldn't with me because I haven't got anyone. Both my parents are dead and I've got no other family.'

Ojo nodded.

'You're the only person who knows where his daughter is and you're on the brink of being deported . . .'

'Exactly – and when that happens, he's terrified he'll lose her for good. The attack on the prison van was an act of desperation.'

'I don't understand,' said Claire. 'If she doesn't want anything to do with him, what's he trying to achieve? All this is just for a father/daughter conversation?'

Benjamin shook his head.

'Spinney treats people like possessions, even his own daughter. If he gets his hands on her – he will *take* her. Do you understand? Whether she wants to go with him or not.'

Claire looked at him, appalled.

'Why the urgency, Benjamin?' said Ojo. 'Why are you only telling us this now?'

'Because I'm worried – I don't think Emma's thinking straight. I think she's getting reckless, and that's the biggest mistake she could make. He won't stop looking for her. If the worst happens and I do end up on a plane in a few days' time, I'm scared about what will happen.'

'You want her protected?' said Lassiter.

Benjamin nodded, looked over at Ojo.

'If I tell you where she is – can you guarantee her safety?'

36

'It looks like she's been lying to her employers about where she was living,' said Ian Towler, the NCA's senior investigating officer, a tall bear of a man who was leading the team investigating the security van raids. He was standing in Skegman's office addressing the DCI, with Finn and Ojo also present. He'd just spent the last hour interviewing Dave McElligott, alongside anti-corruption officers from the Directorate of Professional Standards.

The new intel regarding Emma's identity had been a major breakthrough. Now they knew *why* Terry Merchant had died, what it was that the Handyman was so keen to acquire from Benjamin Ngomo. As soon as he'd received the information from Ojo, Skegman had passed it on to the National Crime Agency, who hadn't wasted any time descending on a Starbucks in the centre of London. The bemused staff there said they hadn't seen the colleague they knew as 'Emma Smith' since her shift had ended earlier that afternoon. After taking her address, the NCA team immediately rushed to a small flat in Dollis Hill, only to find no trace of her there either.

'Did we know Spinney had a daughter – any family at all, for that matter?' asked Finn.

Towler nodded.

'Our most up-to-date intel was that she was estranged from him – has been for some years. Clearly, he wants a family reunion, though none of us realised how badly.'

'There's something I don't quite understand,' said Ojo, addressing Towler. 'I was told you were already *here* when I phoned through the information about Emma.'

Skegman looked awkwardly up at Towler, who gave him a brief nod of consent, and the DCI told her about McElligott. Finn couldn't watch and looked down at the floor as he listened. His own feelings about what had happened were still extremely raw. He was conscious too that Ojo had been McElligott's DI for the past six months.

'You are kidding me,' said Ojo instantly. 'The little bastard – the little *fucking* bastard.'

'It goes without saying that you need to keep this to yourself for the time being,' said Towler. Ojo was about to respond when Finn interrupted.

'Park it, Jacks,' he said. 'We've got an operation that takes precedence right in front of us. We need to focus on that.' He tapped his wrist. 'And get a shift on . . .'

He was very conscious that the rally in Parliament Square was getting closer and closer. The demonstrators would already be on their way to begin their march at the BBC's headquarters in Portland Place and he was keen to get moving before they arrived. Spinney was Towler's problem; Finn was more concerned about catching a killer.

'How long has McElligott been working for Spinney?' queried Ojo, as if she hadn't heard Finn speak.

'Only a matter of days,' Towler replied, and Ojo immediately put it together.

'So Dave helped him with those raids – effectively got Terry Merchant killed?'

Towler nodded.

'He gave them the name of the CHIS, essentially set up the decoy near Heathrow that blindsided us on the day.'

Ojo looked furious, then – just as it had affected them all – her anger gave way to shock as the impact of it sank in.

'Alex is right, Jackie,' said Skegman. 'Right now you both need to be thinking about Daniel Best – and keeping Claire Beacham out of harm's way.'

'How was Claire at the prison earlier?' Finn asked Ojo.

'Reached her limit of how much shit she can absorb, I think. When I left her, she was heading back to Portcullis House to put the finishing touches on her speech.' She turned to look at Towler. 'So what happens to McElligott now? Does he just vanish into a puff of smoke, never to be seen again?'

The NCA man shook his head.

'Not quite. If we can keep news of his arrest from getting out, then I think we might be able to use him to bait a trap for Spinney. We know he has an interest in Beacham and your investigation – we can use that to our advantage. It's a bit of a long shot, but I think we have to try. That's why it's so important we keep this between ourselves for the moment.'

Ojo nodded, beginning to calm down.

'I get it. It's just – we've worked together for a long time. I mean – Dave's a tool, a first-class, grade-A tool, always has been – but I never thought he was bent.'

'None of us did,' said Finn.

Ten minutes later Finn was on his way out of the building. He was trying to think through what Daniel Best might be planning and where he was likely to be right now. The rally had been rescheduled relatively late following Benjamin's return into custody, so he wouldn't have had time to prepare anything elaborate. This was a man grief-stricken by the loss of his son, the pain doubled down by the recent death of his mother.

'Let's not be judging people by their grief, eh?' said Karin.

Finn was about to head to the car park when he checked himself, suddenly aware that this might be the last chance he'd get to talk to Dave McElligott before Towler took him away. He headed back to his office, which still had the same 'do not disturb' notice written in biro taped to the door. An NCA officer was in there with him – it was minor miracle the news hadn't leaked out to the rest of the station yet.

'The NCA want to use you to bait a trap for Spinney,' said Finn, getting straight to it. 'I think Towler's going to come and talk to you again shortly. How do you feel about helping them with that?'

It wasn't a foregone conclusion – McElligott was going to go to prison, there was no doubt about that. As an ex-police officer, things were already going to be very difficult for him in there – betraying Spinney would take that risk to another level. Whatever mitigations were gained by helping the NCA, Finn doubted they'd offset the target he'd be putting on his back.

'I'd be up for that,' said McElligott.

'You understand the risk?'

In the circumstances, it was probably a stupid question.

'I'm going to rot in a cell for God knows how many years now, guv. I'd like to have at least *something* to cling on to – to make me feel good about myself. It might make a difference later.'

Finn gave a small nod to the NCA officer.

'Thank you – I'll let them know.'

Finn rose to his feet and they looked each other in the eye, as if aware this was the last time they'd be able to talk like this. The next time they were likely to meet would probably be in court.

'Wait,' said McElligott quickly. 'There's something I wanted to tell you before they move me. It's a small detail from the last time I spoke to Spinney – it's been nagging at me. He wanted to know all about the murder investigations.'

'You've already told us that,' said Finn. 'We think it's because of Claire Beacham's work with Benjamin Ngomo. He's the only person who knows where his daughter is.'

McElligott looked momentarily surprised as he absorbed the information, then shook his head.

'There's something else. He wanted to be kept informed if I heard anything about Michael Beacham.'

The NCA officer was paying close attention now too.

'Michael? Did he give any indication why?' said Finn, remembering his previous reservations about the man.

'No. I've been thinking about that while I've been sitting down here. I reckon it might have something to do with the collapse of the Doll Street deal. The timing of it seems very coincidental. I can't back this up with any hard evidence – but I think it's possible Spinney was involved in that somehow.'

Finn tried to make sense of it.

'If you're going to launder money – lots of it – high-value property is an excellent way to do it.'

McElligott nodded.

'That's what I thought too,' he said. 'You think I might have a future in this game, guv?'

The information about Michael was rattling around Finn's brain as he made his way towards the front entrance. If there was a connection, it would have to wait. He looked up and saw Jackie Ojo striding towards him in her coat. Marching would be a better word, her footsteps amply illustrating her mood. She saw which corridor he'd come from and guessed where he'd been.

'How's he doing?' she said.

Finn looked around to check they were alone.

'Says he wants to help the NCA.'

Ojo considered it for a moment.

'Bit fucking late now. It was Ray Spinney he sold himself out to – not some street-level drug dealer. There must have been a thought process to it, a point where he could have backed out or even told us where to find the fucker. It was a cold-blooded choice. That's what makes me angry.'

Finn motioned gently at his watch and they both started walking down the corridor towards the car park.

'How's Cassian getting along?' he said, changing the subject, and she visibly brightened.

'Much better, thanks. I had a phone call from the mother of one of the other kids at his school. She was furious – said Cass had been bullying her son.'

Finn looked confused.

'That doesn't sound too brilliant.'

Ojo produced a rare wide beam of a smile.

'Turns out her boy had been giving Cass some grief for a few weeks now. He didn't want to tell me about it and eventually stood his ground. Don't think it got physical – at least not *too* physical – but I gather this lad got the message.'

'Good to hear,' said Finn approvingly, remembering the conversation he'd had with her son the night he'd joined them for dinner.

'He sorted it out for himself which is what's really pleasing me.' She gave Finn a sideways glance. 'By the way – he did mention he'd quite like to go to an American football match with you some time. If you're up for it?'

Finn nodded, rather touched.

'Happy to. Next time there's a game on at Wembley, I'll sort us out some tickets.'

They walked through the main reception area where a handful of stragglers were waiting by the front desk. 'I hope we're still on for that drink on Saturday night,' he added, aware that rather relied on the investigation being concluded by then.

'You're confident,' said Ojo. 'But, hell yeah – if we're in a bar this weekend then maybe even more than one ...' Finn smiled and they went through the double doors and out into the car park. The ground was wet from a recent downpour, the skies an ugly steel grey. 'Incidentally – I've got a request,' she added. 'If the NCA do manage to set a trap for Spinney – I'd like to be part of it, guv. If Dave's involved, I think we've got a legitimate interest.'

Finn thought about it, then nodded.

'Why so keen?'

'Feels personal – because of Dave, obviously, but I've also met Benjamin Ngomo now – and I feel invested in this.'

Finn empathised. They should hate McElligott for what he'd done. There'd be plenty at Cedar House who would when the news broke. But much as he tried, Finn was struggling to feel the anger any more; there was just the personal tragedy of the situation.

'Let's focus on Best right now – once we've got him in a cell, I'll have a word with Towler and see where they're at.'

There was a rumble of thunder above and they both headed away to their cars.

37

Annie Treadwell was standing on the steps of All Souls Church, looking around nervously. Across the road was the opulent five-star Langham Hotel complete with its resplendently dressed doormen outside. A few feet away, adjacent to the church, was the BBC's historic Broadcasting House headquarters. Security guards wearing high-vis jackets were patrolling nearby, eyeing her suspiciously. She peered at them tentatively and then looked beyond at the piazza they were protecting.

Some tired-looking office staff were walking out of the building at the far end, tucking their passes into their pockets. One day, Annie hoped to be one of them. She'd come straight from a lecture at the University of East London where she was studying media and communication, and was fascinated by the brief glimpse through the windows she was getting of the main BBC newsroom.

Delving into her bag, she pulled out the banner she'd made earlier and unfurled it. The words 'Stop the deportation!' were spray-painted in black across it. She smiled with satisfaction at her handiwork then checked her watch. Her friends really ought to have arrived by now and she hoped they hadn't had a change of heart.

'I think everyone's gathering just around the corner,' said a friendly voice behind her. She turned to see a tall bespectacled man with a shaven scalp. He was wearing a long brown raincoat, which looked slightly too big for him. She walked around the curve of the church front, looked where the man had pointed, and smiled as she saw a decent-sized gathering of people carrying placards and banners.

'I was wondering where they'd all got to,' she said as the stranger followed her round. Annie looked up at the darkening sky then down at the flimsy jacket she was wearing.

'It's going to piss down soon, isn't it? I really didn't think this through,' she said. Despite the black clouds above, it was also relatively muggy. Perfect storm conditions, in fact. A new stream of people suddenly appeared from a street behind the church and converged on them. There was an audible increase in the hubbub and she heard someone blow a whistle.

'Looks like we're off,' said the man in the raincoat. Annie hooked her bag around her shoulder, picked up her banner and followed him as he joined the influx. A young man at the front looked around, like a conductor about to start a symphony, then began to shout:

'Show me what democracy looks like!'

A woman next to him answered the call:

'This is what democracy looks like!'

There was a small cheer from the crowd behind and they began repeating the chant as the ragtag group started to move slowly down Regent Street. Annie could see a number of police officers, dressed in full riot gear, discreetly accompanying them now. At first, it seemed like they'd come from nowhere. But as they passed a side street, she saw a convoy of police vans parked one behind another. Above, she could now hear the sound of a helicopter getting closer.

'Typical – what are they expecting, a full-on riot? We're just here to stop a man from being deported. Total overkill,' she said.

But when she turned her head to see if the man in the raincoat agreed, he was gone, lost in the crowd.

Jackie Ojo arrived at the Special Operations Centre in Lambeth and made her way straight to the SOR, the Special Operations Room. A large, high-tech space, it was populated by a dozen or so trained camera operators hunched over screens feeding live images from security cameras dotted around central London. At the far end was a wall-sized screen that dominated the entire room.

The image on it was currently split into four. On one of the feeds, Ojo could see the marchers making their way past Oxford Circus. Another showed the lower half of Regent Street they were heading towards. A third, the feed from Piccadilly Circus and the final one, the scene currently in Parliament Square. Looking around, Ojo could also see print-outs of the various screen grabs of Daniel Best on every desk.

She walked through the room and saw the Gold Commander in charge of the operation and introduced herself. A tall, middle-aged man with dark hair and silver metal-framed glasses, he looked like he could be Finn's slightly more uptight older brother. He greeted her with a glance of irritation.

'Shouldn't your governor be here?' he said.

'DI Finn's at Parliament Square. Given the sensitivity regarding Claire Beacham's protection, he thought it would be better if he was there in person.'

There was some truth to that – though Ojo was fairly sure the commander could guess his real motivation.

'Wanted a piece of the action, did he?' he replied.

Ojo smiled briskly.

'Any potential sightings of Best yet, sir?'

The commander shook his head.

'He'll know *we* know what he looks like. I imagine he'll have taken steps to address that.' He pointed at the big screen where a new single image had appeared, replacing the previous split-screen. From the angle of the shot, sweeping over central London, Ojo could tell it was coming from a police helicopter. 'That's a feed from the camera on NPAS six-one,' continued the commander. 'We're leaving nothing to chance. If Best's out there – we'll find him one way or another.'

The picture flicked back to an overcast Parliament Square and Ojo could see the platform that had been erected there, the spot where Claire would shortly be making her speech.

'I hope you're right,' she murmured.

Finn was striding across College Green and could feel the rain beginning to spit now. He hoped the heavens would open, that it wouldn't just be heavy but biblical. The worse the conditions, the smaller the crowd, the easier this might be. He looked around the square and checked everything was as he expected it to be. He could see Paulsen in the middle distance close to the statue of Millicent Fawcett, talking with a uniform inspector.

As he walked closer, he could see her remonstrating with him and could hear the faint sound of chanting now. As far as he was aware, the demonstrators were still making their way down Regent Street, so he shouldn't be able to hear them yet. He glanced around at the parliamentary estate and over towards Westminster Abbey, but couldn't trace the source of the noise.

Seeing him approach, Paulsen left the inspector and jogged over to join him.

'We've got a problem, guv. There's a separate group of anti-immigration protestors gathering on the other side of Westminster Bridge. We had no advance intel about them at all – and they're on the move now,' she said. Finn put a finger against the earpiece he was wearing and pressed a button on the wire it was connected to.

'GT from MI five-four – are you receiving, over?' he said.

'*Go ahead, MI five-four,*' came the response.

'Have you got eyes on this second group?' he said.

'*Affirmative. There's maybe around twenty or thirty people crossing the bridge. Gold Commander's assessment is there's enough personnel on site to contain them.*'

'Received – thank you. MI five-four out,' said Finn.

He scowled. It was a wrinkle he hadn't been expecting.

'This isn't good – a confrontation creates chaos and chaos gives Best the potential cover to do whatever he's come here to do,' he said to Paulsen.

'We can still stop this,' she replied. 'Seal off the square – call off the rally.'

She hadn't ever really hidden her feelings on that from the start, but before he could respond, the sound of chanting suddenly got louder and they both turned to look at the far corner where the square joined with Westminster Bridge.

A group, nearly all male, was beginning to enter the area now. Police in riot gear were already swarming towards them. They marshalled them to a halt in front of the statue of Winston Churchill. The demonstrators seemed happy to stop; they raised their fists and began chanting, '*Zero tolerance – kick them out!*' in short, sharp bursts. Finn sighed, looked over at Portcullis House and reached for his mobile.

Claire stared out of her office window down at the melee below. She randomly homed in on the face of one of the men chanting by Churchill's statue. He almost looked in pain as he belted out the words, reaching down to find the hate from somewhere deep, before expelling them as force-fully as possible.

'You've done the right thing,' said Lassiter.

Claire nodded slowly. She'd finally, reluctantly, agreed to Finn's plea on the phone to cancel her speech. It had been dangerous enough knowing a killer might have been out there, but she hadn't wanted to incite a potential riot either. The decision made her feel hollow inside though and the fury on the face of the young man outside was depressing her. It seemed to encapsulate the hatred that had been stalking her for the past fortnight.

Her phone buzzed and she looked down, expecting it to be the Whip's office querying if she was still going ahead with the speech. Instead, it was Michael. She let it go to answerphone and tossed the handset on to her desk. He could wait.

'What is the point of me, Grant?' she said, looking out of the window again. Now she could see the marchers carrying placards and banners for Benjamin entering the square from Whitehall. The police were desperately trying to shepherd them away from the other group. She looked for the man she'd been watching earlier – he was now screaming in the face of an officer in front of him who was pushing him back with his shield. Several of the men around him suddenly surged, escaping the cordon and running towards the newcomers.

'What is the point of any of it?' she said.

In the Special Operations Room, Jackie Ojo was watching the chaos unfold. The arrival of the pro-immigration protestors had made things trickier. Officers who'd been tasked to try and pick Daniel Best out from the crowd were now trying to manage an entirely different situation.

'*Sarge!*' she heard someone shout.

320

She looked across and saw a young DC signalling to her. He was standing behind the desk of one of the camera operators and Ojo hurried over to join them.

'Look at this. I think something's happening,' he said.

The operator's fingers were flicking across the keyboard to keep the camera fixed and focused on one particular target. In the middle of the square was a burly-looking man wearing a turquoise sports shirt and tracksuit bottoms. He was holding his shoulder, which rapidly seemed to be shading dark. People were running past, jostling him, and he fell to the grass looking bewildered. Unnoticed in the sea of legs, he then toppled over on to his side.

The DC instructed the operator to pull the camera back to give them an overview. There was another body visible now, a woman lying prone close by, but it didn't seem clear what had happened to her. Near her, a young man stumbled to his knees, dropping his placard, narrowly avoiding getting trampled on.

'Go in closer,' said the DC.

The operator's fingers tapped the keyboard again and the camera zoomed in – a bright red patch of blood was clearly visible on the man's midriff.

'Someone's got a knife,' said Ojo, grabbing her radio.

Finn had retreated to the back of the square, the Houses of Parliament directly opposite, to try and get some sort of sense of what was happening. Above, a police helicopter was buzzing noisily. His main concern was that if Best was there, he might be able to use the confusion to slip away. He couldn't see Paulsen, but the uniform inspector she'd been talking to earlier was using a megaphone, instructing the crowd to disperse.

Finn's earpiece crackled into life and Ojo quickly told him what she'd seen on the camera feed. Finn looked to where she was directing and immediately saw the prone bodies on the ground. Paramedics who'd been on standby for the rally were already rushing towards them. Now he was looking more closely, he could see some of the demonstrators starting to run in panic as they saw people scattered on the ground with blood on their clothes.

There was a new commotion in the far corner where several armed police officers were now sprinting hard towards the entrance to the parliamentary estate.

'GT from MI five-four. What's happening at the main gate?' Finn shouted into his radio.

'MI five-four from GT – someone's broken through . . .'

Armed police from all sides were now hurtling in the direction of the entrance.

'Is it Best?' he yelled into his radio, but there was no response and for a second, all he could see was mayhem.

Paulsen was standing at the corner of the square close to Westminster Abbey, by the podium where Claire had intended to make her speech. She'd heard the same messages on her earpiece and was methodically scanning the scene in front of her. There was a scream only a few yards away and she saw a young woman holding her arm. Blood was leaking out over her hands. Beside her was a bald figure in glasses wearing a raincoat. He turned and Paulsen saw the knife he was holding.

'GT from PS three-three. I've got him,' Paulsen screamed into her radio. 'IC1 male, shaven scalp, thirty to forty years old, wearing a brown raincoat, light blue jeans and white trainers. He's right in front of the rostrum.'

Finn immediately sprinted over towards her. Despite Paulsen's call, there didn't seem to be any officers responding and he guessed that was because the armed units were dealing with the incident at the gate. As he caught up with Paulsen, he caught sight of Best for himself, who immediately held up the knife to the girl's throat.

'One step closer and I'll cut her open . . .' he shouted.

Annie looked too scared to even scream. She was holding her arm, blood flowing down her side on to the grass.

'Daniel – drop the knife. I *know* why you're doing this . . .' said Finn.

'You've no idea why I'm doing this . . .' roared Best, pulling the stricken woman closer now, using her as a human shield.

'Don't be stupid – do you know how many armed police there are here right now?' said Finn. He was acutely aware a camera in the SOR was probably picking this up – that armed officers were already being alerted. He knew once they saw a man holding a knife, things would rapidly spiral, and when the bullets started flying, he couldn't guarantee anyone's safety. The same thought seemed to occur simultaneously to Best. Without warning, he plunged the knife into the woman's side, threw her straight at Finn and ran. Paulsen immediately set off in pursuit as Best headed behind the podium towards Westminster Abbey.

Finn held the stabbed woman and carefully brought her down to the ground. He put his hand over the wound and felt warm blood streaming over it. He called over to a pair of paramedics treating another victim and one raced over to help him. Finn could now see Paulsen chasing after Best and reached for the button on the wire he was wearing again.

'GT from MI five-four – the suspect is escaping on foot, heading west towards Broad Sanctuary. I need urgent assistance *now*.'

Best was sprinting past the front of the Abbey now. Despite the chaos, there were still, bizarrely, sightseers unaware of what was happening on the other side of the podium. He charged through a group, scattering them as Paulsen tried to keep up. A police van sped up Broad Sanctuary and screeched to a halt. Three TSG officers jumped out and Best desperately tried to change course again. Paulsen launched herself at him, dragging them both down on to the pavement. He tried to rise, but she held him firm as the TSG officers swarmed on to them.

38

Six people were hospitalised in total. Three were in intensive care at nearby St Thomas's with one still critical. The Met had formally identified Daniel Best as the Parliament Square terrorist and it hadn't taken the press long to recall where that name had come up before. Historical pictures of Thomas Best's father were already appearing on the rolling news channels as the horrific details of what had happened to the child were recycled once again.

At Cedar House, Finn was in his office preparing for the interview with Best. Earlier – just ahead of the information being released publicly – he'd broken the news of his arrest to Claire. She'd been subdued as much as relieved – pleased that no one else could get hurt now. But she was as interested as he was in *why* all this had happened and he could tell that until that question was answered, she wouldn't be able to put this behind her.

The mood in the incident room on their return had been far from celebratory as well – they'd caught their man but it had come at a price and they all knew it. Things could have been a lot worse, and might yet still be. Finn felt he owed all of them – Claire, the victims, his own team – to make sure they got to the truth.

His concentration was disturbed as Paulsen put her head round his door.

'I thought you'd want to know – the duty solicitor's arrived so we can begin with Best if you're ready?'

He looked up and frowned.

'Are you okay?' he said.

She had an ugly bruise under one eye that was starting to discolour badly and a nasty red weal on the cheek next to it.

'I'm fine – it's all superficial. I suspect I'll have a thumping headache later though,' she said. Finn nodded and rose to his feet. He grabbed his jacket and a sheaf of papers off his desk, and headed over to join her, but she remained where she was.

'What did you mean when you said you knew why he was doing this?'

He paused as he remembered the moment in the square earlier.

'When you're bottling up that much grief – sometimes you just need to be listened to,' he said. 'And in the end, he found a way to make us all listen.'

It took a couple of hours before they were able to interview Best. He'd needed checking over by a doctor and had received some medical treatment for the injuries he'd sustained during his arrest. He wore a bandage around one hand and there were some small cuts and bruises to his face too. Finn and Paulsen were in the interview room with the duty solicitor while Skegman and Ojo were watching via a feed on a monitor upstairs.

'They're calling you a terrorist,' began Finn. 'Is that how you see yourself?'

Best had been sitting quietly throughout the formalities and it had been hard to read what was going on in his mind. Finn suspected the man was still in shock himself.

'Call me a terrorist by all means, but I'm not an extremist,' he said, as if starting a topic of debate around the dinner table.

'Why not?' said Finn. 'I'd say the word fits you perfectly.'

'Because I'm just an ordinary guy and what happened to me would push anyone into . . . places they didn't think they would ever go.'

'So what *did* push you there?' probed Paulsen. 'It's obviously related to Thomas, but why did you go after these three – Mazurek, Vance and Whitcombe?'

Best carefully took a sachet of sugar, tore it open and tipped the contents into the mug of tea that was sitting in front of him. For a moment the only noise in the room was the chink of spoon on china.

'You wouldn't understand,' he said quietly. 'How could you?'

'You clearly hold them responsible in some way,' said Finn, but Best didn't respond.

'I've done a lot of reading about what happened after Freya Appleton and Brandon Challis were convicted of your son's murder,' said Paulsen. 'There was a pretty exhaustive inquiry – a large number of people were held accountable.'

'Like I say – you wouldn't understand,' repeated Best tonelessly.

'I mean, there wasn't just one inquiry,' persisted Paulsen. 'Lambeth Council initiated an internal audit serious case review. The General Medical Council looked at the doctors who'd been treating Thomas up until his death, not to mention the external inquiry ordered by the Secretary of State. Lord Parnell's recommendations were—'

'Don't talk to me about Lord *fucking* Parnell,' said Best, snapping finally.

'Why not? You were quoted at the time as welcoming his conclusions,' said Finn.

'I know. You say these things because that's what the world expects you to do. But you have to understand what it *felt* like. I didn't know any of the people they named – they didn't mean a thing to me. It was like someone needed to be blamed – so they found scapegoats.'

'They weren't scapegoats – they were genuinely culpable,' said Finn. 'I've read through it too—'

Best shook his head, waving a hand dismissively.

'You're not hearing me. I was *told* justice had been done – but it didn't *feel* like it.'

'So we're back to the three people you killed. We know you met with each of them in the months before Thomas's death,' said Paulsen.

Best winced as he remembered.

'I spoke to Mazurek at his office. Told him what was happening – but he didn't listen to me, didn't *think*. So I tried my GP, told her – but she never followed it up – didn't *speak*. And I told that PC, the night I went round to try and get my boy back – and he didn't *act*. Three of them. And all it would have taken is just one to do their job properly and Tom might still be alive now.' He was sitting bolt upright as he said the words, his eyes shiny with emotion.

Finn thought about every conversation he'd ever had with an agitated member of the public, complaints he'd passed on but never chased up. Could all three of them have done more? It was impossible to say now. Best seemed to sense what he was thinking and leant forwards.

'These institutions are supposed to be there to help you. But when it mattered, they failed me – all of them. It was like I saw this country for what it truly is, not what you think it is most of the time. And once you understand that, you can't ever see the world in the same way again. Nothing "pushed me over the edge" – everything just reframed.'

As Finn listened, it was hard not to think of the alternative reality that might have been. The one where Lukasz Mazurek's recommendations had been acted on or Ruth Vance's email

328

had been followed up, where Freya Appleton and Brandon Challis had been stopped. The one where Daniel Best was now quietly raising his son like any other father.

'What about Claire Beacham – what was her connection to all this?' said Finn. 'We know you met with her just before Tom's death.'

Best looked at him as if he were stupid.

'I was told she could help me, that she would listen – that she wasn't like other politicians. That she was someone who would get up off her arse and actually *do* something.'

He broke off, shaking his head as if the idea was now patently ridiculous.

'So what happened?' said Finn.

There was a pause as Best took himself back into the moment.

'I explained clearly to her what was going on, said my boy needed help – that he was being abused and that if someone didn't take action, something terrible was going to happen. And do you know what she did? She cut that meeting short and closed the conversation down.'

Even now, years after the event, there was fury at the memory. Out of the corner of his eye, Finn saw Paulsen frown and sensed she was thinking the same thing as him. This didn't sound like the woman he'd met with, dealt with.

'She said she wrote to you afterwards . . .' he said.

Best snorted with contempt.

'Yeah – she told me she'd *relayed* my concerns . . . a week later, Tom was dead.' His words reverberated around the room. 'I see this woman on television every week, pretending to care – about domestic abuse, that lad in prison and God knows what else. It's all bullshit.'

'Did you go to Parliament Square to kill her today?' said Finn.

The solicitor leant and tried to whisper something to his client, but Best waved him away.

'I've watched her over the years since Tom died, listened to what people say about her. You hear them on the bus or in the supermarket – that she's one of the *good* ones, that she's down to earth, just like you or me.' He shook his head. 'But she isn't. Everything I did was about making her understand that. Maybe I'd have killed her, maybe I wouldn't – what mattered was showing her the truth about herself. And you know what? I reckon I did.'

He sat back and crossed his arms.

'Those people you stabbed in Parliament Square – they didn't do anything to you, or Thomas,' said Paulsen.

'All I did today was speak truth to power – in the only language they understand.'

Finn could see something he recognised in the man's eyes. It was hard not to think about the last six months of his own life, the things he and his counsellor had been talking through.

'Why didn't you come forward, speak to someone? We know your mum died recently – there are people who could have helped you,' he said.

Best laughed.

'Ask for help? Like I did before? Are you taking the piss? I don't *want* to be healed – do you know what it's like to lose a child?' He looked at the two detectives. 'I'll kill myself at some point – that's a promise. Maybe not this week or the next. But one day, when the world looks away again – which it will – then I'll do it.'

'That's how you feel now,' rasped Paulsen. 'People change.'

Best was already shaking his head.

'I won't.'

And Finn knew he meant it.

★ ★ ★

'This could all have been avoided,' said Finn afterwards. He was in Skegman's office where the DCI had poured him a glass of whisky from a bottle he kept for special occasions. 'Three good people dead because none of them pursued Daniel Best's complaints any further. They all passed it on and assumed that would be enough.'

'You can't judge them harshly for that,' said Skegman. 'An angry man making accusations about his ex and her new partner. There's plenty who wouldn't have even looked beyond that. They did their jobs – and had reasonable expectations that others would do theirs. A lot's changed since Thomas Best died though.'

Finn thought about Nina Thornbury and knew that was true. But he wondered about her predecessors, whether even now they truly understood the part they'd played in all this. He gently shook his drink and stared down into the glass as if it contained some sort of truth.

'Is there any update from St Thomas's on the injured?' he said.

Skegman shook his head.

'Annie Treadwell's condition has stabilised.'

In his mind's eye, Finn saw Best thrusting the knife into her body again. At the time he hadn't been optimistic about her chances.

'That's something, at least.' He finished off his drink and held out the glass for Skegman to top up. 'And where are we with Dave McElligott?'

Skegman sighed.

'He's left the building. I spoke to Towler before they took him away – the NCA's going to get him to send Spinney a message on the burner phone he was using. They intend to use his interest in Michael Beacham as bait. If he goes for it, they'll then try and arrange a meet.'

Finn mulled it.

'Spinney's not stupid – he'll smell a trap.'

'Not necessarily. The only people here who know about Dave are you, me and Jacks. Towler thinks Spinney won't be able to resist it.'

Finn shrugged.

'Maybe. Jackie asked me earlier if she could be in on any operation the NCA were preparing.'

'I know,' said Skegman. 'She's been in here asking me the same thing. Towler's open to it – thinks having someone on board who knows Dave might help smooth things. I'm not against the idea – despite everything, he still feels like one of ours.'

'That won't last,' said Finn.

Skegman watched him for a moment.

'You look tired – you should go home and get some rest,' he said.

'I've just had six months sitting on my arse, thanks. Besides, everyone's decamped to the pub – I promised I'd join them for a quick one.'

Skegman arched an eyebrow.

'Drinking with the troops? That's almost borderline sociable behaviour, Alex. All that therapy must have done you some good.'

Finn rolled his eyes.

'Maybe you should give it a go sometime,' he said, heading for the door. 'Might do *you* some good . . .'

But the smile on his face fell away as he strode down the corridor. Whatever victory he was off to celebrate felt extremely hollow.

39

The trap for the Handyman was baited later that evening. McElligott had messaged Spinney and told him that Michael Beacham was a loose end to the investigation that was still being actively pursued. He'd immediately received a phone call back asking him to explain exactly what that meant. McElligott then suggested they talk in person the next day at the same park in Beckenham where they'd met before. A full operation was immediately prepped by the National Crime Agency.

Eight plain-clothed officers would be dotted around the park, with an arrest team nearby ready to move in once Spinney's identity was confirmed. Towler and Ojo would monitor the whole thing from an unmarked police van parked nearby. The expectation was that Spinney would come alone but they were assuming nothing. They hadn't discounted the possibility that he travelled with hench-men, acting as lookouts. For that reason, a couple of armed response vehicles would also be close at hand in case things escalated quickly. Nothing was being left to chance.

McElligott had spent the night in custody at a central London police station. When Ojo arrived for the briefing the following morning, he was in the room just like any other regular officer on the team. As Towler went through the details of the operation, she was watching her former colleague closely. He looked tired and pale, and she guessed he hadn't had much sleep.

After the briefing ended, Towler himself drove Ojo and McElligott into south London for the rendezvous. As they made their way through the traffic, little was said. If Towler had a view of what the other man had done, he was keeping it to himself.

'Do you mind if I ask you something, sarge?' said McElligott suddenly, breaking the silence. They were caught in a jam close to Brixton market and Ojo stopped people-watching to turn and look at him.

'Yes, Dave – what would you like to know?' she said coolly.

'Why are you here? You haven't exactly hidden your contempt for me today.'

That was a bit harsh. She hadn't been overtly unpleasant – she'd simply treated him like any other prisoner in custody.

'What were you expecting – a hug?' she said.

He shook his head.

'I expected nothing – but that's the point,' he said. 'I imagine I'm persona non grata at Cedar House – at every nick in the country now. So I don't understand why *you're* here. You don't have to be – just like Finn, I never had the impression you ever really liked me.'

His bluntness threw her a little, but he wasn't wrong about their relationship.

'Maybe it just doesn't sit right with me to wash my hands of someone,' she said. 'Fuck what every other nick is saying. And frankly, fuck you too, Dave, for what you did – but I'm doing this for myself, as much as for anyone.'

If McElligott was bothered, he didn't show it.

'You've got a son – can you be certain there's no situation where you wouldn't have done the same as me? To protect him, or to secure his future?'

They locked eyes and she didn't answer. This time it was McElligott who sat back and looked out of the window.

At precisely midday, the former detective constable sat down on the same bench in the same bandstand in which he'd met with Ray Spinney before. He was wearing covert body armour for his own protection and fitted with a concealed radio so that he could communicate with the NCA team if he needed to. He waited for a quarter of an hour but no one came. As agreed in the briefing, he then tried to phone Spinney – but there was no reply. After thirty minutes he tried again and after forty-five minutes Towler formally aborted the operation. One of the plain-clothed officers in the park walked over to the bandstand and discreetly handcuffed McElligott again for the return journey. They were about to leave when the prisoner stopped.

'Just give me a second, can you, mate?' he said.

Dave McElligott looked around the peaceful green common for one last time, then walked away into whatever future was awaiting him.

Kenny Fuller watched from the other side of the park and tugged at his ski hat. It was more a nervous tick than because he was genuinely concerned that the scar on the back of his head was showing. He watched McElligott depart with his escort and held his position. When you knew what you were looking for, it wasn't difficult to see who the undercover officers in the park were. Seven or eight different men and women dotted around the place began to disperse simultaneously. He waited briefly then headed for the same gate McElligott and the plain-clothed officer had used to leave. Heading out on to the street, he could see the two men walking ahead. Keeping his pace even so as not to attract attention, he tracked them and watched as they turned into a small cul-de-sac. Out of the corner of his eye, he could see a group of them now standing next to a white van. Discreetly, he pulled his phone out and activated its camera.

'Of course, he knew it was a trap,' said Skegman later as Ojo explained what had happened. 'The old bastard hasn't managed to dodge half the police forces in Europe for Christ knows how long without having a decent nose for these things.'

Finn sighed, not bothering to remind the DCI he'd made much the same point the previous night in the same office.

'How was Dave?' he said to Ojo.

She paused, remembering her last sight of him – being led away, cuffed, head bowed.

'Does it matter any more?' she said.

Finn thought about it and shrugged.

'I suppose he's not our problem now,' he said. 'Do we know how his partner's getting on?'

'I spoke to her this morning,' said Skegman. 'She's still processing it. Part furious with him, part worried *for* him, and absolutely terrified about what it means for her.'

There was a moment as they all took that on board.

'Funny how it all comes back to kids,' said Ojo suddenly.

'How do you mean?' said Finn.

She pursed her lips and blew.

'Dave sold his soul for his unborn child. Daniel Best lost his mind because of what happened to his son. And Spinney's trying to move heaven and earth to find his daughter.'

Finn nodded slowly in agreement.

'On the plus side, the NCA have assured me there's no one else at Cedar House who was implicated,' said Skegman. 'And they've picked up the baton regarding Michael Beacham – if he and Spinney are connected, they can dig into that to their heart's content. As far as I'm concerned, our investigation is closed and we move on.'

He said the words firmly, but Finn shook his head.

'I'm not sure it's going to be that simple. Morale here's rock bottom because of Dave. And then there's Mattie . . . and we haven't really talked about that. She did some excellent work on this – she was the one who first identified Best as a suspect. Are we just going to let her walk away?'

'She wants to be a sergeant – sounds like she's ready to be one, too. You can't stand in people's way, Alex,' said Skegman.

Finn bristled at the words.

'I'll take her out for a beer, guv,' Ojo said gently. 'See where her head's at – nothing's done till it's done.'

'The little bastard sold me out,' said Ray Spinney, looking at the photograph on his phone of Dave McElligott in hand-cuffs. He put the handset back to his ear and glared out of his kitchen window at a small patch of balding wasteland. It was almost as if he were trying to burn a bit more away with his gaze alone.

'How many more of your people do you think they've got to?' said Fuller down the line.

Spinney had immediately suspected a trap when McElligott called and suggested they meet in person, specifying exactly where and when. His reluctance to reveal exactly what Finn's team knew about Michael Beacham had also been a red flag. Simultaneously, the handful of Spinney's remaining other contacts inside the Met had gone quiet.

'I wouldn't like to put a number on it,' he growled.

The NCA was moving and the sense of things spiralling out of his control was there again. Experience and instinct told him now was the time to move on once more. The money they'd stolen in the raids would keep him hidden again for a while yet. But he'd come back to England for Emma, and if there was a principle he believed in, it was that there was always a move you could play. You just had to find it.

He looked down again at the picture on his phone and noticed a woman talking to McElligott. He recognised her – she was one of Finn's team. He'd seen her face in the files he'd been sent on the south London MIT right at the start of this.

'What do you want me to do?' said Fuller.

The original plan had been for all the men involved in the robberies to get well clear of London immediately afterwards. Only Fuller now remained.

'Don't leave just yet, Kenny – I'll be in touch,' said Spinney before ending the call.

He walked over to the kitchen table where his laptop was flipped open and began flicking through some files on its desktop until he found the one he was searching for. A thumbnail of Jackie Ojo appeared and he double-clicked on it. He checked the expanded image against the one on his phone – something about this wasn't quite adding up. Why would Finn's personnel be involved in this? It was the NCA who were leading the hunt for him. He stared at Ojo and an idea began to form. There was *always* a move you could play.

40

Claire Beacham found her husband sitting with a glass of wine at the kitchen table. He'd ordered an Indian takeaway earlier which she'd completely forgotten about.

'I'm sorry, you should have started without me,' she said, sitting down opposite him.

She looked and felt shattered.

'It's alright – I put most of it in the oven to keep it warm. If you're ready though, I'm starving?'

She nodded and he sprang to his feet, swiping a pair of oven gloves from the counter as he went to retrieve the food. 'You were on the phone a long time?' he said.

'I think it's good news. Unofficial word from the Home Office is they're "reassessing" Benjamin's case.'

Michael stopped by the oven and beamed.

'You've forced them into a U-turn – that's fantastic,' he said.

Michael brought the food over and took a seat. She watched as he dived in greedily, spooning an assortment from the array of foil trays into a small mountain on his plate.

The news about Benjamin was a boost, a victory at the end of a week that had battered her from pillar to post. The memory of Lukasz Mazurek's head rolling across the floor of this room was still vivid, but it seemed like weeks ago, not days. Finn had rung her and told her exactly what Daniel Best had said under interview. She hadn't commented, simply thanked him for the information and his efforts on the investigation. But she did remember the day Best had come to see her, remembered ending that meeting early, guiltily remembered only too well why.

'Dig in . . . or I'll end up eating all of this,' said Michael. 'I've got enough of a spare tyre as it is,' he said, slapping his stomach, forcing the bonhomie a little. She hadn't been hungry but the smell of the food was beginning to get to her. Tentatively, she started to take some.

'You said you wanted to talk to me?' she said.

He smiled conspiratorially, tore off a piece of naan bread and chewed on it for a moment.

'I know you feel I've been holding a few things back, that you wanted some explanations from me. Well, now that this nightmare is over, I thought it might be a good time to have that conversation. Especially now that there's something to celebrate.'

He waited for her to say something but she didn't, her face unreadable. He reached down, picked up some print-outs from the chair next to him and passed them across to her. She flicked through them, saw pictures of a vast house, all glass and white stone, a cloudless blue sky above, palm trees and rainbow-coloured plants lining a long driveway. She stared at the images nonplussed.

'The San Fernando Valley. What am I looking at here, Michael?'

And so he explained his plan and how long it had been gestating. The speech was clearly one he'd been preparing for a while, like a pitch at a business meeting. When he finished, he sat back, rewarded himself with a sip of wine and beamed. She looked at him like he was insane.

'This house costs over three million dollars,' said Claire, throwing the print-out back down on the table. 'Where on earth do you think we're going to get that kind of money from?'

'You don't have to worry about that,' he purred. 'I've made an offer. It's a fresh start, a new life. It'll be waiting after the next election – we can be whatever we want to be. After everything that's happened this week, it just feels like the timing's perfect,' he said.

She felt overwhelmed, looked at the pictures again.

'Where's this come from, Michael?' she said. He looked at her, affecting polite confusion.

'You once said you'd like to live in the States—'

'I say a lot of things off the top of my head – what do you imagine we're going to *do* out there?' She held her hands up, bemusement turning to anger. 'We'd need money to live on—'

'Stop worrying about the finances – that's taken care of.'

She looked him directly in the eye as realisation dawned.

'*Taken care of?* Is this what Doll Street was really about?'

He shook his head dismissively.

'I want us to start a family, Claire.' He pointed at the print-out. 'In that house.'

She felt the blood rush from her head, the smell of the food now making her feel sick.

'I can't . . .'

'I know you've always said you didn't want kids. And I believed I felt that way too, which is why I've never pushed the point. But recently . . . something inside me changed. I thought – a different life, a different setting . . .'

She slowly looked up at him.

'You don't understand – I *can't* have children.'

Mattie Paulsen and Nancy Deen were enjoying a cheeky snog on the sofa. Given the week Paulsen had been through, they'd decided to stay in, have a few beers and some pizza, and let Netflix do the rest. As it was, they'd had a *lot* of beer, and the police series they'd been watching had met with Paulsen's unrelenting contempt.

'Everyone's wisecracking – like a nick's full of quick-witted comedians. They're really not – I mean, if I said some of that stuff to Finn . . .'

She'd passed an exaggerated hand over her head. Nancy had started giggling and that's when the snogging had begun.

'It's been ages since we've had a night like this,' said Paulsen, coming up for air.

Nancy groped for her beer can by the side of the sofa.

'Your breath smells of garlic bread,' she said.

Paulsen absently gave her a middle finger and Nancy straightened up as she took a sip from the can.

'So Finn's not happy about you going for this job then?'

Paulsen smiled.

'He's being a big baby. I quite like that. How are you feeling about it now?'

Nancy pondered it for a moment.

'I'm coming round to it, I suppose. I like the idea of more money, obviously.' She took another swig of beer. 'Maybe it *is* time for you to move on. Here's the thing – how far do you want to go in the police? I mean, I can't see you as some sort of management figure. A detective chief superintendent whatever . . .'

'Oi!' said Paulsen. 'Why not?'

'Because you'd be terrible at it. And you know you'd be terrible at it. Managing people, budgets, admin.'

Paulsen frowned, largely because Nancy was right.

'I've never really thought about it.' For a moment she remembered her pursuit of Daniel Best outside Westminster Abbey, her absolute determination to hold him down as the

TSG officers moved in. 'I could see myself as a sergeant though.'

'So I'll say it again – why the rush? You're still out and about doing interesting stuff.'

Paulsen shrugged.

'Don't know what else I'd do.'

'You've changed so much over the last few years,' said Nancy wistfully.

'No, I haven't,' retorted Paulsen. 'I'm exactly the same person – don't get sentimental, it doesn't suit you.'

Nancy rolled her eyes.

'You *have* changed. You used to be all storm clouds and' – she screwed up her face into an impression of Paulsen's familiar scowl of concentration – 'now you're a bit more . . . blue skies and . . .' She gave a goofy grin. Paulsen looked outraged, then began to laugh as Nancy held the expression. They were interrupted by the muffled buzzing of a phone. Paulsen delved into the depths of the sofa and extracted her mobile from under a cushion.

'It's Finn,' she said, checking the display before putting the handset to her ear.

'Something come up?' she said, trying to sound sober.

Nancy made the goofy face again and Paulsen waved a hand at her as he answered.

'Erm . . . no,' said Finn hesitantly. 'I just wanted to say well done. It was your work that led us to Daniel Best. You're ready for a sergeant's job. I'm going to call DCI Khan at the West Command Unit MIT in the morning and give you a recommendation.'

Paulsen smiled the sort of smile she'd never let him actually see in person.

'Thanks – I appreciate that.'

'You deserve it.'

343

'You're fucked off, aren't you?' she said, still smiling.

'Totally,' came the deadpan reply and her smile widened.

'She's right, isn't she?' said Karin.

'Maybe,' said Finn, the grin on his own face still there, as he put the phone down. His evening had been spent processing the events of the week – they'd caught Best, kept Claire safe and no one else had died. But the ghost of Dave McElligott overshadowed everything – together with the accompanying guilt. Calling Paulsen and giving her the credit she was due had made him feel a little bit better. But it would be a while before he got McElligott out of his system.

He was about to settle down in front of the TV with a glass of whisky when his mobile rang again. He didn't recognise the number or the man who greeted him. But it was a voice that stopped you in your tracks – dry as firewood with a hint of old London.

'Detective Inspector Finn?'

'Who am I talking to?' he replied, sitting down at his kitchen table, already sensing this was important.

'A man looking for his daughter.'

It took a split second to make the connection and when it clicked, the voice sounded *exactly* the way Finn thought it probably should.

'Ray Spinney?' he said, any weariness he'd been feeling instantly evaporating.

'I won't piss about,' said Spinney briskly. 'I suspect you have information I want.'

'You want to know where Emma is? And what makes you think I'm going to tell you?' said Finn.

'Because I've been here many times before. Dealt with many men who claim their principles can't be compromised. Until, of course, they are.'

Finn realised that was very true – he was just the latest in a long line of people to receive a cold call from the Handyman. He wondered what he'd be offered first, carrot or stick. That was at least one positive about his situation: neither would get Spinney very far. He had nothing to gain and nothing to lose.

'You're wasting your time – there's nothing you can do that will change my position.'

There came a rasping sound which might have been laughter.

'Do you know what I've learnt over the years? That everyone's got their vulnerability. A need for money or to protect people who are important to them. Which is it with you?'

Finn almost smiled.

'Well ... I've never really been motivated by cash and I've no surviving family for you to threaten. So just like our mutual friend Benjamin, there's not much there for you to work with, I'm afraid.'

There was a pause.

'I'm aware of your circumstances. Words are important to me, Detective Inspector. I am not a man who is profligate with them. When I say *everyone* has a vulnerability, I mean everyone,' said Spinney.

Finn's mind was racing. This was an opportunity and he was trying to form a strategy on the hoof – to use these precious seconds somehow.

'You have no leverage over me and I'm guessing most of your usual sources have dried up. So I think this is something of a desperate move – which tells me more about where you're at than anything I should be worried about.'

'You'd be foolish to underestimate my reach.'

Finn could see how this man intimidated people. He was right, he didn't waste words – he spoke largely in statements, each point punctuated with the same unnerving detachment.

'I don't know – the NCA are determined to find you and you won't leave the country this time – not with Emma still out there. The walls are closing in a bit, aren't they?'

'If you're trying to provoke a reaction from me, I wouldn't bother,' said Spinney. 'Bigger and more dangerous men than you have tried – and died, attempting it. I'd be more worried about what can happen to you. So do yourself a favour and tell me where she is.'

Finn glanced around his empty flat, his eyes settling briefly on the framed picture of Karin sitting on his mantelpiece.

'Shall I tell you what *I* want, Ray? One day, to sit in an interview room, look across the table and watch a little piece of you die inside. That's what I'd like – and I'm a *very* patient man.'

There was a pause, the same type adults use after a child has said something foolish, to let the words dissipate.

'Tell me where I can find her and I'll give you enough money to retire on tomorrow.'

For the first time, Finn could hear genuine frustration in his tone.

'I honestly can't think of anything worse.'

'Very well. You were warned,' said Spinney and the line went dead.

41

'It's hot air – what can he do?' said Finn the following morning. He was back in Skegman's office and felt considerably less concerned by Spinney's threat than his DCI.

'There's a lot he can do, Alex,' said Skegman. 'Ask Terry Merchant's family – or any number of the people he's been responsible for murdering over the years.'

Finn shook his head dismissively.

'Towler's assessment was the same as mine; Spinney's running out of road. For all his talk, his reach isn't as long as it used to be. The NCA has got him on the run and his options are limited. I think the call last night was a last roll of the dice before he disappears again. I'd be very surprised if I'm top of his list of worries.'

Skegman's usually rapid little eyes were centred and still for a change.

'He's a man who doesn't forget things and you've crossed him now. I'll be happier when he's under lock and key.'

There was a knock at the door. They could see Jackie Ojo behind the glass and Skegman waved her in.

'That number Spinney used to call you with last night, guv. I've just been cross-checking it against some of the records we gathered during the Best investigation.'

'That's the NCA's job, Jacks,' said Skegman, irritated.

Ojo shrugged.

'We know he had an interest in those murders – I thought it was fair game.'

Finn looked at her with an unspoken approval.

'What did you find?' he said.

Ojo smiled smugly.

'The same number was used to call Michael Beacham earlier this week.'

Despite Skegman's objections, Finn and Ojo drove straight over to the Beachams. The attraction of dealing Spinney an instant blow was too much for Finn to resist. They'd pass it on to Towler's team later, but his immediate concern was whether Claire might have been involved in this too.

As they made their way across south London, he was pleased to find Ojo in surprisingly good spirits. Given everything that had happened with McElligott, and the worries she'd been having about her son too, it was good to see.

'So what's put you in such a good mood?' he said.

'Plenty,' she replied. 'Cass seems back to normal – as far as normal goes for boys that age – we've taken a killer off the streets and weeded out a rotten apple in the team. Not a bad week, I'd say.'

That was one way of looking at it, Finn supposed. The shitstorm that was Dave McElligott still hadn't hit. John Skegman was metaphorically battening down the Cedar House hatches before getting the formal go-ahead from the NCA to release the news. For the moment, a highly suspicious Sami Dattani and the rest of the station had been told the DC was off with flu.

'Hope we're still on for that drink later?' said Finn.

Ojo chuckled.

'More than one, I hope,' she said. 'We've got a fair bit to talk about.'

'Don't suppose you know if Mattie's been offered an interview for that sergeant's job in Hammersmith yet?' he inquired, trying to sound casual.

Ojo nodded.

'She said she got an email this morning. It's on Tuesday week. I gather you put in a good word for her?'

'Yes,' said Finn, tight-lipped. 'I did.'

Ojo glanced across at him then looked out of the window and smiled.

When they arrived, Finn's concerns that Claire might somehow be involved in whatever her husband had been doing were almost instantly put to bed when he saw the dynamic between them. The cold fury in her eyes, matched only by the terror in his.

'It was a wrong number,' said Michael, explaining with little conviction why Ray Spinney's phone number was in his call list. At that point, Claire had told the detectives about the conversation he'd had with her the previous night. It was when she showed Finn the pictures of the house in California that the pieces fell into place.

Michael watched her give him up with obvious dismay but didn't try to stop her. If she felt any compunction about what she was doing, she didn't show it. Instead, she spoke with the same clarity and strength Finn was used to from her performances in the Commons. Over the last eleven days he'd become so accustomed to seeing her at her most fragile that he'd forgotten that side of her – the tough-as-nails politician. Her husband tried to make eye contact with her while she spoke but she wasn't having it. Once she'd finished, she turned away and crossed her arms.

'Your finances are going to be coming under a lot of scrutiny in the days and weeks ahead – I hope for your sake they're watertight,' Finn warned Michael. He was sitting on the sofa, offering nothing now. Finn doubted he'd add anything more meaningful until he had a lawyer next to him.

'Claire—' he started.

'I didn't know anything about this until last night,' she said to Finn, cutting him off. 'You have to believe that.' It was almost as if her husband had become past tense already.

'The NCA will cross-check everything – but for what it's worth, I do believe you,' said Finn.

Spinney's words on the phone came back to him – everyone had their vulnerability. A lot of people would give their right arms for the kind of affluent lives the Beachams enjoyed, and yet Michael had wanted more. Just like Dave McElligott, he'd engineered his own downfall. Finn nodded at Ojo to proceed.

'Michael Beacham, you're under arrest on suspicion of conspiracy to commit money laundering and for money laundering offences contrary to the Proceeds of Crime Act . . .'

Michael was ignoring her, still concentrating on his wife, but her back remained turned on him – in every sense.

'Are you alright?' Finn asked Claire later. Ojo had taken Michael back to Cedar House and he and Claire were alone now. The mask of cold indifference she'd been wearing had given way to something much more vulnerable now that her husband had left the building.

'No,' she said with a weak smile. 'And I think that might be the first time since this all began that I've answered that question honestly.'

'I can talk you through what's likely to happen to him next if you like?' he offered.

She shook her head.

'I really don't want to know,' she said. 'He's on his own now.'

The emphatic delivery of the words contrasted with the hurt on her face and Finn suspected her true feelings were considerably more complicated.

'I'm so sorry,' he said. 'This is going to damage you professionally, isn't it?'

He stopped himself from saying 'as well as personally'. Her marriage felt like none of his business. She nodded.

'Yes, it will, but I'll live. I'm not even sure I want to stand for re-election next time anyway. Politics is supposed to be a *conversation.* Not tribal war, like two sets of football fans baiting each other. Truth is, I've been feeling disillusioned for a while. I think Michael must have picked up on it.' She exhaled. 'I didn't see this coming though – that he could or would behave like that.'

'California was never going to happen then?' said Finn.

She shook her head firmly.

'Not the way he wanted it. A house full of laughing kids and a happy-ever-after. It was always impossible – I can't have children.' She saw the puzzled expression on Finn's face. 'Michael didn't know – and yes, I'm aware that sounds a bit strange.'

He remembered what Ian Gilfoyle had told him about her struggles with alcohol during their relationship, the allegation of physical abuse, and a thought began to form.

'Did something happen to you?' he said, not entirely sure how to phrase it or even what he was trying to suggest.

'Do you have children?' she countered.

He shook his head.

'My wife died a few years ago before we got round to it.'

Finn surprised himself – he wasn't used to being so candid with people about Karin, but he felt like he could with her. Claire nodded sympathetically.

'My turn to be sorry. I sometimes forget everyone's carrying something,' she said. Finn didn't respond, aware she still hadn't answered his question. 'I do of course remember the morning Daniel Best came to see me. It was the day I had my abortion.'

It took a second for the word to sink in. Finn did a quick bit of mental arithmetic.

'This would have been when you were with Ian Gilfoyle?'

She raised an eyebrow.

'You have done your homework.'

'Our investigation took us into every corner of your life.'

She nodded.

'I never told him I was pregnant. This was before I became an MP and I was very ambitious – I didn't feel ready for a baby and I wasn't sure about the relationship either. Yes, he had a right to know, but I didn't tell him and that's something I think about a lot.'

Finn could easily imagine how overwhelming the situation must have been. Gilfoyle had called her an actress and, in a sense, she was, just not in the way he thought.

'You cut the meeting with Best short to go and have the abortion?'

She was staring absently out into the garden now, almost as if she hadn't heard him. He wondered how deeply she'd buried this over the years. Finn, more than anyone, knew what bottling secrets up could do to you. He'd kept the scale of his own grief from his team at Cedar House for long enough.

'Even on the day, I wasn't sure I'd go through with it. I'd been vacillating all morning and my head was somewhere else. The appointment at the abortion clinic was almost on me by the time Daniel came to my office – I didn't really take in what he was saying. All I was thinking was whether to go through with it or not. I made the decision while he was talking, stuck to it, told him I'd pass on his concerns and then went straight to the clinic. We only met briefly six years ago – so it was hardly surprising that I didn't remember him when he came to the surgery.'

She stopped and looked down suddenly.

'How was I supposed to know?' she said, her voice cracking as the emotion took over. 'How could I guess what the consequence of that day would be?'

'You couldn't know – it was impossible. You can't blame yourself,' said Finn.

She shook her head.

'I'm not just talking about Best – the abortion left me infertile.' Her voice was barely more than a whisper now. 'I developed an infection afterwards. It's very rare that it can be so damaging, but it can happen. I never told Ian what I'd done and for a while, I came off the rails – drank too much, did . . . other stuff I'm not proud of.' She looked up at him with genuine shame. 'And that's something else I need to tell you about.'

'I'm not here to judge you,' he said. 'You don't need to tell me anything you don't want to – the investigation's closed.'

'I owe you the truth,' she said and took a deep breath. 'What happened – knocked the stuffing out of me. I suffered from depression afterwards . . .' She faltered. 'The real thing, I'm afraid – for a time. I don't know if you've ever had any experience of it?'

Finn looked away for a moment and nodded tightly.

'After my wife died.'

Her face softened.

'I was a bit out of control – took it out on Ian . . .' she said. 'More than just verbally . . .' The words seemed to die in her throat.

'I know. He told us about it,' said Finn gently. 'Not with any anger, I ought to say – we pushed him and he was helping us.'

Claire listened then nodded.

'He's a good man and he didn't deserve to be put through any of that. I carry the guilt every day.'

'Everyone has their secrets,' said Finn. 'Me included.'

'I should have told you from the start. I'm sorry.'

The abortion was another question answered, thought Finn, why it had always felt like she'd been holding something back.

Claire's phone buzzed. She glanced down at it.

'That's Grant, I ought to take this.'

She slipped out of the room and left him alone.

Finn could finally see how everything fitted together, but was still finding it difficult to fully get his head around. Now that he had the last piece of the jigsaw, he thought again about Daniel Best. It wasn't just that Best's complaints had fallen through so many cracks. It was that no one had been there for him in the years that had followed his son's death, charting the decline of his mental health. More people had died as a consequence. It was all too easy to imagine something like that happening again somewhere and the thought chilled him.

Claire re-entered the room suddenly looking business-like.

'I'm sorry – I'm going to have to cut this short. Grant's managed to find a window in my diary to get me some time with Benjamin at Cromarsh later.'

She brought Finn up to date regarding the potential U-turn by the Home Office.

'That's good news, surely?' said Finn.

'Yes, but apparently Benjamin's not particularly convinced and still believes he's going to get deported.'

'Which he yet might be, I suppose . . .' said Finn.

She nodded.

'We're so close now and I don't want him to blow this right at the death. I need him at the races for his court appearance, but he just doesn't listen to me. I struggle to get through to him at times.'

She suddenly looked exhausted, as if the combination of Michael's arrest and the memory of her abortion had removed even the last vestiges of her energy. That was something else Finn could relate to – that feeling of running on empty.

'I could come and talk to him with you,' he offered. She looked at him hopefully. 'If you think it'll help?'

42

Jackie Ojo's mood remained upbeat as she left Michael Beacham with the custody sergeant. There was still work to be done before they could charge him, but she'd seen the fear in the man's eyes as they'd booked him in. She'd already phoned the NCA with news of the arrest and had no doubt the evidence in the Doll Street paperwork would be found to move things forwards.

As she re-entered the incident room, she saw Sami Dattani at his desk, studying his screen intently. The rest of the room was also quiet, which was odd following the successful conclusion of a major investigation. It was usually a bit more relaxed with a fair bit of banter flying around. Not today. She wondered if the news about Dave McElligott had leaked. It wasn't impossible and the mood of the place was definitely subdued. Morale would certainly get worse when it became public knowledge. Cedar House would be marked by it too – at best seen as incompetent, at worst, corrupt.

She centred herself – and breathed out. In moments like this, you had to pull back and remember what was important. Her son, her mother – her life away from the job. She would continue to come in and make her contribution. If the place was something of a skip fire for a while, then so be it. She'd put on the blinkers, collect her pay cheque and see it through until they came out the other side.

'Where's the boss?' said Paulsen who'd come over to her.

'Still with Claire, but he should be back by lunchtime – what do you need, Mattie?'

Paulsen looked coy.

'Does he know I've got an interview with the West Command Unit MIT yet?'

Ojo gave her a withering look.

'Are you fishing for something?'

'I just wondered how he was about it. He's being very decent to my face – but I don't know what's *really* going on in his head.'

Ojo smiled.

'He's properly pissed off and doesn't want to lose you. There – I've said it. Is that what you wanted to hear?'

'Maybe a little,' said Paulsen, trying and failing to prevent a pout crossing her face.

'He'll get over it,' said Ojo. 'He hates change and he doesn't always take to the people who work for him.' She nodded at the rest of the room. 'Just about everyone in here respects him, though I'm not sure they all *like* him and vice versa. You've done well on that score . . .'

'I owe you for that,' said Paulsen. 'You've always looked out for me since I came here.'

'You haven't got the job yet. Don't get ahead of yourself . . . no one likes a cocky bollocks.'

They both grinned.

'Not a chance – but I wouldn't mind finding some time in YoYo's to talk about the interview. I could use a steer.'

'You're on.'

Before Ojo could add any more, she was interrupted by the sound of her mobile ringing. Paulsen gave her a quick nod of thanks and left her alone to take the call.

'DS Ojo?' said a voice she didn't recognise. 'It's Peter

Margetson at the NCA; my governor Ian Towler asked me to give you a bell.'

Ojo tried to place him from the briefing, before the abortive attempt to arrest Spinney in the park, but couldn't.

'What can I do for you?' she said.

'It's nothing serious,' said Margetson. 'We think we've located Emma Spinney is all – the boss thought you'd want to join us when we pick her up.'

The boss? *His* boss, maybe. Skegman would, of course, take the view that Cedar House's involvement in this was now over. Sod Skegman, she thought.

'I'd love to,' she replied. 'Thanks for thinking of me.'

'No problem,' said Margetson. 'We reckoned there might be a few loose ends you'd want to tie up.'

She looked around, felt again the downbeat mood of the room, and the attraction of getting out was strong.

'Where is she?' said Ojo.

'Vacant property in Bethnal Green – I can meet you there in around forty-five minutes if you're free?'

He gave her the address and ended the call. She quickly tapped out a text to Finn, then went over to Paulsen.

'The NCA reckon they've found Emma Spinney – I'm off to go and pick her up with them if anyone asks,' she said.

'Don't suppose you need some company?' said Paulsen hopefully.

Ojo smiled.

'Sorry, Mattie, I'm good. I'll see you when I see you.'

The drive across south London to Cromarsh Prison was the longest amount of time Finn had actually spent in Claire's company. For most of the journey, she talked him through what she thought was currently the Home Office's thinking regarding Benjamin. It wasn't all conjecture – she clearly knew people who knew people and was drawing a reasonable extrapolation of where things stood. She also seemed to be parking her husband's arrest in another part of her brain. Distracting yourself from deep emotional pain by throwing yourself into work was something Finn knew a bit about. It would catch up with her later that evening though – he knew that much too.

'Do you mind me asking . . .' he began. 'How did you come across Benjamin's case in the first place?'

She pulled a face as she recalled. They'd arrived at the prison now and were just about to pass through the jail's airport-style security procedures.

'Michael drew my attention to it – said someone at work had mentioned it to him. Benjamin's a constituent of mine – at least according to the address he gave when he was arrested.' She turned to look at Finn, realising. 'Oh God, you're not saying . . .'

Finn was already nodding.

'Ray Spinney? Almost certainly.' He stopped and shook his head. 'He's meticulous, whatever else he might be.'

Claire looked confused.

'I don't understand. Was he using Michael to launder money – or to simply get to me?'

Finn was buckling his belt back on and grabbed his wallet and keys from the plastic tray that had just rolled through the X-ray machine.

'Both. Like I say – there's thought behind everything he does. I suspect he saw an opportunity to use the pair of you to his advantage and didn't waste it.'

A member of the prison staff began leading them down some white-walled corridors. The whole place smelt of paint and detergent and for a few moments there was just the sound of their footsteps tapping on the hard floor.

'I'm sorry,' said Finn, guessing what she was thinking. Nobody likes to be played – least of all a politician, he suspected. 'If it's any consolation, manipulating people is what he does.'

'There's something else,' said Claire. 'If we succeed in keeping Benjamin in this country, will he be safe? It doesn't sound like Spinney's the sort who lets things go.'

Finn nodded.

'If his immigration status changes, then I'd imagine there'd almost certainly be an option for witness protection – the same for Emma as well.'

They entered the visitors' hall, sat down at a table, and a few minutes later, Benjamin was brought through to join them. He looked surprised to see Finn there. Claire began by explaining what she believed was likely to be the sequence of events following his sentencing hearing. If she thought it would lift him, she was mistaken. He regarded them both as if interviewing a pair of particularly unpromising job candidates.

'Sorry – after what happened last time?' He let that hang in the air for a moment. 'I just want to get my court appearance out of the way. I'll worry about the rest later,' he said.

'That's fair enough, after everything you've been through,' said Finn. 'But the most important thing is you stay out of trouble between now and then.'

Benjamin looked at him wearily.

'What do you think I'm doing, having a party in here?'

'No, but there may be people who'll try and provoke you. All we're saying is be careful. Spinney's got nothing to lose.'

'I'll tell you what would make things safer – if you arrested him and ended this. Don't suppose there's any danger of that?' said Benjamin.

361

Claire exchanged a glance with Finn.

'How's Emma doing – have you spoken to her?' she said.

He looked at them warily but didn't reply. Finn smiled reassuringly at him – he'd received Ojo's text earlier and knew she was on her way to pick Emma up.

'It's understandable that you're worried about her safety,' he said. 'We know she's somewhere in east London and safe. We're not here to get information out of you.'

Benjamin laughed unexpectedly.

'Good job. Because I don't know why you think she's in east London – she's not in London at all, as it goes.'

It took Finn a moment to compute the words. When he did, alarm bells began to ring in his head.

The street in Bethnal Green was quiet and out of the way, a strip of ex-council houses close to a small estate. Jackie Ojo parked up and took in her surroundings.. It was a grey and windswept day and the road was deserted. She looked around for someone who might be Margetson but could see no sign of anyone. East London was a patch she knew well – she'd been born in these parts, and for all the change over the years, it still felt the same to her whenever she returned. There was a slight sadness as she remembered her childhood and a father long since passed. She looked around again and apart from a cat tiptoeing along the top of a fence, couldn't see any signs of life. She began to walk down the street, checking the house numbers as she went.

Finn had excused himself and left Claire with Benjamin. He was now in the corridor outside the visitors' hall, frantically searching for the text Ojo had sent earlier. Finding it and confirming the address, he tried to call her – but wasn't getting a signal inside the jail. He ran swiftly through the maze of corridors, out into the car park, and tried again – but even outside, he was only getting one bar on his phone. Swearing, he sprinted to his car, gunned the engine and accelerated away.

After nearly ten minutes on foot, Ojo realised she'd parked up at the wrong end of the street. She was now in a no-man's-land. It would be quicker to continue walking on rather than turning back for her car now. Her phone vibrated in her pocket and she pulled it out, thinking it might be Margetson. She saw instead a WhatsApp from her mother.

Buy onions!

'Right – of course,' she said to herself, shaking her head. There was probably a good reason why her mother couldn't buy them for herself, even if it was hard to fathom what it was right now. It was even more likely that she'd forget altogether she'd even sent the text by the time Ojo got home later. Shaking her head, she carried on walking.

A short distance out from Cromarsh, Finn tried to ring her again – but this time the call went straight to answerphone. His knuckles had turned white around the steering wheel.

'Jacks – if you pick up this message, Emma Spinney is *not* in east London – I think you're walking into a trap—'

His phone buzzed and he immediately broke off, expecting to see Ojo's name on the display. There was a new text message and what he saw turned his blood cold.

You were warned.

He instantly called for emergency assistance, directing it to the address in Bethnal Green. Then, activating the blues and twos on his unmarked car, he put his foot down.

'So sorry – I've been a twat and parked at the wrong end of the street,' said Ojo into her phone. She checked her watch.

'I'm about five minutes late – I should be with you any second.' She was speaking to Margetson's answerphone and assumed he must be en route himself – with luck he was a little delayed too. There were some missed calls from Finn on her phone together with an answerphone message. She was about to listen to it when she noticed where she was.

She'd reached a 1970s red-brick block that had been separated into a row of terraced houses. Seeing the number she was looking for, she walked up to the front door and pocketed her phone. She was about to ring the bell when she noticed the door was ajar. She pushed it open and peered in.

'Emma?' she called.

There was no reply and she stepped cautiously inside. In her pocket, she felt her phone buzz again and ignored it. The house was empty and smelt musty. She opened the door to the living room and instantly an arm like a tree trunk seemed to come from nowhere and curl around her throat. She couldn't move, could feel the body of someone much larger and more powerful behind her. In her pocket, her phone was still vibrating.

'Expecting someone, were you?' said a voice with a slow Liverpudlian drawl.

Finn skidded to a halt outside the house. He'd driven as fast as he could – but even with blues and twos, it was impossible to navigate from south London to east of the river quickly. Several police vehicles had got there ahead of him in response to his earlier call for emergency assistance. An ambulance was also there, its back doors wide open. He knew instantly things were bad because there was no one to be seen and the front door of the house was open too. He could feel his heart beating, a dread at what he might be about to find.

He sprinted past the ambulance into the house where

364

several visibly distressed officers were standing in the hallway. Holding up his warrant card, he roared at them and ran through into the living room. Two paramedics in dark green uniforms looked up as he entered, but there was no urgency about them. There was no movement of any kind in the room. On the floor between them was the body of Jackie Ojo. And as that reality sank in, Finn's fragile heart, so delicately rebuilt, shattered once more into a million pieces.

43

Claire felt like murdering a vodka and tonic. Instead, she took a sip from the carton of coconut water on her desk at Portcullis House and smiled to herself. No more booze – that was one easy decision she'd made overnight. So was accepting the end of her marriage. Michael had been the architect of his own downfall and would have to face the consequences of his actions on his own. Sometimes you needed a relationship to end to be able to properly recognise that it hadn't been working. She was alone for the first time in many years – and she felt lighter and freer for it.

'I haven't seen you smile like that for a long time,' said Lassiter.

'I've just had an email from my contact at the Home Office. It's confirmed – they're going to grant Benjamin indefinite leave to remain. Sounds like if he hadn't handed himself in after Spinney's attack, things might have been different. It's hard to portray someone as a threat to the community when they've been witnessed running for their life.'

'I think you're underplaying your own contribution,' said Lassiter. 'You made the Nasty Party look nastier, made sure the public understood Benjamin was more victim than villain. It all made a difference, I'm sure.'

'They'll only deport him now if he commits another crime, which I can't see happening. It feels like a win, I have to say,' she said.

'Well done, Claire,' said Lassiter. 'You deserve that.'

'I think my reputation is just about still intact,' she replied. 'Despite everything. You've heard the news about Rebecca Devlin, I take it?' Lassiter looked at her, nonplussed. 'She's got a job in the Downing Street press office . . .'

He looked at her, unimpressed.

'She'll get eaten alive,' he said.

'It's them I'd be more worried about,' said Claire.

She glanced out of the window – sections of Parliament Square below were still cordoned off.

'So what now?' said Lassiter.

'What's in the diary?' said Claire.

He arched an eyebrow.

'Plenty. But I thought you might want to take a short break after everything that's happened. You probably should, you know? Give yourself a chance to get your head around it all.'

She thought about it, knew he was referring as much to her personal life as her professional one. The news about Benjamin was a reminder though of why she'd got involved in politics in the first place. She wasn't sure if it offset the guilt she felt about Daniel Best and her husband, but that in itself was a lesson. There were more victories to be had and more to be chased. More to be done, in short, to balance the books.

'Why don't we just take things one day at a time,' she said, 'and see where that takes us?'

Underneath a dull grey shawl of a sky, the sea frothed restlessly against the ferry slowly ploughing its way across the English Channel. The wind was howling around Ray Spinney as he stood on deck staring out at the murky green water. He'd be in Zeebrugge by the afternoon and, unusually, didn't have a clear idea of what he would do next.

It hadn't been too difficult to leave the UK, despite his most wanted status. He always had reserves of fake identities and passports to draw upon, put together by some of the finest forgers in Europe. With a little disguise, he'd caught the ferry from Hull and was travelling now under a Dutch passport. Rebuilding and starting over was something he was well accustomed to and the process would begin again when he arrived in Belgium.

He felt no emotion for Jackie Ojo, just as he hadn't for Terry Merchant and the many others who'd preceded them. He'd come to the UK with only one objective that mattered, and failed to achieve it. Now he was staring that failure in the face, beginning to comprehend the totality of it. He remembered Finn's bravado on the phone – and his belief that he couldn't be hurt. Hopefully he'd learnt differently now. Finn had come between Spinney and his daughter and there would be a further reckoning one day. This wasn't over – not by a long chalk, of that he was certain.

For now, he was alone again but it felt different this time. He could remember holding Emma soon after she'd been born. The three-year-old pointing at the ducks in the park, the nine-year-old in fancy dress, the teenager screaming and slamming doors. As the memories collided, he was unable to stop the tears from coming, and for the first time in years, Ray Spinney sobbed his heart out.

Nancy Deen stood outside the closed door of her bedroom holding a mug of tea. Her free hand went to open it then wavered. She stood, unsure of what to do, then knocked gently. There was no reply.

'Mattie – I've brought you some tea.' She waited but there was still no response from the other side of the door. 'If you want it . . .'

Surrendering, she turned to leave then stopped. 'I'm in the living room if you need anything. Anything at all . . .' she called out. She stood there for a few more moments, feeling her own heart growing heavier with each passing second, then finally turned and walked away.

Initially, Finn had been a model of calm. He'd broken the news to Jackie's mother himself, then stayed with her and Cass until the family liaison officers arrived. While the boy's grandmother had crumpled into agonised silence, the youngster had reacted in stages. At first, there was shock, then came anger mixed with disbelief, and finally, howling tears of anguish. Finn, still struggling to deal with it himself, had found it unbearable.

Skegman had told him bluntly not to return to Cedar House afterwards. Not because of anything he'd said or done, but because he knew Finn was still in shock himself and in no state of mind to be working the investigation. The DCI wasn't much better, to be fair, rasping out the instructions with an audible catch in his voice, but Finn couldn't even summon the fight to argue.

'*Call someone*,' his late wife had urged him as he'd driven home, but he'd ignored her. He was replaying the conversation with Spinney from the previous night over and over in his mind – remembering, too, his all-too-easy dismissal of the threat in Skegman's office only that morning.

This, he thought ironically to himself, might be what his bereavement counsellor would count as a relapse. He couldn't face talking to Murray right now, either – it was too soon for that, even with him. At least he had a support network he could turn to this time. Later, they would play their part, but for now, he just wanted to be alone.

Jackie hadn't just been a colleague; she'd been his friend. An unusual one – they'd lived completely different lives, come from very different worlds until they'd met at Cedar House – but she'd understood him in a way few did. Since Karin's death, she'd felt like family of sorts, though he'd never truly articulated the thought before. It had taken her death for him to truly understand what role she'd played in his life and he hated himself for not seeing it sooner.

The following day was a blur. At around nine in the evening, he went to bed for no other reason than not wanting to be awake any more. He woke just ninety minutes later with the sound of Cassian Ojo's screams of despair still ringing in his head. Walking over to his bedroom window, he pulled back the curtain and watched the quiet street outside.

'*Alex . . .*' whispered Karin.

'Shhh,' said Finn.

He wouldn't be broken by this, he decided – at least not in the long term. He wasn't going to go down that road again. He remembered what he'd said to Spinney:

'*Shall I tell you what I want, Ray? One day, to sit in an interview room, look across the table and watch a little piece of you die inside.*'

For an instant, all he could hear was the sound of his breathing. He dressed, grabbed his coat and made for the door. He faltered briefly, letting another wave of emotion pass through, then walked out into the night.

The End

ACKNOWLEDGEMENTS

I submitted the first draft of this book to my publishers on Wednesday October 13th 2021. I was feeling a little smug – I'd enjoyed writing this one (doesn't always happen) and had fallen a little in love with Claire Beacham after spending almost a year inside her head. Then, just two days later on Friday October 15th came the appalling murder of Sir David Amess the MP for Southend West at a constituency surgery in Leigh-on-Sea. Suddenly, what I'd written seemed to have a whole new and very tragic resonance. As I listened that evening to some of the cross-party tributes to Sir David, one phrase stuck with me. Forgive me – because I'm paraphrasing, but it went along the lines of:

'Far from being out of touch with society our MPs are probably more in touch with what's happening on the ground in their constituencies than they've ever been before.'

It's a view that flies against the popular stereotype and I appreciate there'll be plenty reading this who won't agree with it (goodness knows a lot's happened since I wrote the book!) But the thing that's always struck me when I listen to people talk about politicians is our conviction that we 'know' them. I think, often, we only see a fraction of the true person and I was keen to dig into that. Partly, because recent years have so skewed our view of MPs I wanted to try and move away from the popular stereotypes and cliches – I'll let you decide how successful I've been.

In particular, I wanted Claire to feel relatable. She's a Labour politician because the story needed her to be an opposition MP but I hope she's representative of many of our Members of Parliament across the board – someone, normal and fallible, simply trying to do the right thing. Sometimes a lot of good goes unseen, with actions that make a meaningful difference receiving little press attention – and yes, that includes even those MPs you don't like. Did she stand again at the next election? And if not, what happened to her next? It might be fun to find out one day . . .

Once again, I need to thank the fine people at Hodder for the fantastic continued backing that they give me with this series. Huge thank you's to the guv'nor Eve Hall who's edited this series from the start – and welcome to Beth Wickington who's seamlessly jumped aboard with this book. As ever – a big thanks too to my brilliant agent Hayley Steed for her continued wisdom and support in all things. And a particularly special thanks to police advisor Stuart Gibbon for answering a near endless stream of questions this time around. Each and every email ended with the words 'I think these are the last ones' – which in hindsight was a flagrant lie.

Finally, I suppose I ought to say a few words about the ending of this book. I mean, I *ought* to – but maybe I should just leave you just with this:

'*To be continued!*'